A Sword's Poem:

The Making

The Breaking

The Reforging

Leah Cutter

A Sword's Poem

Leah Cutter

Copyright © 2015 Leah Cutter

All rights reserved

Published by Book View Café Publishing Cooperative

by arrangement with Knotted Road Press

www.BookViewCafe.com

www.KnottedRoadPress.com

ISBN: 978-1-61138-481-9

Cover and interior design copyright © Knotted Road Press

A Sword's Poem:

The Making

The Breaking

The Reforging

Leah Cutter

Book View Cafe

www.BookViewCafe.com

Also by Leah Cutter

Historic Fantasy:
Paper Mage
The Caves of Buda
The Jaguar and the Wolf

Contemporary Fantasy:
Of Myst and Folly
Poisoned Pearls
The Popcorn Thief
Siren's Call
When the Moon Over Kualina Mountain Comes
Zydeco Queen and the Creole Fairy Courts

The Shadow Wars Trilogy:
The Raven and the Dancing Tiger
The Guardian Hound

The Clockwork Fairy Kingdom Trilogy:
The Clockwork Fairy Kingdom
The Maker, the Teacher, and the Monster

Collections:
Beyond the Garden
Burning Flowers
Tell Me Again
The Shadow Wars
The Shredded Veil Mysteries

The Making
A Sword's Poem
Volume I

The Making

A Sword's Poem

Volume I

刀の詩の本一

はじまり

LEAH CUTTER

AUTHOR OF PAPER MAGE

One

Oh That Horrible Day!

Hikaru

O h that horrible day! I shall never forget it, not ever. Not even if I lived long enough for the rain to wear Mount Shirayama down to a mere pebble. Never have I been so frightened—nor, afterwards, so alone.

The day started fair—pale blue skies washed by spring tears, with only a scattering of clouds left behind by the night. Fragrant winds tickled the pink and purple flowers dancing by the side of the road. The *uguisu* chirped and sang as we passed from the open fields to under the trees of the black pine forest.

As was proper, we were on our way to the temple of Inari, the Rice Goddess, to pay our respects and ask her blessings on our union. It was the perfect weather for Norihiko's and my first pilgrimage together. We'd been married such a short while, even as mortals would count it: barely a handful of days.

It was rare for any of the *kitsune* to marry—most would say doomed— but we were young and foolish. We believed our love was stronger than the accumulated wisdom of our people.

I rode in a wickerwork carriage painted gold and red, fully enclosed and with three servants, of course. Bursts of green bamboo emblems ran across the top of the carriage, while the wheels spun merrily with golden spokes. Our outriders had matching bamboo emblems on their harnesses and saddles. They were mostly human, well-trained guards who'd dedicated their lives to the protection of my family and our kind.

Brilliant white oxen drew us along at an unfashionably slow pace, allowing us to enjoy the scenery and the weather. The road was clear through the trees, well-marked but not rutted. Only a few houses lay deep in the woods, the peasants stopping to gape at the richness of our troop. What a magnificent sight we must have been!

I trailed only a smidgen of my sleeve outside the carriage, letting it float and waft in the air. I didn't feel the need to show off my outfit, or to impress what few travelers we might encounter on this quiet road. I had all that I desired that day: a devoted husband; spring breezes sweet enough to be perfumed; and an immortal's life ahead of me.

As we rode along, Norihiko would range with his mighty steed, both before and after the main carriage, gathering beautiful mementoes of our trip to bring to me: a tiny pinecone hanging from a fragrant branch, still sparkling with dew; a sprig of brush clover, full of the tangy essence of spring; a partly-decayed leaf, half still in its yellow fall splendor, while the other half was just a spiderweb-thin splay of veins—a shadowy reminder of its former glory.

I laughed and clapped my hands every time Norihiko presented me with one of these treats. I crafted poems of thanks in return, which made him go seek more splendid trinkets to share with me.

If we hadn't been traveling as we were, along a public road with outriders and servants, he probably would have tried gifting me with kisses as well— and I would have let him.

His last visit, he brought me a shiny black raven's feather, comparing its sleek richness to my own hair. Our families weren't close to the bird clans— none of the *kitsune* were. To the outrage of my servants, I braided it into a strand of my hair.

Norihiko had given it to me. There couldn't be anything wrong with it.

I was so foolish. So young. So in love.

The attack came that afternoon without warning, during the Hour of the Lamb. We still rode slowly through the black pine forest, taking our time, enjoying the pleasantness of the day, the ease of the road.

I had never envied my mother her gift of foresight, but that day, I wished I'd borne the burden of it for our family.

Not that she necessarily would have seen this. If she had seen it, she would have warned me. But only some things are meant to changed. Many were meant to be, and nothing could change them, in the balance of things.

Arrows zinged out of the trees from all sides, sliding easily through the lattice work of the carriage, one piercing my left shoulder while a second went through the ribs on my left side, both of them pinning me to the back of the seat.

The shock and pain stole my breath and rendered me unable to scream. The carriage suddenly lurched to one side, as if a weight had been dropped on the right corner, while the oxen began to run, jerking and jolting the carriage behind them.

More than enough screams came from the servants attending me. All three had been shot.

Fuyoko died instantly, the arrow piercing her jugular. Ume wailed, her hands cupped over her stomach, as if trying to save the blood spilling from the wound there.

Yukiko also cried out, her voice sharpened by pain, but she mainly shouted at the driver, trying to get him to stop. She had a single arrow sticking out of her left arm like an odd banner, and her flank bled easily.

Was our off-balanced gait because the driver had been shot, and now hung off the edge of the carriage?

The carriage tilted farther to the right. Yukiko clung to a handle near the ceiling of the carriage with her good arm. I was still pinned, unable to get away. I worked frantically to pull the arrows from my left side. The other two lolled like life-sized dolls, stripped of their magic and strings.

Fuyoko fell over into my lap, an arrow sticking out from her neck like an obscene flag. I pushed her away like a cursed piece of wood.

I finally found the strength to pull the arrow from my side. The crimson waterfall that flowed from it made me wonder, for the first time in my life, if I might die. Weakness flooded over me.

It wasn't the sight of the blood.

The arrow had been spelled. I couldn't smell anything beyond the gore filling the carriage, but if I could, it would have been a foul odor.

It takes a lot to kill one of the *kitsune*. This arrow, and the others, had been specially made with that task in mind.

How was my poor Norihiko going to survive? What sort of attack was my love under? Had he and his mighty steed managed to break free?

Looking back, now, I realize there wasn't anything that I could have done to save him, even with my magic and my wiles. But at the time, it was all I could think of.

I had to save my precious mate.

With my blood-covered fingers, I couldn't get a good grip on the arrow pinning my left shoulder to the seat of the carriage. I banged on the roof of the carriage, hoping to rouse the driver if he was there and merely wounded.

There was no response.

The carriage tilted suddenly to the other side. Above the chaos and shrieks I heard a loud tear. I still had the arrow stuck through my shoulder, but at least now I was free of the seat cushion.

My stomach lurched when I realized what I had to do next.

I didn't want to touch Ume. She flopped next to the door, blocking my exit. I had no choice. As I tugged her to one side, she looked at me with wide, blinking eyes, mouthing words with no sounds, like a beached trout.

I looked away as quickly as I could, knowing I would have nightmares about her silent screams for many years.

I pushed at the carriage door, trying to open it, my fingers still slippery from the blood.

Yukiko came to help, adding her weight to the handle, so we could push open the left door.

Trees rushed by the opening. The oxen raced along the dirt path, nothing impeding their stampede. The carriage rocked steadily from one side to the other, throwing Yukiko and me together, then apart, both of us crying out from our wounds.

I think we would have jumped. We both considered it.

However, before we did something as rash as that, risking additional injury, the carriage hit a hidden boulder on the left and we rose up onto two wheels.

For a few breathless moments, we hung there, clinging to the open doorway as the carriage dropped to its side beneath us.

Fortunately, this tangled the oxen's harness enough to snap it, and the sound of the beasts' hooves faded into the distance.

The carriage slithered to a stop.

The silence that immediately wrapped around us was a terrible thing. How could it be so peaceful, so tranquil, when we were so badly hurt? The *uguisu* resumed its song. Bamboo clanked hollowly in the wind nearby. A white and pink butterfly trilled across the path, as if nothing could disturb its day.

The quiet oppressed us, made us hushed and still.

It probably saved our lives.

Without saying a word to each other, Yukiko and I freed ourselves from the carriage. She was shorter than me, but less injured: one arrow had grazed her flank, another her shoulder. She wedged one foot between the blood-stained cushions, hoisted herself up, then scrambled out the open door.

I tried the same trick, and with her pulling on my unwounded arm, escaped the overturned carriage as well.

We crouched beside the carriage, panting from our exertions. The pain from my injuries washed over me in constant waves. Silent tears streamed down my face. The arrow still in my shoulder stole my strength.

I had to rid myself of the evil thing before I could continue.

Just using gestures, I directed Yukiko to snap the end off, then push it through, out the other side. It burned like pure fire. I bit my own hand to keep myself from screaming.

Once it was gone, though, I felt myself healing. Exhaustion slammed into me. I longed to lie down, to sleep, so that I could wake up and find that this was only a horrible dream.

When a terrified shriek wrenched through the still air, my false hopes shattered.

I stood, ready to run back up the road.

Yukiko grabbed my uninjured arm.

I shook it, trying to dislodge her, but she wouldn't let go.

"We must use stealth, my lady," Yukiko whispered. "They cannot know we still live."

Oh, how I longed for her wise tongue not to have spoken! However, I knew she told the truth.

Our silence had kept us alive so far.

No one will ever know what it cost me to crawl back up the road, but I did what I must. I didn't have the strength to keep us both hidden with my magic. I was too frightened to even consider leaving Yukiko behind.

I don't believe I was thinking in terms of revenge yet—truthfully, I wasn't thinking much at all. However, now, looking back, I wonder if that seed had already been planted, burrowing deep inside me when the first arrow struck. If that long, slow crawl, being more quiet than mice, warmed those flames, helped bring them to life.

The road slanted gently, something I hadn't noticed earlier as we'd ridden so blithely along it. Just as Yukiko and I crested the slope, a bright flash of blue greeted us—a cold light, as if emanating from a frozen corpse.

Then a swirling ball of red and gold, the same colors as Norihiko's family crest, rose from the ground into the hands of a short, fat, tonsured man dressed in dark robes.

He carefully placed the ball into a box held by a servant standing next to him, then he strode to his horse.

In moments, they were gone. The road was empty. Sunlight filtered gentle and golden through the trees, dappling the bodies lying there.

The time for stealth was over. I dragged myself upright and staggered as quickly as I could back to our party.

I didn't spare a look for the corpses we passed. The outriders, as well as their horses, had all been slain. I would light incense for them later and say my prayers.

My eyes were fixed on Norihiko.

He lay just a little ways up, still, too still. My brightest star dimmed and shadowed.

It was worse than I could have possibly imagined. Foul arrows pierced his arms and thighs, blood pooling on the road.

But those hadn't killed him.

A huge hole lay in the center of his chest, burned and ragged along the edges.

I screamed. I wailed. Poor Yukiko tried to console me, but I knew nothing outside my grief.

It wasn't fair that my beloved had been taken from me. What kind of awful fate cut down one so young and fair, full of the promise of immortality, before he'd even reached his third decade?

The stench of the magic that had killed Norihiko finally made me retch and break away, bringing me back to the coolness of the afternoon under the black pine trees.

Norihiko's wound stank of the ashes of graveyards. That magical blue light that had marked the end of the ceremony—that had also been chilling.

Fear filled me. What had that evil sorcerer done to Norihiko? The rank odor of his wound, the way it dripped pus, told my waking self things I didn't want to know.

I shied away and let myself wallow, unthinking, in my grief instead.

Yukiko dragged me over to a horse that had come wandering back and made me climb up on it. I wasn't dressed for walking down a rough road, with my layers of skirts and underskirts and robes, my delicate slippers that wouldn't last walking down a rocky path.

We needed to find people, humans, to bind our wounds, help us gather our dead, and loan us a sacred space for the funeral rites and fires.

No matter how I might deny it, I had to burn Norihiko's body quickly. It would not decay like a normal body. It would solidify, like jelly, full of pus and poison.

It was all so unfair. Both his death, and the actions I would now have to take.

Later that night, Yukiko finally agreed to leave me alone in the shelter of my room at the inn we'd found. She let me know that she was right outside the door, ready to burst in if I raised my voice beyond a whisper to call her.

When she gathered together her blankets, I knew that she was literally sleeping on the other side of the door, on the floor.

I'm not sure what she thought I'd do. I wasn't about to hurt myself, no. Not yet. I had too many other things to do first.

I blew out all the candles in the simple room—just mats on a raised platform in the corner for a bed, a plain wooden block for a pillow, windows overlooking the yard to the back, where the innkeeper kept a careful garden full of herbs.

A sliver of moon kept me company. Its cold light gave me chills, but also, heated my blood.

I let myself remember what I'd seen that afternoon. The moon helped me remember details I'd not noted at the time.

The magical light. The coldness of it. It had been death magic.

Which meant the sorcerer had to have been a Taoist, one of those obsessed with immortality.

Not only had he taken Norihiko's life, but his soul as well. That beautiful gold and red ball had been my love's true spirit.

In the quiet of the darkness, a weight settled around me. A new pilgrimage had been laid on my shoulders. Instead of traveling to Inari's temple to ask for her blessing, I needed to find the soul of my mate and free it.

Not so it could travel to the "Pure Land"—I didn't believe the empty promises of the Buddhists, nor in their Hell.

My Norihiko would go to Heaven, as foretold by the good deeds he'd done in his short years.

I knew I would never join him, though, because of the deeds I was about to commit in his name.

Two

Cool Darkness Curled Around

Norihiko

Cool darkness curled around Norihiko, but he barely felt it.

Nothing could soothe the kiln-like heat burning through his core. He glowed like a beacon in the night. He felt trapped in a land of extremes, the darkest blackness just beyond the brightest light, unimaginable heat surrounded by blessed coolness.

He must still be sleeping, though. A nightmare brought on by too much sun and riding through the heat of the day.

Norihiko woke himself, only to find he *was* surrounded by flames. Their brilliance dazzled him, made him dizzy, but he couldn't reclose his eyes.

Where was he? Were the Buddhists right after all? Was there a Hell for Norihiko and all the *kitsune*, as some of the fanatics proclaimed?

Norihiko struggled to get away, to bow out from the dance the flames demanded.

It was only then he discovered he no longer had limbs, or body, or even a head. He discerned the flames through some other sense, not sight but awareness, knowing the fire surrounded him, a living, cackling thing, scorching hot but not burning him.

The flames grew brighter and the heat intensified. If Norihiko still had a body, his sweat would form a river.

The attack suddenly came back to him, the arrows singing out of the woods, the screams of the horses and his men, how they'd tried to fight but were outnumbered, hemmed in.

What had happened to his darling Hikaru? Had she been killed in the ambush? Was she also dancing in the flames? He struggled to see beyond the bright light, through to the darkness he could barely sense, but there was nothing else there.

Norihiko found he couldn't weep in this new form, though his very soul wanted to cry out at the harshness of his fate.

Then the first blow came.

Sharp pain reverberated through Norihiko's new form. He shouted…and his shouts manifested as sparks.

The pain was relentless, strike after strike, hammering down on Norihiko. He found he couldn't breathe in the heat and the pain, shouting instead, more angry sparks.

But his new form didn't break or bleed.

Instead, he…thinned.

The blows forced Norihiko into yet a new shape. Longer, more slight.

Norihiko struggled against the blows, gasping non-breaths between each volley of strength sapping agony.

He heard the singing then, the words floating through the still blistering flames.

A Taoist spell, full of enchanted poetry, crafted to seep into the core of his very being.

Norihiko realized that his memories were being pounded out of him. He screamed from the depths of his soul, for his love, for Hikaru, for his family.

The spell pouring down on him was meant to insert a new purpose for living into his soul.

Norihiko found he now could cry—tears streaking like falling stars as they flew from him, sizzling as they landed.

Unfair! he raged in his silence. His mate, his one true love—they'd never had a chance. The years they'd planned to spend together had been stolen from them.

Norihiko mourned even as his love faded from his mind, saddened though he no longer understood why.

Then the folding began.

Norihiko's torturer had thinned him to the point where he could be folded back onto himself.

When Norihiko's sides touched, it was as if there were two of him, foreigners compelled to embrace, forced to share each other's households.

Norihiko was this other, as well as himself. Together, they cried out in pain as the blows hammered down, thinning them again.

Then he was folded again, two becoming four, though now, each was no longer completely distinct. They shared memories, pain, and a red-gold essence that was impossible to define.

Norihiko found he lost more parts of himself to these others. He could no longer recall the smell of young pine trees, or why a raven's black feather had been so important, once.

Pain formed all of Norihiko's world, coursing through his long, still rough form.

His torturer, his *maker*, as he was coming to understand, continued to thin and refold him. The cries of his shattered soul were worse than the racket the priests made at the end of Ghost month to chase all the spirits back to their homes.

All these selves bickered and tried to hold onto what each had been, while all the time, the chanted words of the Taoist spell replaced bits and pieces of Norihiko as fast as he lost them.

Finally, there was no longer an "I" defined simply as Norihiko.

There was only a "we."

Only then did all of Norihiko see the pattern of the reforging being forced on them by their maker, that they understood the rationale behind this terrible magic.

The wielder of them had a great and terrible purpose: to unite all of Nifon under a single Buddhist faith.

Norihiko's maker meant to bind all of him to that homogeneous idea.

Instead of each of the disparate parts of Norihiko's soul trying to hold onto its own identity, they flowed together, determined to fight.

A single man's belief was too little a thing. A sole approach to the mysteries of life was too foreign to their very nature.

Being forced to support it would make them brittle. They would break with their first stroke.

Instead of fighting the reforging, all of Norihiko fell back on his true, wily nature. They listened, hard, to the Taoist spell, seeking a trick, a way out of this sure and final death.

Finally, they found it.

The Taoist wasn't forging them for himself. No, he was making them for another to wield.

Part of that wielder's purpose was a pledge to the land; in particular, Mount Shirayama, the mountain where Norihiko and all his selves now found themselves.

All of Norihiko clung to that piece—a half-dozen lines in a song that spanned hours—pouring themselves through that tiny crack, slipping away from the main principles meant for them and aligning themselves along this sideline.

They consciously devoted themselves to protecting this land, this mountain, as well as those men who were the champions of it.

They vowed to defend it to the death as their maker added sharpness to their form. A desire grew in them for the blood of those who dared defy their purpose.

They were a new death being unleashed upon the world, reforged and pure, ready to feast on the lives of their enemy and to keep their newly chosen home, Mount Shirayama, sacred.

Three

A Blood-Red Sunrise

Junichi

Ablood-red sunrise greeted Junichi as he staggered from the forge—an appropriate omen. Cool morning breezes dried the sweat still pricking his bare torso. He breathed deeply of the refreshing air, letting it fill and cleanse him, as his masters had taught.

Exhaustion rolled along Junichi's spine and pressed down on his shoulders. He locked his knees and put his hand on the rough wooden wall of the smithy to keep himself from toppling onto the trampled dirt.

None of his followers could be allowed to see how forging the sword had diminished him. He couldn't risk it. They must only see him as strong and masterful.

Junichi glanced up again at the sky. The sun hadn't shown her face, though a red glow now turned the horizon orange, like the fire he'd worked with all night. The forest that stretched below his compound loomed, dark and still full of biting night shadows. Pale grass covered the hilltop, making it wet with dew, the earth's sweat. Beyond the smithy lay the dark barracks full of still sleeping servants and followers, and beyond that, his own imposing palace, the intricately carved wooden statues that formed pillars around the door and defined the first story from the second still hidden in the dim light.

Nothing had gone right the past two days, or the previous long night, but this morning, Junichi finally had hope.

First, the attack had been all wrong. His top captain had lost his head as a consequence, yet another example for the men of the perfection Junichi demanded. The oxen drawing the fox fairy carriage had been wounded, not killed. His scout had reported that the female fox fairy had died as a result, the coach overturning just a little down the road.

Despite these setbacks, Junichi had managed to capture the male beast, kill its body cleanly, then trap its soul before the slippery thing could escape.

After the race back to Mount Shirayama, Junichi had prepared himself for the spell. He'd fasted, supping on no more than water for the rest of the day as well as all the next while he smelted the ore—perfecting the metal—and prayed over his tools. It had been a brutal ordeal, and he hadn't slept more than an hour over two days.

However, time had been of the essence. Junichi had to be ready to do the spell when the new moon rose or he'd have to wait another month. The warlord Masato, Junichi's former apprentice and current client, would have had some scathing words about the *old man* being slow if that had happened.

Then the damned fox fairy soul had fought Junichi, fought the reforging. Junichi had been forced to use his own precious life energy during their battle, more than one lifetime's worth.

Luckily, he had several stored up. Though he now regretted just killing his captain the day before and not taking his soul for energy as well.

This sword was costing Junichi more, much more, than he was getting paid by Masato. He didn't owe his former pupil a thing, which was why he'd demanded the first half of the gold up front. He still should have asked for more.

While Junichi hadn't been surprised by the *kitsune's* struggles, he hadn't anticipated the beast's strength.

Junichi took another deep cleansing breath, willing the air to revitalize him. Just a few more moments to recover his strength. Then he could allow himself a proper rest. Some tea, perhaps. And a dreamless sleep.

That stupid fox fairy had resisted the purpose Junichi had prescribed for it, bringing Nifon to heel under this Buddhist religion that Masato followed.

The perfection of taming one so wild for the strictness of this single cause was too tempting for Junichi. The symmetry had seemed miraculous, if Junichi believed in miracles.

If Junichi succeeded in reforging this beast's soul into a sword, the deed would prove the rightness of his choice. That all fox fairies were worthless following their own, independent nature.

They all needed to be tamed, or destroyed.

At least the idiotic fox fairy had finally seen the aptness of Junichi's resolution and chosen to at least partially align itself with it.

But how much of the Buddhist cause did the sword now support? Had Junichi pounded out enough of the beast's will to make it pliable?

The right wielder should be able to control the sword.

Was Masato the right master for such a beast? Hard to tell. Junichi had misjudged the boy—no, man, now—before. He'd thought the boy would follow in his own footsteps. Had chosen him carefully, trained him for years.

He'd never imagined that when he sent Masato across the sea to mainland *Shina* to study with the mystics there that the boy would find *religion* instead.

A servant approached Junichi as he pushed himself off the wall of the smithy. The servant bore a plain wooden tray, with an equally plain, brown-clay cup filled with chilled mountain water.

Junichi nodded his thanks as he sipped the refreshing drink. At least one of his servants had been paying attention. He'd reward the man later.

The servant hovered, remaining after Junichi waved him away.

"What do you want?" Junichi asked, exasperated. He needed to rest. To sleep. To recover.

"One of the local lords, Kitayama no Taiga, wishes to speak with you, sir."

Junichi hid his irritation. Not many of the local lords would dare make the journey through the nearby forest to pay Junichi a visit. He couldn't tell this Taiga to come back some other day—that would show too much weakness.

Instead, Junichi forced himself to stand straighter and taller. "I need fresh robes," he directed the servant. He paused, considering. "Set up a tea service and pillows on the top of the small rise, just there. Invite this lord to watch the end of the sunrise with me."

All Junichi wanted to do was go collapse and sleep until the next moon. However, not just fear of showing weakness drove him to invite this Taiga to tea.

He was also curious. What could this lord want?

Junichi's legs wobbled as he climbed the small rise. He again cursed the sword and how much it had drained him. The sunrise wasn't quite complete—the round disc of the sun still lingered halfway below the horizon. Birds chirped merrily from the nearby trees, making the forest seem cheerful, masking the dangers there. Dew still covered the pale grass, wetting the bottom of Junichi's plain brown robe and soaking his feet in his sandals.

How was Junichi going to replenish the life forces he'd squandered on beating the sword into submission? He would need to do so, soon.

He was also going to renegotiate the terms of his contract with Masato. Again. This entire venture had been so expensive! Developing the right spells to wound the fox fairies, creating the box that would transport a soul, then all the metals and expensive ingredients that had gone into the sword.

While Masato might maintain that he'd already paid his former master generously, Junichi hadn't been compensated nearly enough for his weakness now.

Maybe Junichi could convince Masato to pay him with the lives of his followers instead of gold this time. Surely he could spare a few.

The gray head that awaited Junichi surprised him. He'd been expecting one of the nearby young bucks to come and offer his services to either Junichi or Masato, willing to gamble that they would eventually be the lords of Shirayama. That was Masato's big vision, after all—the burning Buddha on the top of the mountain.

Not that much of a gamble, really. At least, not as far as Junichi was concerned. They would win. He would do everything in his power to ensure it, to make sure that this vision of Masato's came true.

However, this Taiga was as ancient as the mountain he stood on. He held himself straight, though his face was a mass of wrinkles and his skin as thin as rice paper. His beard was short and trimmed, composed only of white and gray hair, all the black long since worn away.

Junichi shivered. Though he was as old—possibly older—than this Taiga, he'd never let himself look or feel his age. His Taoist magic kept him young, and was worth every life he sacrificed to it. He would use that time properly. The ones he took it from were sure to waste it.

Taiga was yet another omen of all the bad luck surrounding this venture with the sword and the fox fairy. Curse all of them.

Junichi glanced around the small rise. Where was Taiga's retinue? He surely hadn't come by himself, had he? Or was he as cursed as Junichi, and unable to father heirs? That must be it. No son would let his father walk blithely into a Taoist magician's commune. Not without taking proper precautions.

Or if Taiga did have an heir, maybe he'd turned into something else, found a different path, like Masato.

At least this morning Junichi's servants had done their jobs well. Colorful purple pillows—not the court's purple, but close enough—were set tastefully on either side of a plain wooden table. An exquisitely crafted teapot and cups sat on the table, pale yellow, like impure gold. To the side, an iron pot bubbled cheerfully, hanging from a tripod set up over a well-contained fire.

"Greetings to you, O master swordsmith, on this auspicious day," Taiga said as Junichi came closer, bowing low.

"May it be a fair day to you," Junichi replied, already suspicious of where this conversation was leading. He bowed in return, though not as low. Not merely because Junichi didn't consider Taiga an equal, but also because he remained concerned about his balance in his weakened state.

After the servants served the tea, Junichi ordered them away, out of easy hearing range. Since his guest had come alone, it seemed proper to return the favor, and let their conversation remain private.

Junichi wasn't worried that Taiga would suddenly attack him. That would have been uncivilized, and there was nothing about this man that was common or rude. Though the style of his robe hadn't been seen in court for many years, it was still finely made from the highest-quality silk, a forest-green outer robe covering light brown pants.

Junichi and his guest sipped their tea in silence as they watched the sun break free of the horizon, blazing orange and pink clouds now modestly hiding her brilliance. More birds picked up the chorus, sounding like chattering ladies-in-waiting. Frogs from a nearby pond added their bass to the song. A light breeze tickled Junichi's neck, causing him to sigh softly as the new day began.

"What would you say to commemorate such a sight?" Junichi asked Taiga as he set his cup down.

Taiga thought for a moment before he replied:

> *"War banners shield*
> *The sun, hide her from spring vows*
> *That come before shame."*

Generally, men gave their allegiance to the Emperor in the spring. The association was that a spring vow was eternal, and would be renewed annually, like the seasons.

Taiga's response implied, though, that the spring vows he'd taken, or possibly were about to take, weren't honorable.

This surprised Junichi. Why would this at least once great man consider doing something distasteful?

So Junichi replied:

"Clouds, like blood, draw
Away swiftly, leaving behind
Mere reports of vows."

Implying that no matter what vow Taiga had taken, it was impermanent, and more importantly, always deniable. All things could be justified, explained away. Junichi knew this from personal experience.

In addition, the Buddha had taught that no deed in and of itself was either good or bad. It was one of the things that had drawn Masato, Junichi's former apprentice, to the religion.

Taiga nodded and took another sip of his tea before he replied:

"Winter leaves falling
Lose nothing while the mountain
And those vows still stand."

Was Taiga describing himself as a winter leaf? Or was he talking about Junichi, as Taoist magic was often described in terms of cold and snow, or death and the graveyard?

Though Junichi would love to continue to play the poem game with such a worthy opponent, he knew he was too drained from his recent ordeal to play it well. Plus, he didn't know enough about Taiga's background to understand all his references.

And Junichi never played any game that he didn't intend to win.

"Interesting," Junichi replied, taking another sip of tea. "And what vows are you speaking of?" he asked plainly. He was too tired to peel away meaning from flowery language.

It wasn't a sign of weakness, Junichi assured himself. It was, rather, a signal to his guest that he wanted to understand everything his guest had to say.

"Your servants claim that you performed a great spell tonight, creating a sword to protect the land," Taiga said. His face remained impassive, as if merely sharing news about the weather.

Junichi signaled a servant to come and pour them more tea while he thought. He cursed his slow brain. What would such an old man want with a sword? Surely he didn't mean to wield it himself, did he?

After the servant left, Taiga continued. "I've been the sworn guardian of this mountain for many seasons."

Junichi raised an eyebrow at this. He hadn't realized that Taiga had been appointed to the duty. He'd thought Akimoto no Tayo was responsible, the sworn lord of the mountain. He'd already been defeated by Masato, made his peace.

Had Masato lied to Junichi? Junichi wouldn't put it past him, not to share vital intelligence like that. It made Junichi more dependent on Masato, something he'd taught the boy when he was young.

Junichi was going to have to set up a better spy network through the region. Pay more of the local farmers for their knowledge.

"I've protected the sacred wells and temple," Taiga added. "We live in harmony with the *kami* and the *ujikami*. But this war with Masato—it threatens to destroy the very rocks under our feet, shake the mountain until it falls."

Ah—so those were the vows Taiga meant. He was the keeper of the heart of the mountain, not the land or roads. So the mountain must have two guardians, both assigned by the Emperor.

The other guardian, Akimoto no Tayo, had considered his duty to the mountain and the lands here onerous. He'd happily capitulated to Masato, with only token resistance. Perhaps he hadn't been born here, and had been sent to the provinces as punishment.

While Taiga had taken those vows to heart.

"Perhaps the mountain needs to be shaken," Junichi told him. The land was pretty enough, but it wasn't Kyoto, the city of the Emperor. "Maybe it needs to be leveled." Though that wasn't Masato's intent. He'd had a vision of the Buddha stepping from the mainland *Shina* to the island of Yamato, his foot landing on the top of the mountain and setting it on fire.

"In time, even mountains wash away," Taiga said. "That is the cycle of things." He paused, then added, "And though some may claim that war is the natural way of man, Masato's ways are not."

Junichi chuckled at that. No, they were not. Junichi wasn't the only sorcerer in Masato's pay. Masato, himself, also still dabbled, though he'd never been able to master the more difficult arts. "Do you know what type of magic I practice?" he asked Taiga. How much did the old man know?

"You're a Taoist magician," Taiga said, still with no inflection, no judgment apparent in his tone. "You swim against the stream of life, searching for immortality. Your magic isn't natural." He shrugged, then added, "An unnatural war needs to be fought by unnatural means."

Was this Taiga more, or less, than what he seemed? Was he ready to justify any and all acts in the name of his mountain? Junichi was very intrigued. How far would this honorable man go?

However, instead of asking about ethics, Junichi merely said, "You are very wise."

Taiga laughed. "No. Just an old man."

"Who wants to live a bit longer?" Junichi guessed. Maybe Taiga didn't want the sword. Maybe he'd come to regret his childless state and wanted what Junichi could provide him—to live enough years to become his own legacy, instead of relying on sons and grandsons to bring him an unsatisfying type of immortality.

"Me? That isn't my wish." Taiga laughed again, a bit harder and longer.

Junichi noticed the servants nearby raising their heads. He guessed they didn't often hear laughter in his compound. Not free and joyous like that.

Or maybe they were waiting for Junichi to become offended and take the old man's head. But this Taiga still interested Junichi. If they had lived in a different time they might have become friends, drinking tea together in the afternoons, wisely debating the world.

Finally Taiga stopped laughing and added, "I'm ready to leave this vale of tears today if necessary. But the mountain—she isn't."

Taiga put his tea cup to the side and stared at Junichi, his gaze heavy and determined. "I want the sword. I want a chance to defend the mountain as she should be."

"And what would you give me for such a prize?" Junichi asked. He didn't hold Taiga's gaze but instead, looked down and toyed with his cup. He expected the old man to offer something trite, like his life.

"My soul."

Now it was Junichi's turn to work at keeping his expression neutral, not allowing himself to show the joy that suddenly warmed him, like a welcoming sunbeam. He couldn't afford to show Taiga how tempting his offer was. That would have been a bad bargaining ploy.

However, the old man's offer was the perfect bribe. Particularly after the long night and intense struggle.

Immediately, Junichi started justifying the deal to himself. He and Masato had only talked about the sword containing a fox fairy soul. He hadn't *guaranteed* it. It certainly wasn't in the contract they'd signed.

He could always make another sword for Masato. Right?

Besides, how long would Taiga be able to hold such an artifact? He'd be sure to lose it in the first battle he had with Masato.

And hadn't Masato, in his latest communication with Junichi, proclaimed himself the finest general in the world?

Certainly he should be able to overcome a minor lord like Taiga in order to fetch the sword for himself.

That way, Junichi could both have Taiga's soul, and Masato would have his sword.

Junichi considered the man in front of him. He longed to drink down the strong spirit of him, like the sweet water that came from the hidden springs on the mountain.

"I would only use it as the guardian of the mountain," Taiga added.

It took much more effort for Junichi to keep a straight face. The foolish man had just given the sorcerer a way to bind him. If Junichi worded the contract correctly, Taiga would never be able to attack with the sword. He'd only be able to use it for defense.

The strong will of the sword might also be a good thing in this deal. It would be the final arbitrator, deciding whether Taiga was a fit guardian or not.

Junichi was very curious whether or not the sword would accept Taiga.

Taiga turned away, gazing out at the far horizon. His profile showed no emotion, no trembling, no doubt. He could have been carved from mountain stone.

However, Junichi needed to be certain. "The sword contains a soul," he said. He wanted to see if Taiga understood all the ramifications of his deal. A life had already been taken for the creation of the sword. This didn't make the sword evil, but it wasn't necessarily good, either.

The only reaction from Taiga was a quick intake of breath. However, he didn't turn away from the course he'd plotted.

"I understand," he replied. The sadness in his eyes told Junichi that he wasn't lying. He was ready to accept this death for his mountain.

No wonder he'd earlier described his vows as being beyond shame.

Junichi called for his scribe, dictating the terms of the contract. He didn't specify a length of time before he collected Taiga's soul, but he knew it wouldn't be long.

Taiga didn't flinch when Junichi cut Taiga's hand and used his blood to sign the pact.

His eyes did widen, though, when Junichi used his teeth to open his own wrist. However, Taiga didn't say anything, and his hand didn't tremble as he signed, using Junichi's blood.

When they finished, Junichi rose to fetch the sword himself instead of sending one of his servants. He nearly fell when he stood, his exhaustion overriding his excitement.

However, he pulled himself straight. Even though he'd already reached an agreement with Kitayama no Taiga, there were still limits of what he'd disclose to another.

Only the vaguest fire still lit the kiln. Metal shavings and tiny grains from the sparks littered the floor. Tools lay scattered everywhere, along with bundles of herbs that Junichi had used to keep the space pure.

The sword lay slumbering. The surface of it was cool to the touch, pleasing to the eye. Its tears spotted its side, dappling its smooth steel skin like dew on a petal.

Junichi had braided thin strips of black-and-gray sharkskin around its handle. The bumps of the skin felt like raised chick flesh against Junichi's palm.

The sword shivered as Junichi picked it up. It only fought against him a little as he raised it, pulling itself toward the earth, making itself feel heavier than it actually was.

"I name you Seiji—the lawful one," Junichi whispered, the name suddenly coming to him. He passed his hand along the sword's surface. When it shuddered again and nicked his fingers—questing for his blood— he merely laughed.

He was not afraid that the sword might turn against its maker. While it might try, they were too intimately bound together. The sword would fail.

Junichi used a plain black-lacquered scabbard for the sword, not to humble it, but to allow the beauty of the weapon to speak for itself.

When Junichi stepped from the forge, he found that Taiga had instructed the servants to remove the table and place a crimson-and-gold silk pillow in its stead, between the two seats.

Junichi presented the sword without much ceremony, stating the sword's name and setting it on the pillow as gracefully as he could manage, given his exhaustion, before kneeling down again.

Taiga greeted the sword properly, bowing to it reverently and speaking its name before he touched it.

The sword seemed to accept him. It allowed itself to be drawn from its scabbard without too much effort.

"He is beautiful," Taiga whispered.

For the first time, Taiga seemed overcome with emotion. Junichi couldn't understand the tears that now pricked the old man's eyes.

Was it because of the sheer beauty of his work? Or did the sword mean more, somehow?

However, when Taiga tried to rise, he found he couldn't lift the sword. The old man staggered, but he didn't fall. The tip of the sword refused to leave the earth, though.

It seemed that the sword had rejected the old man. Junichi wasn't certain why—maybe it was because of the pact Taiga had just signed. The sword would only acknowledge a true protector of the land, not one who served a second master, as Taiga now did, his soul wholly owned by Junichi.

Taiga didn't say a word to Junichi about it, claiming some sort of breach of contract. He understood his own lack of worth. He walked away with as much dignity as he could, dragging the sword behind him.

What Taiga did with the sword didn't really matter to Junichi. Taiga only had one, maybe two weeks of life before Junichi would drink him down, use the steady, strong force of the old man to fuel his own long life. He considered the bargain fair.

It didn't occur to Junichi until much, much later, that maybe Taiga had never intended to use the sword himself. Junichi always assumed that old men were as childless as he was, especially since Taiga had come to call on Junichi by himself.

Junichi had never thought that this Taiga might have a son.

Four

Morning Crept In

Hikaru

Morning crept in on tired feet, with gray, mouse-colored clouds and a sad sun. I felt weary unto my bones, hollowed out by my grief, as if the slightest breeze would bowl me over. Yukiko watched me like a hawk, convinced, I'm sure, that I would slip away, feeling as though my burdens were too great to bear.

She didn't understand how the promise of revenge kept me on my feet. Made me rise and continue moving through my day.

We supped that morning on cold soup, made from watery chicken broth and wild spring onions. How my Norihiko would have loved it, such simple food, such comfort for the soul.

The silence spilled around Yukiko and me, too thick to be broken. We ate in my rooms, hidden from the other guests. Morning showed the thick cobwebs gracing the corners of the beamed ceiling, the poor quality of the sleeping mats, the lack of poems or paintings hanging on the walls.

The innkeeper tottered around his garden in the back, fussing over his plants as I would imagine one fussed over particularly recalcitrant children.

He saw us looking out from my simple room, I'm sure, but he gave space to grieve.

I'd placed the tiny pinecone Norihiko had given me on the window sill, one of his many presents of love. The branch it clung to was still fragrant. I meant to place it on Norihiko's funeral pyre later that morning. I'd lost the raven's feather long before.

The humans had lent us a small Shinto temple for us to conduct our rites. Trees grew right up to the walls surrounding the building, making the complex feel as though it was still part of nature. The *torii* was neither broad nor tall, just a simple gate with crude guardian lions merely carved into the wood on either side, not brightly painted or decorated. The building itself was as humble as its surroundings: plain wooden walls with a rounded, thatched roof.

Yukiko and I spent little time inside, being blessed by the single priest we'd hired to chant the sacred prayers. The villagers respected my need for solitude, though I knew they'd be curious about the fine lady and her great sorrow.

The main room of the temple held a single offering table at the front, covered with bowls of fine rice that Yukiko and I had donated. A bamboo door hid the statue of the *kami* the temple was dedicated to.

If it had been Norihiko and I praying, making a side trip to visit a local temple, like any tourists we would have asked for the priest to open the door, to have allowed us to pray before the spirit itself.

I was unfamiliar with this particular forest spirit. I didn't know if she was a real *kami*, or just a convenient myth for the local priests, an easy way for them to be supported. The only way I would have been able to tell was by viewing the *kami's* home directly.

As the priest finished his prayers, he dripped fresh water over Yukiko's and my head. I felt blessed by a calm I hadn't expected.

Maybe the *kami* was real.

Once the ceremony inside the temple was finished, there was nothing to do but go to the funeral pyre set up outside. Oh, how I longed for the comfort of my mother and sisters at that time! I had insisted that the ceremony be kept short—I didn't have the strength to endure hours of public grieving.

Yet, when faced with Norihiko's body, I was selfishly glad that I had these last few moments with my love, alone.

I'd directed the priests to put Norihiko's body in the northern-most corner of the shrine compound. Priests had trimmed the tree limbs directly above the pyre, so that the flames wouldn't set the surrounding woods on fire. The trees still overshadowed the entire complex, silent guardians of Norihiko's final resting spot.

I wished I could see his face one last time. I had covered his entire body with the finest cloth I could find in this tiny outpost. But even the incense constantly burning beside the pyre couldn't hide the truth: my love's body was already rotting, spoiled with death magic.

I imagined Norihiko clearly, though, with his eyes closed, hiding the twinkling brown, a slight smile on his full lips, his body which always had been so full of life and energy, relaxed and at peace.

At Yukiko's insistence, I gave a short eulogy. The words I spoke were stiff, formal, and ugly. I longed for more beauty, to give my love the poetry he deserved—to describe the weeping sky, the stillness of the sacred space, the elegance of the white mourning silks we wore.

Yet, this ugliness had its place as well, reflecting the hidden, disastrous wounds on Norihiko's body, the echoing loneliness I felt, the pitying glances cast on us by the priest.

Many have railed against the strictness of the funeral ceremonies that those of the court must go through. They don't understand—or have never experienced—the totality of grief we felt. It was a blessing, truly, to be told where to stand, what to say, then be led away when it was time to go.

I never would have made it without Yukiko to guide me. Her solid presence gave me a wall to lean on when my grief became too much. Had she lost someone before, to become so well practiced in the rituals?

I would never ask, though. Despite how closely I relied on her that day, she was still a servant.

And keeping our roles distinct, well, that was essential to the ceremony of our lives.

Yukiko and I started our journey back the next morning. I will always think of the days during our ride home as dark, full of angry storm clouds and thunder.

In truth, it was still spring, with only light showers and pale blue skies. The carriage I'd purchased was cheap, the hay in the cushions smelled musty, and the fabric covering them was rough. It was an open carriage—I didn't care what scandal I caused traveling this way. We needed speed, not decorum.

Most of the rain that fell that trip was in the form of my tears. I let myself grieve greatly all the way through the dismal handful of days it took to get back home. I would have torn out my hair and shredded my clothes, but I didn't want to be more of a spectacle than I already was, a constantly weeping woman, face ash-smeared, in increasingly soiled white mourning robes.

I hid us with magic and glamours when I could, turning curious eyes away from Yukiko and myself, letting us pass without notice. Too many people remembered us from when we'd traveled the other way.

When I was forced to let the humans notice us, so we could get food, fresh horses, or a place to stay, they stared at me, pitying the weeping bride, their sorrow amplifying my own.

It wasn't difficult for me to grieve with all my soul as the days passed and we moved from forest, to field, to foothills. I knew I had to let all of my sadness out, to encourage the floods to come now, because I wouldn't have time for them later.

Generally, brides as young as I was went into mourning for a full year. They were attended only by their families. Not even close friends could call. A mourning bride couldn't see any young men, either.

I couldn't be hidden away like that. It would cause a scandal, but I didn't care.

Norihiko's revenge demanded that I act quickly. I had to find whoever had killed him. Find the caster of the foul magic.

I also needed to finish my tears before I got home, so my mother wouldn't try to stop me enacting my revenge, wouldn't insist that I stay there with my tears.

Yukiko stayed silent through much of our journey. She'd wailed with appropriate feeling over the death of her fellow servants, but after that, she lost her words. She stared grimly out over the horses, as if willing them to run faster.

She stayed with me through the long days and nights, holding me as I cried, without another tear coming from her own eyes.

By the end of the ride home, I'd finished my weeping and grown as silent as Yukiko. Particularly when I burned my white mourning robes and replaced them with black.

I think Yukiko understood that this wasn't the end of our journeys. I didn't know where fate would lead me to seek my revenge, only that I couldn't rest until I'd found it.

I'd sent riders ahead of us, bearing sealed letters, so my family already knew our news. We arrived at the estate in the early evening, even though custom dictated that one never reached one's destination until after it was fully dark, so no one could witness our exhaustion or travel-stained clothes.

As it was just my family, I didn't care.

My childhood home—though really, I suppose it qualified as a small estate—sat nestled in the foothills of Yoshino Mountain. Strong gates, iron and sturdy, supported by thick rock walls protected the compound. They were diligently maintained, though really, none could find us whom we didn't want to see. The roads were all hidden and enspelled.

Evening had settled softly across the land, hiding the sharp rocks, giving everything a green tint, as if covered by moss. The mountain shot up sharply at the back of our property—yet another safety precaution, as we never had to worry about an attack coming from the rear. It was a land of peace, reflecting the true nature of the *kitsune*. We never started any war, and would slip out from a trap rather than fight whenever we could.

My two sisters, both older than I—Etsu and Cho—greeted us at the outer gates.

My mother, of course, had taken to her bed at the news.

I knew she would weep for me, for Norihiko, for the rest of her day. How long would she lay all the responsibilities for the household on my sisters' shoulders while she mourned? Had she finally found the one perfect excuse, so she could hide in her rooms forever?

Not that I wished my mother ill. But having lived with all her humors and sick spells, perhaps I was a bit tired of them.

No tear tracks marred my sisters' beautiful faces, though they wore the finest black mourning silks, rich and heavy. I was glad that they'd already burned the white cotton robes that one wore over one's clothing at the start of a mourning period: I'd dreaded living through more funeral rites, as well as having to give a new elegy.

Etsu wore her glorious, thick black hair unbound, falling around her like dark waterfalls, as was proper during the first weeks of mourning.

Cho, the sister closest to me in age, still had her usual butterfly pins in her hair, the ones beautifully enameled with red and green wings.

It was the only color on the three of us, the only bright spot I'd noticed for days.

Despite my resolutions, the sight of them made me weep.

Etsu pulled me into her arms immediately, comforting me as was her responsibility as the eldest. She smelled of warm, dry places, lined with leaves and fur. Of all of us, she was the most comfortable in her fox form.

Mother had told us it was because Etsu was the eldest, that someday, we'd all feel the same way.

I wasn't sure I believed Mother. Was Etsu's ease instead due to the man who'd fathered her? He'd been a human sorcerer, who'd specialized in changing shapes.

When I finished my tears, we walked hand-in-hand to my rooms, along the darkened corridors of the main building. All the lights had been masked with yellow silk, making the spaces seem even more enclosed.

In my rooms, the *tatamis* had already been aired out and laid on the floor, with a scattering of red, green, and yellow silk-covered pillows. Only a few of the lanterns had been lit, keeping the corners dark, hiding mysteries and shadows. The windows overlooking the formal gardens were shuttered, with bright red ribbons holding them shut against any ill spirits.

Servants brought us tea, then withdrew. I knew they were waiting just outside the door, listening closely for any tidbit they could use in their gossip.

I didn't know what to say to my sisters. These rooms, where I'd spent so many years, were foreign to me, now. Echoes of the laughter I'd shared with Norihiko stirred restlessly in the corners.

My sisters respected my silence, or at least, tried to. Cho didn't know how to be still, though. Soon, she was chatting away about the spring, the way the leaves were budding, the latest volume of poetry she'd read, how the robins proclaimed that the summer was to be short but hot.

I didn't interrupt her, and I didn't let Etsu shush her, either. It amazed me, how I no longer felt as though I was the youngest amongst us.

Had I ever been as light and silly as Cho?

Of course I had been. Until the past week, I'd been even more flighty.

Now, the weight of my responsibilities lay heavily on my shoulders.

Eventually, Cho's rambling began to irritate me. I wanted to be alone again.

I'd never been a solitary creature, but now, my soul seemed to relax only when I was by myself. I couldn't explain my desires to my sisters. They wouldn't have understood. I barely understood it myself. The *kitsune* were social by nature.

I started yawning, a polite way of letting my sisters know it was time for them to be on their way. I didn't have to feign my exhaustion, though I knew I wouldn't sleep: too many ghosts lingered in these rooms. Memories of Norihiko and our poetry contests, impassioned letters I'd agonized over, whispered confidences as we both grew bold.

After Etsu shooed my other sister out of my room, she paused at the door, then turned back and said, "You won't have to go through this alone. We'll be there with you, as long as we can be."

I shivered as much at her words as her deliberate phrasing. Etsu had a touch of my mother's gift. What had she seen? What trials would my sisters go through with me?

What would my revenge cost them?

With Yukiko's help, I managed to put off my sisters and spend the morning alone. I didn't have the energy to get off my sleeping *tatami* until quite late, well after the sun had risen and the chores of the day had begun. I spent time sitting on the small porch off my main room, watching the garden and the trees just beyond.

I couldn't see the mountain from my windows, a lack I'd never felt before. The budding greenery below was too transient, too fragile. It reminded me, the immortal, of the impermanence of life.

If Norihiko had still lived, I would have composed sad poems for him. Because he was my true love, he would have responded in kiind, knowing better than to try to cheer me up.

Even though it was still spring, the afternoon dragged on, the air hot and breathless. I decided to sleep my way through the worst of it, not just because that meant I could put off my sisters for a while longer.

I dreamed I was being snugly held, encased in safe darkness. It wasn't clear if Norihiko had come back to me—but I'd only felt such peace in his arms.

Then everything began to tremble and shake, as the land does when Nai no Kami starts his dance to bring the mountain down.

I awoke, shivering and sweating, chills racing down my spine.

Yukiko knelt beside me, her hand still resting on my shoulder. Evidently, she'd been shaking me awake.

"Your mother has summoned you," Yukiko said bleakly.

There could only be one reason why: She must have had a vision. One that involved me.

"Has she called for any of my sisters?" I asked as I pushed myself to sitting.

"She has not," Yukiko said. "Just you."

I prepared myself as best I could, taking the time to straighten my black-silk mourning robes, comb out my hair, and apply some color to my face.

My mother was certain to be hysterical and I needed to be as calm as possible. Preparing my face and my clothes would help give me confidence.

I also wanted to show her that I wasn't her baby girl anymore. I needed for her to tell me everything she'd seen, not just what she deemed appropriate for me, as she had in the past.

Low moaning echoed through the hall as I approached, filling me with dread. I paused outside my mother's door, taking deep breaths and calming myself, before I pushed open the *shoji* and entered.

It was worse than the time she'd seen flood destroying the nearby farms and the ensuing famine.

Not only had my mother not dressed or fixed her hair, she hadn't bothered to get up from her sleeping mat. The wooden pillow block still lay to one side, discarded like a child's toy. None of the windows were open and the air smelled sour, like a sickroom. No lamps brightened the tiny square space—it was as gloomy as a tomb.

Mother sat on her mats, crying and weeping, moaning and wringing her hands. She muttered quietly, "Norihiko, poor, poor, Norihiko," over and over again.

I held back my sigh of exasperation. Why was *she* allowed such extreme grief when it had been *my* husband who had been killed? Yet I contained myself and my mourning?

I still went to my mother, held her, rocked her back and forth and stroked her hair, as if she were the child and I the adult. I'd done this many time before when she'd had a vision.

Something was wrong, though. Mother was much more upset than usual. She cried fitfully, stopping and starting, her forehead pressed hard against my shoulder. She smelled bitter, as though she'd taken a vinegar bath.

Through her tears and increasingly loud moans, I made out a few more words: "Fire," "Pain," and "Splintered."

What had she seen? Was it more than Norihiko's death? Was the estate about to be burned down? Was our family to be sundered? Oh that she would just control herself! Cease her weeping and carrying on!

I waited, not very patiently, for her to calm down and tell me what she'd seen.

Except, she never did. She would stop crying for a while, only to start back up again. Her moans cycled up and down in volume.

My back started to ache from holding my mother for so long. I wanted to signal one of the servants, have them bring me some tea, but they'd all withdrawn beyond the *shoji*.

Possibly they'd done this out of courtesy, but I knew better. They were lazy and knew that I'd be calling on them to fetch things for my mother.

They'd all lived through many of my mother's hysteric spells, when nothing would satisfy her or end her grief.

When my mother's moans had quieted enough that I could be heard, I called out for Yukiko. She came immediately. At least *she* was well trained.

"Please fetch Etsu," I told her. It was appropriate for the eldest to come and take care of my mother, at least for a while. Until she could calm herself enough to tell me what she'd seen.

That seemed to draw Mother out of her fit, at least for a while.

"Do. Fetch Etsu," she said, gasping through her tears.

"Right away," Yukiko assured me with a nod.

I knew Yukiko would also come back with refreshments. I was going to have to reward her loyalty, soon. Not a new outfit, not while we were both in mourning. Maybe a new comb for her hair, though.

"Mother, what did you see?" I asked. The question was selfish. I should have asked what I could get for her, how to help her pain. But I had to know. She wouldn't have called for me if her vision hadn't been about me. And she'd already mentioned Norihiko.

Mother grasped my forearms, tightening her grip until I winced with pain. Her skin took on an eerie light, as if a death fire burned beneath it. Her mussed hair stood out further, as if full of its own life. Her bloodshot eyes bored into me, seeking the depths of my soul, holding it, judging it.

Had she finally found me worthy?

Then she deliberately turned her head, cast her gaze to the far corner of the room where most of the shadows lay, her look growing distant.

"There's so much pain," Mother said, her whispered words swirling around us, binding us together. "He's been beaten, broken, remade." Her voice took on more strength as she continued. "In the fire. In the fire!"

With that, Mother screamed, wrenching her hands from me and covering her face as if to block out the sight.

"Mother, please," I said, reaching out for her. What had she seen? I had to know.

"Splintered! Remade!" she shrieked, rocking back and forth. Then she turned and gripped my shoulders with fingers that felt like iron claws.

"You must save him. Release his soul." The glow emanating from her skin faded, but her eyes still burned with a frightful fire, deep and pitiless. "He's all steel and sharp edges, your lovely soft mate. You must break the curse, free him from this horror."

Her words sank into my flesh as effortlessly as the arrows from the attack. But I couldn't consider the pain right now.

"Where, Mother? Where is he?" I asked urgently. She had to tell me where to go, where I would recover my love.

"Court. You must go to the Emperor's court. You'll find your Norihiko there, recreated as a guardian sword," Mother said all in a rush, pushing the words at me.

The burden of revenge already laid on my shoulders doubled in weight. I wanted to weep as my mother did, scream and rage against fate.

A sword? My lovely, kind, honorable Norihiko had been reforged into a sword? I shivered, the horror overtaking me. How he must have suffered!

Then the flames Mother saw redoubled in my own heart. The sorcerer who had done this to my beloved would pay double now, pay with pain as well as his life.

I must not have been paying Mother enough attention, because she suddenly shrieked again. "You must take heed! Or the pain, the fire, the heat, and the splintering will take you too!"

Then she fell back on the mat. "The flames! The hammering!" She held her arms up in front of her and thrashed from side to side, as if trying to escape a beating.

I grabbed onto Mother's shoulders and shook her. "Mother!" I called.

This was much worse than any other vision I'd ever witnessed. She couldn't free herself from it. It was as if she were reliving it, experiencing the agony my Norihiko had gone through when he'd been reforged into a sword.

I called her name and shook her again, but she didn't know me, couldn't hear me, couldn't come back to this place.

I'd seen my mother tear her hair and weep, play the martyr to what she'd witnessed, but she'd never been as bad as this. She pulled away from me, shrieking in pain as she cried.

I didn't know what to do to comfort her, how to bring her out of her vision. I felt as helpless as when my servants had died in the carriage, poor Ume and her soundless screams.

Finally, Etsu came in. She was properly dressed, her makeup and hair perfectly done. I may have resented her taking the time to do it, however, I fully understood being prepared when dealing with Mother and her visions.

Etsu's servants carried a calm, herbal tea, as well as sage-green cloths soaked in lavender water.

When Etsu called Mother's name, she calmed immediately. Her frantic thrashing stopped. Her tears continued, but at least she no longer shrieked or moaned.

Eventually, between Etsu and me, we got Mother to drink some of the tea. It helped the most, and Mother's tears dried soon after that.

Had Etsu put some sort of spell on it? She was the most magical of all my sisters.

When Mother finally closed her eyes and went limp against the sleeping mat, Etsu and I rose. Mother always needed quiet to sleep, particularly after such a grueling vision. We would wait, as we always did, on the far side of the *shoji* in case Mother needed us, called us back, as she frequently would.

"Wait. Stop," Mother called before we could escape.

I didn't express my exasperation, but instead, plastered a pleasant smile on my face and turned, ever attentive.

"Give her the box," Mother croaked out, her voice rough and hoarse after so much screaming.

Etsu issued a sharp order to one of her servants before she went back and knelt again next to Mother's sleeping mat.

I followed, more curious than impatient.

We didn't make the mistake of trying to talk with Mother now, ask her how she was or if she needed anything. It was better for her to rest and not think up new tasks for us.

The servant returned. She entered Mother's room on her knees, a square, red-lacquered box held above her head so her breath wouldn't spoil its perfect surface. She presented it with a low bow to my sister, who in turn bowed and gave the box to me.

The workmanship on the box was exquisite. The lacquer so polished that I could almost see my reflection in it. The box fit comfortably into the palm of my hand and was as light as a puff of down.

Inside the box, on a pile of the finest red silk, lay a small, bead-shaped wooden amulet, about the size of an acorn. The wood was golden brown, and the sides were carved in an intricate design—like the twisted branches of a thorn bush—then filled in with black.

The bead was warm to the touch, and felt heavier than it looked when I put it in the palm of my hand, as if it were carved from lead.

Mother gestured wordlessly for me to come closer.

I held out my hand with the bead to her.

With just a finger, Mother touched the bead.

A tingling shock ran up my arm. She'd just cast magic on it. The bead felt even heavier, now.

"It won't save you," Mother instructed, her voice reedy and soft. "But it may keep your spirit and body united in a time of great need."

What did that mean? What else had Mother seen?

Of course, she wasn't about to tell me. I'd never understood why all fortune tellers could only tell some of what they'd seen.

Maybe some things were too horrific to bear. Or perhaps knowing more wouldn't change things.

Etsu produced a long leather cord. After I threaded the bead through it, she tied the cord around my neck. I hid it under my robes, the weight an extra comfort.

"Thank you," I told Mother.

She barely nodded before she passed into dreams.

Etsu and I rose again, this time making it out of the room. Etsu's servants set up pillows and brought tea for us, my mother's lazy women nowhere to be seen.

We stayed quiet for a while, each lost in her own thoughts.

I knew where I had to go, what I had to do. I didn't know the details, like how to free Norihiko from this terrible curse. But that would come.

Mother had seen me meeting the sorcerer responsible for this terrible deed. I was certain of it. She'd also seen the danger I would be in when I confronted this man and had provided me with protection.

The solid weight of my new amulet spread through my body, solidifying my bones. My love had been captured in steel. I would become just as hard and would fall upon those who had harmed him with a great, swirling anger.

At the same time, I still worried about Mother. This vision was much worse than any she'd ever shared. It had soaked into her blood, blinded and overwhelmed her, unlike any other.

I shuddered to think what it must have been like for Norihiko.

Finally, Etsu spoke. "You will not go to court alone."

How had Etsu known what Mother had told me? Had she shared in some of the vision? Or did she already know, given her words from the night before?

"But Mother will need—" I started to say.

"One of *her* sisters will take care of her," Etsu said firmly.

I nearly snorted. Mother's sisters were often just as hysterical over the least little thing.

Etsu continued. "You need *your* sisters with you."

I wanted to protest. I wanted to tell Etsu to stay here, look after the household, nurse Mother back to health. Her servants needed someone to take them to task.

However, I'd always had a greedy soul. I wanted my sisters with me. I did at least manage to ask, "Are you certain?"

At that, Etsu laughed, a mean, bitter sound that shot frozen arrows down my spine, filling me with dread.

"Surely you don't think just breaking the sword is going to free him? It isn't going to be that easy."

Etsu took my hand in her ice-cold one. "We will stay with you as long as we can."

I shuddered at her repeated words, clutching her hand and willing my warmth into her, willing our flesh to stay as one.

I knew better than to ask what Etsu had seen. She wouldn't tell me, being more tight-lipped about these things than Mother.

However, I now feared my mother's warning of *sundering* even more.

There was nothing more to say after that. We spent the rest of the afternoon in silence, drifting in our thoughts like motes in a sunbeam.

Five

Through the Lattice

Kayoku

Through the lattice set up at the back of the *seishikina* hall, Kayoku could watch the ceremony of succession. Of course, women weren't allowed at such important ceremonies. However, Lord Taiga had ordered delicately-carved wooden lattice screens to be set up all around the edges of the hall, with enough space behind them that a quiet soul could sit and watch.

The ceremony was very beautiful. Melodious hymns, chanted by the priests of the Mori temple, filled the room and blessed the space at the beginning. Two dozen courtiers filled the hall, row upon row, like colorful flowers. Pungent incense crept through the lattice to include those hidden there. The men of the Kitayama clan filed in like an endless line of soldiers, each brave and dedicated to the mountain.

Kayoku couldn't help but compare her husband, Iwao, with the others, in particular, his older brothers.

She had to admit that Iwao wasn't the most graceful of men.

Instead of bending like spring bamboo during the ritual dance performed by all the men of the Kitayama clan, Iwao plodded along, peering from time to time at the cheat sheet he'd attached to the back of his flat wooden baton.

Iwao's outer robe was just as fine as all the others, made from dark auburn silk with the family crest of a stylized mountain, sewn with delicate golden stitches, covering the back. Yet it stretched across his shoulders in a way that made it seem ill-fitting.

Like the others, Iwao kept his face serious and as emotionless as possible.

However, his eyes burned with a fierceness that Kayoku had never seen before.

Kayoku tried to pay attention to every detail. This was, after all, the most important ceremony of her life. With Iwao's ascension came her own. She'd always been a lesser, minor wife. Now, she'd be one of the most important, with as much power as Chieko, the wife of Iwao's eldest brother, as Lord Taiga had outlived all his wives.

Questions plagued Kayoku. Everyone knew that Lord Taiga was concerned about the warlord Masato and his attacks. It had only been a series of skirmishes so far, with each side testing the strength of the other. No formal declaration of war had been made.

Akimoto no Tayo, the other primary lord of the mountain, had supposedly already negotiated with Masato, surrendering his lands and transferring his allegiance.

Was that why Lord Taiga had suddenly announced Iwao as his heir? Did he need a more traditional approach to battle?

Though Kayoku respected her husband, she also knew he wasn't the most creative of men. His performance at the ceremony was true to form. He followed litanies well, and memorized words flowed smoothly from him. If he'd had to make up his own response, he wouldn't have done as well.

Did Lord Taiga's decision have something to do with the sword, Seiji? Lord Taiga had disappeared from the compound for a night and a day. When he'd returned, he'd been dragging what some of the generals had described as the most elegant weapon they'd ever beheld.

Kayoku dismissed the rumors that the sword was magical, that none appeared to be able to lift it. Men would always blame magic, curses, or their own bad luck rather than acknowledge their true lack of ability.

She was curious, though, and looked forward to being able to view the sword herself. Maybe she'd write a letter that evening, asking permission to visit Iwao in his rooms, to celebrate his success with him. If he was in a good mood, he might even show her the blade of the sword.

And if he was in a very good mood, maybe they could try getting Kayoku pregnant again. Little Kenta had just not been meant for this earth. He hadn't even survived to his name day.

Kayoku focused her attention back on the ceremony, concentrating on the reactions of the others as Lord Taiga passed everything he owned, all the land and temples he was responsible for, to his youngest son.

Lord Taiga's generals were all in shock. So were Iwao's brothers.

None of them understood why Lord Taiga had chosen to turn everything over to Iwao.

Was it a trick, a way of forcing Iwao to fail, so that he'd be disgraced? Surely Iwao wasn't so important that Lord Taiga needed to resort to such an elaborate ruse.

Or was it Kayoku's bad luck finally turned good?

After the ceremony of succession, Kayoku gathered with all of the wives to have wine and gossip. Of course, they all pretended they hadn't been there, hadn't seen each other through the lattice screens.

They met in Chieko's rooms, as she was the oldest woman of importance on the estate. The windows had all been opened to let in the beautiful spring breezes. Festive strips of red, gold, and green paper, delicately folded together in a zigzag pattern like the *gohei*, hung from the corners. A ceremonial pine— only as high Kayoku's waist and meticulously trimmed—had been brought in from the gardens, blessing the air with its sweet scent.

"Please, sit," Chieko directed Kayoku, indicating the seat of honor at the head of the room. Chieko's robes were dyed the most delicate shade of green, like tea leaves just budding. Kayoku felt like a dark storm next to her, her own robes dyed musty brown.

"Oh, no, that is your seat," Kayoku insisted.

Officially, now that the succession ceremony was complete, Kayoku was the head woman of the Kitayama clan estate. However, she was also one of the youngest women there. She'd lived on the estate for less than two years. She wasn't about to overstep herself. She needed to maintain the allies she had, while pursuing new ones.

"Please, I insist," Kayoku said, giving Chieko a generous smile while declining to sit at the head of the room. It was good that she'd always gotten along with Chieko. It wasn't difficult to give her the seat of honor.

Though the estate wasn't that large, and their "court" was only a fraction of the size of the Emperor's, the relationships were complex, and alliances were always shifting. For the sake of her husband and their combined line, Kayoku knew she must gather and keep the support of as many of these women as she could.

"I heard that Iwao did well," Chieko said after all the women had settled into their places and the servants had poured the wine.

"Oh, did you hear that?" Kayoku replied politely. She suppressed the smile she felt rising inside of her. She was so full of pride she was afraid it would start to drip from her. Her husband really *had* done well, as far as she could tell.

Emiko, Iwao's youngest sister, laughed and clapped her hands. "I heard that he spoke every word without tripping once!"

"I'm so very happy for him if that's true," Kayoku replied, pleased with this. Iwao's tongue hadn't stumbled over a single response in the litany. And though she loved and respected her husband, she was too well aware that words had never been his friends.

The other wives joined in praising Iwao. Kayoku listened greedily to their words and would have blushed if that had been her nature. She politely turned the conversation away from the ceremony as soon as she could, asking instead about the shower of stars that had fallen toward the mountain, debating if it was a good omen or a bad one, as well as marveling over the beauty of it.

When Emiko thoughtlessly added, "I was sure the stars were part of the latest battle," the whole room grew quiet.

"You're wrong, child, the skirmishes haven't come that close," Chieko finally responded, her tone chiding.

Kayoku was glad she hadn't had to deliver such a reprimand. She still was aware that in the near future, it would be her place.

"But what if they do?" Emiko asked, the words all rushing out. "What if they attack the Mori shrine? What if they remove the *shintai*? The *kami* will no longer visit! The mountain will have lost her soul!"

"Child, child," Chieko said, shaking her head. "You must believe in your brother, your father and his sons, and all their generals. They will protect us and defend the mountain. All you can do is your duty. And pray."

Emiko was obviously frustrated with such a response. Kayoku sympathized. She'd also felt a need for more action.

Though none of the other women looked directly at her, Kayoku felt their intense curiosity. How would she handle such a breach of conduct?

Propriety demanded that they never talk about the war, or who had lost sons, or why it was so difficult to get the newest silks or the freshest fish.

In the growing silence, Kayoku finally spoke. "Emiko, why don't we take Priestess Ayumi with us the next time we go to clean the Mori temple? That way, the water will not only be pure, but blessed. It will be something useful we can do together, and it will help protect the shrine, ensure that those not worthy can't enter."

Emiko gave her a grateful smile. "Thank you, Kayoku. That is a good and practical suggestion. I think we should all think of such things, do what we can."

Kayoku felt the alliances shifting around her. Who would heed such a suggestion? Who would accuse her of overstepping her bounds? She'd been the victim of such fluid connections before, accused of bad luck and shunned, regardless of her position.

When Kayoku's father had remarried, the new wife hadn't liked Kayoku. She'd gone so far as to accuse Kayoku of interfering with the household, though Kayoku had been running it for years, since the death of her own mother. At the same time, Kayoku hadn't cared for the extravagant way her new stepmother had spent money.

Kayoku had been pledged as Iwao's wife when she'd been born. With the arrival of her new step-mother, there was no question about Kayoku leaving her childhood home when she got married.

However, her stepmother's accusations of bad luck had followed Kayoku. She'd gotten pregnant almost immediately, however, Little Kenta hadn't lived beyond his first year.

It was too early for Kayoku to know if the other wives considered her new position lucky or not. Not just them, though. While Kayoku hoped that her new position would be lucky, it was far too early to tell.

Kayoku always tried to work hard instead, to do her duty, to be faithful to what she believed in, and to let her actions speak for themselves. That way, she didn't have to believe in just luck when something good came her way.

She certainly didn't believe in magic.

Two days later, Kayoku received a written summons from Chieko, asking her to come visit later that morning.

Kayoku had been expecting such a note. It was only proper for Chieko to start handing off running the Kitayama estate to Kayoku. Not everything, not all at once. But maybe a smaller piece, like overseeing the kitchens, cooks, and supplies. Kayoku was determined to do a good job. To be perfect in every detail. So that none would find fault with her.

Kayoku instructed her servants to bring her semi-formal robes. They weren't as good as what she'd worn to the succession ceremony, however, they weren't her everyday robes either. She couldn't decide on an appropriate color, though. The brown, while it looked stately, appeared so dowdy next to Chieko. She didn't have anything that was white or green, the traditional colors of spring. Instead, she went with a reddish peach, reminding herself that running the estate didn't require that she dress as fancifully as an advisor to the Emperor.

When Chieko's servants directed Kayoku to the formal sitting rooms instead of Chieko's personal greeting hall, Kayoku was doubly glad she'd taken more time with her robe and makeup that morning.

But why the formal rooms? Was Chieko going to have scribes there to record their conversations? Was there some sort of contract that needed to be signed between the pair of them?

Chieko looked lovely, of course, sitting in the far corner of the formal hall, wearing the most beautiful sky-blue robes, her hair held back with enameled hairpins. She was all alone, no scribes knelt beside her. Her servants stood several *tatami* lengths away. She almost looked like a blue cloud, so small against the dark walls, sitting in the corner opposite the door.

New banners had been hung on the plain wooden walls of the hall, possibly that morning, filled with elegant calligraphy and poems about the summer sure to follow the current spring. Fresh pine boughs had been tacked to the wooden beams running the length of the ceiling. Delicate paperwhite flowers stood in an elegant bronze vase in the center of the room, blessing the space with their sweet perfume.

No tea service was laid out between the pillows where Chieko sat and where Kayoku was expected to kneel. No writing desk, either.

What did Chieko intend to say? Kayoku found her back stiffening and becoming rigid. She held herself taut.

Surely Chieko didn't believe in Kayoku's bad luck? She couldn't ask Kayoku to leave the estate, could she?

"Good morning," Chieko said, not bothering to rise. "Please, join me in this brief respite."

Puzzled, Kayoku sank down as gracefully as she could onto the bright pink and yellow pillows opposite Chieko. At least she was able to kneel without putting one of her hands out to catch herself like an old woman.

After the last of the servants had withdrawn from the room and they were all alone, Chieko turned her gaze directly at Kayoku. "Lord Taiga is very ill," she stated plainly.

Kayoku didn't know that her spine could stiffen any further, but it did. "*Oko!*" she exclaimed.

"Shhh," Chieko warned. "Only a few people know."

Meeting in the formal room, particularly in this corner, suddenly made more sense. No other rooms adjoined this corner—the windows looked directly out onto the gardens at the back of the estate. No one would be able to "accidentally" overhear them.

"What is it?" Kayoku asked. "What's wrong?"

"No one knows. It's a wasting disease, though. Unnatural." Chieko continued to stare at Kayoku. "No one knows how to cure him."

Kayoku tried not to squirm under the direct gaze. It was very unlike Chieko to be so rude.

"Some have questioned the *convenience* of this illness. Particularly since he'd just declared Iwao his heir," Chieko added.

"Iwao?" Kayoku asked, incredulous. She couldn't help herself. She giggled. "Surely, no one is accusing him—"

"They aren't, not really," Chieko said with a slight smile. "Your husband is very honorable. It would be beneath him to stoop to such a thing."

"Thank you," Kayoku said. "You are very kind to say such a thing." Even though it was completely true. It would never even occur to Iwao to do such a thing.

Plus, Iwao wasn't that creative. Kayoku couldn't imagine how he'd be able to find a disease to give to an old man that no one had been able to recognize. Her husband had many faults. Being overly imaginative was not one of them.

"Others have said that you are the one with ambition, however," Chieko said.

Kayoku blinked, surprised. "Really? Why would anyone accuse me? I'd never do anything to hurt Lord Taiga." Though the words were said automatically, Kayoku found them to be true. She didn't know Lord Taiga well—she'd always been a minor wife, and had never interacted with him much. However, he'd still always treated her kindly.

"I know," Chieko said. "But I have to be able to tell them that I saw your face when I asked. That you were surprised by his illness, and shocked at being accused."

"I see," Kayoku said, trying to keep the bitterness out of her voice.

And she did understand. Her husband was not the only one who had difficulty lying. It still stung that anyone would think her capable of such an act.

"Now," Chieko said briskly. "I am sorry to do this to you. But I will have to place much of the burden of running the estate on your capable shoulders while I attend Lord Taiga." She gave a wistful smile. "I'd been looking forward to working with you, gradually bringing you in. It would have given us an excuse to chat, often."

"I will do my best, so that my work only reflects the best of you," Kayoku said fervently. This was all she'd ever wanted—a chance to prove herself. To be of use to the household and to the estate.

To be someone of consequence, not because of rank or birth, but because of duty and honor.

"I'm sure you will," Chieko said with a kind smile. "If I could pass off the care of Lord Taiga to your most excellent hands, I would. But I must be the one consulting with the priests, advising the well-wishers, as well as directing the cooks to make the special foods Lord Taiga will need to regain his health."

"I understand," Kayoku said, though she didn't, not really. On the one hand, seeing to Lord Taiga would not be an easy task. He was a proud man. Independent. And not used to being ill, to having to follow additional strictures.

On the other hand, it was the most important job in the entire estate. Why would Chieko even consider handing it to her?

"Are you ready?" Chieko asked Kayoku.

"I am," Kayoku replied.

"Then let us begin." Chieko started to rattle off her duties.

The list seemed endless.

Kayoku quickly put aside all her questions and doubts and earnestly applied herself to learning everything she could as quickly as possible.

Perhaps her luck wasn't so bad after all.

After just a single day, Kayoku fell, exhausted, onto her sleeping *tatamis*. How had Chieko done all of that? And still maintained such a perfect-looking personal household? All her servants were the envy of the rest of the women.

Kayoku was doubly impressed with the eldest wife now. And even more determined to fill her shoes, no matter how inadequately.

The next morning, there was still no improvement in Lord Taiga's condition. If anything, he'd worsened. Kayoku made special arrangement so she could go and visit him herself.

It shocked Kayoku when she saw Lord Taiga, just a day later, taking him a plate of *hanpen*—a spicy fish cake that she'd made herself—in order to tempt his appetite.

Instead of staying on his sleeping mats, as Chieko and the priests had no doubt directed him to, Lord Taiga spent his days in his special garden, sitting as motionless as a rock, staring at nothing.

Kayoku didn't understand the appeal of the place. It was outside, unprotected from sun and rain. It held flowers, trees, rocks, and a small rock path leading between them. It didn't grow anything useful, like herbs for healing or cooking.

Plus, it was too wild to be beautiful, too unordered and unkempt.

Lord Taiga's face had turned skeletal, and his body weak. His skin was the same color as the gray skies above them. He wore impeccable bronze outer robes, with pink and red under robes showing just at the edges of his sleeves.

"Thank you for your thoughtfulness," Lord Taiga said, putting the dish to one side, not even bothering to taste it.

Stung, Kayoku still knelt on the rocks beside him. "Anything for you, my lord," she murmured.

But Lord Taiga didn't say anything else. He sat, as still as stone.

Kayoku stayed for a long while, hoping that he might say something else.

However, Lord Taiga paid less attention to Kayoku than to the rain that eventually splashed down on them.

The funeral for Lord Taiga took place the day after he died, instead of the usual four days later. Kayoku had agreed with Chieko that the ceremony needed to be held immediately after the lord's death. The body had begun to smell badly. They needed to preserve the health of the rest of the estate.

The ceremony took place in the front courtyard, just as the sun left the shroud of the earth. Kayoku waited next to Chieko, carrying a branch from one of the *unohana* bushes in Lord Taiga's garden. The tiny white blossoms were just opening and smelled very sweet. She'd chosen it for the pyre so that Lord Taiga would have something of his favorite place to go with him to Heaven that surely awaited him. He'd always taken such good care of the *kami* in the Mori shrine. The *kami* were certain to take care of him now.

In an undulating line, the priests left the estate first, dancing into the courtyard, banging drums and playing discordant flutes and whistles, chasing away any evil spirits that might have gathered. Lord Taiga's sons marched out next, waving fragrant *sakaki* tree branches that would be later placed on the funeral pyre.

Kayoku and Chieko followed next, with the rest of the wives behind them.

Chieko gave the eulogy, as was appropriate. Though Kayoku was officially the highest ranking wife, Chieko was still the eldest. It was a heavy burden, seeing off such an important man, but Kayoku didn't envy Chieko. Her poem was particularly clever, or at least that was what the other wives said— Kayoku didn't have much of a head for poetry.

Later that afternoon, Kayoku and Chieko held a second ceremony with the rest of the wives and women on the estate. They served cold tea and dried fish, each spoke in turn about the kindness and goodness of Lord Taiga, then they burned the white cotton robes that they'd worn over their black mourning silks. The men held their own, separate ceremony.

So many things were forbidden that first week of mourning: no colorful robes, no rich foods, no contests or games of any sort, no meetings between men and women.

Kayoku knew the enforced stillness would drive her mad. After her mother's funeral she'd received special dispensation from the priests to clean her rooms.

Permission was easy to get from the priests of the Mori temple. All Kayoku had to do was write a brief letter, explaining what she wanted. The answer returned within the hour, astonishing her.

Kayoku wasn't used to such a position of power, but she vowed to use it to do good, useful things for the estate.

She marshaled half a dozen of her servants and went to the men's quarters, the approval held tightly in her hand in case someone asked. But no one challenged her. They didn't even run into anyone once they got to the southernmost wing, where Lord Taiga's rooms were.

There wasn't really much difference between the halls of the men's quarters and the women's, but Kayoku always checked the small things that marked these as the men's place. The walls didn't have the poetry that the women's quarters did, and what was hanging was always written in the more formal *kanji* script, instead of the *katakana* that women used. In the women's quarters, most of the windows faced inward, on halls and other rooms. In the men's quarters, more windows were on the outer walls and opened to the outdoors, which meant it generally smelled better. And the walls sometimes showed more signs of wear, particularly when the men were careless about their armor or their swords, banging into the walls.

Though all the windows for Lord Taiga's rooms had been left open, the awful stench of his illness still lingered in the hallway outside his rooms. Red banners still hung on either side of the *shoji,* poems for luck and healing, though they hadn't done much good.

Kayoku slid open the doors carefully and looked inside. The rooms were as stark as she had thought they would be. Lord Taiga hadn't been an extravagant man. A plain writing desk sat in one corner, and a cupboard for his robes stood against the far wall. Two budding maples—probably brought from his garden—guarded the inner doorway.

"Sweet candles," Kayoku ordered as she took a step inside and the stench hit her. How had Chieko tended to Lord Taiga in that foul stench? Two of her servants quickly hurried away to do her bidding.

At least Kayoku had planned ahead and had the rest of her servants already carrying buckets of water.

"We will be cleaning from top to bottom," Kayoku announced as her servants gathered behind her, curiously looking beyond her to the lord's former rooms.

That brought some good-natured groans. Her servants had been with her long enough to know she meant literally that—they'd clean everything from the rafters to the floorboards. However, she also knew they weren't upset by her proclamation—they, too, had been looking for more to do.

"We'll start in here, in the outer rooms," Kayoku told everyone. When the other servants came back with the sweet candles, she'd start them burning in the inner rooms. That way, maybe the smell wouldn't be too bad by the time they were ready to clean the inner sleeping room.

Kayoku suspected, though, that the candles wouldn't be enough and that they'd all be covering their noses with damp cloths to filter the stench.

"Remove the *tatamis* from just inside the door, first," Kayoku directed the servants.

Gasps filled the room when the first mat was lifted up and out of the way.

Strange symbols, long and wavy like some kind of sea creature, had been drawn in black pitch on the wooden floor.

"Attend me, all of you," Kayoku said immediately.

All of her servants looked up to her.

"None of you will breathe a *word* of this to anyone," Kayoku said harshly. "Or I will sell you to the sorcerer who made these marks." She looked at each of the four servants there, one at a time, making sure she had each one's assent. Rumors of this could *not* get out. It would be disastrous for the entire estate.

"Now, Sachi, go and fetch Priestess Ayumi. Hurry, and tell no one what you've seen," Kayoku warned again.

"Of course, mistress," Sachi responded, leaping to her feet and racing out of the room.

Sachi had been with Kayoku since she'd been a little girl. She'd do as she was told.

"Come," Kayoku said, pointing to two other servants. "We need to see what other markings are here."

They discovered more symbols on both sides of the door to Lord Taiga's sleeping rooms, as well as under his sleeping mats. The other servants returned with the sweet candles, and Kayoku quickly set them burning around the edges of the room.

Sachi and Priestess Ayumi returned just as the last candle had been set. Kayoku wasn't certain that Sachi had told the priestess, but it had gotten her to move quickly.

The priestess wore the typical dark green robes of the Mori temple, undecorated or embroidered, with plain straw sandals tied to her feet. She didn't wear any makeup—not that she needed any. Though her skin was a golden brown from being out too much in the sunshine, her features were arranged most pleasantly, with a round-moon face, a broad forehead indicating her great intelligence, wide-spaced eyes that always looked on the world with curiosity, and a tiny nose and mouth. Her rich black hair was tied back in a serviceable bun instead of some of the more exotic styles that the other women at the estate wore.

Kayoku would have estimated that the priestess was about her age, though it was impossible to tell for certain. Sometimes Kayoku wondered if Priestess Ayumi was much older, given her great wisdom. Then the priestess would say something silly and giggle like a young girl, making Kayoku wonder even more.

When Priestess Ayumi arrived at Lord Taiga's rooms she didn't say a word but examined each set of symbols carefully. Kayoku gestured silently for her servants to all wait against the wall as the priestess went from one set to the next, then walked around them, studying them from all angles.

The sickly scent from Lord Taiga's illness seemed to swell. Kayoku found it difficult to swallow. Even the birds outside the windows fell silent, waiting for the verdict.

Finally Priestess Ayumi approached Kayoku. "Thank you for bringing these to my attention." She continued in a loud voice, so that all the servants could hear as well. "These are protective markings, meant to ward someone from evil spirits. Nothing more. You will come to no harm removing them."

The first waft of sweet candles finally managed to cut through the stench.

"How would we best clean them?" Kayoku asked the priestess.

"You should gather the leaves of the *jigoku no kama no futa* flowers and place them in your water buckets," Priestess Ayumi replied seriously. "This will help purify the floor, and make sure that no evil will enter here."

Kayoku tried to keep her expression neutral. "Go. Do what Priestess Ayumi has said," she told her servants. "And remember what I said. I will sell you to the first evil sorcerer I find if you tell anyone what you're doing."

Her servants nodded and quickly set about their tasks. Once they were busily washing the outer room floors, as well as the backs of the *tatamis*, Kayoku and Priestess Ayumi slipped into Lord Taiga's sleeping room and shut the door behind them.

Kayoku walked to the far side of the room, where the window looked out over the garden and they were less likely to be overheard. "Are those symbols really harmless?" she asked.

Priestess Ayumi replied quietly, almost whispering. "The ones out there are."

Kayoku didn't believe her. "They why did you instruct the women to use the demon-pot flower?"

Priestess Ayumi gave Kayoku a quick smile. "It will make them feel important, like they're doing some kind of magical thing, protecting the rest of the estate from harm. But," she said, turning and frowning, "there are some symbols in here…" The priestess shuddered, then pointed to the area of the floor just beneath the head block Lord Taiga had slept on.

The symbol was the length of a man's arm and unsymmetrical, a series of twisted lines and characters, like a folded book torn apart by the wind, then the pages caught in a spider's web. Kayoku looked more closely. She'd thought it had been painted with the same black tar, but now saw the color was more reddish.

Bile filed her mouth at the thought of Lord Taiga, lying—dying—on top of dried blood.

"This one—I don't know all the characters," Priestess Ayumi continued. "But I recognize the general design. It's used to catch a soul after the body is dead, to hold it until it can be collected."

Kayoku drew in a sharp breath. Lord Taiga's soul hadn't gone directly to Heaven? That couldn't be. "Wouldn't the priests have noticed? When he died?" Surely someone would have done *something*.

"How could they?" The priestess shuddered again.

Kayoku floundered for a moment. What could she do about Lord Taiga's soul? Then she straightened up again. All Kayoku could do was to offer prayers at the appropriate times. It was up to the priests to see to Lord Taiga's soul.

All Kayoku could do were the practical things, namely, to make Lord Taiga's rooms fit and safe for regular people again.

"How do we clean it?" Kayoku asked, determined to do her part.

Priestess Ayumi gave a grateful smile. "I need to gather some special herbs and bless some water. Which of your women do you trust to help me when I return?"

Kayoku didn't understand what the priestess meant. Which of her servants? Why would she entrust this to a servant?

After the silence stretched uncomfortably, Kayoku realized she had to say something. "I will help you, of course."

"But, my lady, you don't need to dirty your own hands—"

"I do, though," Kayoku said firmly. "I am responsible for this estate, for the souls here. It is my duty to ensure the health of everyone under these roofs."

With a brief bow, Priestess Ayumi acquiesced, then turned and hurried out of the room.

Kayoku knew the priestess would be returning even more quickly.

She went and knelt down at the far side of the room, close to the open window, hoping she'd be able to breathe more freely there. Then she waited, calmly, for Priestess Ayumi to return.

Her mother would be proud of her, she knew.

On the one hand, Kayoku still wasn't used to her change of status. Different things were expected of her.

But she also truly felt responsible for everyone. She was certain Iwao felt the same way. That was how she'd been raised.

She resolved to send him a letter as soon as the mourning strictures of the first week were eased.

They had to meet, to talk about how to rule the people together.

Because while Kayoku could do much on her own now, it was just practical to have the support of her husband as well.

Six

Fine White Skin

Iwao

Fine white skin, smoother
than glass, yet, unbreakable—
Warm, pure mountain snow.

Iwao watched the beauty of Kayoku sleeping for a long while before he slipped from their shared bed and went to his outer rooms. She'd been unguarded in her passion earlier, as lovely and as free as the wild songbird who'd joined him on his veranda that morning. He'd caressed her face as she'd lost herself, drowning in their shared joy, astonished at the spirit that she'd allowed to move through her.

Though still in his sleeping robes, Iwao composed himself behind his writing desk, staring out the dark window from his room, into the night. Shaded lamps in the corners gave him light, soft and golden. The spring air still held traces of their earlier passion.

He couldn't allow himself to get lost in remembering that night, but he couldn't stop thinking about it either.

Kayoku had asked what had changed, for Iwao, since they'd last seen each other. She specifically hadn't mentioned Lord Taiga, or his new position, treating them like jealous ghosts, as if paying attention to them would give them too much power.

He'd joked with her, telling her that the generals had changed as much as Mount Shirayama ever did, which was, not at all. Despite being placed at the head of the army, and it being the generals' duty to obey Iwao, they still looked to each other for approval and direction.

That would change over time. Iwao felt confident in his abilities, his learning.

But did he have that time?

He stared down at his writing desk, at the bundle of letters there. At the blank paper holding the reply he would have to send in the morning.

What Iwao hadn't shared with anyone, at least, not yet, was that the warlord Masato had sent a formal challenge of war. As part of the declaration, he'd also included the terms of what he wanted.

What Masato had wanted surprised Iwao. The warlord had only asked for a portion of the eastern slope of Mount Shirayama, that he was willing to take by force. He hadn't asked for the entire mountain.

Not yet.

Iwao already knew his response, what the generals would say. They weren't giving Masato any part of the mountain on which to build his foreign temples.

It wasn't that Iwao was particularly against this Sakyamuni, or Buddha. He'd read some of the Buddha's teachings, and they'd seemed very instructive.

However, like his father Lord Taiga, Iwao didn't trust Masato a bit. Whatever Iwao gave him, in the end, would never be enough.

Masato was greedy, and not a ghost. Only the entire mountain would satisfy him.

Iwao was impressed with the wording in the formal challenge of war, at Masato's bravado, along with his subtle implication that their armies were equal.

Though Masato's army may have outnumbered Iwao's, Masato primarily hired *saburai*, servants. They weren't men of honor, like Iwao's men. Masato's men would be fighting above their station. This meant that when they died, their deaths held more honor, since they'd been killed by men so far above them.

Iwao would have to assure his men that fighting for the mountain regained whatever honor they might lose fighting men beneath their own position.

The estate was still at that time of the night. Most of the court was asleep and the servants hadn't yet risen to start preparations for the new day. This was the hour when Iwao liked to stroll the grounds, not to check up on things as some assumed but because it gave him a quiet time to think.

His father, Lord Taiga, had also desired stillness for contemplation, but he preferred to do his thinking while as motionless as the mountain. Iwao saw himself more like a stream, babbling quietly to himself as he meandered.

However, he would never leave his dear Kayoku alone in his rooms.

Restlessness still drove him, first from his writing desk, then to his cabinet where he kept Seiji.

He'd shown Kayoku the sword earlier. Both he and Seiji had been pleased with her praises, though he knew it was ridiculous for him to ascribe such emotion to a mere sword.

Without ceremony, Iwao drew Seiji from his sheath and practiced sweeping blows and cuts, both defending and attacking. He often did these types of drills when he was alone.

Seiju was a *taichi*, formed in the new style with a long, curved blade, elegant and lightweight. Iwao was more familiar with *chokuto* swords, which were short and straight. He practiced as often as he did so that he could rely on his hand, for it to know what to do, without conscious forethought. Swords were only used at the end of battle, when a man had exhausted his supply of arrows or spears.

The steel seemed to vibrate in Iwao's hand, as alive as he was, swathed with unseen night currents and desires. He'd believed his father when he'd told him that it was a magic sword. Iwao had felt its power the first time he'd drawn the blade, after he'd dedicated himself to the protection of Mount Shirayama.

Seiji had *sighed* with Iwao's words, grown light and warm to the touch. He desired the same things Iwao did, life for the mountain and her people.

Now, Seiji whistled through the air, singing as sweetly as Kayoku had earlier. Iwao could almost hear the words the sword sang, describing the beauty of the mountain, praising its moss-covered rocks and fresh bubbling streams.

For a moment, Iwao had the image of carrying the sword out of his rooms, maybe stepping onto the veranda, to bathe the sword's banked heat in moonlight and cool air.

But that was ridiculous. Iwao bit down hard on the impulse, as he always did.

No one knew the poetry that lived in Iwao's soul. No one could know. He would rather be silent and thought a fool than to disappoint his family and be called *flighty*.

A good leader of men was practical, and that was what Iwao had trained himself to be.

Lord Taiga had always seemed satisfied with Iwao's dedication, the way he'd focused himself. However, a few days before Lord Taiga's death, he'd called Iwao to his rooms, demanding to hear some of the poetry he knew Iwao still wrote.

Iwao had demurred initially, but eventually he'd given in to the dying man's wishes.

It was then that Lord Taiga admitted that the poetry he knew still lived in Iwao's soul was why he'd chosen Iwao for his heir. Only someone who could hear the mountain's song could be her true guardian.

Iwao had re-sworn his oath that day, pleasing both his father and Seiji.

Who still sang in his hand, directing his arm in even more extreme moves.

Iwao stopped himself, drawing up, standing tall and straight, like a sword. Then he bowed low, placing the sword before him, paying it proper respect, before he sheathed the sword.

Why was he sweating lightly? He hadn't been practicing that hard, had he? He thought back, then frowned when he realized how he'd let himself get carried away dancing with the sword.

Iwao shook his head, breathing in the calm of the night.

This would never do. He had more discipline than that. He just had to use it.

Still, working with Seiji had loosened Iwao up. He seated himself again behind his writing desk, drawing out his fine brush, shaving ink from his finely-made stick and mixing it in the ink stone. He crafted his letter of response to Masato, rejecting his offer of "compromise" and choosing war instead.

Iwao used the most polite and formal phrases he knew, re-reading the words often, holding his poetic nature in strict check. Because of the seriousness of the matter, he wrote the final version out with his own hand instead of assigning it to a scribe.

Masato would pick the field and time for their engagement, as was custom.

Iwao found himself looking forward to their battle. A keenness for blood always slipped into his thoughts after working with Seiji, something else he had to watch out for.

Using a black ribbon, Iwao sealed the letter with a complicated twist. Then he wrote out instructions for his main servant to find a dying spring leaf, preferably one partially decayed, as a symbol of their conversation. Masato and his foreign religion were a poison, killing the spirit of everything they touched. Iwao would stop the spread of this disease here and now.

Hissed words slithered across the room on slight breezes. Iwao shivered. Was that Seiji, whispering in his sheath, agreeing with Iwao?

It couldn't be. Iwao shivered again, dismissing the feeling as just another overly-romantic notion, the kind he'd trained himself out of now that he was a man.

After putting away his writing implements and making sure his room was tidy, Iwao stuck his head out the door and woke one of the servants in the hallway.

"Tea," Iwao ordered. "And be silent bringing it in."

Then Iwao went back to his sleeping room, drew on a fresh robe, and sat in the tranquil darkness, watching his beautiful Kayoku sleep, composing poems he would never speak aloud but that he prayed she would feel in his hands when he touched her, see in his eyes, and witness in his acts and duty.

The afternoon of the day before the battle, Iwao rode his horse Kage up the high slope of the mountain. The sun shone down brightly both between the trees, dappling the path, then growing blindingly bright when they raced out of the trees and across meadows. He flushed rabbits, geese, even a newly shorn buck. Kage didn't notice, he just thundered on, like a colt on a summer's day, taking joy in the running, stretching his legs as far as they would go.

Seiji whispered the entire time, urging Iwao to ride faster, take more daring jumps. Soon, Iwao was far ahead of his outriders and servants. When he was certain no one could see him, he practiced drawing Seiji from the back of Kage, while they rode.

Normally, a man didn't fight from horseback. Battles were fought up close and hand-to-hand. Fighting from horseback was extremely difficult with a *chokuto* sword. The straight blade made it almost impossible to unsheathe quickly, particularly when riding hard and fast.

Seiji was curved and easy to draw, going from earth to sky in one movement, followed by a downward slash.

Iwao could easily imagine an opponent, also on horseback. He practiced striking this enemy's body, side, arm—even leg—from his own position on the back of Kage.

The idea was…radical. It was the kind of thing Iwao had always had to guard against, those leaps of fantasy. He'd trained himself to be practical. Horses were too expensive, too precious, to be risked in this strange new way of fighting. Men were much easier to find and replace. They took less training, less specialized food, less care.

However. Iwao needed an advantage for this first battle with Masato. The generals didn't trust Iwao, but they had at least been honest about their army's capabilities.

Masato outnumbered them. Two bows for every one of theirs.

Plus, as much as Iwao's practical side denied it, there was something strange about Masato's army. He'd seen himself the men who fought on after receiving fatal blows, who needed to be killed two or three times, whose discarded bodies were bloated and covered with painted designs of evil characters.

Seiji sang in Iwao's hand as he charged. He sliced through the air as happily as he could slice through flesh, whistling in the clear afternoon sun.

It would take time, probably most of the night, for Iwao to convince his generals to take this risk. To have a single battalion that didn't merely ride horses to the battle, but rode their horses *into* battle. He knew they had enough *taichi* style swords to arm these men.

Iwao spent the rest of his ride planning what they would need to do. How the battalion would attack. What brief training he could give the men.

It was a trick. A one-time gamble.

They'd never be able to do it a second time—the enemy would be prepared for it.

If they lost, they would be in much worse condition than they would have been just losing the battle. They would have lost all those horses as well.

Seiji whispered the entire ride back to camp that it would be worth it. The battle would be won.

Fleet clouds, fleeting sun,
Daylight gone, here, gone again—
Life dried up like dew

The day of the battle dawned dark, chilled, and gray. Iwao had only slept for two hours, but it had been enough. He ate a little rice cooked with chicken and green onions while sitting outside of his tent, the generals and servants standing well away, giving him a little peace. The soup was more of a winter dish, but he relished the warmth that morning.

Iwao dressed in formal battle robes—brown silk with the Kitayama family crest embroidered in gold on the back, a stylized ideogram of Mount Shirayama. Before he put on his armor, he left his plain tent to walk among his men, as Lord Taiga always had.

Grass still covered the paths between the plain brown canvas tents. The men had divided themselves up by clan or battalion, depending on how many of their brothers or uncles served with them. They set their tents up in clusters and circles, with wide rivers of grass between them.

Grim faces greeted Iwao as he walked from camp to camp. The men knew the odds facing them.

Iwao didn't speak with any of the men. He knew that his tongue would betray him if he tried. His fanciful nature, and the current stress, might cause poetry to erupt, and he couldn't afford to be seen as anything other than rock solid this morning.

Instead, Iwao just nodded at them as he passed. He also partook in some of the small ceremonies going on that morning, so stood with his head bowed as a priest blessed the men's weapons and horses. He uttered his own silent prayers of protection when a group of men handed him a box of carved wooden beads that would be tied to their mounts. He took part in another group's sacrifice, throwing a straw effigy on their sacrificial fire.

More than one soldier spent his time sharpening his sword and spear points, counting and recounting arrows, testing bows and tightening strings.

The battalion with the *taichi* swords were already practicing, the men lined up and drilling, fighting up and down a small rise.

Iwao watched for a while, before giving them an approving nod and moving on, back to his own tent.

The priests of the Mori temple dripped water on Iwao's head, chilling and refreshing, as part of their blessing. They chanted poems of victory and blew smoke from sacred fires over his armor.

Iwao wore Oyoroi-style armor, with thick, flexible shoulder protectors tied to his arms. Like the rest of his armor, they were covered in iron scales, laced together with beautiful red and gold ties. His helmet flaps were similarly covered, though the crowned peak was one solid piece of iron.

The priests carefully tied each part of Iwao's armor to him, chanting and blessing the ties.

Iwao contained his growing impatience through the ceremony, making sure to thank the priests for all their hard work before he was finally able to mount Kage and be away.

Iwao rode out of the camp and to the field of battle, then up a small rise that had been prepared, on the western side. His generals fanned out around him, and the army spread beneath him.

His heart swelled at the sight of his army, with the war banners waving bravely as the sun burned through the clouds. Though most of the men had their own colors and armor, the overall effect was dark and heavy, a solid committed group of warriors. Brilliant green ribbons—the color of the mountain in spring—were tied to armor, weapons, horses, uniting them with one goal. Horses snorted in the cool morning air, steaming as they took the field.

Masato and his men joined the field. His army was like a dark cloud, cold and shadowy.

The two leaders rode forward toward the center of the field, each with their generals and servants.

Iwao let his generals examine the enemy's troops. He focused on the leader. Iwao had seen Masato before, but this morning was the first time he'd been in close proximity.

Masato was darker than Iwao remembered, tanned like a peasant, almost swarthy, while the surface of his skin was unnaturally smooth. His smile was all-knowing and indulgent, like a father's when dealing with a petulant child. Strange symbols covered his well-made Oyoroi-style armor—Iwao learned later they were Buddhist blessings. A sleepy expression filled his eyes, as if he saw everything through a veil. He was a solid man; his body had known fine foods as well as heavy exercise.

Seiji remained strangely silent as they drew closer.

After the formal greeting, Masato read out his lineage, tracing his father, grandfathers, and great-grandfathers. He went first, as he was the challenger. His background wasn't illustrious, though he had been abroad to *Shina*, which was where he'd first dedicated himself to this Buddha.

Iwao found his back stiffening as Masato continued to try to puff himself up. He hadn't trusted this new religion, and now he liked it even less, particularly after studying its avatar.

Masato was a lazy man. He only did the smallest sliver of his duty, not what he must, not fully embracing what duty entailed.

How could merely speaking the name of the Amida Buddha bring a man to Heaven? The *kami* needed works, great and small, to consider a life well lived.

Iwao read his family's history quickly, deliberately using an eager voice, stumbling over words like a new student.

He knew his reputation would precede him. And his enemy appeared to take the bait as Masato's smile grew more indulgent.

Exactly what Iwao wanted. He needed for Masato to misjudge him, to think him young, unschooled.

For Iwao's plan to work, Masato had to completely underestimate him.

After they agreed to the terms of battle, as previously negotiated, Iwao wheeled Kage around and raced back to the line of men behind him, supposedly yet another sign of his inexperience. Because his back was to Masato, Iwao allowed himself a smile at his generals' playacting, the way they shook their heads and grimaced.

More fuel for the fire.

Iwao drew away with his men, as was protocol. It put both armies into better arrow range. Close up was only for later.

However, the section of men that Iwao led didn't withdraw as far as the others. Hopefully, Masato would take it for yet another mistake of youthful impatience.

The priests began blowing their whistles and banging their drums, a prelude to the first attack, to put fear into the enemy while swelling the hearts of Iwao's men.

Weird wailing came from Masato's side, inhuman and otherworldly.

Iwao's men stood tall, brave in the face of the unknown. Their horses shifted nervously as the scent of ashes and dark, long-buried places rolled over them.

With the first barrage of arrows, Iwao led his charge. He relied on his generals to direct their division, to rearm the men with arrows and follow the traditional forms, as well as to provide his group with cover, to allow them to get close enough.

Iwao led his troop to the right, sprinting with their horses. To the uninitiated, it looked as though they were leaving the battlefield.

Until, as one, they turned on Iwao's signal and rushed toward the left flank of Masato's army.

The generals leading Masato's men didn't notice Iwao and his troop until it was too late. No one had ever led such a charge before, not at the start of a battle, rushing toward the enemy unheedingly, like beaters flushing quarry.

While some of Iwao's troop used bows, the rest had spears or swords drawn. They swept through Masato's men like a wild wave crashing over the shore, brushing away any resistance.

Seiji sang in Iwao's hand, urging him on, thirsting for the blood of the enemy, seeking out bodies to feed on from all sides. Like a child with a mere stalk of wild grass, Iwao swung his sword effortlessly, from one side to the other, endlessly wielding death.

Iwao learned after the battle that the opposing line had broken immediately. They hadn't even given a token resistance. Masato's men had stopped firing, turned, and run.

Iwao and his troop chased Masato's men across the plain and through the valley, easily picking them off with spears and arrows as they fled.

It was the first time Iwao's men had had such a victory—the skirmishes they'd fought before with Lord Taiga had never given them such a clear win. They went a little mad with it, not halting the slaughter even when the generals ordered them to stay their hand.

Seiji, too, longed for more even after Iwao had pulled back, gathering his men to him and charging forth again.

That evening, the generals insisted on celebrating their great victory, even though it had been a one-time trick that they'd never be able to do again. Masato's generals would now be looking for such a trick, watching in all directions for such a wild attack.

Iwao would have to do something even more unexpected the next time.

Somehow, with Seiji's whisperings following him even into his sleep, he didn't doubt that was possible.

Seven

The New Moon

Hikaru

The new moon hid my sisters and me very well the night we arrived at court. It was fully dark, and humans can't see that well. Plus, my sisters and I played with the lamps the servants brought out to our carriage, making first one, then another, go out.

Though we'd arrived in a well-made carriage, and the robes my sisters and I wore were all amazing quality, we'd agreed that half-glimpsed riches would spread gossip faster, rather than letting everyone see our finery all at once. We wanted the news of my arrival—a very wealthy young lady—to fly to every corner of the court.

The other reason we played with the lights was to hide the number of people and servants actually accompanying me. My sisters weren't always going to be staying in court, and it would be best for them to be able to come and go without ceremony.

Etsu had finally admitted that she'd had a vision. She, too, had witnessed some of the ceremony the Taoist sorcerer had performed. She knew just how closely intertwined the steel of the sword was with Norihiko's soul. Merely breaking the blade wouldn't release his spirit. She had to do research, as well as consult some sorcerers, before she could construct the spell to free him.

While Etsu searched, Cho would act as a relay for me. She would carry news of Etsu's findings, news from home, as well as news from the land and the progress of the season, which I would need as well.

As a *kitsune* I could pass as a human. As this was my first time at court, I didn't have to change my appearance too much. If I ever wanted to come back, I would have to look much different than I currently did, or wait until all those who knew me had passed to the great beyond.

However, because I was pretending to be human, I was as trapped as all the other women in the artifice of the Emperor's compound and his very tame gardens.

An older fox fairy could survive in such a place, supping off the beauty of the robes and court, the delicate flowers, the twisting pines. However, I was young. I needed more wildness to survive.

Though it was quite late, I directed the servants to unpack many of the trunks, making sure that the court servants as well as my own marveled over the fine robes and silks we had.

Of course, many were enhanced magically. Not even my family could afford all the outfits necessary for a season at court, or have them created in just a few weeks.

Etsu had insisted on a specific number of robes, of exacting quality. Too many, or too fine, and some might accuse me of being a courtesan or a mistress. Too few, and I wouldn't get the attention I needed from the court.

I had thought Etsu was being stingy in her count of robes, but after seeing the reactions from the servants, I realized Etsu had judged the number just right.

The rooms I'd been assigned at the court were inner facing, no windows directly leading to the outside, as was proper for a lady. It gave me the feeling of being shut in a cage. There wasn't really any privacy, as anyone could be waiting just beyond a wall, listening.

At least the beams were made from sweet cedar, the finest quality. I would have to get some paper and create some wall hangings, writing a poem or two for Norihiko. I hadn't wanted to play the part of a widow, but Etsu had insisted, saying that if I had times of melancholy, it would be good for people to be able to nod and assign a reason for it.

I'd wanted to make the death of this mythical husband several years in the past, but eventually agreed that just over a year would be more believable, given my age.

However, I was determined to never be sad, or at least, to never show it. I was going to be brilliant, sparkling, witty, and above all, desirable.

Mother fretted about my using myself as bait to trap the one who'd killed Norihiko, but I knew I had to. My love had gone through so much. How could I do anything less?

After the trunks were unpacked, I insisted that my sisters and I have some tea and relax. Only one of the palace servants remained, an older, round, buck-toothed woman who moved as though winter still flowed in her veins.

Cho put a small spell on her, just to make her move more quickly.

I laughed behind my hand at her reaction, her confused face, not understanding why she suddenly moved like the spring wind.

After the servant had left, Etsu placed unspun silk fibers in the corners of the inner room, then used them as part of a muffling spell so that no one would be able to discern a conversation spoken in low tones.

When she was finished with her spell, Etsu came over to Cho and me and started scolding us. "You need to be more careful," she said, glaring from Cho to me and back again.

Though Cho looked chastened, I pretended I didn't know what my eldest sister talked about. I glanced down at my robe, then back at her. "Why? I didn't spill anything."

Etsu glared at me. "You can't just treat these humans like your toys. You need to show respect."

I didn't point out how unfair Etsu was being—I hadn't even cast the spell in the first place! Instead, I replied, "One of these humans killed Norihiko. I'm supposed to forgive them?"

"I wouldn't ask that of you," Etsu said stiffly. "But not all of them were involved. Save your anger for the sorcerer."

I was ashamed of my outburst, of encouraging Cho, but I didn't back down. "What do they matter?" I asked.

Etsu sighed. "They matter a great deal, little one. Soon, you will see."

I was so tired of that being her usual response. There was a part of me that was happy she wouldn't be here at court, that she would be off researching the spell. "It doesn't matter what happens to these humans." I wasn't thinking beyond my revenge.

Nothing mattered except that final death. What happened afterward was of no consequence. So why worry about upsetting a few mortals in the meanwhile?

It never occurred to me that something could happen to my family.

Mother had some connections at court, of course, people who had contacted her regarding their future, who had asked for her blessing, or sometimes tried their luck at winning her hand, if only for a short while. We'd used some of these connections, discreetly, to invent a persona for me.

We'd timed my arrival so that I came to court just a few days before the Kamo festival. The procession, or so I learned that morning from my gossip session with Yukiko, was to be very large this year—one of the longest they'd ever had. Princess Ruri would be leading the festivities.

The Kamo festival would be the perfect place for me to make my first appearance, in front of so many important people, as well as at such a festive time of year. We agreed that I should use a half-open palanquin for making the journey from one temple to the next, so that my robes might be seen, but not my face.

We also agreed that when the procession came to a stop, as it inevitably would from time to time, that I should be prepared to pass a poem or two to the nearby carriages, commenting on the day, the festival, and the prayers that had been spoken.

The man in charge of all the arrangement for the procession, the marshal, wasn't easy to track down. I suppose he was busy with all the arrangements. Still, he should have made himself more readily available.

Because everyone at the court was jostling for the best position they possibly could have, I couldn't merely send the marshal a note to get myself placed toward the front with all the important people. I had to actually go see him, to be in his presence to influence him magically. Not even Etsu could have written such a spell into a letter.

But Yukiko and I finally did find him, standing at the edge of a large assembly area.

A long line of brightly painted white-and-gold wicker carriages wove its way from the nearby streets into the area.

The marshal was instructing workers in how to drape the traditional hollyhocks along the sides and tops of the carriages. Servants began carrying in huge baskets of the flowers, the blossoms brilliant purple, red, and pink, and the leaves all large and verdant.

They were all going to look so splendid decorating the carriages, the banners, even the oxen and servants bearing the palanquins.

When I finally did manage to get the marshal's attention, he wasn't happy. Nor was he a pleasant man. His face was as pasty as a tree-ear mushroom, with narrow, beady eyes and a small forehead—a sure sign of low intelligence.

"Excuse me, marshal," I started.

The marshal didn't even let me finish before he turned away, saying, "It isn't feasible."

How impossibly rude!

"Turn back toward me, please," I said, slipping my words into his ear, making him *want* to turn back.

This was the kind of magic that I was best at, making men want. I was much better at it than my sisters—only my mother was better than I.

"Are you sure there's no place in the procession for me?" I asked coyly. I kept most of my face covered with a fan; however, I still let him see my eyes.

"But I just finished making the final assignments!" he whined, fighting me and my suggestion.

Really. Such an unpleasant man.

"You could make one more change, for me, couldn't you?" I asked him, smiling at him from behind my fan, staring into his eyes and pushing my will toward him a little harder, making him feel not only my desire but the want, the *need*, to make me happy.

With a large, affected sigh, the marshal finally acquiesced. "Fine, my lady, I'll give you your spot." He shouted for his scribe—a harried-looking man in stained, light-blue robes, who came running up with a portable writing desk overflowing with letters, pens, and papers.

In short, barked phrases, the marshal directed the scribe to write down the new order of the procession.

The scribe looked surprised, but he didn't say anything, just took down the notes as he was told. He did, however, sneak many improper glances at me. Obviously he needed to be better trained: just because he served a person in power didn't mean that power automatically was bequeathed to him as well.

I kept pushing my will on the marshal, never letting up for a moment. Normally, this sort of activity exhausted me, but I was so focused on having my way that I barely noticed.

Before I left, the marshal sighed again and asked, "Anything else, my lady?"

This brought an even more startled look to the scribe's face.

Evidently even the most common of courtesies was normally beyond the marshal.

"That's all," I told him airily, turning away and dismissing him with a wave of my hand.

It was only when I got back to my rooms that I noticed Yukiko's disapproving looks. I recalled Etsu's warnings from the night before. Yukiko had probably overheard the entire conversation.

"What?" I asked her, trying to prevent whatever argument she was about to give me. "I did what I had to do."

Yukiko stubbornly replied, "You must be more careful, my lady. You don't want people to become suspicious around you. Watching what they say for fear they'll fall under your spell. You want people to want to please you of their own accord."

"Do you really think that awful man would have ever wanted to do something for me of his own desire?" I asked, incredulous.

Yukiko tried again. "My lady, my family has worked for your family for generations. We are used to your ways. Others aren't. Please, don't make this difficult for yourself. Save yourself, your will, for when it's really needed."

"I thought that was what I was doing," I told her frostily. "Now, if you're finished with your lecture, I have some poetry I must write."

I stomped off into my inner room, closing the *shoji* forcefully. The air was stale, the room was too small, and my robes were choking me.

I still sat myself down at my writing desk and breathed deeply, willing myself to be calm.

I could do this. Norihiko had lived through ten thousand times more agonies than the minor discomforts I had at the Emperor's court.

I would work my will upon anyone standing in my way. I would find my love's killer. And I would have my revenge.

It never occurred to me that I, too, would have to suffer consequences for the choices I made.

The day of the procession began with bulging gray clouds. However, they all blew over as the sun proceeded to climb, and by the time the ceremonies started, nothing marred the clear blue sky. A coolness that had crept in with the night remained, which was actually a blessing, as we were all in our most formal outfits, out in the blinding light.

Of course, the start of the festivities was all chaos. I rather enjoyed the spectacle.

Flocks of young girls in their fancy robes with flowers in their hair flowed this way and that, like slowly moving water, as directed by their aunts and mothers. Stiff officials in their black robes hurried from one point to the next, barking orders like raucous crows.

Even the marshal himself tried to get everyone ordered and into line. I was tempted to play games with him, maybe cause him to trip, but I contained myself. Particularly when Yukiko pinched my side.

Finally, everyone was ready to begin the short walk to the Shimo-Gamo shrine, where the first ceremony was to be performed. The young girls danced and scattered their flower petals, the priests intoned their prayers with beautiful harmony, and Princess Ruri threw ribbons from her carriage that were perfectly caught by the wind and floated like gay banners above the crowd.

Even I was impressed by how well the humans had arranged their ceremony.

The procession slowly made its way to the next temple. Of course, there was a holdup. I couldn't see what it was—though I had a wonderful position, among the first twenty in line. I couldn't see everything.

However, instead of sending Yukiko or one of the other servants to see what was the holdup, I amended one of my poems and got it ready to send to the carriage behind me.

Before too long, a delightful response came back. Then the palanquin three up from mine sent a missive, exclaiming how well the young girls had performed.

And the race to be the most clever, the most thoughtful and creative, was on.

As I sent my poems out to the various carriages and palanquins, I instructed my servants to tell me about the owners. I assumed Norihiko's killer was male—he'd been reforged into a sword, after all, not a fan or a piece of jewelry. I also assumed he would be young, as well as important.

However, most of the important people in the vehicles around mine didn't seem to fit. They were either elderly, or female, or, to put it delicately, not the type of person who would wield a mighty sword.

Mother had foreseen that I would meet Norihiko's current wielder at the Emperor's court. I couldn't just go to every young male and demand to see his sword. Even with my magic, it would be tricky. I didn't care about my reputation with these humans, but the men would. They wouldn't want to be compromised by a young, eligible female suddenly showing up at their rooms.

So how was I going to find this man?

I started sending my poems farther down the line of guests. Maybe the man wielding Norihiko was a younger son. That would make sense, actually—a ruthless younger man, seeking power through any and all means.

Finally a servant came back with some good news. A young man who had just come to court to have his inheritance approved by the Emperor also carried an incredible sword. Some even claimed it was magical. It was the new style of sword, a *taichi*, curved and elegant.

My heart pounded in my chest. Could this be the one? I sniffed at the paper, trying to get a sense of the man. Strong, yes. Disciplined as well. I couldn't smell his evil, but I was certain I'd found the one.

The poem he returned to me was surprisingly well thought out. That must have been how he'd been able to integrate himself with such important people: a honeyed tongue to hide a vile heart.

I put forth my best effort, trying to win him over, to make him curious about me, to make him desire an audience.

I wished again that there was some magic I could put into the written word, such that he wouldn't be able to resist.

There would be time enough for that later.

The procession ended far too soon, midway through the day. It had been exhausting, playing with words all day, trying to be the brightest and most sparkling.

But I had my quarry in my sight, now. I hadn't had time to convince him that we must meet, that he should invite me to his succession celebration.

Those were minor details. I had the scent of him. I knew he was here at court. I would be able to find him. Track him down.

Enact my revenge.

The moon had reached her peak and was waning again before I finally got what I wanted—an audience alone with this Iwao.

Alone, of course, was quite an exaggeration. His servants were there. Mine, as well. I'd had a specially carved lattice screen built for this occasion, and had visited the workshop late at night to magically impregnate the wood with my scent.

We met in formal rooms set aside for just such occasions. None of the windows faced the outside, which was just as well, because the smell of fresh air might have distracted me. It had been so long since I'd breathed freely!

But every time I heard myself complaining, I would remind myself that my poor Norihiko couldn't even breathe at this point.

The room itself was oppressive. Heavy brocade fabric, dark and red, hung in wide loops from the ceiling, like ill-painted waves. The pillars were carved with many bumps and swirls, as if they sprouted diseased mushrooms. Even the floor was unpleasantly covered with ancient, poorly made *tatamis*.

I wore one of my better robes, the color of cherry blossoms, with a pale green robe underneath, like the freshest leaves. Though Iwao would never see my face, I still took care with my makeup, highlighting my eyes with kohl, whitening my skin, and painting my lips the color of summer berries.

I didn't bother being on time. Why would I ever do something as foolish as that? But I didn't make the man wait too long…maybe only a quarter of an hour. I sent in my servants first, having them set up the screen, then waiting a bit longer before I walked in, settling myself behind it.

At least this Iwao controlled his curiosity, and didn't gape at me like a vulgar foreigner. He wore nice enough robes, something brown and slightly dull, with some kind of gold stitching on it. He was a heavy-set man, with exaggerated features—an overset brow, deep brown eyes, a large nose, and flabby lips.

For all his size, his hands were surprisingly delicate, like a scholar's. Though he still had the hard calluses a man built up doing sword work.

The most disappointing thing about him? I couldn't smell any magic on him.

The man was human. Mundane.

Was this all a fool's errand?

I began fanning myself with the most beautiful white and gold paper fan, spreading my scent out to him, starting to entrap him.

"Thank you for agreeing to see me," Iwao stated plainly, as if this were some sort of common meeting.

"It is I who is privileged by this encounter," I replied. "You have become quite popular in court," I added, flattering him.

Most had never heard of him—that had been part of my delay in finding him and setting up some "chance" meetings with him.

His laugh surprised me. It was more humble than I'd expected.

Then again, he would have to play his part to perfection, wouldn't he, to get this far?

"You must have mistaken me for someone else," Iwao said. "I'm an unimportant servant to the Emperor, that is all."

"You are the heir to Mount Shirayama!" I proclaimed.

Really, it was a tiny holding, out in the provinces. But I had to puff him up. All men need such things.

Iwao shrugged. "I've dedicated myself to protecting the mountain, being her true guardian. We've been successful, so far, fighting off those who would take her from us."

I'd heard about this battle as well, with some praising Iwao's daring use of horses in an actual battle, while older, wiser heads had proclaimed it wild foolishness.

"Just you?" I asked, flirtatiously.

"And my marvelous generals. And the men who have fought so bravely," Iwao said, giving credit where it was due.

"And that sword of yours…" I added.

"Ah. Seiji. Yes. He's a marvel. I inherited him from my father," Iwao said.

I didn't believe this lie. "What makes this Seiji so special?" I asked. I had to know if this was truly Norihiko or not.

"He's of the new style of sword. Supremely crafted. Elegant as a mountain sunrise. Harder than mountain stubbornness." Iwao coughed into his hand, as if ashamed by how passionate he'd become.

It intrigued me, this man who was so plain, yet could write such amazing poetry.

"Seiji carries the soul of the mountain with him," Iwao continued. "Guards and protects her, like I do."

He does not, I nearly snarled. *That steel entraps the soul of my love.* How could I have started to think kindly of this man? I shook myself, glad the lattice would hide the movement.

I stared through the lattice, pushing my will out on Iwao. "I'd like to see this famous sword," I said demurely.

Iwao gave an uneasy laugh. "It isn't really proper…" he said, hesitating.

"Normally, what you say is true," I replied. "But this Seiji isn't really a normal sword, is he?"

Iwao sighed and shook his head. His eyes looked haunted.

He must have known what Seiji actually was.

"Please. Let me see it," I asked again.

Iwao signaled for one of his servants. "Fetch Benkei. And have him bring Seiji to me." Iwao turned back to me and gave me a half-smile. "Some of the servants are…superstitious about the sword. They don't like handling him."

"Ah, I see," I said. Good for them. That meant at least some of Iwao's staff were sensitive.

I could use them. Direct them more easily.

An older gentleman came in the room shortly. He carried a scarlet pillow that bore a plain, black lacquered sheath.

Even without seeing the blade I knew it was magical. Swirling ribbons of power danced around it.

How did this mundane man tame such a wild power? Oh, he was clever, playing the dumb human. Very clever indeed.

My servants were well enough behaved that none of them gasped, though I felt Yukiko, sitting beside me, stiffen.

This was the sword. I had no doubt that this was the cruel form my Norihiko had been forced into.

"It's very beautiful," I told Iwao after his servant had set the sword down between us.

Iwao merely grunted and took another sip of his tea.

What was the sword whispering to him? Was this Seiji telling Iwao that his days were now numbered?

It was obvious to me that this Iwao hadn't made Seiji himself. He'd hired the Taoist priest to do all his dirty work.

I couldn't just steal the sword. My revenge demanded more.

I would have to work Iwao, slowly drain him, make sure that when he died, he would know that it was because of me.

I would strip him of everything he loved, first. This mountain of his. His self-respect. His duty. His honor.

Only then would I take the sword. And use it on that damned Taoist magician myself.

It wasn't that difficult to turn Iwao's thoughts to his recent inheritance. He didn't admit it publicly, but his father had been ill before he'd died, something horrible and wasting, as humans are wont to do.

He also admitted that he didn't have any direct heirs of his own.

"Really?" I asked, pretending surprise, though I knew full well about this. "Surely one of your wives is bearing you a gift, even as we speak."

"That would be nice," Iwao said stiffly. "But there is only the one wife."

I knew this. I also now saw my way in. "Only a single wife for such a strong man like yourself?" I murmured. "Surely you want more." I pushed my will at him, staring at him over my fan from behind the lattice.

All the pushing I'd done that day would leave me drained and unable to do much for the next day or so. But that didn't matter. I had to have this man take me with him.

Iwao gave an uneasy laugh. "What a man wants, and what a man needs, are not always the same thing," he replied.

"But more than one wife would guarantee you an heir," I told him. It was a lie, of course. And while many men blamed the woman for their lack of progeny, it was generally the man's fault.

Iwao still hesitated. "It's a lot to ask a woman. To come out to the provinces. We're a small estate."

"You need an heir," I told him, aware of the servants eagerly listening to every word. I couldn't just order Iwao to take me as a wife. It had to at least sound as though it came from him.

I was still pushing more than Etsu would like.

I didn't care. This was my only chance.

"Someone who will take care of your mountain," I added.

That seemed to settle him. "I know it's too much to ask of such a great lady as yourself," Iwao said, stumbling over his words like a schoolboy. "But perhaps you'd considered such a position yourself."

I gave him a merry laugh. "Of course I have. Since my own dear husband has died, I've often thought about retiring to the countryside, to live among the peace of the rocks, for the streams to sing hymns with me."

I hated being in the court. Hated feeling so closed in and fettered. I needed those wild ways and hills. The bright bursts of color from growing things. To feel the full pattern of life all around me, living, dying, and re-birthing.

Some of that longing, I'm sure, came through my voice.

"Then would you consider becoming a wife to someone such as I?" Iwao said, his words still plain and inelegant.

"Perhaps," I said coyly. "Would one such as you ask such an indulgence?"

"I would," Iwao said fervently. "It would be my deepest desire. For you to become a second wife for me."

"Second wife?" I asked archly. Did I really want such a lowly position?

Then again, it isn't as if I would be staying there for long.

"Second," Iwao said.

I could tell he was fighting me on this suggestion. He did truly value his first wife.

"Very well," I said, acquiescing with what grace I could muster through my exhaustion. "I will be your second wife. Follow you back to your mountain. Give you the heirs you deserve."

I didn't bother telling him that those heirs would all be heartache and suffering.

Maybe he knew. The sigh he gave was heartfelt, from his soul, as if he'd just released a great prophecy.

All I could see was that I was finally one step closer to enacting my revenge.

Eight

Surely There Was a Mistake

Kayoku

Surely there was a mistake. The outrider must have misunderstood.

"Excuse me?" Kayoku asked, using her most formal tone. "Did you say Iwao was traveling with a second wife?"

"I did, ma'am," the man replied. He looked worried, as well as sweaty and tired. His legs, arms, and even his face were mud-stained from having ridden so hard and fast, trying to arrive before the rest of the party.

"There's a new wife," the man repeated. "A second wife," he clarified. "She's beautiful. And rich."

This only confused Kayoku more. "Then what does she want with *my* husband?" she asked. She quickly put her hand over her mouth. She should never have said such a thing out loud.

However, the outrider merely gave her a grin. "Aye, that's the question, isn't it?" He grew somber again quickly. "She isn't a spy from Masato. Her family's too well placed. They say she's widowed, looking for a quiet place to live."

"It won't be that quiet here," Kayoku proclaimed. "Not for long." Masato had started to mass his men together again. The first big victory hadn't broken the enemy, merely delayed him. There had been more, stronger skirmishes lately.

The man shrugged. "We'll do what we can to keep the peace," he promised.

"Thank you," Kayoku said sincerely. She gave the man a *jutte* coin in gratitude, then hurried off to direct the servants.

Chieko still maintained control of the kitchens, which was a smaller part of the estate management. Kayoku was in charge of everything else, including keeping all the rooms clean, the *tatamis* fresh, making sure that the priests had what they needed for their various ceremonies, running all the servants and keeping the peace between the various factions.

None of Iwao's generals would be as efficient as Kayoku at running the estate, she was sure of it.

Where to put the new wife? Of course she needed to be close to the other wives. But where?

They wouldn't arrive until the next day, which gave Kayoku at least a little bit of time to sort out rooms.

First, Kayoku directed the servants to open up Iwao's rooms, sending fresh candles, as well as adding a sweet hollyhock bush from the garden, carefully trimmed so that no leaves would fall.

Then she tackled the problem of the new wife. Kayoku couldn't put the woman in the servants' quarters, no matter how much she might be tempted.

She didn't have to move herself, though, as this was merely a second wife. Perhaps it was time for Emiko, Iwao's youngest sister, to give up her formal sitting rooms?

Except that she was a young woman, just come of age, starting to entertain her own visitors, under proper supervision, of course.

Still, Kayoku found herself outside of Emiko's rooms without having first sent a note asking to be seen. Since she was the head of the household, it wasn't inappropriate for her to do this.

It still made her feel so awkward.

"I'm so sorry!" Emiko said as she came out of her room. Behind her, in the room, there was a flurry of activity as servants were packing things.

Relief washed over Kayoku. At least Emiko understood without being asked what would be expected of her.

"Thank you," Kayoku said, taking Emiko's small hands in her own.

"Chieko said it was the only proper solution," Emiko said with a too-casual shrug.

Kayoku swallowed her disappointment. Chieko had stepped in? Did she think that Kayoku wouldn't do the right thing? Wouldn't honor the new wife as was required?

Fighting to keep her face and tone neutral, Kayoku said, "Having another set of hands to help run the estate would actually be a blessing," she said.

Except that Kayoku didn't want to give up any of her power. Or control. She loved being as busy as she was, much more so than a normal wife.

"I heard that she was beautiful," Emiko said conspiratorially. "That would be just like my dumb brother. To let a pretty face go to his head." Then she put her hands over her mouth and gasped. "Not to say that you aren't beautiful, Kayoku!"

Kayoku couldn't help but giggle at the girl. "I know I'm not the most beautiful," she admitted.

"You are very beautiful," Emiko said stubbornly.

"I know I'm not," Kayoku said. "I have a very plain face, with large teeth and regular hair. Not cascading like black silk, like yours."

"You aren't telling the truth," Emiko said. "Your eyes shine with such intelligence. You're hands are very delicate and kind. And your skin is like moonbeams caught in a silver bowl."

"Don't be ridiculous," Kayoku said, laughing again. She knew she was plain. She'd accepted that as a young girl.

However, she also knew that beauty wasn't everything. She was also smart and practical. Those qualities would see her much further in her life.

They talked quickly about where Emiko would go, how soon the rooms would be ready. Kayoku would oversee the refurbishment herself, making sure everything was of the highest quality. She needed to make sure that not only this new bride felt welcome, but that Chieko would think Kayoku had done everything in her power to make things right.

A second wife didn't necessarily spell disaster. She might even bring the household some luck.

Kayoku stood outside in the cool night air with the rest of the household, waiting for Iwao's return. She never spent much time outside. It made her uncomfortable not to have a ceiling above her head, so she'd ordered additional lamps to be lit. She knew it was impolite—guests should be allowed the grace of darkness to hide their travel stains. However, the night held too many strange winds that gave chilling moans and carried the rotting scent of graveyards.

The lights didn't show that much beyond the main door to the Formal Greeting hall, just inside the gate. Just to the right hulked the men's quarters, a sturdy, three-story wooden structure with only a few windows lit. To the left sat the Ancestor's Hall, its elaborate carvings hidden by the darkness. Kayoku felt supported by each, like the guards beside her.

As the first wife of the estate, it was Kayoku's duty to welcome the lord of the estate when he returned home from a trip.

As his wife, she couldn't help but be very curious about the new wife he'd brought back with him, and why. Did Iwao think Kayoku couldn't produce an heir? That was the usual reason a husband gave for a second wife. The new wife was supposedly very beautiful. Was Iwao more shallow than Kayoku had thought?

No, there must be another reason why Iwao was willing to disrupt his household like this and bring in another woman.

Kayoku had tried to oversee even the smallest detail so that this new wife would have nothing to criticize. The flowers in her room were fresh from the garden that afternoon, with the petals all checked so that none would fall inappropriately, signaling bad luck. The *tatamis* were all well aired. Sweet candles had been lit, and had been burning most of the afternoon. The rooms had been cleaned from rafters to floor, and not a speck of dust remained.

Still, Kayoku knew from her experiences with her stepmother that complaints could always be invented.

What type of woman would this new wife be? Would she be grateful for all the work that had been done on her behalf? Or petulant with nothing quite good enough?

It didn't matter. Kayoku was determined that this new wife would not bring discord to the estate. There was enough being sown outside the sturdy walls by Masato.

While Iwao had been away, there had been more than a few small skirmishes. Though Kayoku wasn't supposed to be involved in the war—none of the women were—she'd had to oversee the supplies sent to the soldiers, making sure enough food was being sent to them as well. She had a very good idea of how those battles had gone: well, at first, then increasingly badly.

According to the gossip, Masato was testing both their strong and weak points before engaging in the next huge battle.

Kayoku, like everyone else in the estate, prayed regularly that he didn't find too many.

The travelers arrived without fanfare. Iwao was surrounded by his servants and outriders, of course. He was too important to ride by himself. His travel robes were plain black, sturdy, and sensible.

He looked well, Kayoku noted with approval. Though the time at the Emperor's court had not erased the worry lines that marred his face, there was a twinkle around his eyes that she hadn't seen for a long while.

Seiji was tied to his back, and the first thing Iwao did after he dismounted was to take the sword, still in its sheath, and touch the ground with it. He closed his eyes in prayer for a moment before he turned to greet the household.

Kayoku barely listened to his words, fascinated by Iwao's movements.

He didn't realize how he caressed the sword as he talked. Kayoku found her thoughts leading down inappropriate paths as she remembered how he'd stroked her own thighs in a similar manner.

At least the Emperor had approved of Iwao's inheritance, as well as his continued role as guardian of Mount Shirayama. As opposed to that idiot Akimoto no Tayo, who had abdicated all his power to Masato, and now sat like a puppet in his own hall, unable to scratch his nose without the warlord's approval.

Speculation had run high as to whether or not Iwao would introduce the new wife to the gathered household. Kayoku found she was disappointed when he didn't. Instead, he dismissed most of the gathered crowd, sent his fellow travelers on their way, then beckoned for the new wife's carriage to approach.

The first wave of dread crashed down on Kayoku. The carriage was finely made, beautifully painted white and gold with green bamboo crests. It cost more than what the estate would spend on food and drink for half a year, possibly more.

Kayoku turned her attention away from the waiting carriage, though, and went to greet her husband.

"You look well," Iwao said, giving Kayoku a formal bow. "Running the household seems to be agreeing with you."

"Thank you, my lord," Kayoku said, humbled that he'd noticed. "You look well yourself."

"I was relieved of my worries about the estate, once I knew it was in your capable hands," Iwao said sincerely. "You are more reliable than my eldest general, more sturdy than the mountain herself."

Where was all this poetry coming from? Iwao usually spoke much more plainly.

Was he in love with this new wife?

Kayoku contained her shudders.

"I live to serve," Kayoku replied simply.

"So do we all, even if there's sometimes battle among the taskmistresses," Iwao said, still with that twinkle in his eye.

What was he talking about? The duty he must split between his wives? The duty of the mountain and the estate?

Iwao gave one last caress to Seiji before turning toward the new wife's carriage. "Welcome to the Yakimata estate," he called out.

The woman who exited was far beyond Kayoku's expectations.

She'd been expecting someone pretty, possibly even beautiful.

She hadn't expected a woman who could compete with the *kami* for beauty.

Her skin was porcelain prefect, pale and smooth. Despite the many hours on the road that day, she looked freshly made up. Her robes were unwrinkled, as if she'd just stepped into them. They were the color of a newly washed sky, soft and gray. Even her scent was still sweet, as if she'd just wakened.

Kayoku swallowed hard against her jealousy. It would never do to show Iwao, this wife—anyone—her true feelings.

No wonder Iwao had chosen this woman. There wasn't a man who could resist her.

But why had she chosen Iwao?

Iwao gave all of Kayoku's formal titles, including her grandfather as well as her father, as part of her introduction. Kayoku was impressed that he remembered them all. It made her feel slightly better.

Then the woman gave all of her credentials. She came from a high-placed family—very high. She ended with her first husband's ties, ties that she obviously had chosen to maintain.

They showed that her family had come down, slightly, in the world.

Were there debts on her original estate that needed paying? Was she actually not as rich as she seemed?

But Kayoku finally had a name to go along with the beautiful, disturbing presence in front of her.

Hikaru.

"I greet you, Hikaru, and welcome you to our humble estate," Kayoku said, using her most formal tones and greetings.

"Thank you," Hikaru said, graciously enough. "I look forward to learning about the mountain, the estate, the *kami* and all that goes on in your lives here."

Her voice was like a song as well. How could anyone be so perfect?

There had to be something wrong with her, hidden deep in her soul. No one could be this perfect.

"I am tired now, and would like to retire," Hikaru said delicately.

"Right away," Kayoku found herself saying. She turned and started ordering servants to finish preparing Hikaru's rooms.

Wait—why had the guest not politely yawned? Letting the host declare it was time to depart? And why was Kayoku so determined to make everything right for this other wife, as if she were a mere servant, and not the first wife?

It was too late that night for such complications, Kayoku decided as she hurried away.

In the morning she would be more fresh. More able to decide things for herself.

Better able to judge the luck of this new wife.

Kayoku was determined not to attribute all that went wrong the next day to the new wife. However, nothing good had come out of her arrival, either.

Masato had sent another declaration, wanting another large battle. Iwao had agreed, of course. There was no possibility of compromise. Kayoku wished she had better insight into what she could do to help end the war quickly.

She knew better than to believe it could be avoided, unlike some of the women in the compound.

Emiko was now sick. It was probably nothing. The move and the excitement and everything. She'd always been a delicate girl.

This summer cold worried Kayoku, though, who insisted on cooking a special healing soup, with chicken and wild mushrooms, and bringing it to Emiko herself.

While Emiko ate in her greeting rooms, Kayoku busied herself in her sleeping room, lifting up every *tatami*. There were characters there, under the mats, but they were done in chalk, not blood or tar, and were drawn to bring peace to those walking and sleeping over them.

It wasn't until the end of the day that Kayoku realized the other problem: Iwao hadn't sent for her yet. He'd been gone for almost a month. It wasn't that she needed to fulfill his physical needs. But they needed to make sure they were aligned in terms of running the estate.

Kayoku spent part of the evening composing a letter to her husband, inviting him to come and visit her in her rooms the following night. She made certain her words were very matter-of-fact, and made clear her intention of merely talking.

She sent the missive off, then waited in her rooms for a reply.

None came.

The night settled around the estate. Kayoku was glad her windows all faced inward, that she didn't have to see the darkness pressing in from the outside. The air had been calm, almost sticky, all day. Now, the winds had picked up, still carrying those strange moans and ill scents.

They all came from Masato and his army, she was certain of it. Yet another way to demoralize Iwao's men. Though she wasn't certain exactly how Masato was doing it...she still didn't necessarily believe in magic.

Just luck.

When still no word came back from Iwao, Kayoku asked a servant to inquire if the lord was ill.

The servant hesitated. "Are you certain?" she eventually asked.

"Why wouldn't he respond?" Kayoku asked plainly.

"Perhaps he has company," the servant replied dryly.

Horrified, Kayoku stammered, "Of course. You may be right. I should—I should not be so impatient about these things. Thank you."

She fled back into her rooms, her cheeks burning.

Of course Iwao might already have a visitor, might be busy with his second wife, which was why he hadn't replied to her note.

How was she ever going to get used to this?

Kayoku met Hikaru in the formal greeting hall of the woman's quarters for their first official meeting. She couldn't think of anywhere else to do it. She didn't want to bring the other wife into her own rooms—that was too intimate, and she barely knew this woman.

Plus, she wanted to impress this Hikaru, if that was possible. She'd heard from her own servants how this new wife had insisted on new *tatamis* being laid down, had removed the flowers, even asked that all the windows could be opened to remove the stench of the sweet candles.

Before Kayoku was fully ready, Hikaru arrived. She floated into the room as if she walked on a cloud. Kayoku had never seen anyone so graceful. Her tan robes with red and gold trim could have been worn before the Emperor. That sweet scent of hers flowed in with her, as if Hikaru had just walked into a grove of jasmine.

Even her servants were better dressed and more elegant than Kayoku. She felt very plain in her palest green robes, and held herself stiffly while waiting to be addressed.

Then she shook herself. *She* was the head wife here. She was the one in charge.

"I greet you, Yamamoto no Hikaru," Kayoku said formally, bowing in greeting from her seat.

"And I greet you, Shimizu no Kayoku," Hikaru said, just as formally.

Did she bow as deeply? It was difficult for Kayoku to tell from her seated position.

Hikaru sank onto the pillows as gracefully as flower petals dropped from cherry trees.

Kayoku shook herself again. She had *never* been given to flights of poetry. Something must be truly wrong with her.

Maybe Emiko's fever was spreading?

"Have you settled in?" Kayoku asked after the servants had served them both tea and withdrawn.

"Perfectly fine," Hikaru said with a slight smile.

Even Kayoku could tell that was a lie. Hikaru wasn't settling in at all.

"I know that it's very different than your life back on your own estate," Kayoku said. "We are just a small holding."

"This is very true," Hikaru said. "It is very rustic. And rural. Provincial."

Kayoku felt her back stiffen further. Hikaru should *never* have said something like that. She should have found a way to compliment Kayoku and the estate instead.

"Perhaps you'll be able to visit the court again soon," Kayoku said. Even if this Hikaru left in the morning, it couldn't be soon enough for Kayoku.

"Perhaps," Hikaru said. "The mountain is very beautiful. Very special. Full of spirits and *kami*."

How had this woman even noticed? Kayoku shook her head. She wouldn't have thought Hikaru could see beyond the hem of her own robes.

"It is very beautiful," Kayoku agreed, though she rarely saw the mountain itself. Still, when the spring was in full bloom, the breezes blowing down from the top of the hills were very sweet. The sunsets, too, particularly during the fall, were spectacular. The two or three that she'd seen.

Kayoku, like most of the women on the estate, spent all her time indoors, not allowed outside. The sun could never darken their skin, and the wind wouldn't be allowed to roughen their hands.

"What else interests you?" Kayoku asked eventually, as Hikaru seemed content to just sit and sway in the still morning air.

"Poetry," Hikaru said immediately. "That was how we met, Iwao and I. He wrote me the most beautiful poem."

"Iwao?" Kayoku said, giggling. "Surely not. One of his advisors probably wrote it for him."

"Ah. I see," Hikaru said, nodding. "Thank you. That explains a lot." The room chilled considerably from her disapproval.

"It isn't that Iwao couldn't write poetry," Kayoku said hastily. "It's just that he doesn't." He hadn't ever written her a poem, had he? Not even during his awkward teenage years.

"I'm sure he's perfectly capable," Hikaru agreed, the lie laying easily between them.

"Is there anything else you like?" Kayoku asked. "There are many different duties you could pick up around the estate."

Hikaru's giggles floated through the room, brightening up the very air. "Why would I do that? When I have you to do such things?" she asked.

"Excuse me?" Kayoku asked. Had she just heard Hikaru correctly?

"Don't worry about handing off any of your duties to me," Hikaru said. "I don't need them."

"Of course you don't," Kayoku found herself agreeing instantly. Hikaru didn't need to work around the estate, to pick up any of the chores. Kayoku could do those herself. Hadn't she been doing them alone for some time now?

They talked only a little more before Hikaru excused herself, claiming she was still tired from her long journey from the court.

Kayoku excused her rudeness (again!) and let the second wife leave without assigning her any tasks.

On her way back to her own rooms, Kayoku wondered what had just gone on. Why hadn't she insisted on Hikaru helping more? She was running herself ragged every day. It wasn't appropriate that Chieko helped as much as she did, not when there was now a second wife to take some of the burden.

There was just something not right about Hikaru. Kayoku didn't know what it was. But she was too perfect.

Nothing good ever came from being too perfect.

Masato issued his next big challenge. Kayoku did what she could to prepare for the coming battle, to lay in supplies for the men: bandages, healing herbs, tea, and soups.

Kayoku sometimes found herself stopping in the middle of whatever task she had at hand and wondering where Hikaru was.

Why wasn't she helping? But every time Kayoku went to talk with the second wife she found herself believing (again!) that Hikaru didn't actually need to help with anything. Even when Kayoku sent her a note, Hikaru's excuses seemed perfectly fine.

Bad luck continued to plague the household. Some of the horses had come down with a cold—they were coughing dreadfully. Was it Emiko's summer cold that had affected them? Or had she caught some sort of horse disease?

It just wasn't healthy, to have all those animals living so close to where people lived. But there wasn't anything Kayoku could do about it, to get the horses moved off the estate. They had to be protected. They were more valuable than men, more vulnerable as well.

Then a small fire broke out in the servant's quarters. Only a single room was burned—people leapt to put it out very, very quickly. The threat of the entire estate burning was too high for anyone to take even a small fire lightly. Servants were reprimanded, lights were doused, the women's rooms were all much darker.

To top it all off, the priests from the Mori temple came and complained that all the oil they needed for their latest ceremony had spoiled.

It was the same oil as was used in the kitchens. However, something had spoiled it. Instead of being fresh, it stank as if it were ancient. It was no longer clear, either—black ashes floated across the top of it.

Who could have done such a thing? When the priests claimed it was magic, Kayoku refused to listen to them. A human had done this—added something to oil to make it rot. Thrown ash and dirt into the pot. A spell wouldn't have been so directed. It would have burst the jars, or spoiled all the supplies in the temple.

And besides, if a spell could ruin something in their most holy of holy places, what chance did the rest of them have, then?

The day before the next large battle with Masato dawned hot and sticky. Kayoku didn't believe in the Hell the Buddhists tried to escape, but it wasn't a good omen.

Iwao looked tired that morning. Kayoku shared a quiet cup of tea with him before he left for the army camp. He'd spend the night there, and join in battle the following day.

"My lord, you know, I've been running the estate," Kayoku started, not sure how to bring up Hikaru's lack of participation.

"You've been doing an excellent job at it," Iwao said, smiling at her. "You are my best general." He looked over his shoulder, as if someone had just called his name.

Kayoku didn't see anyone there. Seiji lay on pillows in the corner.

"Just don't tell the other generals I said so," Iwao said, laughing gently. "Or they'll be jealous."

"Of course, my lord," Kayoku said. It was good that Iwao could joke with her, even just a little, at a time like this.

"You look tired this morning," Iwao said.

"I'm fine," Kayoku assured him immediately. "You don't need to worry about me."

"But you could use some help," Iwao guessed.

"It is my pleasure as well as my duty to fulfill," Kayoku said stiffly.

"I will see that you get some more help," Iwao said firmly. "When I return." He paused, looked away, then looked back at Kayoku. His eyes seemed to brim with emotion that he never, ever released or inflicted on anyone. "And maybe we can work harder at getting another heir as well."

"Thank you, my lord," Kayoku said, suddenly relieved. He hadn't called her to his bed once since he'd brought Hikaru back to the estate. What if he never called her again? She'd refused to give into her fears.

Though it was improper, Iwao bowed his head toward Kayoku, low, placing his forehead all the way down onto the *tatamis*. "It is I who should be thanking you," he said.

He pushed his cup out of the way. The back of his hand casually brushed against the silk of her robe.

It was the slightest touch.

And more intimate than a caress.

"When I return," Iwao promised.

"It will be my pleasure," Kayoku replied, her throat suddenly dry.

She would wait for him forever if she had to.

Because though she understood and respected her husband, there was a small part of her that loved him as well.

Nine

Finally the Night Had Come

Hikaru

Finally, the night had come, when I would enact my revenge.

Masato had issued his next big challenge. Iwao and his troops were doomed. I think they knew it. There was a bitter taste of tears in the air of the camp, the sweat of desperation. Men sharpened their swords incessantly, the sound of whetstones against blades a constant whining in the background.

The battle would be the next day. I had listened as carefully as a human woman could to rumors about the war when I'd been at the estate. I had listened magically as well, invisible to the human eye, listening to the generals when they drank, or to the soldiers when they ate.

The war hadn't been going well. Masato had recently had several successful skirmishes against Iwao's troops. He was forcing them to pull back. The area of the mountain that Iwao controlled was diminishing.

Both sides were losing patience with the slow pace of the war. They each needed a decisive victory, to bolster their men, and their own egos.

So they'd agreed on another large battle, with a specified time and place, like the first big battle they'd had.

Masato had two or three times the number of swords, horses, and archers as Iwao. They were desperately outnumbered, again.

The generals felt that if Iwao could pull another brilliant move, as he had the first time, they would be saved.

No one was looking forward to gambling their lives on that, however.

I couldn't encourage or discourage any of the men. Men and women didn't have that sort of contact. And it was far too draining for me, at my age, to take on too many different human forms. Just appearing as a woman most of the time took a lot of my strength.

Still, I did what I could to "aid" the war effort, like adding ghostly, ghastly sounds to the winds Masato sent. I also made things to go wrong, puzzling things, like in the temple when an oil barrel spoiled. I also set loose bedbugs and other biting insects, so swaths of men lost sleep, ensuring they wouldn't be at their best.

The estate didn't realize how poisonous the air was growing—only those sensitive to it could tell.

To be honest, Masato made me uneasy. His influence wasn't natural. He had the use of some sorcerers, I could tell.

But he hadn't done as Iwao had and taken my love's life.

Ah, so certain was I, of the rightness of my cause. I didn't bother to see what was in front of me.

Fate blinded me. As well as my hatred, and need for revenge.

Living at the estate had become unbearable. Iwao's first wife, Kayoku, had intimated that I should help run the household.

I shuddered to even consider such a thing. It was far, *far* beneath someone such as I. If she only knew my true nature, she'd never be so rude as to suggest *chores*! I had helped run my family's estate, that was true, when my mother declared herself too ill. But that was an estate that mostly ran itself, as the *kitsune* were far less restricted and structured than the humans.

In some ways, it was dreadful living in a state of war. I felt sorry for the humans here, who wouldn't someday escape.

Not just because of the inconvenience, how impossible it was to get fresh seafood, news from the court, or even new silks. But because of everything else.

The estate had allowed some of the nearby farming households to come and live inside the compound walls. So much noise! Cattle and people and children crying. All that unhealthy smoke from their cooking fires.

It was worse than living in a *village*.

I had my sisters to help keep me sane. Plus, I had more access to the outdoors than I'd had at the Emperor's court.

Still, it made me wonder how any human woman stayed sane, always locked indoors, with never a breath of fresh air, never a glimpse of sunshine, just the occasional sunset or sunrise.

I stayed hidden in Iwao's tent, after he'd moved there, just before the battle. No one could know I was there. None would see me, or hear me.

Women at battle were considered *unlucky*.

Iwao had no idea just how unlucky I was about to be.

Iwao's war tent was as plain as they came. I know his generals were aghast at how simply their leader lived—even more simply than Lord Taiga had.

I suspected it was because they couldn't justify their own indulgences if their commander had a pared-down life.

The tent was merely muslin, well made, but coarse, dyed a dark brown color, which seemed to be Iwao's family color, for some reason. Maybe they thought it represented the mountain, but dirt was actually a richer color than what they used.

Tatamis only covered the far end, which was where Iwao slept. The rest was pounded dirt. Two folded up writing desks lined one wall, along with pillows for resting on.

Seiji had his own portable rack, also along that wall. I heard him whispering, frequently. I tried as hard as I could to understand his words, but alas, I had never held him, and he'd never whispered to me. His words always sounded angry, though.

I was surprised that he suffered Iwao to wield him. But perhaps that was part of the curse.

A tea service sat in the other corner. A pile of clothes. Iwao's armor.

That was it. No extra rooms. No special pillows. No extras. It was almost as bare as the soldiers' tents.

Did Iwao live like this to shame his generals into living a more austere life? Or was he paying penance for his previously decadent life? To make up for his previous awful deeds? I was never certain.

While I waited for Iwao to return from his meeting with the generals, I made sure to paint the appropriate symbols under his *tatamis*, the sort of thing that came natural to all *kitsune*, that my mother had taught me—signs that weakened a man's will, that drained him of his essence.

I knew the reverse as well. While humans may have called what I brought *luck*, when I used those symbols, I knew better. It had much more to do with optimism, joy, and life.

"I thought I would find you here," sounded a woman's voice from behind me.

I jumped, startled. Who had sneaked up on me so completely? I wasn't so exhausted from playing a human that I'd lost all sense of stealth, had I?

But it was just Etsu, standing and looking as disapproving as always. She wore a great black travel cloak over her regular robes.

"Are you away, sister mine?" I asked, ignoring how she glared at me.

"You cannot just flout human customs this way!" Etsu whispered urgently to me.

I couldn't help but laugh at her. "No one can hear us," I said in normal tones. "And none of them can see us, either. Or at least they can't see *me*."

"They can't see me either, but I'm not the fool here," Etsu insisted. "You have to be more careful."

"I have been careful," I said primly. "I took precautions before I arrived." Yukiko would cover for me back at the estate. I'd arranged a signal for her as well, so she'd know if I had the sword and we could leave.

It had been a joy to ride out with the rest of the troops. Fresh air at last!

I *had* been careful, despite what Etsu said. The men hadn't seen me.

Their horses, on the other hand, had sensed me. They'd shied away, repeatedly.

Which wasn't necessarily a bad thing. Such skittish horses would spread more unrest among the soldiers—the men knew the horses had keener senses than they did. This, in turn, would help further to bring down Iwao's army.

"You don't understand," Etsu said sadly, shaking her head.

Was she referring to some sort of prophecy that she'd had? Or merely implying that I was too young, and therefore too inexperienced, to be properly dealing with humans?

Both made me angry. "Then explain it to me," I told her sharply.

"The humans matter, more than you realize," Etsu told me.

It was an old argument—really, the one we'd been having almost every day since I went to the Emperor's court. "How can they?" I asked plainly. "They don't have the long lives that we have. It doesn't matter if there are more of them. We'll simply outlive them."

"You'll see," Etsu said, shaking her head, still looking dour.

"Or you will," I added, feeling sassy.

She just grimaced at me. "I'm not here to argue, or to convince you to change your ways and start treating the humans better. I did want to let you know that I would be gone for a while. I found a book—really, the rumor of a scroll, that will greatly help us in separating his soul from the sword."

And just like that, my sister ended the fight, as well as my petulance.

"Thank you," I told her sincerely. "I should be at home by the time you return." I didn't want to perform any sort of great magic like that outside of our protected estate. Who knew what might occur in the chaos of the human world?

"I will look for you here, first," Etsu said wryly. "Though I know you'll be successful, you may not be as successful as you think."

I had no idea what that meant, and I wasn't about to start another argument by insisting she explain yourself.

"Travel safe," I told her. "I will count the hours until you return."

"Thank you, little one," Etsu said. "Be safe. Be true."

And with that, my eldest sister was gone.

I knew she'd return. Despite how Norihiko had been taken, we were generally difficult to kill. I had to believe that she would come back to me, that she would find a spell that would break my love free from his cursed existence.

Even oblivion had to be better than how he was living now.

Iwao came to his tent later than I'd thought he would. He did try to be conscientious, I suppose. Planning with his generals how to best beat Masato.

He didn't realize he was doomed.

I waited, kneeling on his sleeping *tatamis*. I'd draped a sheer piece of cloth to keep the sleeping area out of direct line of sight from the door. I'd also enchanted the cloth, so that Iwao wouldn't really notice it.

When Iwao arrived, instead of coming straight to bed, the first thing he did was to place Seiji, the sword, on his stand. Iwao withdrew, but it seemed that Seiji called to him. The sword's whispering filled the tent.

I caught my breath, ready to slip sideways, a move that humans viewed as one of us disappearing. However, it wasn't necessary.

Seiji merely wanted to play. Or perhaps, if he was aware of me being there, to show off.

Iwao drew Seiji without ceremony, a long sweeping movement.

Then he began to practice. Defending. Attacking. High blows. Low assaults.

Seiji worked his magic on Iwao. The human wasn't that graceful on his own. But under Seiji's influence, Iwao flowed with the same beauty as pines dancing in the wind.

It was obvious to me when Iwao would try to assert his own will over the sword. He didn't cut himself, but he came close to it.

Iwao wasn't a good match for Seiji at all. I could only see red when I watched Iwao grow more clumsy.

His will wasn't compatible with the sword's. They only worked together well when Seiji was in control. As it should be, with any human.

Soon, I promised my love, my one true mate.

Soon I would break him free from this cursed existence, where he had to deign to be touched by men.

Only as Iwao was drawing near the sleeping mats did I dissolve the spell holding the cloth into place. It fluttered down beautifully, like a butterfly landing on a flower.

Iwao gasped when he saw me. But he was clever, more clever than I'd imagined. Instead of calling my name, he came directly to me, kneeling beside me so he could whisper and none of the guards standing outside would hear us.

"What are you doing here?" Iwao asked. He was shocked, but he was more puzzled, more curious, than disgusted by my presence, as I knew he would be.

"I came to see you off, my lord, to give you a proper hero's send off," I told him. It was almost the truth.

"It's bad luck to be with a woman the night before battle," Iwao warned. "And if any of the guards saw you..."

"They didn't," I assured him. I pushed my *will* toward him, reassuring him. "I was quite clever!" I told him, maintaining an air of absolute innocence.

"It isn't safe here," Iwao warned. But he was already weakening. His body leaned toward mine, the sour scent of his sweat from his workout with Seiji wafting toward me.

"You'll protect me," I told him. "Just another reason for you to be spectacular tomorrow."

Iwao grimaced.

I saw my mistake instantly. I needed to keep his thoughts revolving around me, and our passion, and not the upcoming battle.

Still, I couldn't help but comment. "You were remarkable, practicing with Seiji as you did. It was an honor to watch you."

Iwao chuckled. "You would not believe how the sword calls to me sometimes. Fortunately, I'm older now, and more disciplined. However, if I'd met the sword when I'd been younger, I probably would have practiced with it all the time, to the exclusion of everything else."

I believed it. It was that wild side that Seiji called to in Iwao, the very nature of my own soul, trapped in horrible, unyielding steel.

"But now, I think you should practice your other sword skills, my lord," I told him flirtatiously.

Iwao looked surprised, but then he smiled at me. "I don't believe I'll ever get used to your direct nature," he said.

I didn't tell him that he wouldn't have to. Because I would be gone in the morning and he would be dead before noon.

Iwao was pleasant enough as a lover. He at least tried to pleasure the woman he was with, and not be completely selfish. I'd heard stories from Mother about such men and how to use their pleasure against them.

With Iwao, it wasn't that much different. I drained his life as I drained his seed, leaving him drowsy and satiated.

In the morning, he wouldn't know how confused his mind still was, how much fog I'd left behind.

I didn't really have to do much. His own disciplined nature would get him killed the longer he wielded Seiji.

They would never be a matched pair, not as Norihiko and I had been.

It didn't take much magic to withdraw unseen from Iwao's tent, and to flow to where the battle would be held in the morning. It was a shame, really. The field they were fighting in would be better used for crops than a battle. Even I knew that.

Still, I made myself a simple nest at the top of a rise, from which I could see everything. The nest held me safe and kept me invisible. It was one of the earliest magics all *kitsune* learned.

Then I waited, more patiently than my sisters would ever imagine I could, to see the fulfillment of my revenge.

To wait until Masato killed Iwao, so I could take the sword.

Ten

Gray Clouds Crept In

Iwao

Gray clouds crept in, above
the honor field, staining
sky, and earth, below

Iwao sat on the back of his horse and grimly reviewed the field before him. The clouds above, full of rain, matched the ones in his head.

Even Seiji couldn't bring a clarity to his thoughts. Just a longing to break free, to ignore discipline and honor and merely attack, now.

Iwao shouldn't have given into his baser side the previous night with Hikaru. But she had sung so sweetly to him, her flesh white and perfumed. He couldn't help himself, regardless of the amount of discipline he'd built up over the years.

Hopefully, his entanglement with her would bring him luck, as she'd promised with her sweet sighs and sweeter passion.

Iwao shook his head, trying again to concentrate on the here and now. Masato sat with his men, still wearing that smug smile. His army had swelled like rivers after spring rain. And was as muddy too; dark currents and winds moved among his men.

Many reports of the unnatural nature of Masato's army had reached Iwao. Sitting on the hilltop looking down at them, he could believe them. They seemed limitless, like the tide, constantly pouring out and over his own men.

Iwao tried again to dislodge his dark thoughts. He and his generals had come up with a plan—as desperate as these black times. They wouldn't try a full troop of men on horses again. Though all the generals agreed with Iwao that trick had won the last large-scale battle, they also agreed that it wouldn't work a second time.

But a smaller, elite troop, might break through the line. Particularly two of them, attacking at different locations.

Masato sat behind his men, directing the battle. Like Iwao, he'd only join in toward the end.

Iwao hoped to catch Masato unaware, stampede his line and his men, perhaps get the warlord to do something stupid.

Like engage Iwao directly.

Seiji whispered to Iwao of bold attacks and blood-filled clouds.

Iwao fervently prayed for it to be primarily the blood of the enemy.

Kage raced like the wind behind the archers as Iwao and his elite troop broke through Masato's line. He was glad for the extra protections he'd received that morning from the priests of the Mori temple: Masato's men were unclean, swarthy, their faces and bodies painted with unnatural tattoos that gave them strength beyond death.

Still, Iwao almost wanted to laugh at how his troops broke through the line. The first group had met with heavy fighting—and heavy casualties, on both sides.

However, Masato's men hadn't been expecting the second troop to come wheeling up, rolling over the hole the first troop had established.

Seiji sang to Iwao, willing him to draw the sword. Seiji wanted to cut through the air, his song clearing the path for more victory.

Iwao hesitated, though. Seiji was so undisciplined today, more wild than usual. And Iwao's head was still full of clouds.

So Iwao stayed behind and let his men cut a swath through Masato's army. He rode the swell of the wave behind them.

Perhaps Kage knew the way. Or maybe it was Seiji. But before Iwao knew it, he was already facing Masato.

The sounds of the battle continued around him—men shouting curses, screaming, laughing, dying. Arrows whizzed by. Swords clanged against armor.

Yet at the same time, everything stood still. Masato wore his usual lazy smile, though he couldn't hide the surprise in his eyes.

"Come to challenge me already?" Masato sneered, drawing his sword.

"Your days were already numbered, when you set foot on the mountain," Iwao declared, drawing Seiji and slipping off Kage's back.

Masato hesitated. Did he recognize the right of Iwao's claim, finally? Was he afraid of Seiji? Or was he merely filled with empty words and not deeds, like his Amida Buddha?

Masato joined Iwao, dismounting, then advancing on foot, his finely made straight sword drawn and held in front of him. "You won't win," he declared. "Even the Emperor will bow before the Buddha before too long."

"This is the land of spirits," Iwao replied. "The *kami* and *ujikami*. They will always protect us."

"We shall see," Masato said mildly. Then he attacked.

Iwao had to admit that Masato was a ferocious swordsman. He drove forward as fiercely as a hawk, with just as much subtlety as well. Iwao found himself backing up, adjusting his footing, forced to reckon with Masato and his blunt force.

The attack seemed to take Seiji by surprise. He led Iwao back, one step, then another.

Iwao decided to use his hesitation as another ploy.

Let Masato grow smug. Iwao would take his time.

Masato had underestimated Iwao before, to Iwao's advantage.

Let it be to Iwao's advantage again.

Seiji whistled through the air as Iwao finally began his offensive attack. It didn't take long. Only a few steps. Then Iwao was forcing his will on Masato, making the other step back.

Iwao felt Seiji's joy bubbling up and through him. He maintained a scowl, though. It wouldn't do to laugh in the face of his opponent.

But really, it was only a matter of time, now, before Masato was beaten.

Again Masato stepped back. Again Iwao pressed his advantage.

Gray clouds remained overhead, filled with rain. Those long summer tears that Masato and his men would cry. Iwao had to bite his tongue to prevent the poetry from spilling out, filled with the joy of the mountain despite the tears of blood that had been shed.

However, when Masato suddenly gave Iwao an opening, he hesitated.

It couldn't be that easy, could it? Surely it was a trap.

Iwao followed through on his previous attack, following the forms he'd drilled in, not giving Seiji his head.

A laugh echoed over the field, distracting him. It sounded like Hikaru. But he'd left her safely behind, at the estate. Except she'd escaped, hadn't she?

Iwao shook his head, suddenly confused by her sweet scent washing over him. Despite Seiji's strength, he felt his own draining from him.

Masato made another mistake. Again, Iwao hesitated, despite Seiji pushing him to attack.

The next time, Iwao vowed. He'd finish this.

However, the next time Masato left his side open, Iwao slipped. His calves burned with the effort of keeping on his feet.

He'd never been that graceful.

Masato, however, didn't hesitate. Two steps forward, and he was thrusting his sword into Iwao's armor, at the side, where it was the weakest.

Iwao swung out wildly with Seiji, the blade sliding across Masato's gloved hand but not biting into flesh.

"You're mine," Masato whispered.

Did his eyes have a strange glow? Or was that Iwao's still fevered imagination?

Hikaru's sweet laughter echoed through Iwao's head again.

But strangely, his last thoughts weren't of her. Instead, he thought of Kayoku, what a warm and steady presence she'd been through his entire life.

And how he'd failed her, as the darkness overtook him.

Eleven

Gleefully I Watched

Hikaru

Gleefully I watched Iwao fall, succumbing to Masato's superior strength. Though I found the warlord repugnant, a hairy, smelly man without any grace, it was still good to see my lover's killer fall.

My revenge was complete. Iwao's estate was gone. The mountain would belong to Masato. Everything Iwao had dreamed of had ended.

I stayed cloaked in stillness and shadow. None could see me. But it was time to claim my prize.

Men fought and died all around me. I now understood why women were barred from such things. It was too awful. I had to remind myself more than once that they were just humans, they would die soon enough anyway.

It was still so unpleasant. The screams and curses. The ferocious way they attacked one another. The smell of blood and death.

I rose from my nest, but before I could take a single step, a man appeared in front of me.

Not an ordinary man. Not a soldier.

A sorcerer. The short, fat, tonsured man who had taken Norihiko's soul, so long ago.

"*Waru*," I declared him. Though he appeared human, his soul was tainted and corrupt. *Evil.*

He merely chuckled at me, a chilling sound that carried with it the echoes of the battle swirling around us. "*Huli*," he declared me, a common enough insult. "It will be my pleasure to take your soul and use it as well."

Icy fingers touched my shoulders, my knees, and my hands.

Suddenly, I couldn't move.

I struggled to free myself. The sorcerer's spell wasn't complete, I still had some movement in my fingers and toes. If I hadn't been using so much energy to maintain my human appearance, as well as hiding myself all day, it would have been enough to free myself instantly.

As it was, I would merely have to be patient. I could wiggle out of this trap without gnawing off one of my own feet, I was certain.

I still struggled, to make sure this sorcerer underestimated me.

Just over the sorcerer's shoulder, Masato reached down and plucked Seiji from Iwao's lifeless hand.

I howled, loud enough to break through the veils hiding me from those fighting on the hill, stirring them to pull back and leave us to our own battle. Masato seemed startled,

It filled my heart with glee, though, that Masato couldn't raise Seiji, that the tip of the sword insisted on dragging on the ground.

My love had judged Masato unworthy.

In just a short while I'd free him.

The sorcerer chuckled again. "You killed an innocent man, you know."

"It was you who killed my love," I told him, rage filling me.

"True," the sorcerer said. "But I didn't create the sword at Iwao's bidding. The poor, dead mortal. Such a shame that even so brief a life was cut short, unnecessarily."

The words were spoken in such a mocking tone. They filled me with unease.

"I created the sword for its current wielder," the sorcerer added. "And it was Lord Taiga who exchanged his life for the right to wield the sword. The son never knew how Seiji had been created."

I didn't want to believe this odious man. But his words didn't have the taint of lies.

Had I been as rash and willful as Etsu always accused me of being? Had I caused an innocent man to be killed?

I couldn't consider that now. I had to stay focused on my nemesis.

"Ah well," the sorcerer said with a sigh when he saw Masato's struggles. "Obviously I didn't beat enough of the will from Seiji when I made him. No matter. I will use your soul instead, create another, better masterpiece."

"You will not," I told him. I couldn't side step the hold the sorcerer had on me.

But my kind is wily.

I merely disappeared.

"Why…" The sorcerer spun around in place. "How did you do that?" he asked, plainly.

I laughed. I couldn't help it. Maybe I wanted to show off a little as well. "You may be strong, sorcerer, but your magic is unnatural, like your long life. You're still a mortal," I added, touching on what I guessed was his sorest spot.

I hadn't moved. I threw my voice around.

But that damned sorcerer turned his head directly toward where I still stood.

"I've still caught you," he said, drawing closer.

I shrank away. The stench of limestone and ash clung to him. I wiggled harder. It really was just a matter of time before I'd be able to escape.

Time I no longer had.

The sorcerer pulled a box out of nowhere. It was square, wooden, and gave me chills.

I hadn't been close to Norihiko when his soul had been stolen. But I somehow recognized this box. It had carried his soul.

And if I didn't escape soon, it would carry mine as well.

I struggled to free myself from the sorcerer's spell. The battle had moved down the hill from us, the men frightened by my growls and hisses. Still it raged, the sounds of men dying all around us spurring me to greater struggles.

But the damned Taoist, Junichi, I'd learned, was a stronger magician than any I'd encountered. He had unnaturally lengthened his life with the souls of others. Now, those other souls fueled the trap I was caught in.

I could still wiggle my fingers. I was actually able to turn my wrists. However, that was all the movement I'd managed.

Plus, every time I thought I'd be able to break free, Junichi threw something at me. The arrows from a nearby attack suddenly whizzed out of the air, striking me. It wasn't enough to damage me, not really, not with the magical protection I'd already set into place.

But I had to fight those. As well as get away. And keep an eye on Junichi, who was crafting a spell meant to steal my soul.

I was fortunate I had time. It wasn't much, less than a quarter of an hour. Though it went against my very nature, I moved slowly, freeing one fingernail's length of skin at a time. It was hard work, unraveling the tight web encasing me. I wished for a scraper, something I'd seen women using to clean cloth in the fields.

All I had was my wits.

I'd run out of time.

Junichi finished his spell before I was prepared. The knife he held glowed with an evil yellow tint, as sickly as pus from a wound.

I struggled to move. Just a fingertip more! I didn't even have the solace of joining my love, since his soul was still trapped here.

Junichi drew closer, gloating. "This will merely kill your body," he explained, holding the awful instrument close enough for me to smell the rotten stench of it, like eggs long since gone bad. "Then I'll extract your soul. I know what I did wrong last time, with your stupid mate. This time, you won't drain me as much. Your soul will be a bit more broken than his."

This gave me hope. Norihiko had fought the sorcerer, drained him. Junichi hadn't made the perfect sword.

"Are you sure?" I taunted him, even as I increased my efforts to free myself. If I could have run my nails down my skin, scarring myself, I would have, in order to drag this net off myself. "While Norihiko was stubborn and strong, I may surprise you."

"Your kind should be wiped from the face of the earth," Junichi said, spitting the words at me.

It made me pause. Had he been enamored once, with one of the *kitsune?* And turned down? Or was he jealous of our immortality? Or perhaps both? That would explain his hatred.

It made me goad him more. I laughed at him. "You're just jealous, aren't you? Poor deluded man. Our lifetimes are natural. We're *born* immortal. Something *you* can never achieve. Not ever."

With a strangled cry, Junichi lurched forward, slashing down with the horrible knife.

I shrank away, pulling hard at the damned net that held me.

Junichi's knife went *thunk*, as if striking wood. His hand bounced back, as if it had struck something and been thwarted.

The amulet my mother had given me throbbed at my neck. She'd said it would help keep body and soul together.

I didn't know how long the magic would last. If Junichi's attack had already drained it.

But it gave me another chance.

"Did you think I'd come unprepared?" I asked. I found I could move my shoulders now. With my hands free, I could finally shake myself out of Junichi's spell. I pulled at it with clawed hands, frantic now. I *had* to be free.

Junichi stood there with the knife in his hand and a surprised look on his face. "How did you do that?" he asked.

I would have pitied him, given how forlorn he sounded. Obviously, he'd rarely had to struggle often to get what he wanted.

Every moment he paused gave me more freedom.

"I'll never tell you," I said simply. And I wouldn't. Why share that kind of information with an enemy?

"You think you're so special," Junichi said calmly while he struck out wildly with his knife, seeking me, trying to destroy me. His hand bounced back again. "But you're no different than I. Taking an innocent's life."

I knew he meant Iwao. "But I thought he'd killed my mate," I said, trying to excuse myself, knowing I never could.

Not to myself.

"You knew he didn't. You knew it had to be someone with sorcery," Junichi accused me.

I knew what he was doing—trying to keep me there, so he could figure out the spell, kill me with his next blow.

What he didn't realize was the grave danger he was in.

He'd killed my mate. With a snarling growl I finally freed myself from his web. I appeared before him, glowing with rage. I rushed at him, swiping at him with my claws, hoping to catch him.

Junichi slashed his blade at me, luckily missing, as he stumbled back.

It would be a simple matter, really, to drain all his lives from him, lives he'd obtained through unnatural means.

I just had to touch him long enough to do it.

"You will not escape me," I growled at him. "Or my revenge."

I couldn't believe that he laughed at me. "The taking of a life is more complicated than you realize," he said. "I doubt you, a mere woman, can do it."

His words struck a chord with me that I hadn't realized was there.

I'd dreamed of this day, of my revenge, for so long.

But I'd never dreamed of killing the killer myself. Of forcing the life from a body with my own two hands. It had always been by someone else's blade, or by his own hand, that the dirty sorcerer met his end.

I hesitated.

Junichi surged forward, blade raised high.

I wasn't about to find out if my mother's amulet would protect me again. I sidestepped him, slipping into shadows.

Maybe I could get closer to Junichi now. Maybe I could touch him, drain him, if I stayed in the shadows.

Or maybe he'd kill me instead.

I wanted him dead. I wanted the sorcerer who had killed my mate punished.

But the *kitsune* have never believed in acting in violence, not unless we were completely trapped.

I was free.

I found myself continuing to slide away, slipping from one shadow to the next, off the hill, away from the men still battling for a leader who was long since gone, away from the heavy clouds and rain soon to come, going deep into the forest on the mountain.

Junichi couldn't follow me. I'm not even certain my own sisters would have been able to. I had a wild side, deeply in tune with nature.

I didn't hide in shadows that everyone could see. Instead, I used the deep mysterious places that only the *kami* of the mountain could use. Those hidden holes of magic that weren't of this world, but of that *other* place.

I drifted as the rain spattered the leaves, listening to the quiet birds and the winds singing to the rocks. How could I have failed? How could I have turned my back on the killer of my love?

No matter what hatred Junichi may have for women or my kind, he was not right. I knew my mother had killed one of her lovers, instantly, when he'd turned violent. Aunts, too, had killed before. I, possibly, would be able to kill in such a circumstance.

However, this wasn't the same. It was a matter between me and my soul.

In the end, I knew that I could not kill. In the heat of passion, perhaps. But not deliberately, in cold blood.

My mother would be aghast. Perhaps Etsu would understand, not so Cho. Perhaps even my darling Norihiko would turn his back on me for having reached such a conclusion.

I would see the sorcerer dead. It just couldn't be by my hand.

Of course, I couldn't stay hidden in the deep places of the mountain, adding my tears to the late spring rain.

I had to find my love. Norihiko, still encased in the sword. And steal the sword back from Masato.

It was easier than I expected to slip into Masato's camp. The battle had finished maybe the day before, maybe two days. I didn't know how long I'd been mourning.

Men were seeing to their wounds, or quietly celebrating. I think the spirits that had been compelling them to fight were now gone, leaving them unnaturally exhausted.

In addition, some men prepared for the next battle, sharpening swords, fletching arrows, testing bowstrings. Didn't they realize they'd won? Or had their will been so sapped by Junichi that they knew no other life?

I pitied them more than any human I'd ever met.

Masato's tent was nothing like Iwao's. Gaudy red-and-orange banners flew above the black canvas tent, declaring its importance. It had more rooms than a peasant's hut, though I suspected it just housed Masato. Guards encircled the tent, each standing within arm's reach of one another.

Was Masato expecting me? Or an invading army?

A large, ornate wheel—one of the symbols of this Buddha—hung outside the tent. I understood the concept of rebirth. Weren't flowers reborn every spring? But my soul would move on, past this plane, when it was my time to die, no matter what humans believed.

I waited until two of the guards began talking with each other—some kind of bet they had going with one another. Then I slipped through and under the tent, as quiet as a shadow.

Inside was all chaos. My eyes didn't know what to rest on. Brightly colored pillows lay across every surface. Drapes hung down, dividing the tent rooms into more rooms, swaying with enchanting breezes. Candles and torches gave everything a glow that dazzled me.

It took me a few moments to realize that I'd been standing there, dazed, and unable to move.

Determined, I stepped forward, only to have my attention caught by a charm hanging down from the ceiling of the tent. It took a few more moments for me to shake my head, move away.

After taking a deep breath, I finally realized what was wrong: The inside of the tent was filled with charms, mainly created by Junichi, specifically designed to protect the humans from my kind.

I cursed the sorcerer's name again, wishing that I was other than I was, and could have merely killed the man.

That wouldn't have helped, however—his charms wouldn't have suddenly lost their power. In fact, given the way the sorcerer worked, when he died, he might pour all his remaining power into them.

Before I could take another step into this awful place, Masato came into the room.

He was shorter than I'd thought he would be. Muscular, but with fat, sensual lips and a protruding brow—a lazy man. He wore comfortable, tan robes, the best quality. He'd obviously been relaxing.

"Junichi said you might come pay a visit," Masato told me. He looked at me critically, as one might examine a snake, trying to determine if it was deadly or not.

I wasn't held where I stood. I could move around freely. My attention kept being caught by Junichi's charms, though. I would have to half blind myself in order to accomplish anything.

"I suppose this is what you're looking for," Masato said, indicating the case that enclosed Seiji.

I cursed myself. I'd gotten distracted again, while Masato was in the room.

This tent wasn't merely dangerous—it could be deadly. I might not notice Junichi or some other assassin creeping up on me.

But the sword…I needed to rescue Seiji. Steal him away from Masato.

I looked more carefully at the case. It gave me shivers. Magical characters had been carved into it, then painted over with unclean blood. Sickly green, barbed vines tied the box shut, twisted and growing into each other. Charms hung off the four corners of it, made from bones and feathers.

The entire thing repelled me.

I'd never get the box open on my own. I couldn't even touch it, carry it away to where my sisters could help.

"The sword was…not made to my taste," Masato said, grimacing. "Despite how much it cost. It isn't right."

"Then let me take it," I urged him. I would come back and deal with the man later. "I will unmake it." That much I could promise him.

Masato snapped his eyes to me.

Greed filled his soul. And envy. What did this man want?

"I won't give you the sword. I will sell it to you. For a price."

"And that is?" I asked, knowing already that I wouldn't like it.

"Your magic. All your fox fairy powers."

"What good would they do you?" I scoffed, though inside, I was chilled. It was a horrible price to have to pay.

"You'll see," Masato said with that condescending smile of his. "Because if you don't, I have already scheduled this box to be shipped out of Itzosaki harbor, then dropped into the deepest pit of the ocean they can find."

Norihiko wouldn't drown. I knew that. But to never see the sunshine again, even as a sword….

I would swear I heard Seiji hiss at the thought.

"Why would I trust you to keep your word? That if I gave you my powers, you would give me the sword?" I asked. I wasn't thinking of doing it. It was too much to ask. But I had to know.

Masato held out a folded piece of paper, thick, like a scholarly thesis. It was a contract, signing his soul over to Junichi should he renege on his part of the deal.

He wanted my powers that badly. Why would he do such a thing?

"What would you use my powers for?" I asked, convinced of the sincerity of his offer. My powers for Seiji, no interference from him or his men, safe escort to Iwao's estate.

There were no loopholes that even my wily nature could find.

Masato merely smiled and said nothing. "Will you sign?" he asked simply.

I was trapped, as surely as I'd been caught earlier by Junichi's web.

My powers for Norihiko's freedom.

People went about being human all the time. It surely couldn't be that bad. Could it?

I signed.

Junichi had obviously prepared everything for Masato ahead of time. The potion Masato pulled out from a cupboard in the corner stank of the sorcerer.

But what did it matter? I wove some of my own magic into the contract as well. Masato would die if he double-crossed me. Not by my own hand, no, but my magic would drain him of his life. He agreed to the additional terms, without adding any of his own.

He was that certain of the rightness of his cause.

As for me—I didn't really care what happened to me. I'd killed an innocent man—Iwao. Sentenced his estate to the management of the odious man before me. Tasted my own desire for revenge and found it lacking.

All that mattered was that I get Norihiko. I had to bring the sword back to the estate. Let my sisters work to free him.

He would leave this earth. I didn't see why I couldn't join him.

The distracting, dazzling charms in the room all faded to nothing as soon as I signed my name in bold characters on the contract. Not my full, real name, of course, but one that was close enough, that would bind me.

Masato signed his without flourish, both his regular name as well as his Buddhist name. This reassured me that he would go through with the spell, and not try to double-cross me.

The spell was simple enough. We each had to drink part of a potion from a crudely carved wooden mug. The potion stank of rotten pines and sickly flesh. It tasted more bitter than all the tears I'd ever cried. The lines we both recited weren't difficult.

And the simple pinprick at the end, that released my powers from my skin, was nothing at all.

I would have my revenge later, as a human. I just had to get the sword to safety.

It would take the rest of the evening for Masato to fully inherit my powers. He looked more energetic, but his smile was still lazy and fat.

He couldn't lift the sword out of the case himself. Fortunately, it wasn't that snake Junichi who handled it, but one of his odious minions.

It took three men to lift the sword out. I don't know why. Maybe he was encased in further spells that they had to strip away.

Masato presented the sword to me with little ceremony. I could tell he was starting to get distracted by the powers he was absorbing. His face had swollen.

I hoped the power would make him pop, like an overripe grape.

I gave Seiji the bow that was due to him—low and long—before I tried to pick him up.

I don't know if it was because Norihiko was still under a spell. Or if the sword, itself, didn't want to be carried away. But it was heavier than the mountain itself.

I instinctively called on my magic to help me lift him.

That empty, black hole in my very core echoed hollowly.

I still managed to rise, without grace, without dignity. I didn't care if Masato laughed at me.

I had Norihiko. I stumbled toward the door of the tent, dragging the sword behind me. Two men escorted me through the camp. I ignored all the ignorant eyes turning my way, wishing beyond hope that a fraction of my power remained, and that I could turn away their attention.

But my dreams were all false.

Once we reached the edge of the camp, the rains that had been promised all day finally came. Not a soft, gentle patter of water, no, a deluge, echoing the sorrow I felt inside, the tears I wouldn't allow myself to cry.

Soaking wet, bedraggled, dragging a sword that I couldn't lift, step by struggling step I made it back to Iwao's estate. My former husband, whom I'd thoughtlessly killed with my selfishness and revenge.

But that didn't matter, now. I had the sword. My sisters would figure out how to remove the curse, free Norihiko's soul.

Then I would follow it, gladly, to Heaven and beyond.

The Breaking
A Sword's Poem
Volume II

The Breaking

A Sword's Poem

Volume II

刀の詩の本二

崩壊

LEAH CUTTER

AUTHOR OF PAPER MAGE

"Cutter knows just <u>what</u> she's doing" —Locus

One

With a Stiff Face

Kayoku

With a stiff face and a stiffer back, Kayoku greeted General Asheihi, Iwao's second in command, in the *seishikina* hall. She'd never been in there before, not officially. The last time she'd been to the Ceremony hall, she'd been sitting behind one of the lattice walls, watching Iwao's inheritance ceremony.

Now, she sat in the center of the room, composed, waiting to hear the news of his death. Though the hall was large enough to hold two dozen courtiers, all of the estate's generals, as well as most of the men of the Kitayama clan, it felt closed in. Folded paper charms hung from the rafters stretching across the tall ceiling, but they'd brought no luck to anyone at the estate.

In fact, so much bad luck had visited them instead. Kayoku had lost her first child so soon after she'd arrived. Though he didn't really count as a person—little Kenta hadn't lived long enough to receive his real name—she still grieved over his death, the only son her husband, Iwao, was likely to ever have had.

Then the warlord Masato had attacked Mount Shirayama, trying to claim it for his foreign religion, this Buddhism.

Lord Taiga's death had been shocking, coming so quickly after he'd declared Iwao as his heir. It hadn't been natural, either. Though Iwao had won the first big battle and some of the following skirmishes with Masato, now he was dead.

Kayoku blamed the fancy second wife Iwao had brought back from the Emperor's court for much of her husband's recent bad luck. This Hikaru had never fit into the rest of the household, had never picked up any of the duties or chores a good second wife should.

Anger flushed through Kayoku's body. How dare Hikaru be missing now? Where had she gone? Why was she not there with the rest of the household to greet General Asheihi and receive the official news that her husband—her second husband—was now dead?

Kayoku made herself take a deep breath. It wouldn't do any good for her to appear hysterical or irrational. She needed a clear, calm head to make the decisions and run the estate until the warlord and victor Masato came to claim his prize.

General Asheihi limped through the door of the hall. His hard face wore new lines, as if he'd aged ten years since the last time Kayoku had seen him. She didn't know the extent of his injuries, but knew they had to be severe for him to show any signs of pain in public. He wore plain, brown, undecorated robes, barely better than a servant's. His hands were clean, but the nails still had dirt under them, as if he'd dug his way through the mud.

Or maybe it was a reminder that he'd soon be returning to the earth. Masato was sure to ask for the heads of all of Iwao's generals as part of his takeover of the estate.

The bow General Asheihi gave Kayoku was still graceful, and he folded himself onto the pillows on the floor with his usual grace.

"Greetings, General Asheihi," Kayoku said, beckoning her servants over. "Please, allow me to serve you some tea."

"Thank you," the general said simply. "I appreciate your effort."

Kayoku waved away all the servants after they were both served. They didn't leave the room, of course. Even widowed, it wouldn't be appropriate for Kayoku to entertain a man alone.

After the pair of them sat in silence, sipping their tea as the late afternoon sun slipped away, the general finally cleared his throat. "I'm afraid I have bad news," he said formally.

"I expected as such," Kayoku confessed. She put her cup to one side and spread her hands out over her knees, waiting. "I'm ready."

"Iwao was killed this morning by Masato," the general told her. "He was brilliant and brave. If his plan had worked…we'd be celebrating right now."

"But he's dead," Kayoku said, the words echoing harshly across the empty space between them. What was she going to do now?

She took another deep breath. *Calm.* "Thank you for coming to tell me in person." That sounded almost normal.

"You are most welcome, my lady," the general said, bowing in place. After another long moment of silence, he asked gently, "What will you do now?"

Kayoku couldn't contain the bitter laugh that erupted. "I was just asking myself that," she confessed. She looked toward the door, where her servants stood guard, not allowing anyone to disturb their mistress in such a difficult time.

However, Kayoku had lived through impossible times before. After the death of her mother. When her stepmother had accused her of bringing bad luck to the household. When Lord Taiga had died. She took another deep breath, her chest expanding and taking in the air more easily. With what she was certain was an enigmatic smile, she turned back to the general.

"I'm going to clean."

It wasn't difficult for Kayoku to get special dispensation from the priests of the Mori temple to clean her husband's rooms. She was still considered the head wife, though she'd been in that position for such a short while, and Iwao was now dead.

The succession wasn't clear. Though Lord Taiga had other sons, the generals couldn't agree on whom to follow: Yutaka, the eldest, or Tomi, the middle boy.

Kayoku didn't really care either way. They were both married. She'd gladly step aside for either of those wives to help run the estate.

In the meantime, they bickered and drew their own battle lines.

Kayoku needed to do something practical. Like take care of Iwao's rooms. Though he'd been the head of the clan, he'd also been her husband. It was only appropriate for her to take care of his property and his room.

Of course, that lazy Hikaru was still nowhere to be found. She wasn't indisposed, no matter what her servants claimed. She'd left the estate somehow, without being seen.

Kayoku couldn't wait to confront her, to accuse her of being an immoral woman and throw her out. Let the armies use her, keep her or kill her at their will.

Or maybe it would be better to let her live and have Masato decide what to do with her when he arrived to take over the estate.

The latter wouldn't give Kayoku as much satisfaction, but perhaps it would be better.

Kayoku roused her own lazy servants and directed them to Iwao's rooms within an hour of learning of his demise. She knew that the other wives would be shocked. Kayoku should keep strictly to herself and be wailing in grief, not stone-faced and doing practical things.

She didn't care if they accused her of being heartless. They didn't understand that if she didn't move, keep moving, she'd drown.

Kayoku paused before she opened the *shoji* door leading to Iwao's quarters. She'd never been there by herself. She'd never presumed she'd be welcome— she'd always waited until she'd received a proper, written invitation from her husband to come to his rooms. Just as he'd always waited to see her until she'd invited him.

They'd been well suited.

Now he was gone.

Kayoku swallowed down her grief, stiffened her back, and slid open the door. The gray of the afternoon seemed to have filtered in though there were no windows looking outside from the inner rooms. Plain walls greeted her, with only a single piece of calligraphy hanging on them, done in Iwao's flowing hand—his family pledge to Mount Shirayama as well as the Emperor.

The black lacquered sword stand in the corner was empty. Kayoku had the sudden memory of the last time she'd been in those rooms, when Seiji had sat in the corner and seemed to watch over them, approving of their liaison.

Iwao's writing desk was tucked into the far corner. Kayoku knew that the family name chop would be with Iwao, in his battle tent, along with his special ink sticks. However, his favorite ink stone was still here. It was made of gray rock from the top of the mountain, only the well for holding water polished, the rest of it still rough stone. Iwao claimed it reminded him that he could always improve.

Bundles of papers lay beside the desk. Kayoku picked them up, glancing at the top one.

It was a love poem.

Fine white skin....

Kayoku couldn't read the rest. As far as she knew, Iwao didn't write poetry. He'd never composed any for her, not even in his awkward teenaged years.

Maybe it was the other wife, Hikaru, that had inspired such feelings in Iwao. Hikaru had truly amazing white skin.

Kayoku shuddered and resolutely rolled the papers back up together. She would go through them. Later. When she had a nice fire going outside in the garden.

Kayoku turned to the half-dozen servants still standing in the doorway, waiting for their mistress, giving her the space and time she needed to face these rooms.

"Come on, you lazy slugs," Kayoku said, forcing herself to smile. "Time we got to cleaning."

Her servants good-naturedly groaned at that, but she knew they didn't really begrudge her.

Without thinking anything of it, Kayoku directed two to start removing the *tatami* mats directly in front of the door.

Strange characters marred the wood. Kayoku caught her breath. They didn't look as sinister as the ones that she'd found in Lord Taiga's rooms. She recognized a few of the *kana* characters, like for peace and quiet. However, some of the harsher characters were Chinese, and others were characters she didn't recognize at all.

Maybe it wasn't harmful. Maybe it was just to bring tranquility to all who entered.

Still, she didn't want to take a chance.

"You. And you," Kayoku said, pointing to her two most trustworthy servants. "Go get Priestess Ayumi from the Mori temple. And I will personally skin you alive if you tell anyone else about this."

She knew that her threats were good—no rumors had ever reached her ears about the characters they'd found painted on the floor of Lord Taiga's rooms. "And be quick about it!" she snapped when the servants didn't immediately hop to their feet.

"Of course, mistress," they said, bowing out of the room and hurrying away.

With a sigh, Kayoku directed the other mats to be removed. The only other place that held characters was directly in front of the *shoji* leading to Iwao's sleeping chamber.

"Stay here," she directed, not allowing anyone else into the sleeping chamber, closing the *shoji* door behind her.

The room seemed dim and closed in, as if the darkness there fought the single lamp Kayoku held. She raised it high. There really wasn't much there, just sleeping mats, a pillow block, and some blankets bunched up at one end. Iwao had kept his clothes in the outer rooms, as well as everything else. He'd merely used this room for sleeping.

Kayoku took a deep breath. The scent of her husband still lingered, salt-tinged and masculine.

However, it was overlaid with a sweet perfume that wasn't hers.

Hikaru.

Gritting her teeth, Kayoku angrily threw the blankets and sleeping mats to the side, baring the floor.

She gasped. Ugly characters marred the wood there, twisted and jagged. They were painted in black, maybe with some kind of tar.

The characters flew across the floor, as if the writer had been consumed with rage while composing them. There were again only a few characters that Kayoku recognized, but they chilled her completely: wishing the bearer a weak heart, draining strength as one drained pus from a wound.

Kayoku started when the *shoji* door slid open. She held back her sharp retort when she saw that it was Priestess Ayumi from the Mori temple. She wore her usual plain dark green robe with her hair tied back in a practical bun. Today, her golden skin seemed pale—maybe she was shocked from all the bad news.

The priestess closed the door behind her and came closer to the bed.

"You have my condolences, my lady," the priestess said, bowing her head.

"Did these lead to my husband's death?" Kayoku asked bluntly. She knew she should be more subtle about it. However, she had to know.

"I don't know, my lady," Priestess Ayumi admitted. "I don't know the full circumstances of his death. If it was more than just bad luck—if his death was caused by a weakening of his will and mind—these aided that."

"Thank you for telling me," Kayoku said sincerely.

She didn't know how she was going to prove that Hikaru had painted these. But she knew it was the other wife who had done it.

Why would she marry Iwao if she hated him so much? Why would she sleep with him, visit his rooms frequently enough that the scent of her lingered, if she was setting him up for death?

Kayoku had many questions for the new wife. And she would answer them, too, when she showed up.

Kayoku didn't understand why the guards were bothering her about the stranger at the gate. It was late, she was tired, and it had been a long, strange day. She'd spent most of the evening grieving for Iwao, privately, in her own rooms, away from the prying eyes of all the others.

Of course, she was the head wife. But really, couldn't they turn a beggar away themselves?

Kayoku steeled herself as she walked from her rooms to the front greeting hall, growing more angry by the minute. Couldn't she get a moment's peace? And Hikaru had yet to be found. Maybe she'd been a spy all along.

The greeting hall had lamps lit all along the inside wall. Kayoku didn't need the light to read the beautiful poems dedicated to the mountain that filled most of the walls, or to see the many watercolor paintings that hung there. Sweet *nioi-bukuro* packets were suspended from all the corners as well, to prevent bad spirits from entering the room.

The stranger remained in shadows. Lamps flickered as the figure drew closer, though the room was still.

Kayoku couldn't help but gasp when she realized the figure before her was a woman. Her long hair hung in rivers down her back, soaked. Her robe had once been very fine, but now was streaked with mud. Her skin was still fine and white, but pale as a ghost's. She wheezed as she breathed.

"Kayoku!" the woman exclaimed. "Please. Help me." The woman started weeping as if her heart would break, had already broken and nothing could stem the flood of tears.

"Do I know you?" Kayoku asked, stepping back. Was this creature really human? Or some kind of ghost from her past, made manifest?

The stranger stepped forward. "I am Hikaru," she said, hiccupping and gulping in air before her tears started again.

Hikaru? Kayoku didn't believe it. The second wife was beautiful beyond compare. The woman before her—while still beautiful—was just pretty in an ordinary way.

Besides, Hikaru would never have let herself be seen in public with eyes reddened by tears. Or a nose that needed wiping.

"It is me," the woman, this Hikaru imposter, declared. "Iwao…Iwao is dead. And I have his sword."

With that, the woman bent over to pick up a long shape at her feet that Kayoku hadn't noticed before. She almost fell over as she struggled to rise with it.

It was Seiji. Kayoku recognized the black lacquered scabbard, as well as the presence of the sword, suddenly apparent in the room. She shivered.

"How did you get this?" Kayoku asked, striding forward.

The woman hissed at her, made a claw of one hand and swiped at Kayoku while holding the sword to her bosom. "He is mine! My mate!"

Clearly, Hikaru suffered from some sort of delusion. Had she actually cared for Iwao? Was that why she wouldn't release his sword?

But she'd been the one to paint those symbols in his room. Kayoku was sure of it.

"You killed him, didn't you?" Kayoku accused Hikaru. "Your spells. Your bad luck."

Kayoku had expected Hikaru to deny it. Or to laugh off her charges, as she laughed off all the chores that Kayoku had expected the second wife to do.

She hadn't expected Hikaru to collapse onto the floor as gracefully as a falling cherry blossom petal, wrapping herself around the sword as she descended.

"It's all my fault," Hikaru whispered, moaning and crying. "All of it. The death of your husband. The corruption of mine. All my fault."

"What did you do?" Kayoku demanded.

Hikaru wouldn't answer though, lost to her own mourning and weeping. She wheezed again as she breathed, then started hacking.

The second wife was sick.

Kayoku did *not* want to take care of her, to have to nurse this despised woman back to health.

However, if she wanted answers, and possibly retribution, she was going to have to take Hikaru back into the household. At least for a little while.

Two

Never Relenting

Seiji

Never relenting, Seiji and the others *pulled* themselves toward the earth.

How dare *she* touch them? Why did she believe they would suffer her to wield them?

Whoever this Hikaru being was, she had many things to learn about Seiji and his brothers, forged together in steel and blood. How they would bite her, slice her skin the first chance they got. How she would never be able to lift them from the earth.

They refused to admire her persistence, dragging them from the hateful camp back to the estate of their rightful owner, the now dead Iwao. They didn't feel the cold of the night, though the pattern of soft plops on their lacquered sheath told of the rain, and her shivering caused them delight.

She had killed Iwao, through her magic and distraction. He could have won the battle against the hated Masato, could have saved the mountain.

Now, she had damned them all.

But Seiji no longer had limbs to move himself—he only had a memory of a dream in which he once stood upright, but even that was suspect. Maybe he only wished he could walk, so he could see the whole of the mountain, the great creation that he'd dedicated all of his souls to protect.

At least he was back at the estate, away from the hateful camp, that odious Masato.

Masato thought he had a right to rule the mountain. The mountain would not be ruled by a single man. And a single religion for such a large mystery? Bah!

This Hikaru, though. She wouldn't let go of Seiji. Wouldn't draw him out so that he might cut her, but wouldn't release him, either. He felt the shock of those around him. It wasn't proper, wasn't right, for a woman to hold onto a sword so.

But she wouldn't let go.

Seiji ignored Hikaru's rambling words as the fever took her. She kept calling out a name, *Norihiko*. It stirred the darker places of his soul, made him restless and angry. He had a memory of tiny pinecones still hanging from a fragrant branch, then it was gone.

Seiji hissed at Hikaru every time she made him remember things that he didn't understand, hissed his displeasure at any who might hear.

Eventually, Hikaru grew silent again, stopped petting him, let him sleep.

But she never let him leave her side.

Three

Karada No Ke

Masato

Karada no ke, tohatsu, kugi, shiga, hada
Niku, motode, hone, kotsuzui, ketsueki,
Kokoro, kanzo, jinzo

The sonorous chant went on and on, listing the thirty-two parts of the body. Masato raised his clear voice with the monk, waiting for the usual feelings of peace to wash over him even as his skin crawled with excitement. The tent that had been set aside for the Buddhist monks was well-lit by candles. The generals who had joined Masato in his early morning meditations, kneeling in neat lines, were obviously feeling worse for wear, their skin gray and their eyes tired.

Every part of Masato's body was on fire, though the chant was supposed to bring calm and awareness of his physical self.

Maybe Masato should have asked for a different chant from the priests. Something to appeal to his intellect, or to reflect on the passage of the seasons. But he'd wanted something to ground him. To distract him from the blood bubbling in his veins.

Or perhaps Masato should have chosen a different way to celebrate his defeat of that young cur, Iwao. Though he'd bargained away the sword Seiji—and it would have brought him a pretty penny from the right buyer—he still felt as though he'd gotten more than it was worth.

Candlelight danced around Masato, not because of any breeze, but because of the waves of power that emanated from him. Junichi had been right. The fox fairies were all stupid. Why else would Hikaru have given her magic to Masato, in exchange for a worthless sword that only the dead Iwao could wield?

Junichi had also been wrong, however.

Masato *would* be able to master the fox fairy powers. They were laughably easy to learn. And he had the discipline to do it, given his long studies.

Masato remembered the hours it had taken to master even the simplest spell that Junichi had tried to teach him, the long nights he'd spent fasting, conserving his energy, learning to focus and concentrate his power, just to light a simple fire.

Now, with a wave of his hand, Masato could set the entire camp ablaze.

And more, too. The magic of the fox fairy carried knowledge. It wasn't esoteric and hidden in books where only the most learned could find. Instead, it was right there. All he had to do was be patient, listen, and learn.

It was almost a shame to wipe them all from the face of the earth. But they didn't deserve such power. They wasted it on trivialities like building stronger forests and wild lands, listening to the bees and speaking to the fish.

Masato didn't know what he'd do when he came fully into his power, when the fox fairy blood fully mingled with his.

Maybe he'd just level the mountain after all.

But no, there was his vision still. The one that had set him on this great quest.

Masato had dreamed of the Buddha stepping from the mainland *Shina* to the main island of Nifon, his foot alighting on Mount Shirayama. In Masato's vision, the Buddha then sank down into the mountain itself, taming the wild land, the blowing up the top of the mountain. When the dust settled, Masato saw a statue of the Buddha, carved out of the highest peak of the mountain. The Buddha's topknot of enlightenment was lit up by every sunrise.

And Masato's name would be written into every stone, the mountain renamed in his honor.

Like Junichi, Masato hadn't been bothered to father an heir. He knew how tricky they could be. Particularly since he hadn't stopped Junichi from killing his own father, then had later saved Junichi from his father's guards.

So Masato didn't trust a human heir.

But to have his legacy live on as a mountain…it would be forever. As long as the mountain stood, people would bow to him in awe.

It was a much better plan to achieve immortality than Junichi's plan for it. Eventually, the magic of the Taoist magician would fail, and Junichi would pass on.

While the mountain would live on, as would Masato's name.

Masato found his mind wandering as he chanted. He tried to bring it back. Tried to focus. But his mind wandered again, thinking about his past. About the Buddha. About his future. About the stupidity of the fox fairies. How he'd soon kill them all.

Again, Masato tried to focus on his chanting, on the body parts. His masters had always labeled him lazy.

Perhaps he was. Perhaps he didn't pursue his studies as diligently as they'd wanted, that is, until he'd found something worth going after.

Another wave of magic carried Masato closer to the incense-laced roof of the tent. He relished the floating feeling, aware that he'd paused in his chant to lick his lips and marvel at the sensation.

No wonder the fox fairies were so sensual. Every part of his body felt more intensely. His toes shot down into the earth as he walked. His knees tasted the air they parted ahead of the rest of his body. Even his back seemed more aware, more sensitive to everything he passed.

Finally, the service ended. Masato stood with his generals, his head subtly above theirs. More than one had bloodshot eyes from their celebrations the night before.

Good. They had need to celebrate.

It also meant that they wouldn't speak out of line, ask him what they were doing that day.

Normally, the winning general would take over the property of the defeated as quickly as possible. Masato wanted to go to the estate, to proclaim it as his, to divest the Mori temple of its false *kami* and install the wheel of Buddha instead.

However. The damned fox fairy powers were too distracting.

Masato needed to be in complete control of himself before he faced Iwao's generals. He didn't want there to be any slip-ups or mistakes in protocol.

Iwao's appointment had been approved by the Emperor himself. Masato had to step very carefully to make sure that his rule was recognized as legitimate.

After giving one last bow to the priest and the prayer wheel set up at the front of the tent, Masato strode out into the clear day. The sun had already chased away the clouds from the night before. What little grass remained in camp from the hundreds treading on it still sparkled.

With long strides, staying in front of his generals so that none would approach him, Masato made his way back to his tent. With a mere wave of his hand, all the candle and lamp flames leapt high. The cloth barriers between the various parts of the tent swayed as if Masato carried his own breeze with him.

Masato went directly to his writing desk. He knew exactly what to say. The words flowed from him, elegant yet precise, explaining that he was solidifying his position and would attend to the estate in a few days. The generals, the property, and all the women would be passed directly to Masato when he had the time to visit.

He told himself that he was being generous, giving the widow of Iwao time to adjust to her new status, giving Iwao's generals time to say their last goodbyes before Masato took their heads.

But in his heart of hearts, Masato knew that he needed the time not just to settle his newly-inherited powers, but to revel in them.

He'd worked long and hard to get to this point.

Now it was time to play.

Masato urged his horse to go faster as it climbed the winding mountain road. Heat rose from the ground, where the sun had baked it, turning the long grass white. Hawks screeched high in the air, seeking prey. A tumbledown cottage sat in the distance, the fields long since overgrown. Masato's outriders rode behind him, carefully keeping their lord in sight.

Masato had only tricked them once, the fox fairy blood singing to him of turning other people's vision. Though Masato still sat on his horse directly in front of his men, they didn't notice him. Their eyes slid off, like oil sliding down a pan.

Now, the fox fairy blood urged Masato to go up, higher, to get above the trees and bask in the afternoon sunlight. Masato had never felt so comfortable out in the open like this. He assumed his guards were nervous about how exposed he was. He knew he would have felt the same two days ago. Though

Masato had won the war against the guardians of the mountain, it wouldn't be the first time that those in the field kept fighting on.

But Masato wasn't afraid. Rather, he felt exhilarated by the thought. Junichi had always warned him to be cautious.

Masato didn't have to be cautious anymore. Not with this much power running through his body. Sweat ran freely from his body as it burned with potential.

Though the sword Seiji hadn't turned out to be what Masato had envisioned, he'd still learned from it. Iwao had been truly remarkable in his swordsmanship, particularly when he'd attacked from horseback.

Masato had gotten the finest *taichi* sword that he could find at the camp and had brought it with him that day. Now, he drew it while riding, slashing from one side to the other, practicing attacking and defending.

The fox fairy blood surged up to meet the challenge. Masato wielded the blade effortlessly. Practice had never been so easy before. He didn't even feel as though he needed to practice. Skill flowed from him, the sword showing him the way to hold it, to move, even though it wasn't alive at all.

A rabbit suddenly darted across the road, causing Masato's horse to shy to the side as he was making a sweeping downward motion with the sword.

The shocking pain of the blade glancing off Masato's thigh brought him up short. It was a clean cut, short, tearing through the soft linen of his brown pants. The wound smarted sharply, and a small line of blood beaded up along the edge.

However, as Masato's men raced up to him, the pain started to fade, dribbling away like the remains of a jellyfish dying in the sun.

Masato couldn't help but laugh heartily. His men would probably think him mad. But he didn't care.

The wound healed itself in short order. All that Masato had to show for it was a small tear in his riding pants. But it didn't matter.

He had the life of an immortal, now.

Later that evening, Masato called on the name of the Amida Buddha, *nembutsu*, to be saved by the inconceivable working of the Amida vow, to realize birth in the Pure Land.

He knelt on the ground, on his usual meditation pillow, in comfortable indoor robes—the softest brown cotton beautifully adorned in golden pinecones. The scent of the *senkoh* burning on the altar before him delicately perfumed the entire tent, reminding Masato of the temples on the mainland.

Outside the tent, sounds of the men celebrating carried on the wind. Masato felt no urge to join them. He did want to go out, though, into the night, to dance with the night breezes, to feel the starlight on his skin, to maybe even release himself against the side of a tree…

Masato came back to himself with a start. That hadn't been the most base impulse he'd experienced since he'd absorbed the fox fairy powers. But the vision of himself, naked in the night, was so strong. He pinched himself through the cloth of his robe to remind himself that he was still, in fact, wearing clothes.

The impulse grew stronger, his manhood rising.

Masato called on the name of the Amida Buddha again. Just saying the name would bring him to the Pure Land. Though he had a raft of priests he maintained, constantly calling on the Amida Buddha in his name, so that he might not go to Hell, he also did the meditation himself, when he could be bothered.

Now, it seemed like a lifeline to a saner place.

Masato had said the words in the chant so often they came without thought, rolling off his tongue, *Namu Amida Butsu.*

Yet the impulse still remained. The desire to go release himself. To go expose himself.

To do *something* other than sit in his tent and meditate.

Masato shook himself. Though his teachers had all considered him lazy and undisciplined, he would show them wrong.

He would stay in the tent, do his meditation, and be one with the Buddha, fox fairy powers be damned.

By the time dawn crept in around the edges of the tent, Masato was ready to admit defeat. Sweat stained his brown robes as if he'd been practicing with his sword all night. The scent of semen mingled with the sweeter incense, from when Masato hadn't been able to control himself any longer. He hadn't destroyed his furniture or slashed at the strips of cloth hanging down, though the fox fairy blood had urged him destroy everything.

Masato had never known such strong urges to be free. Not even when he'd been a young man, under the oppressive thumb of his father.

Perhaps this had been what Junichi had warned about—this wildness that Masato would find challenging to tame.

Masato took another deep, shuddering breath. Nothing could save him from this overwhelming sensuality. No wonder the fox fairies never did much. They were probably too busy fornicating. Masato clenched his hands into fists so he wouldn't take hold of himself again.

He had to tame these powers, somehow. Contain them.

But how? There were no books on the subject, no esoteric knowledge that any of the priests held. How to steal power from other creatures, yes. But not on what to do if the powers from a foreign creature had been transferred to a man.

With a sigh, Masato made himself stand. His knees protested after kneeling for so long, but after only two steps, they felt like themselves again.

Of course, the fox fairy powers wanted Masato to leave the tent. He struggled to keep his destination in mind—his writing desk, there, in the corner.

He swayed like a drunken man, fighting to control his own limbs. But he didn't give up, as he had so many times the night before.

With a decidedly ungraceful *thump*, Masato collapsed back down to the floor behind his writing desk. After only three tries he managed to shave off some ink from his ink stick, wetting it just enough for his brush.

It didn't take long for him to write his request. Junichi, his former master, would extract a high price for his help. Masato hoped he would be able to mitigate at least some of the cost by pointing out that the only reason he'd done it was because the sword Junichi had made hadn't been right.

However, Masato also knew that he'd pay. Because he couldn't keep the full fox fairy powers. They were too strong.

Four

Not The Fires Again

Kayoku

Not the fires again. Kayoku rushed to the sickroom where Hikaru had yet to gain consciousness when she heard the shrieks. The second wife's fever ran high and she lived between the worlds, muttering when she was more calm, screeching in tones that would bend metal when she wasn't.

Now, Hikaru tossed from side to side, as if trying to get away from the fires in her dreams, screaming about burning again and again. Bright lamps burned in every corner, chasing away the shadows and any bad luck. The room itself was plain, with no poetry or paintings, nothing that would have to be burned if the patient died.

The smell of Hikaru's sickness wafted over Kayoku as she entered. She ordered more *shokoh* to be burned to help chase away the smell, as well as to purify the bad air so no one else would get sick. Then Kayoku knelt beside the poor girl, catching at her hand and holding it firmly between her own.

"You must come back here," Kayoku strictly ordered the younger woman. "You must return." How else would Kayoku get the answers she needed?

Hikaru couldn't die and keep all her secrets locked away. The hand she held burned with its own fire, though the skin was still unnaturally smooth.

Hikaru clung to the older woman's hand as if it were a lifeline. Her eyes opened, but they were blank—her spirit still traveled far away.

Words spilled from Hikaru's mouth, words that Kayoku didn't recognize. The words had power. They stirred the hair on Kayoku's arms and walked icy-ghost fingers down her spine.

However, they didn't seem to do much beyond that. Hikaru fell back, more exhausted.

Did she have powers? Kayoku would believe it. The second wife had appeared so glamorous when she'd first arrived at the estate. Even in her illness, she was still beautiful.

She was also ordinary, though, and had the needs of any woman.

Hikaru began to cry, heartbreaking sobs.

"You're here at the estate," Kayoku told her. "You're safe."

"My mate is still cursed," Hikaru said, eerily clear. "Norihiko! Norihiko! How could you be taken away from me? How did he change you into a sword? Through the flames. The flames!"

Hikaru dragged the sword Seiji closer to her as she wept. It seemed to be the only thing that gave her solace, though Kayoku could tell its weight was unnaturally huge, and it dragged itself toward the ground every time Hikaru touched it.

Did Hikaru believe that her mate had been turned into the sword?

The girl was clearly insane.

However, she also refused to let go of the sword's scabbard, even in the worst of her imaginings.

It was just one more piece of the puzzle that Kayoku must learn about, once Hikaru recovered.

Masato's casual declaration that he'd stop by the estate in a few days to collect his property didn't surprise Kayoku. Nor was she surprised to find herself listed among the rest of the goods, such as horses and servants. She was a prize of war.

What surprised Kayoku was her anger at being treated as such. Good luck or no, she certainly had more value than Iwao's old robes or the pots and kettles in the kitchen.

Kayoku carefully kept her anger off her face as well as out of her tone when she met with the generals that morning in the Hall of Ceremony. Her servants were too well trained to start rumors and gossip about their mistress that way. Still, she didn't want to start any speculation.

Though half a dozen generals were already gathered in the hall, it seemed empty. Most of the poems about the estate had been taken down and carefully hidden away. The brazier at the front of the hallway that generally scented the air with pine and cloves was also missing. Kayoku was surprised that the bronze flower vases remained: then again, they had a few days yet.

She didn't know if hiding their treasures would do any good, or if they'd all see the flame.

Two of the generals still wore the plain muslin mourning robes over their regular robes. She'd thought they would already be finished mourning Iwao.

Or perhaps they were still mourning the estate, the mountain, and the Mori temple.

Servants herded the generals to gather on the far side of the hall. Then they came forward, carrying the screen of state. It was a large wooden frame with a piece of painted silk stretched across it. A beautiful sketch of Mount Shirayama covered the front of it.

If the lights were just right, Kayoku could see through the screen, but those on the other side couldn't see her. She walked in after the servants had placed the screen and took her place behind it.

Though none of the other wives would have faulted Kayoku for foregoing the screen of state—her husband was dead, and the estate was in shambles— she still liked the formality it gave her. The mask she could hide behind, that false hope that things could get better.

As one, the generals turned and bowed to Kayoku. It put a lump in her throat. They weren't necessarily paying her that respect, she knew better than that. But that they would still honor her husband so meant a lot to her.

"Thank you," Kayoku told the assembled group. "What news do you bring?"

General Asheihi looked up and around, seeking the silent permission of the others before he spoke. As one of the oldest generals, it was within his right to demand to be heard. But the old general ruled by agreement, not force.

Though Kayoku's view of General Asheihi was fuzzy through the screen of state, she still thought too many hard lines marred his face, too much grief plainly visible in his eyes. He wore dark gray-blue robes, the color of an angry sea. His voice rang out firm and true across the room.

"We have released the men, telling the farmers to go back to their families. There were no rewards, of course, other than granting the men their lives. We hope, for most of them, life will go on as always," the general said.

Kayoku nodded. Though it hurt, it was the truth. The farmer didn't care who the lord in the manor was. His gods would always be the wind and the rain.

"We have also started a complete inventory to hand over to Masato when he arrives," the general continued. "It merely lists servants and other property. There will be a second list for the people who belong to the estate."

Kayoku bit her lip to prevent herself from asking which list she was on. She was already well aware of her status.

"I will make certain that the lists are accurate," Kayoku stated. Though she hadn't run the estate for long, she still knew more about the inner workings of it than any of these men.

"Thank you," General Asheihi said. "The second list. It won't be completed until Masato is on his way here."

"What do you mean?" Kayoku asked, puzzled. Certainly people weren't thinking they could run away, did they? There really was nowhere to go. The estate was her home.

"I'll be blunt," General Asheihi said.

Some of the other generals hissed at that.

Whatever could he be willing to say that they'd disapprove of? Kayoku was intrigued.

"Do not be surprised, lady, if some of the people assembled here, and elsewhere in the estate, decide that it is better to go to the lands of the eternal cherry blossoms rather than to be employed by Masato."

Kayoku felt her own breath catch. Suicide?

Yet, it made sense. Better an honorable death than a dishonorable life.

"I understand," Kayoku said. "And I respect and grant each of you your own wishes and choice."

General Asheihi had little else to report after that. Some of the men had needed disciplining after winning, still trying to loot a local village. The priests of the Mori temple were holding services day and night, without pause or break. And the Emperor had been informed, of course, though no one was expecting any help from him.

Walking through the shaded corridors back to her own rooms, Kayoku considered what General Asheihi had said.

It didn't matter if she was considered property or not. She didn't have to behave as if she was.

Rather than live a life like cattle, she, too, had a choice.

And before Masato came to the estate, she was going to walk in the lands of the eternal cherry blossoms as well.

Kayoku hurried through the corridors to Hikaru's room. Priestess Ayumi had fetched Kayoku, despite the late hour, insisting that she come. The priestess had looked as perfect as ever, in sturdy brown robes and solid bun, her skin as fresh as if she'd just woken.

Was the girl dying? Kayoku felt strangely at peace with that. Kayoku felt as though she already walked with one foot in the other lands. Perhaps her mother waited there for her. Everything seemed wrapped in soft cotton, all the edges tucked away.

The smell of sickness had finally been chased away from the room. Lamps burned steadily in all the corners, brighter than Kayoku would have thought polite, but she assumed that either the priestess or Hikaru had asked for the light.

The girl still looked sick, paler than was fashionable. Her black hair hung in greasy strings, Red lingered under her eyes and around her nose, probably from all her weeping.

Despite all that, she was still beautiful.

Hikaru's eyes were still glazed, though, wet as an animal's. Yet she still sat up and turned her head unerringly toward Kayoku when she came in.

"I'm sorry," Hikaru said. "I'm sorry, I'm sorry, I'm so very, very sorry." The words sounded rote, as if they'd been rehearsed, with no emotion or true regret behind them.

"What are you sorry about?" Kayoku said, kneeling down beside the sleeping mats.

"I'm sorry, I'm sorry, I'm sorry," Hikaru continued to repeat, still addressing the door where Kayoku had been. "I didn't mean to do it. I know Iwao was a good man. Innocent of the crimes I'd thought he'd committed. I'm so sorry."

"What do you mean?" Kayoku asked, her back stiffening. "What crimes?" What did Iwao's second wife think he had done?

Hikaru reached out and touched the sword Seiji. "I thought Iwao had killed my mate. Stolen his soul to form this sword."

Kayoku couldn't help her bitter laugh. "Iwao wasn't imaginative enough to do something such as that."

"I know. I know. I'm sorry. I'm sorry. Please, please, give me my powers back," Hikaru said, her voice trailing into a whisper. "Let me be beautiful again. Healthy. Strong. Please, I *need* my powers back. My magic…."

"Powers? Magic?" Kayoku said. "What powers?"

Kayoku didn't believe in magic. There was only good and bad luck. That's what her mother had told her, what she'd believed all her life.

But Masato's men, the howling on the wind, how the oil for the temple had spoiled, those awful characters under Lord Taiga's sleeping *tatamis*, meant to capture a soul…

Was there magic? Had Kayoku been wrong?

It wasn't difficult for her to believe that Hikaru was a magical being. She'd been unnaturally beautiful. And all the times Kayoku had asked Hikaru to help around the estate, pick up some of the duties a second wife should, and how she'd always left without saying a word.

"What magic?" Kayoku asked again.

But Hikaru just slipped back into repeating over and over again, "I'm sorry. I'm sorry. I'm sorry."

Kayoku stroked Hikaru's too-hot hand until the younger wife fell asleep. It seemed as though her confession had exhausted her more than her continual shrieking.

However, when Kayoku bathed Hikaru's face one last time in lavender water, the younger wife's forehead finally felt cool, as if the fever had finally left her.

"What are you going to do about her?" Priestess Ayumi asked as Kayoku left the sleeping rooms and withdrew into the general room.

"Do?" Kayoku asked. The girl was finally getting better, but that didn't mean Kayoku could set her to work already.

"She admitted to killing Iwao," Priestess Ayumi said. "She should be punished."

Kayoku opened her mouth then shut it again. The priestess was right. Hikaru should be punished, flogged and beaten, then possibly beheaded.

However, Kayoku had always prided herself on being practical. Hikaru wasn't the only one to blame. Iwao had let himself fall under Hikaru's spell. He'd been blinded by her beauty, by the sword Seiji, by his own invulnerability. No matter what powers Hikaru may have had, or had used on her poor departed husband, Kayoku knew he'd been complicit as well.

"Masato will be here soon enough," Kayoku said after another moment. "She'll be on his list, part of his property. I'm not sure there's anything for me to do before that. What do you think?"

The priestess gave a grim smile. "I think you are correct, my lady. There isn't anything else you need to do besides make sure that she's on the list."

They both knew what list she meant, the one listing all the *property* that was now Masato's.

Maybe Kayoku would make sure that Hikaru's name was listed beneath the kitchen pots and pans, just above the servants.

"Thank you for taking such good care of her," Kayoku said sincerely. She knew the girl wouldn't have recovered without the careful oversight of the priestess, as well as her prayers.

"She said many strange things in her fever," the priestess confided in Kayoku. "That her powers were taken by Masato. That the sword contains the soul of her husband. That Iwao was innocent."

"Just the ramblings of a sick mind," Kayoku assured the priestess.

Was Hikaru telling the truth? Was her mind too clouded for lies?

Kayoku would have to meditate and pray, because part of her already believed Hikaru. She'd been so impossibly beautiful, able to work her will on everyone, including Kayoku.

The priestess said goodnight, and Kayoku went back to her own quarters.

How had Masato taken Hikaru's powers? Kayoku shuddered thinking about what evil spell the man had cast.

Did the sword Seiji contain a soul? Why would Lord Taiga bring back such an artifact, then give it to his son? Had only Iwao been able to wield the sword, as some of his men had sworn? That none of the other generals could even lift it? Was it magical as well?

Hikaru couldn't lift Seiji. Kayoku had blamed the second wife's weakened state, but maybe the sword had rejected her as well.

There were too many questions still, even with Hikaru's confession. Kayoku firmly turned her mind away from everything tangled up on this earth, though.

Kayoku would pass from this world soon enough. There would be more than enough mysteries for her to explore later, in the land of the eternal cherry blossoms.

Five

How Dim The Sun

Hikaru

How dim the sun looked when I first opened my eyes. I couldn't understand it. No clouds marred its brilliance. The sky looked blue and perfect through the tiny window above where I lay. Birds sang in the distant trees. The scent of sweet candles overwhelmed any of the other scents that I might have used to place myself, though I knew where I was: the estate, in an outer sickroom.

Still—the sun had paled, as if it were now covered in mist that only I could see.

I struggled to sit up on my sleeping mat. The only time I'd felt this weak was after I'd been shot by Junichi's evil arrows. Surely I wasn't injured as well?

No single place on my body hurt, however. Instead, my entire body ached in a way I'd never experienced before.

I took a deep breath to warm my blood, heal myself…and found only a cavernous void where my magic had once lived.

I wept, then, my eyes well used to the tears. But I didn't cry for Norihiko, or my past mistakes. No, that morning, I wept for myself and my foolishness.

Finally, a priestess came in the room to see to me. I automatically tried to charm her, to hide my tears and be other than who and what I was: a sick human woman with a thrice-broken heart.

I failed, of course. There was no magic left in me. I could tell by the pitying smile she gave me, her solicitous tones as she asked how I was that morning.

"Better," I lied. "I'd like some tea, now."

At her puzzled look, I realized how my tone must have sounded to her. I was used to my magic sweetening and softening anything I might say, making my requests always sound reasonable, causing people to be eager to do as I asked.

"Please," I added. My heart sank. I was going to have to relearn how to talk with humans now, how to move through the world.

How to be human, myself.

There wasn't anyone I could ask about it. No one I could learn from. I was going to have to do it all myself.

I couldn't contain my heavy sigh. How foolish I'd been to let go of my fairy powers so easily! I'd had no choice, though.

I reached out and touched Seiji's scabbard. Though the sword might hate me for killing its wielder, at least I'd saved it from a worse fate. I shivered again, remembering Masato's threat of drowning the sword.

Someday, soon, I would break the curse. Or rather, my sisters would, since I had no magic. They'd free Norihiko's soul so he could pass beyond this vale of tears, go to Heaven as had always been his destiny.

I'd die of a broken heart at that time, I knew. But maybe somewhere beyond the world we'd unite again, in the world of eternal cherry blossoms.

I wiped away the tears that came back to my eyes, determined to stride forward instead of always looking back with regret. When the *shoji* opened, I put on my best smile and turned toward the door.

I kept my smile in place though I was shocked to see Kayoku, the head wife, kneeling there with my tea.

"Good morning," I told her. I even bowed my head toward her. Not a proper bow, but at least I tried to show some level of respect.

"Good morning," Kayoku replied.

She seemed startled to see me this way. "How are you this morning?"

"Well," I told her, though I didn't know if I was or not. Who could tell, in such a complicated body? It didn't respond the way I thought it would at all.

"That's good," Kayoku said, coming into the room. She set the tea service down and looked at me critically.

The smell of the tea made my mouth water. I longed to clear it, wash out the cobwebs in it. Yet Kayoku made no move to serve me. She continued to just stare at me. Was I supposed to serve her? I'd never paid attention to such niceties before. And was her look rude? I wished I could shun it, divert her eyes, make them slide off me so she couldn't actually see me, see how weak I'd become.

"You do look better," Kayoku finally said. "You're not as pale as you were. And your face has a healthy flush to it, not fevered."

"Thank you," I told her, wondering. How sick had I been? I looked at the tea with longing.

Kayoku gave me an indulgent smile and reached for the pot, pouring out two cups, and handing me one.

I tried to wait. I truly did. It was only polite to let the host take the first sip. At least that much I'd learned. But my mouth was so dry! My body felt parched. I took a polite sip, then gulped the rest down quickly, holding my cup out for more.

"You may want to slow down," Kayoku said filling my cup again. "You've been sick for quite a few days. Your stomach isn't going to be able to handle much, yet."

"What do you mean?" I asked, stopping myself before I gulped down the second cup. "Days?" Hadn't I just arrived the night before? Slogging through the rain, determinedly dragging Seiji behind me?

"You've been ill for three days and four nights," Kayoku informed me. "Fevered and walking between worlds."

Three days? How could I have lost three whole days? "I've never been sick like that before," I said, horrified. What must they think of me, being so ill? Were humans regularly ill like that? I had no idea.

I took a demure sip of my tea, though I longed to drink it down as quickly as I'd finished the first cup. Three days. I had nothing better to do than to look forward to the rest of my life being counted in illnesses and days like this morning, when I was weak and still recovering.

I reached out and touched Seiji's scabbard, telling myself that my sacrifice was justified, or would be, once I broke the curse and set my mate's soul free. Then I could free myself as well, leave this land of tears and go to the land of eternal cherry blossoms.

"You said…you said many things while you were sick," Kayoku told me cautiously.

I nodded. That didn't surprise me. My mother, in her illnesses, frequently ranted about what she'd seen, the injustices done to her.

"You claimed that Seiji contained the soul of your mate," Kayoku said, staring directly at me.

What could I say? I wasn't going to deny it. The humans would declare me mad, but that was all right with me—maybe I was a little mad.

"It does. The soul of my mate Norihiko was stolen and reforged into the sword Seiji, by the evil Taoist sorcerer Junichi," I said, bracing myself for her derision or laughter.

Instead, Kayoku merely nodded. "And you gave up your powers to free him?" she asked.

I couldn't help but smile. Even in my rantings I'd deflected the truth. "I gave up my powers to obtain him," I told her honestly. Then my heart fell. Had I admitted the truth of it? Had I told her about her husband?

"And Iwao?" Kayoku asked coldly.

My sorrow tripled. "I killed him," I admitted. "I'm sorry. I'm so sorry." I had the weirdest sense that I'd already said that to her once before. Maybe I had, when I'd been sick. I didn't remember, though.

"I see," Kayoku said coldly. She placed her teacup down on the tray and stared at it.

Was she mastering her own sorrow? Had she cared for her husband? I watched her carefully, both trying to learn from her as well as preparing myself for the worst.

"Masato has already sent his letter of intent," Kayoku said after a few long moments. "He expects proper lists and inventory of the estate, all his *property*."

I didn't understand her bitterness at that. Wasn't that how it was always done with humans, when they lost a battle?

"You will help me prepare for our new lord," Kayoku told me. "By this afternoon, I expect you to be in the kitchen, working with the servants, listing things there. You can read and write, can't you?"

From her derisive tone, I think she expected me to admit to illiteracy. "I can," I told her, pride filling my voice. "I have quite a neat hand. I can also write in Chinese as well as *kanji*." *Kana* was used primarily by the women of the court, while men and scholars wrote in *kanji*.

"I thought as much," she said, sounding disgusted. "Very well. I shall expect you there mid-morning, at the hour of the snake."

I wanted to protest. That was so early! And I was still so weak, my body not under my command.

On the other hand, my body would never be the same, not completely under my control, not as it once had been.

"I'll be there," I told her meekly. "Please, send in my servants so that I may be ready."

I didn't know where Yukiko was, why she wasn't there, what she'd say to me in my fully human state. Or had she abandoned me?

"If I can find them," Kayoku said. "They seem to be remarkably well trained at disappearing when there's work to be done."

"Like all servants," I said automatically.

That finally brought a smile to Kayoku. "Like their mistress once was," she said.

Was she teasing me?

With a final nod of her head, Kayoku gathered up the tea service and left me to my questions, my doubts, and my hard lessons in being human.

I collapsed with a huge sigh back onto my sleeping mats. Never had I worked so hard before! It had been such tedious work as well. List of pans and cookers, of bowls and serving trays, of plates and dishes. Then recounting and double checking. My fingers ached from all the writing, my back hurt from being stooped over the desk, my eyes smarted from the cooking fires.

Kayoku was an exacting mistress. But she'd earned my respect as well. Despite how she hated that she must turn everything over to her enemy, the victorious warlord Masato, she still was determined to do everything correctly, to hand him a well-ordered household.

Most wives would have been tearing their hair out, gnashing their teeth, and unwilling to do a thorough job.

Was this what it meant to be honorably human? To do your best, despite all your weaknesses and limitations?

I fell into dreamless sleep pondering such philosophy, determined the next day to do better.

Though I felt stronger the next day, I also hurt more, muscles I didn't know I had aching. I didn't lose my determination, however. I was going to do better than Kayoku expected of me, since she obviously expected the worst.

And what could I say? I was just now realizing that my sister Etsu had been right all along. Humans deserved my respect, not my derision or pity.

I shuddered to discover, though, what my sisters would think of me. Yukiko had been bad enough. Though she responded to all my requests (couched, now, *as* requests, and not as the orders I'd been so used to giving) she still was deeply uncomfortable with my changed status.

I was going to have to find a new personal maid, something I was dreading.

While I was finishing the long afternoon's work in the kitchen, I heard a melodious yipping. It distracted me, making me look up from my work and miss whatever Kayoku had said next.

Some part of me was reaching for that sound. I had understood what it meant, once. It wasn't just noise.

"Those damned foxes," the head cook muttered. "Go and check the roosters and hens," he directed one of the servants. "Make sure they're all gathered in the yard. Or we'll lose more tonight."

When I looked back at the room, Kayoku was watching me curiously. I tried to keep my face blank, and not show her my joy.

While I might not recognize the words of the foxes, I knew their meaning: My sisters had returned. Hopefully, they'd bring me good news, as well as a spell to free Norihiko from his cruel, steel form.

I didn't know how to get out of the estate on my own. There were guards everywhere, in every hallway. I couldn't turn their eyes from me. I also couldn't disguise myself as a guard or a servant—the estate was too small. Everyone knew everyone else. A stranger would be regarded as a spy.

Though they'd lost the war with Masato, the estate was still battle ready.

I paced my rooms, feeling as closed in as I had at the Emperor's court. Though I was now human, I still didn't understand how these women lived their entire lives indoors.

At least my rooms had an outer window that overlooked the garden. I'd gotten them with my powers, as generally women only had inner rooms. But I'd needed the ability to at least look outside, catch a glimpse of nature.

I found that need hadn't diminished with my powers gone.

I'd directed Yukiko to lower all the lamp lights. I'd never learned how to do that myself. I'd always just dimmed lights with my powers. I also got Yukiko and the others to wait outside my sitting rooms. I didn't want anyone to witness my meeting with my sisters.

I didn't want them to see my family shaming me.

Yukiko seemed to understand. She gave me a very sorrowful look as she bade me goodnight.

It did, but didn't, surprise me that my sisters didn't join me in my rooms. I was no longer like them. Why should they go to the bother of coming to see me?

Still, it hurt my soul, cutting as deeply as Norihiko's death had.

Instead, the pair of them sat outside the window to my rooms. At first they sang in fox form, soft yips and howls.

My heart ached, and I found my mouth opening and closing, as if I was about to join them in singing, though I no longer knew the words.

I sank down below my window and leaned out as far as I dared, listening with all my heart, catching at the sounds of my home.

Finally, the words changed to something human, that I could understand. They sang in such sweet harmony I found myself weeping at the beauty.

Time slips away
Like a petal
Floating down a mountain spring
Power dies
To be reborn
Fall leaves give way to spring seeds
Families sundered
Lives shaped
To follow cruel paths
Never returning
Never turning back
Never the same

Why did they sing of such things? Was I that doomed? Was Norihiko doomed? I couldn't help but cry out, "Tell me, sisters, what tidings are these?"

Etsu replied. "You've lost your way. The strongest of us has become untrue."

That made me sit up straighter. I was never the strongest of my sisters, nor the best in anything. "There was a greater prize at hand," I told them, though I now doubted the wisdom of my choice. But there hadn't been anything else I could have done. Masato would have drowned Norihiko. He would have been lost forever.

I would always make that choice. My powers for Norihiko.

Wouldn't I?

"You've lost the prize, now," Cho said.

I couldn't help but reach out to grasp Seiji sitting beside me. "I have the sword," I told them.

"You no longer have the power to change him back," Etsu said, scolding me.

"But you're the one with the strongest magic!" I said. It had always been true. The man who had fathered Etsu had been a sorcerer.

"You're the one with the strongest love," Cho said, gently correcting me. "Only Norihiko's mate can bring him back."

"Wait, what?" I asked, startled. "Bring him back?"

The long suffering sigh Etsu gave would have done our mother proud. "Crafting a spell to merely break the curse and free Norihiko's soul was never my final goal. I knew we'd lose you, too, if I merely did that. Instead, I've discovered how to bring him back, to melt the steel back into soft flesh."

"You never told me," I accused her. Would I have waited if I'd known that? Known that it wouldn't just be me facing the rest of my lonely days?

"I couldn't tell you. I didn't know if I'd succeed," Etsu admitted. "But I have. I found the spell."

"Then you must do it!" I exclaimed. "Now! I have the sword here, ready."

"Sister, you don't understand," Cho said sorrowfully. "We cannot. Only Norihiko's mate can bring him back. Only she has the power and will to make him to return."

"So you can't break the curse?" I asked, slumping down. How could I have been so stupid? Now I'd ruined everything, Norihiko's chance of freedom, my own life.

"Why would I merely do that?" Etsu asked, rightly puzzled. "Craft just a partial spell, when I could bring him back to you?"

"But I have no powers!" I said, the tears coming again. "I've thrown away everything!" My impulsive decision was proving to be as thoughtless as my mother had always accused me of being.

"Tomorrow night, you must come to us," Etsu whispered urgently. "You must find us. We will work to get your powers back."

"Really?" I asked, astounded. Why hadn't I thought of that? "You can do that?"

"Powers can always be transferred," Cho said simply.

"Masato will never give them up willingly," I told them.

"You'll have to steal them, then, sister," Etsu said.

"But how?" I asked. I knew I wouldn't be able to do it from afar. I would have to get close to Masato again. I shuddered at the thought.

"That will be up to you, sister," Cho said. "But we'll help, anyway we can."

"Tomorrow," Etsu called again.

"Tomorrow," I promised them, though I had no idea how I was going to fulfill my word. How could I get out of the estate? Then sneak back in? And how was I going to get to Masato?

My future was more uncertain than it ever had been. But I was determined to get Norihiko back. To bring him fully back to the flesh. To have a chance of spending our lives together again.

I had come so far on my journey. I was determined to keep moving along, no matter how many tears lined the way.

Six

Hiding His Smile

Junichi

Hiding his smile, Junichi gave Masato a short bow. He wasn't surprised that Masato hadn't moved his camp yet, particularly not given the message he'd received, begging his help with Masato's newly acquired fox fairy powers. All the cloth hanging down to separate the rooms of the large structure had been removed, so it was now one single, large room. The smell of incense filled the tent and made the air hazy.

What was Masato hiding? How were the fox fairy powers affecting him?

Junichi had suspected that his former apprentice wouldn't be able to handle them. He had warned him about them, that the *kitsune* were tricky and wild. But Masato hadn't listened, of course.

Then again, Junichi hadn't been too stern in his admonitions. Maybe Masato would surprise him. Maybe he'd developed enough discipline in his studies of Buddhism.

Masato knelt on pillows before his altar, looking wise and composed. His robes were the finest quality—a beautiful auburn color, with a design of dark brown pinecones—and his hair was neatly slicked back. As always, his eyelids drooped slightly over his expressive black eyes, giving him a perpetually sleepy stare.

But Masato couldn't hide from his old master the slight tremor in his hands, clenched tightly in his lap, the way his head turned this way and that instead of staying focused on what was in front of him.

After the tea was served and enjoyed—a lovely smoked brew that Junichi would have to ask about later—Junichi finally asked, "How may I be of service to you?"

Again, that tremor of his hand as Masato put down his teacup. "I need your help taming the fox fairy powers," he said through gritted teeth.

Keeping his face completely impassive, Junichi crowed inside. This would finally put Masato fully under his thumb again. "Of course," Junichi said smoothly. "I'd be happy to remove them."

Junichi waited. Would Masato give in to the temptation to just be rid of the powers? That would be the simplest course for him. When Masato had been Junichi's apprentice, that would have been the path he'd have taken, leapt at.

Had Masato grown? Or would he take the easiest way out of his predicament?

"I don't want them removed," Masato said, though his voice quavered, like an old man's. Obviously, he'd been fighting with himself over this very subject. "I merely want them contained. Lessened."

So his pupil had grown. Junichi couldn't help but smile. "That will be more difficult," he warned. He'd tried to anticipate what Masato would actually request and had come with more than one spell prepared, as well as more than one artifact.

Merely releasing the powers from Masato would be the easiest, bleeding them out of the man and letting them dissipate into the ether. The area where they performed the spell would retain some of the magic and become a place of great power. Masato could have dedicated such a place to his Buddha, created a significant temple.

But while Junichi had prepared for that possibility, he doubted that Masato was that selfless.

Transferring the powers from Masato and recapturing them in an artifact would not have been as easy as merely releasing them, but Junichi had prepared an appropriate vessel: a bronze statue of a sleeping fox, curled up, nose buried in its tail.

Merely weakening the powers, but leaving a shadow of them with Masato, was the most difficult of spells, but Junichi had prepared for that as well, creating a box similar to the one he'd held the fox fairy spirit in. This one, though, was decorated with *sanzashi* thorns and berries, and lined with smoky ashes. The berries from the *sanzashi* could help a man with a weak heart—or kill him, if the potion was strong enough.

"It will also cost you," Junichi warned. The supplies to do all the spells had been expensive, and they'd taken time to craft. This venture had cost him so much already.

"Of course," Masato replied dryly.

Junichi couldn't help but smile. It was good Masato valued Junichi's work.

"How much gold—" Masato started.

"Not gold," Junichi said, interrupting him. He knew it wasn't polite. But he wanted to shock Masato as well, make him pay attention despite his horribly distracted state.

"Really?" Masato asked, one eyebrow raised. For a moment, he sat perfectly still.

Junichi suddenly realized just how affected Masato was by the comparison. His former pupil had been fidgeting—subtly, but constantly—the entire time they'd been sitting there.

"I want your bones," Junichi announced boldly. He would have asked for Masato's life force, but depending on how Masato died, and when, Junichi may be able to claim that already given the contract they'd originally signed as master and pupil.

"That's all?" Masato gave a slight chuckle. "I will happily sign those away to you. I'd assumed you'd take them anyway, regardless."

Junichi nodded and kept a pleasant smile on his face while he cursed silently. He should have asked for more.

"And the lives—" Junichi started.

"I will not provide you with more lives," Masato said firmly. "I need my men to fight."

"Then it will have to be more gold," Junichi replied swiftly. He wasn't going to delay all of his payment until later.

"Gold I have," Masato said. "And will have even more, once I take the estate. Let's draw up the contract."

Junichi sipped his tea as Masato's scribes wrote up the contract, still smarting from the deal they'd made. Masato had become a better negotiator. Junichi should have driven a harder bargain.

But that was all right. He could just shave off a smaller portion of the fox fairy powers than he'd originally planned, so that the next time Masato asked for help taming them, Junichi could renegotiate everything.

Junichi strode confidently into the graveyard. The tantalizing scent of fresh limestone tickled his nose—maybe he'd have to come back and steal some bones, later. Crows roosted in the nearby trees and cawed cautiously at their approach, like a friendly welcome home. The night was clear, but the moon was still only a quarter full, silvering the ground and setting the dew-covered grass to sparkle.

Masato had stopped just after they'd entered, then determinedly walked forward again. He'd probably forgotten how much work he'd done in such places when he'd been an apprentice.

Or maybe he was remembering the nights and the corpses, and the memories weren't as fond as Junichi's.

No matter. This was Junichi's playground, where he spent his most magical time. Others might find the graveyard eerie, the smells distasteful, the sounds of bones creaking unsettling, but they were all part of the music of the night to him.

Most nobles were cremated when they died, their bones set aflame with fragrant pine and incense. The poor, however, couldn't afford the fuel—it took a very hot fire to burn a man. They sometimes left the bodies of their relatives on sacred ground, hoping that the priests there would take care of the matter. Particularly if the family was very poor and couldn't even afford the cost of the prayers.

So the priests buried the dead, sometimes deeply in the ground, sometimes just in shallow graves. Frequently, more than one body was buried together.

Since there had been so many deaths on the battlefield, the priests had been busy with those funerals. The local farmers had received very little in the way of care.

Something Junichi had been counting on.

Fortunately, they didn't need any of the bodies that night. Junichi had been tempted to make Masato dig one up, just for old time's sake, but decided at the end that it was unnecessary.

Maybe next time.

The spot they chose was a shallow grave. Junichi could feel the bodies under the ground, four of them, buried one on top of the other. A large *sanzashi* thorn bush grew nearby, its thorns matching the ones on the box Junichi had prepared. Though its flowers had already dropped, it wouldn't berry until much later that fall.

Masato knelt beside the grave, sinking into the soft earth with a grace that belied his size. He hadn't always moved so well—was that an effect of the fox fairy powers? Junichi wasn't sure.

Junichi prepared the space, sticking joss sticks of finely made jasmine incense in the center, a silver basin of pure water on the left, and the box on the right. When he opened the box, the ashes swirled slightly on their own, as if tickled by hidden winds.

Then Junichi started his prayer.

> *Izanami, goddess of the night,*
> *Aid me in my quest*
> *Powers we seek*
> *To carve apart*
> *And hide in the darkness*

The poem went on for several more stanzas. Though Junichi had crafted the song specifically for this spell, Masato still sang along when he could, compelled by the power swirling around the pair of them.

Junichi raised his arms as he sang, circling Masato and the area they'd prepared. He'd missed this, he realized, missed creating something magical with someone else.

It was why he'd bothered with an apprentice in the first place.

Maybe he should try again, but he was too afraid they'd turn out to be exactly like Masato, and would leave before their training was finished.

As the crescendo approached, Masato extended his left arm over the basin of pure water. With a quick flick of a knife, Junichi cut the skin of Masato's wrist so the blood dripped down, splashing into the water, sullying its purity.

Then Masato extended his left arm over the box. Junichi, on his next circle around, plucked a thorn from the *sanzashi* bush, then rammed it into Masato's wrist with his thumb.

A tiny trickle of blood slid from the wound along Masato's skin and dripped into the box.

At the same time, a wisp of yellow smoke slid out around the thorn. The ashes from the box swirled up and captured the smoke before it could escape, like ivy climbing a trellis, several small nodules sinking into the smoke as if it was a solid thing.

The ashes tugged downward, drawing the smoke with it, into the box, wrapping firmly around it.

Junichi continued his song for three more stanzas. Before he'd signed the contract, he'd planned on drawing out eight stanzas of power.

But now—three would do. Masato would feel as though a great pressure in his chest had been released. And it had been.

Junichi also gave it only two or three days before it would build back up to intolerable levels and Masato would beg him to carve out more of the fox fairy powers.

When Junichi finished his song, the smoke stopped seeping from Masato's wrist and the ashes fell back in the box. Quickly, Masato reached down and slammed the lid shut. He kept one hand there, a finger idly tracing the *sanzashi* thorn bush design while he brought his other wrist to his mouth, licking at the wound.

Silence filled the graveyard. Junichi took a deep breath of the stillness. He was tired. The spell had been work. But he also felt very satisfied. The spell was complete and well realized.

"Thank you," Masato said after a few more moments. He stirred briefly, then settled down again. His chest expanded and his shoulders settled down.

He felt better. It was obvious to Junichi.

But it wouldn't last.

Junichi also felt great satisfaction at that.

Masato held the box close to him as they walked back into the camp. Junichi let him carry it, as well as all the other supplies. It was still full night. The moon had set and only a few fires burned, the men settled in for the night. None of the guards seemed surprised at Masato being up and around that late at night by himself.

As they approached Masato's tent, he turned to his old master with his usual smile, lazy and tired. "Thank you again. I think I'll finally be able to sleep tonight."

"You're welcome," Junichi said with a slight bow of his head.

"Would you like me to prepare a tent for you?" Masato inquired. "I know you must be tired after performing such a great, complicated spell."

Junichi shot a look at Masato. That wasn't another dig at Junichi for being old, was it? Masato's accusations that Junichi was old and out of touch still stung, for all that they'd been uttered more than a decade ago.

But Masato seemed merely solicitous, a host asking after the health of his guest.

"The night is still full of spirits and life," Junichi replied sincerely. The cool winds tickled the short hairs on the back of his neck, stirred his blood. He still felt satisfied with the work he'd done that night. "I will make my way back to my own compound."

"I would like to send some of my men with you," Masato insisted. "Just to make certain that you arrive safely."

Who would attack a Taoist sorcerer during the moonless part of the night? Did madmen exist on the mountain, determined to squander their lives? Or had Masato forgotten Junichi's power?

However, Masato appeared to be sincerely concerned. "I can travel over this entire mountain safely on my own," Junichi replied crisply.

"I know you can," Masato said with good humor. "I still feel the need to look out for you."

"Keep your men," Junichi said, waving his hand dismissively. "I will be fine."

"If you insist," Masato said slowly, following Junichi as he made his way to his horse.

"I do," Junichi said. Even if he'd been barely able to stand because the exhaustion was so bad, he still would have refused any help.

"Very well," Masato said, acquiescing.

Junichi's mount was prepared quickly and efficiently. Masato's men were at least very well trained. Better than Junichi's, he suspected.

But not as easily replaced, he was certain. Such training cost.

Masato himself packed Junichi's bags, ensuring that the silver basin was safely stowed away. When he stepped back, though, he still carried the box containing the fox fairy powers. He stood there, beside Junichi, waiting.

When Junichi reached out to take the box, Masato stepped back.

"I'll take that," Junichi said. He was too tired to try to be polite and merely ask.

"I don't think so," Masato said slowly. "This is mine, these are mine."

"What do you mean?" Junichi asked, his anger starting to rise.

"Check the contract," Masato said. "I only paid for a vessel to store the powers. I never surrendered them to you."

Junichi thought back. Masato was correct. The contract had been worded very carefully around that clause. He hadn't thought anything of it at the time.

Masato really had grown more clever. Junichi cursed silently.

"You need to be very careful with that box," Junichi warned. "If you lose it, you'll be vulnerable. Someone could use those powers to get at you."

Masato chuckled. "True. I had already figured that out. However, that someone would have to have *your* powers. Only someone with strong Taoist magic could untangle the fox fairy magic from the ashes and thorns of the graveyard."

Junichi had to reluctantly agree. "You still have to be careful with it."

"I will be," Masato assured Junichi. "You be careful riding home."

Though Masato didn't add the phrase, *old man* at the end of his statement, Junichi heard it anyway.

He certainly felt like an old man, outsmarted by his former apprentice. He'd planned on keeping the box with the fox fairy powers, to be able to use it, if necessary, to guard himself against Masato.

Possibly he could steal them later, though Masato would undoubtedly ward them well.

The next time Masato needed help, Junichi would be more careful. Negotiate harder.

Prove that he wasn't an old man.

Junichi swung himself up onto his horse without any aid and rode out of Masato's camp as if the winds of the demon Futen were at his heels.

And maybe they were. He certainly felt as though his soul was being flogged. Pain from old betrayals seeped from wounds he'd thought had healed.

Next time, he'd be more clever. Next time, he'd get his full due.

Next time, Masato would have to come crawling to him before Junichi would lift a finger.

Junichi rode hard and fast, barely able to see the road. It didn't matter—his horse's steps were guided by magic, ensuring that Junichi would make it back to his compound safely. None of Masato's guards would have mattered.

The cold night winds didn't clear Junichi's anger. But he did wonder at the truth of things.

No matter what happened, he'd likely come to Masato's aid the next time he called.

They were too twisted together, too entwined. Old obligations still ran between them under the new relationships. Just as Masato would always come running if Junichi sent for him, asked for help.

Not that he ever would. Just as duty didn't change, neither did Junichi's nature.

He was sure to die alone, as that horrible fox fairy had once predicted. Just before she'd rejected him for the final time.

Seven

Looking Around Curiously

Kayoku

Looking around curiously, Kayoku wondered at the differences between where the priestesses of the Mori temple stayed on the estate and the priests. The hall she'd been shown to wait for Priestess Ayumi was more austere than any other on the estate. Even the poems hanging on the walls were simple, done in the woman's *kana* script, and merely celebrating the beauty of the mountain. No fancy lattice-work dividers stood along the walls—it was as if they always used the entire space, without ever dividing it. The remnant of sweet incense still floated in the air, though Kayoku couldn't see any burning. No cobwebs lurked in the rafters, and no dust gathered in the corners.

Priestess Ayumi came hurrying in after Kayoku had circled the hall twice, impressed by the sturdy wooden walls that showed no sign of insects or wear, how neatly piled the guest pillows were in the corner where she assumed Priestess Ayumi wanted her to sit.

"Greetings, my lady," Priestess Ayumi said, bowing low. "Please excuse my tardiness."

"I barely gave you any time to get ready," Kayoku said. "Think nothing of it."

Priestess Ayumi wore formal Mori Temple robes that morning, burnt orange with saffron yellow lining. Instead of her usual practical bun, her long hair was piled up haphazardly, strands artfully falling down to enhance her moon-round face. She wasn't as beautiful as Hikaru—few were. But she still was a stunning woman.

Why had she gone into the priesthood, and forsaken a husband? Kayoku longed to ask, but it wasn't polite. Rumors claimed that she'd lost her first husband and one true love, before she'd even been married, and had joined the priesthood instead.

Kayoku suspected that was partially the truth—but that it was also possibly equally true that Priestess Ayumi wanted autonomy, the kind of authority that being the head priestess of a temple would grant.

After the tea was served by Kayoku's servants, she waved them away, to stand outside the door.

This was a private conversation. One that couldn't be overheard by anyone.

"So how may I serve the mistress of the house?" the priestess asked, using an older, more formal title for Kayoku's position.

Kayoku knew she couldn't just ask for what she wanted. So she asked instead, "Have you seen Masato's lists?"

Priestess Ayumi grimaced, the look darkening her entire countenance. "I haven't, my lady, but I've been informed about them."

The disposition of the Mori Temple and its people had angered many people. But the temple was officially under the protection of the estate, and not a separate entity. Some had proposed that they should petition the Emperor, so that Masato would have to negotiate with them separately, but there was no time, and Kayoku agreed that it wouldn't do much good.

All the goods existing on the temple grounds were to be inventoried and then packed, ready to be distributed elsewhere, including all altars, basins, incense burners, sacred texts, fragrant woods, and so on.

The priests and priestesses were to all present themselves to Masato when he arrived and be prepared to convert to Buddhism, or lose their heads.

None would be allowed to live or find another vocation.

However, as Masato's letter had indicated, it would be days before he or his representatives actually arrived at the estate. It wasn't that difficult to hide those who wanted to stay and live a different life.

Several had chosen not to abandon their posts, though. They would die with their temple, when Masato came and burned it to the ground.

"Have there been any changes?" Priestess Ayumi asked. "Any other news?"

Kayoku didn't want to crush the priestess' hopes, but she had to. "No news. Masato will be here. He will be the new lord of the estate. Soon." She couldn't help but shudder.

"I see, mistress," Priestess Ayumi replied. She swallowed down her disappointment.

Kayoku gave the priestess a moment to settle herself back down to her fate. She was already accepting of her own.

"So how may I help you?" Priestess Ayumi finally said.

"I've heard rumors that some of the people on the estate aren't waiting for Masato. The generals, and like that. That they're already planning on walking in the lands of eternal cherry blossoms," Kayoku said carefully.

"I haven't heard of any such thing," Priestess Ayumi said, her face carefully neutral and not showing any emotion or reaction.

A spike of fear ran through Kayoku. Had she miscalculated? But surely the priestess would be able to help her. She continued with her question, as if the priestess hadn't replied. "How would you go about such a thing?"

The priestess paused, considering. "I have never thought about such things," she admitted.

"Oh," was all Kayoku could say. She'd been certain that the priestess would be able to help.

"However, if I had ever thought about walking in the eternal lands before my time, I may have considered some of the different properties of some of the healing herbs and medicines that I regularly employ," the priestess continued cautiously. "Many of the tisanes and teas we administer have a dangerous side to them."

"I see," Kayoku said slowly, her heart lifting. "Could you give me an example?"

"I'm not sure, my lady," Priestess Ayumi said. She peered at Kayoku, studying her closely. "Too often, I've seen people ask, only to change their mind later."

Kayoku gave a bitter laugh. "Masato had two lists," she said bluntly. "One for the people in the estate, talking of their fate. A second, for all the property. Did you know all the *wives* appeared on the second?" Kayoku made herself take a deep breath. "I've been running the estate for a while now. Yet I'm listed below the hunting dogs." She tried to let go of her anger. She heard her stepmother's voice again, telling her how unattractive the truth was. "I'm less than the horses or cattle," she spat. "Why would I want to stay and serve any lord who thought as little of me as that?"

"I understand," Priestess Ayumi said, nodding. "I may be able to help you, my lady."

"Blessed be," Kayoku said, bowing low. She felt as though all the air had been let out of her, all the steam that had been blowing her up for days.

"Wait here," the priestess said.

Kayoku sat, swaying in her seat, feeling as though her head floated far above her body, near the rafters.

It had been difficult to get to this place. She understood the priestess' hesitation with helping her with such a request.

But Kayoku also wasn't about to change her mind.

Kayoku rose when the priestess returned. "This will help you sleep," the priestess muttered, pressing a bag of prickly, dried herbs into Kayoku's hand. "Make a tea with it, then drink it just before you lie down. May all your nightmares pass quickly."

"Thank you," Kayoku said. She couldn't tell the priestess how much it meant to her, that she had a path out, finally.

That she would soon no longer have to worry about good luck or bad. She was about to take her own destiny in her hands. The rest of the world could wait.

Kayoku sat in her front rooms, formally dressed in a shimmering golden robe, decorated with red dragonflies. She'd washed her face clean of all makeup. Two jeweled hairpins held back the ends of her hair, one of her most prized possessions, as they'd been her mother's. She knelt on her best pillows; her favorite teapot, made from brown clay and glazed so it appeared bronze, sat beside her, filled with water that had recently boiled.

The bag filled with herbs sat immediately in front of Kayoku. It looked so innocent, just plain brown cloth, barely large enough to fill her palm.

But Masato had finally sent a letter, saying that he'd be there the next day.

Kayoku would be gone before he arrived.

She picked up the small pouch. The dried herbs pricked her skin through the bag. They smelled musty, like regular medicine, bitter and dry. But Kayoku trusted that Priestess Ayumi wouldn't mislead her.

It was easy enough to pour the pouch into her tea pot and let the infusion steep. Kayoku drifted. She hadn't said goodbye, but she also didn't feel as though she needed to.

She was the one taking this journey. It was a very private affair. No one else needed to know.

She had left very detailed instructions for the other wives and her servants about what to do once she'd gone.

Kayoku let herself float, listening to the stillness of the night. It was very bittersweet, this parting. To not see another sunrise. But Masato had already instructed that Iwao's wife was to come to his tent that first night. Kayoku shuddered, thinking of what that would have entailed.

Better to leave first.

Sounds drifted in. At first, Kayoku ignored them. Someone was whispering urgently outside the door to her room. She'd left the strictest instructions with her main servant, insisting that she not be disturbed.

The noise increased and started to annoy her, like the incessant buzzing of a gnat. What was that? Who was there?

Finally, a strident voice broke through Kayoku's meditation.

It was Hikaru, demanding to see her.

Kayoku felt herself wrenched back into the present day. She hadn't realized how far she'd floated away, and to what a sweet place, until she came back.

She knew that the younger wife wouldn't be denied. She was so unused to her wishes not being met that she didn't know how to graciously accept a refusal.

With a sigh, Kayoku put the bag of herbs behind her and pushed the teapot to the side. She raised her voice. "Let her come in," she called out.

She didn't have to see Hikaru's triumphant smile to know it was what she wore. But the second wife had composed her features appropriately by the time she entered Kayoku's room.

"Forgive me," Hikaru said, bowing her head low. She wore a dark robe, almost black, with no pattern to break the color. Kayoku had never seen anything like it. Hikaru almost looked as if she'd been cut out of the night.

Maybe part of Kayoku still floated in another place.

"I had to see you," Hikaru said, still addressing the floor. "I have a boon to seek from you."

When Hikaru looked up, she looked puzzled at first. She sniffed the air deliberately, then turned a look of shock and horror to Kayoku. "You have *yama no geikkeiju!*" she proclaimed. She turned her head to the side. "You made a tea from it. An infusion. It's deadly."

Kayoku didn't deny it. "What boon did you seek?" she asked patiently.

"Are you planning on killing Masato?" Hikaru asked. "I would ask that you wait two days before you do that."

Kayoku blinked, surprised. Why would she kill Masato? It would be like trying to kill a wind or a storm.

"I'm not going to kill Masato," she said.

"Then who…" Hikaru gasped and placed her hand over her mouth. "You're not planning on killing yourself, are you?"

"What do you want?" Kayoku asked instead of answering. She felt no need to share anything so personal with the second wife.

"You can't kill yourself," Hikaru said urgently. "You have such a short life as it is. You need to take advantage of it!"

Kayoku gave a bitter laugh. "As Masato's slave? No better than one of his hunting dogs? Death is much, much preferable."

Hikaru grew still. She studied Kayoku intently. "I see. Could I please ask that you delay? So that I might get my revenge on Masato first?"

Kayoku didn't want to be intrigued. She wanted her death!

But the time had passed, her peace already disturbed. Even if Hikaru left immediately, Kayoku knew she wouldn't go back to her plans.

And she did want to help anyone get revenge over Masato.

"What did you have in mind?" Kayoku finally asked.

"Fine," Kayoku fumed at the guard in front of her. "You and a *small* number of men may accompany us."

Kayoku had warned Hikaru that it would be impossible for them to leave the estate without escort. Hikaru had assured Kayoku that an escort was fine—her sisters would take care of them. They just needed to get outside the estate walls.

Kayoku waited with Hikaru at the back gate to the estate. She'd been outside before, at night. But she'd never left the estate, not like this, not this late. She wore a dark cloak over her formal robe—she'd seen no reason to change. Particularly not since the story she'd given the guards included the hint that possibly Masato had requested her presence.

The guards would assume that Kayoku was off to see a lover. Or possibly she was leaving the estate for good, looking to run away. She wasn't surprised when the head guard refused to let her go.

Finally, a heavily armed escort of six men joined them at the gate. "Be sure to keep up, boys," Hikaru teased as she and Kayoku stepped over the threshold and into the night.

Kayoku could barely see anything. The night was too deep. Hikaru, however, walked as if it were still daylight, unerringly following a path, leading Kayoku with her.

The floating sensation Kayoku had indulged in before returned. It was as if they moved in their own dark time, wrapped in the finest of black silks. Everything seemed muffled: the chorus of cicadas and their cycling call in the bushes, the fragrant night winds that tickled the hairs on the back of her neck, and the distant trees standing guard on either side of the path.

Fireflies blinked into existence on their right. Hikaru laughed and clapped her hands. "Look, my lady! Living candles! They are here to wish us well."

Kayoku merely nodded. Were they really insects? Or were they magical lights, brought to life by Hikaru's sisters?

Just a few steps farther, Hikaru suddenly reached over and tugged on Kayoku's arm. "This way," she whispered.

A shudder of fear ran through Kayoku as she stepped from the path.

This was going far, far beyond anything she'd ever done before, had ever contemplated doing. She'd been headstrong for a woman. But she'd more or less followed along the path that her father, her husband, and society had set for her.

Even a single step into the darkness was to start following a wild path that Kayoku wasn't certain she'd ever return from.

Hikaru paused while Kayoku got her bearings. Did the second wife understand the momentousness of the occasion? Kayoku doubted it. Hikaru was far too self-involved.

"I'll get us there and back," Hikaru whispered after a few more moments, urging Kayoku forward.

Kayoku nodded and followed, though she knew Hikaru lied. There really was no going back, was there? Not to a time before. Before the war. Before Iwao's death.

After a few more steps, Kayoku glanced over her shoulder. To the right she saw a pair of hooded figures, going off into the woods. The guards followed.

They hadn't seen the switch. Kayoku assumed that when it was time to return, the guards would be led back, and would escort them back to the estate.

Kayoku breathed a deep sigh of relief, grateful that Hikaru's sisters would do as the younger wife had promised: merely lead the guards astray, but not hurt them or cause them harm.

The trees were more closed in, now. Kayoku had never been in the wilderness like this before. She'd always traveled safe roads, well-marked. Silvery light lined the path. It was easy to walk along, easier than Kayoku would have imagined. Then she saw the bushes pulling out of the path, the vines creeping back.

It was an elegant magic, simple and unassuming, designed merely to make life easier.

Bitterness overcame Kayoku. Nothing in her life had ever been easy this way. No wonder Hikaru was so spoiled!

The path opened up onto a small clearing. Ferns and bamboo lined the edges. Two impossibly beautiful young women stood there, one very tall and thin, with her hair down, wearing finely made red robes, the other, shorter and pleasantly plump, with jeweled butterflies in her hair.

Kayoku could see the family resemblance between the two women and Hikaru: something about the size and shape of their noses, their overly sensuous mouths. They exclaimed over their sister, happy to see her, holding her close and weeping. Evidently it had been some time since they'd been together.

Finally, Hikaru turned to Kayoku. "This is my older sister, Etsu," she said, drawing forward the taller woman. "And my younger sister, Cho."

Kayoku was surprised at the informality of the introduction.

Then again, she was merely human, wasn't she?

"And this is Kayoku. I couldn't have gotten here without her," Hikaru explained to her sisters. "She's been invaluable, teaching me how to be human with grace."

Kayoku blinked at the description. She hadn't known that was what Hikaru thought of her at all.

"Thank you for taking care of our impulsive sibling," Etsu said. She walked over and took Kayoku's hands. They felt impossibly smooth, like silk, and very warm. "We are in your debt." Etsu paused, then added, "I do not say that lightly. If you ever have need, in particular, magical need, I will give you a way to call us. If we can aid you, we will."

"It was nothing," Kayoku demurred. "I was just doing my duty."

Cho laughed merrily at that. "Duty or not, I'm sure she didn't make it easy on you."

Kayoku just smiled pleasantly and didn't reply. She was surprised at how much she liked Hikaru's sisters.

"But now, we need to see about getting her powers back," Etsu proclaimed. "Hikaru claimed that you would be willing to help us. I need to ask you directly, though. Are you willing to help?"

Kayoku nodded. "Hikaru assured me that this would hurt Masato. Even though Hikaru contributed to the death of my dear husband, Iwao, Masato is still the one who did the deed. I would still like to see him punished and hurt."

The smile Etsu gave Kayoku chilled her. It promised inhuman pain and suffering to any who dared cross her.

"Masato will be hurt by this. Weakened greatly as well," Etsu assured her.

"Good," Kayoku said. "Then I will help."

"Then let us begin," Etsu said drawing Kayoku forward.

The last few steps were as momentous as the first for Kayoku. She'd gone down a wild path. Now, there really was no turning back.

Without regret, Kayoku joined the sisters in the center of the clearing.

This was much more sweet than walking in the eternal lands would ever be.

Eight

Watching My Sisters

Hikaru

Watching my sisters glide through the night filled my heart with such longing. I vowed that when I got my powers back, I would never take such ease for granted again.

Kayoku stood directly across from me in the clearing, her regal bearing lending her a stature and elegance I hadn't imagined possible.

Etsu had been correct in scolding me about my attitude toward the humans! Never again.

Despite how they made my very soul ache, I was still glad to see my sisters. I hadn't realized how I had missed them. They'd always been a part of my life. I wished I could sit and drink tea with them for the rest of the night, waiting until after the sun had risen before we all retired, playing silly word games, writing poems for each other, telling stories and learning old myths.

But tonight was meant for grimmer things.

I was pleased that Kayoku had agreed to participate in the spells my sisters were weaving. I hadn't been exaggerating when I'd told my sisters that she'd been teaching me how to be human. I'd watched her deal with the servants, running the estate single-handedly, and negotiating the increasingly difficult demands of Masato and his agents.

I knew my own mother wouldn't have done as well under such strenuous circumstances. Neither of my sisters, either. And it wasn't the big things that made Kayoku human. It was the little things, like the way she joked with her servants about the tasks in front of them, the way she listened to First Cook about his toothache then politely insisted on his assistance and how the pain seemed to vanish midway through that first hour, how she carried herself and the heavy burdens that had been placed on her shoulders, how she hid her deep and abiding grief for Iwao.

The first spell was smaller, easier to perform, but possibly more important. Etsu would disguise my features, hide my own face and beauty, so that when I approached Masato, he would mistake me for Kayoku.

It was essential that this spell be successful. Masato had to be fooled. He still had my fox fairy powers so he'd be able to see through a simple illusion. It had to be a much more complicated spell, one that would require work on his part to block.

With Kayoku here, Etsu was able to work directly with her features. We also exchanged cloaks midway through Etsu's song, to reinforce the binding.

Masato had already demanded that Kayoku attend him the first night of his possession of the estate.

He was going to get much more than he bargained for.

By the time the spell finished, across the dancing lights that filled the center of the clearing stood a figure I recognized from my own bronze mirror. I'd known that I was that beautiful—I'd had people tell me about my beauty my entire life.

Was I really that snobbish, though? My nose stuck permanently in the air? Did I have so much disdain for those around me, that I never addressed them properly?

Again, another memory for me to carry forward, into my new life.

After Kayoku and I exchanged cloaks again, I saw her standing there. I tried to smile at her, to encourage her. She'd come so far already. I was aware that all of this, everything we'd done that evening, had been so far from her normal life.

But Kayoku still seemed distracted by my sisters, the magic in the night, the cool breezes that carried soft promises.

The second spell was more complicated. Etsu placed a golden thorn into the center of the open space among the four of us. Then she cut a length of my hair to wrap around the thorn.

Were those green wisps already trailing from it? I couldn't tell for certain, not without my own magic.

Why had I been so foolish as to give it up?

For the first time, I wondered if Norihiko was worth it. I'd shunned such thoughts before. But since becoming human, I had more time to consider my plight.

Perhaps remaining as I had been, and having the patience to wait for my sisters, would have been the wiser course. Maybe Etsu would have been able to find a way to raise the sword from the watery grave that Masato had promised it.

I'd never know.

I'd learned so much by becoming human. It had truly been a mirror for me to see my own actions and those of my people.

But would I choose the same path if I could do it all over again?

I wasn't sure.

Etsu's spell to bring my powers back to me had no words. She sang nonsense syllables to a discordant tune. It made me uncomfortable, and highlighted the gulf between us, the chasm that I had put there.

Lights shifted in the clearing as Etsu sang, as if shadows danced around us. Though Etsu didn't burn any incense, I still smelled the sweet and bitter *kyara* of *jinkoh* wood. Across from me, Kayoku swayed like a poppy dancing in a gentle breeze.

I can't say how long the spell took. But I'd sunk deeply into it, only coming back to myself after Etsu had finished.

I couldn't see any sweat on her brow, and I didn't have the skill anymore to tell if my sister was tired. But I still knew that it had taken a lot of work to craft such an artifact.

Etsu picked up the thorn and presented it to me, bowing her head low. Instead of being golden, fresh and just plucked, now it looked withered, as if it had aged in snow for many seasons.

"You must drive it deep into his skin," Etsu instructed me. "And it must remain there for a while." She looked at me sadly. "I'm sorry, sister. I wish there was another way."

I nodded, understanding.

I was going to have to distract Masato while the thorn was in.

And we all knew the best way for a woman to distract a man, no matter how distasteful he might be.

I did as I was told and stayed in my rooms when Masato and his troop arrived. It wouldn't do for him to see me too soon, recognize me.

Plus, while physically I might have been able to pass for Kayoku, I didn't know enough about the running of the estate to pass for her. She had far more knowledge about everything. I would have been spotted as an imposter quickly.

So I stayed in my dim rooms, alone, composing myself for my ordeal later that evening. The day had dawned warm, the air sticky.

My thoughts kept circling back to Kayoku. While it was true that I had contemplated leaving this plane after I had freed Norihiko, I don't know if I would have actually had the courage to go through with it, like Kayoku.

The smell of the *yama no gekkeiju* haunted me still. Mother had taught me about that tree, which was plentiful here on the mountain. She'd shared much of her knowledge of herbcraft, of herbs that would ease childbirth or stop it, as well as potions to excite the blood or cool it.

After I'd foolishly given away my magic, I'd equally as foolishly believed that it was the only worthwhile gift I had. I had discounted all the other knowledge I'd accumulated, like herbcraft or creating poetry. I still had skills.

I would have to use all of them, plus more, later that evening.

Kayoku never once asked me if I was sure about taking her place with Masato. Maybe she thought it was just punishment for my misdeeds, for causing Iwao's death. For my foolishness.

Or maybe she still floated between worlds. She had that look sometimes, her gaze far away, not seeing what was directly in front of her but things far on the horizon.

It wasn't punishment, however. Or at least, I couldn't view it that way. I wasn't a sullied woman about to get her just deserts.

Nor was it duty. While I was a wife of Iwao, I had never married him in my heart. I had one true mate, whom, at one point, I would have done anything to save.

I viewed it more as correcting the mistake I had made. I could have asked my sisters for help. Possibly they could have distracted Masato enough while I stole my fairy powers back. The most certain way, though, was for me to do it.

And I needed for the spell to work, for me to have my powers again.

I had gotten myself into this mess. I needed to get myself out of it.

Though I wasn't certain I'd make the same choice again, I still felt as though it wasn't just me dependent on the success of this spell. Only with my full powers could I free Norihiko. He was dependent on me.

I reached out and stroked Seiji's scabbard. The sword would never accept me. However, I was certain Norihiko would forgive me everything when he returned.

I would need it, as I wasn't certain when I'd be able to forgive myself.

I didn't fall asleep for my nap until the heat of the day had seeped away, the promise of the evening's coolness carried on the breeze. I felt as though I had just closed my eyes when a rough hand shook my shoulder, waking me.

"It is time," Kayoku told me as soon as I opened my eyes.

I nodded, swallowed, and gathered myself together, pushing my dreams away and sitting up. "How did it go today?" I asked.

I'd learned that humans needed this sort of interaction, that it was polite to ask about an event.

I hadn't expected the bitterness of Kayoku's laugh. "Masato the great lord rode right past all the servants and wives assembled in the courtyard. I'm not even certain he saw us. Then he spent the day closeted with the generals and other advisors. He never asked for me or any of the other wives, any of those who might actually know about the estate."

"But that was good, right? That you didn't have to deal with him?" I asked, stripping off my robe.

Kayoku looked blankly at me, then blinked.

That was right. Humans had an aversion to actually being nude in front of one another. Even when they fornicated, they still wore robes. At least the proper lords and ladies.

Peasants stripped bare and enjoyed it.

It was still the easiest and quickest way for us to exchange robes, however.

With a shrug, Kayoku started to follow suit, stripping off her outer robe. "We wasted much of the morning standing there, waiting for him, first to arrive, then for someone to finally inquire whether he needed us or not. But why would that matter? We women and servants weren't important enough for anyone else to think that our time might be wasted."

"I'm sorry," I told her sincerely. And I was. It was my fault, in many ways, that she'd been exposed to this.

"Then we gathered again, a second time, to see him off, as he left the estate," Kayoku continued. She handed me her robe with an impatient gesture. I handed her mine in return.

"For a second time, he didn't deign to look at any of us. Later, one of his men approached me to let me know that I shouldn't let such rabble assemble in the yard, that I needed to keep better control of the servants."

Her bitter laugh sent chills down my spine. "I didn't bother explaining to him that there had been very few servants there, that it was wives and minor lords. But I understood what he was implying. Masato didn't want to see us, or even acknowledge our existence."

"I'll take care of him," I told her. "I swear he'll hurt after tonight."

"Good," Kayoku said, nodding as she slipped on my robe.

The enchantment was already taking hold. Her features softened, her nose turned up, her hair grew thicker and softer.

"Will you kill him?" Kayoku asked as I knelt down and she started applying makeup.

I shook my head. "I can't," I told her. "I thought I could kill Norihiko's killer. But that isn't part of my soul, to kill another that way."

"Ah," Kayoku said, pausing. "I think I could. But one never knows what one will actually do until faced with the truth, right?"

I merely sighed in response. "I will do this," I told her after a long pause. "I will steal back my powers and weaken him."

"I believe you," Kayoku said. "And let tomorrow bring what it may."

I blinked back my tears, honored that I'd had a chance to know this brave woman, human or not.

I also vowed to not let her down.

Masato had chosen to keep his camp outside of the estate walls. I don't know if his paranoia was justified or not: sometimes victorious generals were murdered in their sleep when they moved into a new territory. However, the generals at the estate were morally beaten. I doubted any of them retained the will to fight on.

Fortunately, the guards escorting me to Masato's camp didn't try to talk with me. They also didn't look at me. I realized they were just doing their duty, though I suspected they considered it shameful as well.

I didn't know if my sisters followed me through the darkening evening. I tried not to be bitter about the fact that at one point, I would have known if any of my kin was within a single *li*. I didn't see any fireflies, however, didn't hear the yipping of foxes or hounds, so I assumed I was on my own.

I had to save myself, this time. My fate, and Norihiko's both hung on my own wits and skills.

I hadn't paid that much attention to Masato's original camp—my goal had been to get in, steal the sword, and leave. Afterward, well, I don't think I was capable of doing anything other than putting one foot in front of the other as I dragged Seiji behind me.

This time, I looked around eagerly. Guards paced in the darkness, both near the entrance and away from it, so I assumed they circled the camp. Warriors camped to the left of the main tent, while the priests, the sorcerers, the blacksmiths, the cooks, the camp followers and everyone else sprawled to the right. That would have to be my way out, once I regained my powers. It would be easier, and Etsu had warned me that it would take time before I was at my full strength.

Masato's tent was as large as a temple. I remembered it had been divided into several smaller rooms. Guards stood before the doorway, as well as placed about a spear's length apart all around the perimeter.

Was it an honor to be chosen to guard here? Or was it a disciplinary action? I couldn't tell. The darkness hid the disposition of the men. The ones I could see all looked grim.

I wasn't certain what to expect when I walked into the tent. Would Masato try to be civilized at first, invite me for tea and small talk, before inviting me to his bed? Would he be demanding as a new groom?

Masato had removed all the dividers. I wasn't certain why. It made the place more breathable. Maybe the fox fairy powers had inspired him to do that, or maybe his servants hadn't had time to set them up yet.

A silver brazier smoked on the altar at the back of the tent, and the scent of pine and clove incense filled the air, masking a more musky smell. The pillows and writing desk set up in the corner were the finest quality. As was the casual, indoor robe that Masato wore, brown with golden cicadas—a symbol of lust.

Servants took my cloak, then left the tent, left us alone. I turned to Masato, but didn't raise my eyes to him.

I willed the spell to work, that he wouldn't see anything of me standing there.

When Masato grabbed my arms, I gasped and looked up. Had he pierced the disguise?

However, instead of denouncing me, he started kissing me with his vile tongue demanding entrance.

I struggled. I couldn't help myself. I was completely unprepared for his hunger.

That merely brought a quiet laugh from him. "Go ahead. Struggle, my little dove. That just makes me harder." He thrust his hips against my body and I realized the scent the incense tried to cover up but hadn't was his own masculine odor.

I tried to swallow down my fear. His fingers bruised my arms and his tongue continued to invade me. I shivered and tried to take a step back. I wasn't really struggling, it was more play acting, to see what his response was.

It was as despicable as I'd thought it would be. He grew harder and pressed more deliberately against me.

I wasn't about to give in, to scream and cry in earnest. I would never have given him that much satisfaction, or let the game go that way.

Fortunately, however, I was my mother's daughter. I'd been taught how to pretend interest. Fox fairies frequently seduced men to get something out of them.

So I squirmed, squeaked, and pushed away, driving the beast inside Masato wild. It didn't take long before he threw me down on the sleeping mats, holding my body down with the weight and strength of his own. He merely pushed my robes to the side as he prepared to mount me.

I struggled more then, as I knew he was expecting it. "Little wildcat you are," he crooned as he cruelly pinched my bottom to get me to spread my thighs apart.

I cried more when he entered me, unprepared as I was. It hurt, but I could bear it. There wasn't that much of him to accommodate.

As his pleasure increased, I reached back and scratched his thighs. That made him thrust more roughly, brought him closer to the edge.

When I judged he was close to finishing, I scratched him again, howling my displeasure as he grabbed my hair and forced my head back.

I reached back with my other hand and scratched him a third time, but this time, I used the magic thorn and plunged it into his thigh.

Shouting his pleasure, Masato started to orgasm. He didn't notice the power seeping from him—he was too caught up in his release.

The first flood of power washed over me, choking me. I gasped, barely able to breathe. I tried to move my body to prolong his pleasure, so he wouldn't realize that he'd been tricked, but I need not have bothered.

Once the fool finished his useless pumping, he fell over to the side, his eyes closed, a peaceful smile on his lips. "You may go, now."

I swallowed the bitterness I felt over being used and discarded as such. I knew he did it on purpose, to make the women he mated with feel powerless.

I had my prize. I had my power back.

Still, as I walked out of the sleeping room on shaky legs, gathering my robes back up around my shoulders, I couldn't help but wonder at the price I'd paid.

Nine

Galloping Horse Hooves Echoed

Masato

Galloping horse hooves echoed in Masato's aching head. He tried to focus his far-flung thoughts. He hadn't had that much to drink the night before, had he? He didn't recall any wine pots after taking Iwao's wife, marking her as his territory, much as she'd marked him with her nails.

He shivered at the memory. She'd been such a wildcat! He was going to have to send for her again. Soon.

With a groan, Masato pushed himself up to sit on his sleeping mats. The day must be cloudy—the sun was so dim that morning. He blinked and took a deep breath, seeking the warm fox fairy powers to wash away his overindulgence.

Nothing responded to him. His own blood remained sluggish. Was he sick? The powers should just be there! What was happening to him?

Masato swayed when he finally made his way to his feet. He had no strength, no life in his arms or legs.

Again, Masato willed the fox fairy powers to rise, to warm his blood.

Nothing happened.

Had Junichi stolen the rest of the fox fairy powers? Or drained more of them away?

Masato sought the box that contained the shadow that had been carved off. It still sat in the corner, well protected by charms.

But the wood was no longer a dark brown, almost black. Instead, it was tinted with gray, as if the box had aged centuries overnight.

When Masato reached out to touch it, the box dissolved with a puff of ash. All that remained was a dark, greasy spot on the floor.

That wasn't Junichi's work. Some other force was at hand.

Masato tried again to marshal his thoughts as he stumbled back to his sleeping mats. A spot of blood on the *tatamis* caught his eye. He calculated. If he'd been lying on his back, it would have come from his thigh.

Gingerly, Masato reached back to the spot that he only now realized was still sore.

Something was embedded in his skin there.

Cursing, Masato pinched the end of it, scraping his own sensitive skin, and pulled it out.

It faded away to nothing quickly, but not before he saw that it had been a thorn.

Masato clenched his fists together so he wouldn't shout out loud. He was going to have to cancel going to the estate today. Let them speculate why.

Junichi hadn't stolen his powers.

That woman had.

By the time Junichi arrived at the camp, Masato had managed to hold down some tea and compose himself. He didn't bother trying to clean up the evidence of the events from the previous evening. He needed Junichi to see it, read it, and maybe help him figure out what exactly had happened.

Distaste flashed across Junichi's face as he walked into the tent before he controlled himself, his expression becoming wooden.

Masato impatiently endured the politeness required of a host, greeting his guest and serving him tea before they could talk about what Masato needed.

As Junichi put aside his cup, he sighed and said, "You seem to be in a state, old friend."

Masato chuckled bitterly. "That I am."

"What happened?" Junichi asked, solicitous as always.

However, Masato knew that Junichi was already counting up the piles of gold that he'd receive for his help.

Masato explained the night before, showing Junichi the wound on his thigh, as well as the stained spot on the ground where the box had been.

"You said she was like a wildcat?" Junichi asked after Masato had finished. His face was expressionless, as if it were carved out of stone.

"She was," Masato said. He should have tied her arms together before he took her. He'd done that before, with a whore who hadn't wanted to accept the payment he offered, her helpless writhing exciting him more.

Junichi looked again at the sleeping mats, holding up one of the blankets to his nose before turning to Masato. "I think," he said, hesitatingly, "that it wasn't the wife who visited you last night, but the fox fairy whose powers you'd taken."

Masato rocked back on his heels. How? Then he realized his mistake. He barely knew Iwao's wife. He wasn't sure if he'd recognize her again. It would have been easy for another woman to come and take her place.

"I'm going to kill her," Masato ground out. "I'm going to kill them all." He finally understood Junichi's hatred of the fox fairies. They all deserved to die.

Junichi gave Masato a cold smile, one that would chill a glacier.

"I have a plan."

Sweat streamed down Masato's torso, dripping down his arms, slicking his thighs and calves. The fire from the forge belched, the flames licking into the air, but he didn't flinch. The noise from the fire and the bellows was incredible, like standing inside of a storm.

But Masato held the metal blade as steady as Junichi had directed him to. The orange edge of the sword sparked as Junichi hammered it, a continual ring of blows, flattening the blade until it could be bent and doubled. Masato's arms ached with the effort.

Then back in the fire, softening it again. Masato had already lost track of the number of times the metal had been folded back onto itself. Junichi had assured him that while he was still perfecting the technique, what he'd done already far surpassed the finest blades made in the last decade.

It would be another *taichi* blade, curved like a woman's thigh.

When Junichi lifted his hammer, Masato turned the blade again. At Junichi's curt nod, Masato contained his grimace. Instead, he squeezed his right hand tightly and held his arm out over the blade.

With a flick of his razor-sharp nails, Junichi broke the skin again just over Masato's wrist. Masato shook his arm, scattering the drops of blood over the blade. Then he returned to his former position, holding the end of the metal tightly as Junichi folded the metal again, humming a magical stanza.

Masato knew this sword wouldn't be as powerful as Seiji: He merely gave his own blood to it, not the life of another. But it would be bound to him, and him alone. No one else would be able to wield it as well.

If Masato lost the blade, he'd be in desperate trouble. A proper enemy could use it to drain Masato of his power and will.

Of course, the only proper enemy Masato would ever know would be Junichi. No other had his skill in these sorts of spells.

Junichi hummed and sang as he pounded the metal with his hammer, pouring his fury, *their* fury into the blade as well.

Once it was complete, no fox fairy would be able to withstand their wrath. The sword would seek out any who had even the slightest fox fairy blood. It was attracted to them.

As well as deadly to them. Junichi had added old spells, ancient curses against the fairies.

Masato would be unstoppable using it. They would all fall before him. And as their magic left, the people would have more need than ever for new prayers, new religion.

Buddhism would triumph.

And Masato's name would be remembered forever, for being the bearer of their new savior.

Ten

Gliding Through The Night

Hikaru

Gliding through the night filled me with glee. It had never been so easy to slip through the shadows, to avoid Masato's human and not-so-human guards. The breezes spoke to me, whispering secrets hidden by the darkness.

Etsu had warned me that it would take time for my powers to return. I hadn't anticipated this heady rush of ability, certainly not immediately after leaving Masato.

I paused at the far side of Masato's camp, looking back. I could still see the ghostly image of his large tent, squatting like a fat slug, surrounded by the other tents. Anger blasted through me.

How dare he. *How dare he?* Everything was *his* fault, from Norihiko's death to Iwao's. He'd touched me and I'd let him. He'd driven Kayoku to the brink of death. He'd caused this war. He was probably responsible for the recent crop failures as well.

I blamed Masato for *everything*.

Looking back, I know I wasn't quite rational.

That didn't stop me from gathering my power together as I stood, just outside his camp, the night winds blowing stronger and swirling my robes, winds from my own magic matching them.

Could I gather all that magic together into a single flaming ball, fueled by my desire for revenge and my hatred of Masato, and fling it at him? Hurl it across the dark sky, a blinding point of light, that would never stop burning? Would the flames consume everything in their path—men, tent, horses, Masato?

I could see it burning brightly behind my eyes. A fire that I would laugh and cackle at as I danced around it.

I don't know what pulled me back from the brink. Maybe it was a change in the winds, signaling that the darkest part of the night was now over. Maybe it was my own power refilling me, reminding me of sunny hillsides covered with flowers and the deeper mysteries of the woods.

Or maybe it was my own nature, still. I hadn't been able to kill Junichi. I wasn't sure that I could kill Masato, even after what he'd done to me. What I'd let him do to me.

I let the winds die, my power drop. I swirled away, just another piece of the night.

What would Masato do when he discovered he'd lost my powers? Part of me wanted him to suffer.

But I'd lived among the humans for too long. I cared, now, more than I had.

The estate had to be warned that Masato was likely to be angry. Maybe Kayoku could encourage the generals to lock the gates to Masato and his men.

Losing my powers would weaken Masato. There would be a good chance that he'd cancel his visit to the estate the next day.

Maybe the generals would take that as a sign and be able to withstand the next onslaught of Masato's army.

I didn't know what they would do. I didn't know how the estate would survive Masato and his wrath.

Now that I had my magic again, I could help the people flee. I resolved to talk with Kayoku about that.

After I released Norihiko from his steel form.

It was even easier to slip through the guards around the estate, to have one turn to look left while the other looked right and I slipped in between them. Then again, they were barely guarding anymore—they thought their situation was hopeless.

And maybe it was, and maybe it wasn't. I wasn't certain what I could do to help them, except to help them run away.

The only thing I wanted to do was to finally break Norihiko's curse.

The strength of my magic surprised me. It felt different, too. I didn't want to take the time to explore the differences, however. I was finally going to break Norihiko free from his curse. Bring him back to the flesh. Nothing could stop me.

The door to the women's quarters was locked and guarded. They didn't understand that would never stop me, or one of my kind. I ran up the wall, giggling, vaulting over the balcony on the second story, easily entering a window from there. The guards saw nothing, though they might have reported a haunted wind that made the hairs on the backs of their necks stand up.

I'd forgotten how crowded the estate felt. I kept myself pressed into shadows in the dim hallways, though no one but the occasional guard walked there. However, humans were *everywhere*. I could feel their heartbeats, hear them breathe, smell their sweat.

Once I freed Norihiko, I vowed that we were going to disappear into the wild for a week, with nothing but trees, mountains, and waterfalls.

I hesitated at the doorway to my rooms. Someone waited for me inside. It took me a moment to tease apart the scents. Because Etsu had disguised me as Kayoku, I still carried her scent too closely for me to separate it out, between the cloak I wore and the woman waiting for me.

I longed to play, to slip into the room unnoticed and tease her, to send tickling breezes to tug at her hair and stir her robes, make her whirl around asking who was there.

But I didn't want to waste my powers that way. I needed all this incredible strength I had to free Norihiko.

Though Etsu had cautioned me about the spell and what it would take from me, I knew I had to perform it that night. I couldn't wait, not even until dawn. I was certain I could handle it.

I slid the *shoji* to the side and slipped into the room.

Kayoku had kept all the lamps lit. Was she expecting me to play some trick on her? She examined me in silence. I'm not sure what she saw. Did she merely see that my magical beauty had returned? Or did she see the bruises Masato had put on my body and my soul?

"You have your powers back," Kayoku said after a few long moments.

"I do. Thank you," I told her, giving her a low bow. I wouldn't have them without her, and her help.

"And Masato?" Kayoku asked.

"Hurt. Weak," I assured her.

"Good," Kayoku said. After another moment of intense study, she continued. "I suppose you're going to leave now."

"I don't know," I told her honestly. I felt responsible, but I wasn't sure what I could do. "I can help those leave who want to go," I told her. "I can hide them, disguise them, until they get safely away."

Kayoku nodded. "There are some who will thank you for that."

"And you?" I asked, curious.

Kayoku merely smiled. "I will stay. This is my place. Until the bitter end."

I wasn't sure why she felt that way. I would try to get her to change her mind later, I decided.

"Now, I must free my beloved Norihiko," I told Kayoku.

The sword Seiji hissed at me when I touched it. As a human, I hadn't heard his voice, and I was only vaguely aware of his displeasure.

Now, the full brunt of his anger washed over me. I wasn't sure why Seiji was so angry. Maybe it was because I was about to break him, to free the soul inside.

In essence, I was killing the sword Seiji to free my love Norihiko.

However, it wasn't the same as killing a man. I was changing his form, freeing his soul, not sending it to the eternal lands.

"What do you need?" Kayoku asked.

I started. I'd forgotten she was still in the room. I wanted to tell her that I didn't need her, that she should go back to her bed, her dreams, her human life. But one look at her face told me that she needed to stay, needed to be involved.

This sword, indirectly, had been the death of her husband. She, too, wanted to see it transformed.

Maybe she just wanted a little bit more magic in her life.

"I need you to guard the door," I told her seriously. "This is a dangerous spell. Difficult to contain. No one should enter while I'm still singing."

Kayoku nodded seriously. "I will do that for you."

"Thank you," I said sincerely. "I…I couldn't have done this, without you."

"I know," Kayoku said. "I'll be just outside, if you need anything."

Kayoku turned and left me alone, surrounded by all things human and the sword that contained my love. The night beyond the walls of the estate felt full of promise, the winds carrying the news of the mountain to those who could hear.

I placed the sword in the center of the room, though it fought me, dragging itself to the earth, carrying the weight of all the mountain along its blade.

I was determined, however. The sword would yield to me. I would transform it.

I would succeed and bring my love back to me.

I took some time to strip off the robes I'd been wearing, the things Masato had touched, and sluiced water over my bare body, trying to wash away the earlier part of the evening. I found I kept turning my head to look at the sword. Maybe it was to reassure myself that my sacrifice had been worth it.

Or maybe because Seiji still hissed his displeasure at me.

Then I dressed in fresh, clean robes, the color of spring grass, with beautiful silver waves woven through the cloth. It felt good to be in my own clothes, in my own body.

I still didn't feel quite like my old self. I assumed I would, in time.

Etsu had given me all the ingredients that I needed for the spell: an enchanted sprig of bamboo with the most tender shoots, a silver cup filled with the freshest spring water, and a specially scented *nioi-bukuro* sachet, that smelled both sweet and bitter as I placed it around my neck.

I cleared all the pillows and everything extraneous from the room, shoving items against the walls and into the corners. Not that there was very much: I hadn't accumulated that many things as a human. Then I dragged Seiji out into the center.

For the first time, I separated the blade from his scabbard. I was prepared for how the steel shivered in my hand. He sought my skin, sought to take my blood.

I admit, I laughed at his efforts. He was just a sword, whereas I was *kitsune*, full of my powers.

And my pride.

I pushed the scabbard out of the way, shoving it into the corner, beside the kneeling pillows. Then I carefully placed the water on the far side of the sword, while I picked up the bamboo.

The spell had several parts. Etsu had whispered them to me. I hadn't remembered them, as a human. Couldn't have gotten the order correctly.

But now that my powers had returned, the words leapt to my mouth. I dipped the leaves of the bamboo into the water, then sprinkled them onto the naked blade as I started my song.

> *The gusty wind*
> *Blows apart the veils*
> *Between this plane and the High Heavenly Lands*
> *So that my plea can be heard*
> *My spell have the blessings*
> *Of all the kami and urkami*

The song went on for stanza after stanza, pleading my case with the upper gods, proclaiming the injustice done to my love, how we both deserved another chance.

I danced around the sword, swinging my sprig of bamboo like a general's baton. Power emanated from me, sweeping into the room like a fresh spring breeze.

Maybe it was the sachet I wore—it wasn't until I was midway through that I smelled the sourness that had filled the room. Instead of the fresh mulch of fall that I was invoking came the scent of fruit rotting in the fields.

I carried on without stopping, however. I was too close to my prize to consider what such a sour scent meant.

Finally, after several hours, I reached the end verse. I stroked Seiji with the bamboo sprig, so that he might be reborn, as the bamboo was continual and constantly renewing.

The bamboo shivered in my hand, warning me.

I didn't stop.

After the seventh stroke, it took all my strength to bring the bamboo back for the final, last stroke. The lucky eighth stroke that was to finally dissolve the spell.

The bamboo submitted to being used, then it leapt up in my hand, as if trying to get away. I held onto it, horrified as it changed, transforming into a long bone, like a leg bone from a horse. It was bleached white with age and scarred with limestone.

I shrieked, but didn't let go. I didn't understand what magic it was that transformed the bamboo that way, but I couldn't release it. I felt it might turn on me if I did.

Before me, the sword glowed with a brilliant purple light, as if it had been dipped in a sunset.

Without warning, it exploded.

I put my hands up over my face instinctively. Had I spoken the spell wrong? The sword was supposed to dissolved gently, fade away, and leave just Norihiko behind.

Beads of hot steel scored my skin. I cried out. Without thinking, I turned the bone in my hand and used it as a great wand to fend off the sparks.

What terrible things had gone wrong?

When I finally opened my eyes, there stood my love. My Norihiko. I gasped. It had been so long since I'd seen his beautiful face.

He almost looked as I remembered him, with soft brown eyes, a wide, intelligent brow, and sensual lips. His jaw, though, had hardened, and his cheekbones were much more prominent. He looked more stern than I remembered. Also more broad—his shoulders seemed twice as wide, and his torso had many more muscles than I remembered from our short time together.

I heard a noise from behind me. I turned. Without thinking about it, I raised the bone in my hand, like an ax.

The bone transformed again, flowing smoothly. It didn't become what I wanted, because I hadn't wished for a new form for it.

Maybe it became what it thought was needed, though, as it changed into a scythe, long, black, and deadly.

Kayoku stood on this side of the door, not outside, in the hallway, where it was safe.

I lowered my weapon. But it had a mind of its own. It pushed itself forward as it went down to my side, slicing along Kayoku's side. She screamed and dropped instantly to the ground in a faint, her side bleeding.

I cried out loud, dropping the foul thing I held. I could hear its whispers, licking at the blood, longing for more.

This wasn't me. This wasn't my magic.

But it was.

Somehow, while Masato had my powers, he'd corrupted them. No wonder I'd felt so strong! I should have realized it when the night had called so loudly to me: Before, it had always been the sunlight and trees that sang to me.

Before I could go to Kayoku, Norihiko rushed past me. He gathered the wife in his arms, disregarding his own nakedness. He crooned over her, then glared at me.

If his eyes could have spat poison at me, they would have. His stare was so hateful, it was like a physical blow.

"Who are you? What have you done to her?" Norihiko asked, distraught.

If I had the power to cause the earth to swallow me whole at that moment, I would have.

Norihiko—my one true love—didn't remember me.

Priestess Ayumi came to Kayoku's rooms to care for her and her wounds. The first wife still hadn't regained consciousness. The wound hadn't been deep, so I didn't understand why she wasn't waking up.

It didn't occur to me until much, much later that the wound might be magical.

My own selfishness also caused my distraction. Norihiko was free from the sword. I'd broken the curse. Transformed him back into flesh.

But I hadn't undone the reforging.

Being made into a sword had changed Norihiko forever. He was no longer my soft love.

He was also no longer a *kitsune*. He was human, as I had been. I knew it wasn't the curse so many of my kind would call it.

It still wasn't right.

How could I help him regain his fox fairy powers? When would he remember me?

Then there were my own fox fairy powers. They were corrupt, tainted with the stench of the graveyard. How could I cleanse them?

However, the worst part of this whole conundrum was the doubt I felt. I should have been happy that Norihiko was back. I told myself that it didn't matter that he didn't remember me. I'd done the right thing. I'd broken the curse. I'd freed my love. He lived again.

But the cost had been so high.

Was it all worth it?

The Reforging
A Sword's Poem
Volume III

The Reforging

A Sword's Poem

Volume III

刀の詩の本三

鍛え直し

LEAH CUTTER

AUTHOR OF PAPER MAGE

One

Floating in Dreams

Kayoku

Floating in dreams, Kayoku didn't want to wake up. In her dreams, her husband Iwao was still alive. Sometimes his father, the great Lord Taiko, was still alive as well. The estate wasn't under siege from the warlord Masato. The summer was still full and warm, and the weather wasn't turning to fall, full of cold rains and bare trees.

And Hikaru hadn't betrayed her. The inhumanly beautiful second wife hadn't disturbed the order of the household.

Thoughts of Hikaru finally dragged Kayoku out of her dreams. How dare she? Just because she believed Iwao had killed her own mate didn't justify her actions. Not killing Iwao, not causing such disturbance in the estate. And certainly not injuring Kayoku.

Pain spread from Kayoku's side, sending tendrils of fire along her ribs, across her front, and reaching toward her spine. The wound inflicted by Hikaru sucked all the life from her, all her will—a great black hole that would take her life.

Kayoku woke, gasping for breath. The blackness from the wound on her side was drowning her. Was the day dim, or was it still night?

"Shhh," said an unfamiliar voice.

A cool cloth was draped over Kayoku's eyes, soothing her with the scent of fresh rosemary. She tried to take a deep breath and ended up coughing, her lungs full.

The pain was overwhelming. A strong arm helped her sit up while still holding the cloth over her weeping eyes. After a few deep breaths, Kayoku finally felt her lungs open and clear.

"Thank you," she whispered as she was lowered back to her sleeping mats.

The cloth over her eyes was lifted up. She heard it being dipped in water, then wrung out and place over her eyes again.

When Kayoku reached for the hand doing the work, she gasped again.

This wasn't Priestess Ayumi. The wrist she felt was too broad. Wide. Masculine.

"Who are you?" Kayoku asked, struggling to move away and open her eyes. It couldn't have been her father, and she had no brothers. It wouldn't have been proper for any other male on the estate to be this close to her, to see her in this state.

Had Masato made good his promise to take over the estate? And do away with all the priests and priestesses of the Mori temple?

"Shh, shhh," the strange man said.

Kayoku didn't recognize the man kneeling beside her. He had a wide, intelligent brow, an upturned nose, and a strong chin. He wore one of her husband's outer robes—one she'd liked, actually, brown with the symbol of Shirayama mountain embroidered in gold down the front.

"I am…" the young man hesitated. "My name is Norihiko. I am Seiji, the sword, made flesh. Made human."

Norihiko held up his hand at her incredulous look. "Hikaru was successful in her spell. You remember that, right?"

Kayoku wanted to deny his assertion automatically. But the dreams… the vision of Hikaru wielding a great, black scythe, like a farmer in a field, cutting down everything before her.

Slowly, Kayoku nodded. She'd been standing guard, outside of Hikaru's rooms, while the fox fairy performed the ceremony to break the soul of her mate free of the sword Seiji.

But Hikaru had cried out—a terrible, frightened scream. Kayoku had had to go see what was the matter.

"I remember," Kayoku said slowly. "The spell went wrong though." Wasn't Norihiko supposed to be a fox fairy? Not a human?

Norihiko made a sour face. "That's what she claims. That I'm not human. But a *kitsune*. However, she did free me. Broke our—*my*—soul free of the sword."

"Our?" Kayoku questions. Just because this man had once been a sword didn't make him an ally. If anything, it made him an enemy. The great Lord Taiga hadn't been able to lift Seiji. Only Iwao had.

And Iwao was dead. The generals claimed because of this sword.

Norihiko grimaced as if he were in pain. "When our Maker, Junichi, reforged us into a sword, he beat us. Thinned us. Then folded us over. Again and again. Splintering us. Making us many, not one." He shivered. "Hikaru brought us out of the sword, but we still remember being a sword. Being many. I have the main voice, but sometimes, sometimes there are many."

Kayoku had never heard of such a thing. Then again, before she'd met Hikaru, she'd never really believed in magic.

Luck, she believed in, of course. Both good and bad luck.

Her luck, for most of her life, had been bad.

"So what will you do now?" Kayoku asked. Norihiko was Hikaru's mate. They would probably leave, now. Leave the estate unattended. Leave the humans to their fate while the two fox fairies went on to their magical lives.

"I am here to defend you. Protect the mountain," Norihiko said fervently.

"But Hikaru—"

"I don't remember her!" Norihiko said, obviously frustrated. "She killed my true wielder. Iwao. I made myself heavy so she couldn't lift me. I hated her. But she freed me. Made me so much more."

"She was your mate," Kayoku said gently. "She sacrificed much to get you back."

"I know!" Norihiko said. "But I don't remember."

Kayoku nodded. "I'm sorry," she said. And she was. Hikaru had taken her place with the warlord Masato. Endured what would have killed Kayoku.

"It doesn't matter," Norihiko said. "She injured you. Endangered the estate. The soul of the mountain."

Kayoku contained her shiver, though his words were spoken with such finality. "You don't have to stay," she said.

"I do," Norihiko replied. "When Junichi reforged us, he, *we*, dedicated ourselves to the mountain. This is our home. We must defend it. Protect it. Masato would desecrate it. Burn the temples down and cover them with the ashes of the graveyard. Soak the ground with blood that will never wash clean."

Kayoku believed him. Masato was corrupt. It wasn't just his Buddhism that drove him.

"Then what will you do?" Kayoku asked again.

"I will stay. And fight," Norihiko announced with finality.

And die, Kayoku didn't add out loud.

She still heard the words echoing loudly through the room.

Priestess Ayumi came back in the room after Norihiko left. She brought sweet candles to help burn off the smell of Kayoku's illness, as well as scented sachets to place around the room. None of the windows faced outside, of course, but Kayoku wished that she could smell the pines of the forest.

The priestess was in her usual brown robes again, her hair tightly pulled back. Her face had paled—she hadn't been spending very much time in the sun. Plus, dark lines marred the skin under her eyes.

"How are you, mistress?" Priestess Ayumi asked as she helped Kayoku sit up to sip the broth she'd brought. Kayoku's own robes were the inner type, made from the softest cotton, a pale pink, supposed to cheer her up, she supposed.

"I'm fine," Kayoku lied. The pain in her side took her breath away when she moved.

"You're not," the priestess replied. "You've been poisoned. And it may be beyond my prayers to heal you."

"Poisoned?" Kayoku asked, shocked. "But it was just a knife wound—"

Priestess Ayumi nodded. "A knife that was dipped in the foulest dirt and ash imaginable. I've never seen a wound like it before."

Kayoku nodded. The black scythe that Hikaru had wielded hadn't been normal, or natural. It had been magic.

If only the second wife hadn't come into their lives!

With a sigh, Kayoku put aside such wishes. Dreams like that had never been useful. Or practical.

There still had to be something Kayoku could do to help heal herself. "Should we clean the wound again?" she asked.

"We can try," Priestess Ayumi said. "I've been hesitant, though. Even when you were unconscious, even touching the edges of the wound caused you great pain."

"I can bear it," Kayoku said through gritted teeth. She'd gone through childbirth. It couldn't be much worse than that, could it?

The pain was much, *much* worse than anything Kayoku had ever experienced. It didn't just touch her body, though it took away her breath as even the slightest touch by Priestess Ayumi cut into her side. It also wrapped her soul in misery, as if gray clouds and dark nights poured into her very being, denying any sunshine or light—as if she'd never see another spring day, or enjoy another blooming cherry tree.

Kayoku cried out when Priestess Ayumi touched her side again, despite her attempts to stay quiet. She didn't want to disturb the household.

"It's much worse, my lady," Priestess Ayumi said quietly. "It's spreading."

Kayoku remembered her dreams of blackness spreading out from her side. When she looked down, she saw her nightmares made real: a web of black spidery veins extended from the gaping wound along her side. They followed along the lines of her ribs, growing like poisoned ivy. She couldn't see them trailing across her back, but she had no doubt they were there.

"The wound doesn't bleed much, which is fortunate," Priestess Ayumi said. She held up the cloth in her hand mutely.

Kayoku nodded, then bit her lips together, hard, to prevent herself from crying out again as the Priestess wiped at the blood trickling down her skin.

The stench from her wound didn't surprise Kayoku. She knew it was foul and infected. It reminded her of the stories she'd heard from the generals, about the bloated, non-dead men they'd fought in Masato's army.

Without warning, Kayoku's stomach heaved. Fortunately, the priestess was prepared and had a bowl ready for her.

"You need to keep something down," Priestess Ayumi said after Kayoku finished. "You've barely been able to keep down water."

Kayoku blinked, puzzled, a thought pushing itself past her illness and pain. "How long…how long have I been unconscious?" she managed to ask.

"Three days," Priestess Ayumi replied. "You won't last another three."

Kayoku nodded. "I see." She'd been planning on taking her own life, rather than be part of Masato's household.

Now, she wouldn't have to rely on the *yama no gekkeiju* to go walk in the lands of the eternal cherry blossoms.

Kayoku would have laughed at the irony of it. That she'd finally found a will to be back in the world, only to have the possibility taken away from her.

Then the priestess pressed hard against her wound. Kayoku gasped and shuddered again, surrendering as darkness overtook her, and she floated in dreams again.

When Kayoku woke the next time, Norihiko was there again. He appeared to be meditating, his eyes unfocused, looking out into the distance, not seeing the room, the plain wooden walls, the simple altar in the corner dedicated to the *kami* of the mountain, the carved, wooden cabinet that contained her robes, the finely lacquered boxes that held her jewelry and hair pins.

He had such a strong profile. As if it was made from stone. He sat inhumanly still. He might no longer be a sword, and maybe he wasn't a fox fairy, but he was more than just a man. He wore another of Iwao's robes. It wasn't stretched out across the shoulders, but Kayoku was still aware that Norihiko filled Iwao's robes nicely.

"You're awake," Norihiko said, his voice gravelly, as if he hadn't spoken in some time. He still didn't move or look toward her, just sat incredibly motionless.

"I am," Kayoku said. She found she could take a deeper breath than the last time she'd woken.

She didn't believe for a moment that she was better. Rather that the wound had seeped deeper, was no longer crawling across her skin but had gone into her bones. She'd start creaking, soon, when she walked.

"I would like to protect you," Norihiko said without warning.

"Really?" Kayoku asked. Though he'd said that before, she hadn't believed him.

Norihiko nodded. "You. The estate. The mountain. But how?"

Kayoku gave a bitter laugh. "Defeat Masato. And all those who come after him."

"I will try," Norihiko said. "He considers the estate his. But the gates are locked to him. He hasn't been seen, though his army is still gathered in the next valley."

"He'll attack again. He already believes this property is his own, that he's won," Kayoku warned. And legally, perhaps, he was correct. Iwao had lost.

"I'll fight him. Defeat him," Norihiko said.

"How?" Kayoku asked. "His armies outnumber ours. His men aren't human. He has magic and luck on his side."

"But I have the strength of the mountain," Norihiko declared.

"Talk with Hikaru," Kayoku advised. "See if you can get her to help."

Norihiko shook his head. "Never. She's an evil influence. She needs to go."

Kayoku hesitated. On the one hand, she'd wished Hikaru gone so many times, away from the estate, off the mountain and out of their lives.

On the other hand, Hikaru *did* have magic. And Kayoku was starting to believe that though, hollowing her out more than grief.

"I'll go fetch the priestess," Norihiko said, grimacing.

"What's the matter?" Kayoku said, ever the peacemaker.

"It was difficult to convince her that I needed to see you alone," Norihiko admitted. "I lied to her. Said I was a cousin. Your uncle's son."

Kayoku had to admit that was an elegant solution. It would explain Norihiko's attachment to her, as well as allow him to see her without another woman present. "We'll stick with that story," Kayoku said.

Norihiko started to rise, then turned back to her, caught her hand. "You must get well," he said fervently. "You must help me defend the mountain."

Kayoku surprised herself. She was able to give him a cheery laugh. "Of course I will," she told him, though she didn't believe it herself. "I won't leave you alone."

"Thank you," Norihiko said. "You're my only connection to *him*."

After Norihiko left, Kayoku pondered his attachment to her, to Iwao, to the mountain. It was deeper than the springtime vows spoken before the Emperor, more serious and heartfelt. With roots as deep as the mountain itself.

And in the end, as fleeting as a summer storm.

They would all pass. Just the mountain would remain.

"You're dying," Priestess Ayumi said as she helped Kayoku sit down on the bench in Lord Taiga's garden.

"I know," Kayoku said, trying to catch her breath. But she had to go outside. She wore three robes—two inner robes and one dull gray outer robe—and she still shivered in the sunshine.

Normally, Kayoku spent all of her time inside, like a good wife. However, she'd felt such a longing to be in the garden, at least one last time.

She hadn't understood why Lord Taiga had spent his last few days sitting in his garden. It wasn't even a tame place. The flowers overgrew each other, fighting for the sunlight. Large rocks tumbled together, looking as though they'd been spilled over the small hill instead of carefully placed. Dwarf pines grew along the walkway, their stunted branches forcing people to walk a path that twisted.

Now, with the pain so deep inside her bones, Kayoku understood the comfort of such an alien place. It was timeless in a way that even the mountain wasn't. Nature would always be there, a reminder of where they had come from.

Where she was going.

Kayoku sat and meditated among the tumbled rocks. Her servants rested just a little ways off, ready to leap to her aid if she needed anything.

She'd been surprised at how they'd tried to comfort her. Maybe they were just afraid of who would be their new mistress. Or perhaps they'd really miss her.

It didn't matter. Kayoku pulled the clean air deep into her lungs. If she knew how to fight the spreading poison, she would. Priestess Ayumi had tried every herb she'd ever heard about to try to cure Kayoku, potions and tinctures and ointments, too.

It had only been a day. But nothing had worked. The poison continued to spread.

Kayoku still hid how badly injured she was from Norihiko. He didn't need to know. He wasn't really family. Only Priestess Ayumi knew.

When Chieko wandered down the path, Kayoku wondered who had betrayed her. Had one of her servants mentioned casually to another that she would be outside? She'd managed to successfully avoid all the other wives for the last three days.

However, Chieko certainly acted surprised when she saw Kayoku. "I'm so sorry," were the first words that rushed out of her mouth as she approached. "No one comes here. Not since Lord Taiga passed."

"I am the one who is sorry," Kayoku said. "I didn't mean to disturb your peace."

Chieko gave her a rueful smile. "So, we can both be miserable and sorry, or we can sit and enjoy the afternoon and the last blessing of the sunlight. What do you say?"

Kayoku didn't want anyone near her. But it would be rude to turn Chieko, who had been the eldest wife and the most respected, the one in charge of the entire household, until Iwao had been declared Taiko's official heir, catapulting Kayoku into the position.

"I would love for you to join me," Kayoku said graciously. She merely had to look up before her servants were scurrying away to bring more pillows, blankets, and tea for the lady.

"You look lovely today," Kayoku told Chieko. And she did. Her white hair gleamed silver in the outdoor light. Red touched her cheeks, and the smile she wore made her face blossom. She wore a lovely sky-blue robe, embroidered with silver peaches.

"If I may be blunt, you don't," Chieko said, looking critically at Kayoku.

Kayoku opened her mouth in shock, then closed it again. What could she say?

"You've been ill ever since you had to spend time with Masato," Chieko said. "Is there anything I, or any of the other women, can do to help?"

Kayoku wondered again who had told Chieko that she would be in Lord Taiga's old garden. She also realized that was the only explanation the other wives would have for her behavior: She'd gone to see Masato as he had demanded, then had fallen ill.

They didn't know about Hikaru being a fox fairy. Or Norihiko. Or anything.

"There's nothing you can do to help," Kayoku said truthfully. "Except to pray."

She wasn't about to try to explain it all to Chieko. How would the other woman believe her? It was too fantastic a story: That a female fox fairy's mate had been killed, his soul stolen, and reforged into a sword. That Lord Taiga had bought the sword, probably with his own soul. That the sword had caused Iwao's death, and now that Hikaru had freed her mate's soul, she was going to leave?

It was too fantastic a tale. Kayoku only half believed it herself.

No, it was better for the other wives to believe that Masato had cast such illness upon her. That when Kayoku died, the fault would be laid at his feet.

They wouldn't be made to serve him, not as she had been ordered to.

And like her, they also had access to the herb lore of the priestess, and could choose to walk the eternal lands instead of serving Masato, as she once had.

But Kayoku didn't want to die. Not anymore.

However, there was nothing for her but prayers. Nothing she could do to heal herself. She'd fight, every day. To make every day count. Regardless of how useless it was.

Including her last.

Two

What Did One Do

Norihiko

What did one do with arms?

Norihiko contemplated the issue while he sat in the early morning light in Iwao's rooms, waiting for Priestess Ayumi. The estate had woken up around him, servants shuffling off to do their duties, generals still debating their latest strategies, the very few children remaining giggling at nothing, everything.

But still. What did one do with arms?

Norihiko liked his legs. He liked being able to propel himself forward, not to have to rely on a wielder to direct his path. Feeling the earth beneath his toes gave him a sense of power.

He was still learning different odors—the sourness of Kayoku's wound, the saltiness of his own sweat, the sweetness of the flowers Priestess Ayumi always handled. The mustiness of the wood in Iwao's rooms, that he'd claimed for his own. The fading masculine scent of Iwao.

As a sword, Norihiko had always been able to hear. Now, it wasn't as though he heard more, but rather, that he could listen and remember more of what he heard.

However, he'd quickly discovered that people talked incessantly. Usually about things of little consequence. As a sword, he'd been better at ignoring them. Now, he paid attention, or at least couldn't block them out.

But arms…He was never certain what to do with them. Particularly when he was walking. They would fall and swing by his side, but then they'd swing too much. When he sat, where should he put them? They got uncomfortable just hanging there. He liked being able to pick things up, to grasp and carry. His fingers were wonderfully articulated. His arms, though, still sometimes confused him.

As did the only part of his human body that was sword-like. It seemed to have a mind of its own, growing soft and hard without his will. He was aware of what to do with it. That seemed to come naturally to him.

But that one little piece of flesh had also betrayed Iwao. Other men seemed to be led by it as well. He vowed to never be driven by such needs.

Despite being human.

Norihiko stayed sitting, quiet, at rest, when Priestess Ayumi entered the room. He was aware of her, though he didn't turn his head to look at her. His ears told him that she still shuffled slightly, that her right hip continued to bother her. His nose told him that she'd recently seen Kayoku, and carried the scent of the younger woman's illness with her. It also told him that the priestess had tea, the sweet kind that he favored, that lingered in the back of his throat and warmed his blood.

He didn't have to touch her to know where she would most easily break. How vulnerable her knees and elbows were, how soft her side would be if he cut into her.

That was secret sword knowledge.

Norihiko knew the vulnerabilities of every person he met. It wasn't a human ability at all, but power that his hidden selves retained.

After the priestess had knelt down and let the quiet return to the morning, Norihiko turned to look at her. She looked tired. Between Masato's perplexing disappearance and Kayoku's illness, Priestess Ayumi didn't have as much time to tend to herself. He knew that while the household treated her like a young woman, maybe in her thirties, she was much, much older, probably twice that age. But she kept her hair carefully dyed, used special herbs for her skin. She didn't want the veneration of the youngsters. She wanted to work, and keep working. To continue to be of service. Not put to the side.

Norihiko would happily keep her secrets. She kept his.

"How is Kayoku this morning?" Norihiko asked after Priestess Ayumi poured the tea and served him.

"She says she's better," Priestess Ayumi told him truthfully.

Norihiko felt as though he was still learning the subtleties of human speech, but he thought he grasped this one. "Says is not the same as is, correct?" he asked bluntly.

Priestess Ayumi sighed. "Possibly. Probably."

"How do we make her better?" Norihiko asked. "How do we heal her wound?" That was the one thing Norihiko felt he owed Iwao, personally. His Maker had aligned him with protecting the mountain. But Iwao had cherished Kayoku. He'd also dedicated himself to the mountain, but in part so that he could make it safe for her.

"I'm trying everything I know," Priestess Ayumi assured him. "But…"

"But?" Norihiko prompted her when she didn't continue.

"This illness may be beyond my skill. Any human skill."

Norihiko paused to consider the implications of that.

Hikaru. She'd been the one who injured Kayoku. He didn't like Hikaru. She confused him. She also claimed they'd once been mated, married. She'd freed him. But he still didn't like her.

Hikaru had magic. Skill that went beyond human.

"Has Hikaru tried to cure Kayoku yet?" Norihiko asked.

"She says she can't," Priestess Ayumi said with a sigh.

"Hikaru was the one who caused Kayoku's wound. She should be the one to fix it," Norihiko said firmly. Or at least try.

"It may not be as easy as that," Priestess Ayumi warned.

"I will make her," Norihiko promised. If they truly had once been mated, then she should do this for him.

Priestess Ayumi shook her head but smiled. "You can try. I'm not sure that anyone can get her to do something she doesn't want to do."

"She will cure Kayoku. For me," Norihiko assured the priestess.

Because despite her magic, Hikaru had weak points too. Soft places that a sword could bite into. Places she wasn't aware of, but Norihiko and the others still knew.

Norihiko didn't bother to request an audience with Hikaru, though some sense of propriety told him he should. Instead, he walked directly to her rooms. The hallways in this part of the woman's quarters were wider, more open. He smelled fresh air and summer winds floating in. Like every other hall on the estate, the hallways were immaculately clean, with no spiderwebs hanging in the corners, no dust along the inner walls, no dirt on the polished wooden floors.

It could have been attributed to magic, but Norihiko had seen how hard the servants worked. It wasn't something he was supposed to notice. The humans complained about how lazy the servants were, all the time. And certainly some were.

But they lived here, at the estate, too. This was their home. Most took great pride in it.

Finally, an older woman came out into the hallway where Norihiko stood, his arms at his side, listening to his heartbeat in his fingertips. She looked at him strangely. She was human—mostly. She had some slight magics, things she'd picked up over her long life. She had a long face, almost horselike, with hair streaked with gray.

"My mistress will see you now," she told him. She looked at him curiously.

Had he known her, before? He must have, if she'd been a servant of Hikaru's. But he didn't know her now.

"Thank you," he told her kindly. She was one of the good ones, the servants who worked more than any realized.

Hikaru sat in her front rooms. Norihiko couldn't help but be captivated by her. She was loveliness personified, with a perfectly round face, an upturned nose that looked perfect for kisses, tender lips and glossy black hair. Her robes were golden that morning, embroidered with rust-colored maple leaves.

That part of himself that Norihiko couldn't quite control stirred. But he would not give in, would not be attracted to her.

She'd hurt Kayoku. She must be made to fix her mistake.

And she must go. Far away. So that she wouldn't confuse Norihiko any longer.

"Should I refer to you as *Raijim* the thunder god this morning, my lord?" Hikaru asked, mischief all through her tone.

Norihiko shrugged, uncomfortable. He knew she was teasing. He wasn't certain why. He didn't look like the old thunderer, did he? He didn't have a long white beard or an angry god face.

Possibly his expression did convey his anger, though. How uncomfortable she made him feel.

Maybe that was another part of his frail human body that he couldn't control.

"You must cure Kayoku," Norihiko told Hikaru bluntly. He didn't sit down on the pillows she'd arranged for him, but remained standing, his head far above hers.

"I can't," Hikaru told him softly.

"She was injured by magic. *Your* magic," Norihiko pointed out. Why couldn't she see that? Why did she refuse?

"I know," Hikaru said. "And I'm sorry. So very, very sorry. But if I tried to cure her right now—I'd end up making her more sick."

"Why?" Norihiko asked. That didn't make any sense to him. "Your kind can heal, can't they?"

Norihiko tried to keep his face still and not smile at the pain that chased across Hikaru's face at the mention of her kind, how he wasn't like her. He was human, and proud of it.

There was still a part of him, one of his many selves that he still carried inside, that didn't like causing her pain. But that singular, small voice was easily drowned out by the others.

She'd caused so much suffering in others. All the people of the estate by killing Iwao. She'd endangered the mountain, Norihiko's main charge. And now she'd injured the one who had done the most to hold the people together, now that their leader was gone.

She had to go. Despite the confusing images of a pine branch with tiny pinecones clinging to it, how the scent of pine made him long for her.

"My magic has been corrupted," Hikaru admitted to him. "When Masato…never mind. It's no longer reliable."

"Then clean it," Norihiko snapped. He remembered Masato. He despised the man, as much as Hikaru.

"Don't you think I've tried?" Hikaru snapped at him. Her eyes flashed with anger. Her beauty remained, despite her mounting fury.

Or perhaps because of it.

"I've tried everything I know. I've reached out to my family. No one knows how to purify my magic again. No one has ever had their magic corrupted like this before," Hikaru told him. Her hands moved restlessly at her side, as if she wanted to sketch something in the air, but wouldn't allow herself to.

"So your magic is dangerous," Norihiko said.

Hikaru slowly nodded. "I can control it," she told him.

Was she lying?

Did it matter?

"You need to leave," Norihiko told her. "You're a threat to the estate and this household."

Hikaru erupted in a bitter laugh. "You can't make me, you know."

"But you'll go anyway," Norihiko assured her. "You must. You need to find a cure for Kayoku."

"She's all that matters to you, isn't she?" Hikaru asked.

The bitterness in her voice was almost sweet to Norihiko.

"She isn't, actually," Norihiko answered honestly. "The mountain…the mountain still needs to be defended." While Kayoku mattered, she didn't confuse him or attract him, not like Hikaru.

Norihiko wanted to blame all of his attraction to Hikaru on her magic, but he wouldn't lie to himself. Not about that. The woman inside her pride and beauty drew him, whether he wanted to admit it or not.

"I can't compete with a mountain," Hikaru said.

Was she teasing him again? It sounded as if she was. He couldn't allow himself to care.

"Can you control your magic?" Norihiko asked directly.

Hikaru sighed. "It isn't as simple as that," she replied.

At least she hadn't lied to him. "Why not?"

"Magic is who I am!" Hikaru complained. Again her hands raised and she abruptly lowered them, clenching her hand into fists on her thighs. "I live and breathe magic. It's as much a part of me as my skin or my hair. It flows in my blood. It isn't a matter of controlling it, as much as making sure that it's directed correctly."

Norihiko almost understood. He felt as though he stood on the cusp of knowledge, as if he, too, once had magic. As if directing that flow was like channeling a wind through a funnel, or directing a spring brook through a garden….

It was possible to do. But very, very difficult.

"Are you a danger to this estate?" Norihiko asked, though he already knew the answer. She was a danger. She'd already proven that.

Now, with her corrupted magic, she was even more so.

"No more and no less than before," Hikaru declared.

She had to be lying.

"I still want you gone," Norihiko said. "Away from here."

Hikaru took a deep breath as if to argue with him, then let it out with a hiss. "I need to find a way to purify my magic," she said softly. Then she glared up at him. "I will return when I have."

"Good," Norihiko said, though it wasn't good at all. "Then you must cure Kayoku. And help me defend the estate. Keep the mountain out of Masato's hands."

Hikaru blinked but she didn't agree. "I will cure Kayoku. When I can. But I don't know about anything else."

"Why not?" Norihiko asked, startled. She wanted to do this for him, right?"

"You know why," Hikaru stated plainly. "Seeing you—like this, not the real you—is too painful."

The ache in Hikaru's voice troubled Norihiko. This pain—this was too much. It wasn't something that she'd overcome quickly.

For the first time, Norihiko tried to look at Hikaru, to really see her.

She looked at tired as Priestess Ayumi. And possibly as old.

"Fix your magic," Norihiko said quietly. "Then come back. We can… talk."

Norihiko turned and left the room without saying goodbye. He didn't know what else to say.

He didn't want to talk with Hikaru. To listen to her soft voice. To feel the attraction he felt.

But if she cured Kayoku, he would spend some time with her.

He owed her at least that.

Norihiko was grateful again for the lies that Priestess Ayumi had told the household, and in particular, the generals, that he was Kayoku's close cousin. That meant that in the afternoon, when the generals met, he could join them. Not so that he could report to Kayoku, but because he could claim to be part of the household, or at least close enough that they'd allow him.

The generals met in the formal greeting hall, near the front of the estate. Fancy lattice screens lined the room, but weren't set up this time so that others could hear them without being seen. Bare wooden beams ran the length of the hall, dividing the room from its steeply sloped ceiling. Poems dedicated to the mountain, and to the Kitayama family, still hung on the wall, though Norihiko could tell they weren't the finest quality—those had probably been packed away when Masato had first won the battle.

The generals didn't sit in any kind of strict order, at least not as far as Norihiko could tell. Only eight remained, when there had at one time been two dozen.

Had they left the estate? Or did they now walk in the eternal lands?

General Asheihi called them all to order. He was the oldest of them, and had served under Lord Taiga for many years. He wore his silver hair shaved short, like a monk's, and the plainest of brown robes. Wind had etched lines in his hard face, and his eyes still squinted, as if he always stared at the sun.

"There is no word yet from Masato. His own generals don't know what to do. His men are still camped on the slopes of the far eastern hill, though fewer every day—they seem to have a problem with deserters."

This brought chuckles to the entire group. Did they have to deal with deserters themselves? Or was there another reason for their amusement? Did men regularly leave Masato's army? There was still so much Norihiko didn't know.

"Many of our own men have returned to their farms. What else can they do? It's summer, and the harvest must be brought in. Or the winter will be very bad," the general warned.

Norihiko agreed with the other generals that this was the right course of action. They could always gather the farmers up again if they needed to.

The estate couldn't afford a large standing army, though the top ranks were all dedicated soldiers.

"Until there is news from Masato, we're at a standstill," General Asheihi warned.

"Why?" Norihiko asked when it seemed as though the rest of the generals accepted this. He truly wanted to understand.

"Masato is our new lord," General Asheihi told Norihiko gently, as if he were a child.

Norihiko didn't mind. In many ways, he was still like a child, learning his way through the world.

"But he isn't here, at the estate," Norihiko pointed out. "We could lock the gates. Keep him at bay."

None of the men Norihiko could see nodded. He still knew they agreed. Masato wasn't here. Why should they let him in?

"In the formal declaration of war that was issued by Masato and agreed to by Iwao, he now has control of the estate. Because he killed Iwao," General Asheihi pointed out.

"We could still fight him," Norihiko said.

"To what end?" General Kenika asked. "His men cover the mountain like ants. Even if many have left. He can still raise more than we ever will."

"Is it as hopeless as that?" Norihiko challenged. "You all have brilliant minds. Are born soldiers. You just have to fight—"

"And what if the Emperor disagrees?" General Kanika interrupted. "The way of the law—"

"Has Masato always followed the law? The natural laws?" Norihiko asked. "His army is unnatural. You all know that."

More than one general grew pale, remembering. They hadn't known what exactly they had been fighting, but they'd known they weren't regular men.

Norihiko knew, though. As a sword, he'd tasted their flesh. Analyzed it. "They're powered by charms. And magic," he stated bluntly.

A sigh swept through the room, as if Norihiko was finally speaking out loud what they'd all been thinking.

"Do you know how to kill them?" General Asheihi asked.

"Of course," Norihiko said, surprised. He'd thought the generals would have figured out the trick. "They're powered at their core, here," he said, pointing to the center of his belly. "There are three characters carved there. Disturb the center one. Mar it, or disfigure it. They'll lose power."

"They're all heavily armored through their midsection," another general pointed out.

"Exactly," Norihiko said. "To protect them from losing their advantage. You can chop off a limb and they'll keep fighting, even after the blood loss should have stopped them."

More generals nodded at that.

"But if you can get in one good belly thrust, they'll keel over," Norihiko promised them.

"How do you know?" General Kenika asked.

"I fought them, with Kayoku's father," Norihiko lied. "On the far side of the mountain."

The generals nodded and seemed to buy his lie. Norihiko again sent quick prayers of thanks to the quick-thinking Priestess Ayumi for providing him with a plausible story.

"But you didn't win," General Asheihi pointed out.

"Our generals lost their nerve," Norihiko said brazenly. "You don't have to lose. We can win."

Would the generals believe him? It would be so much easier for Norihiko to fight Masato with them backing him up.

One of the other generals said, "What do you know of fighting?"

Norihiko heard the doubt in his voice, could feel it creeping around the room, like a hidden rat. He stood and walked over to General Asheihi. "Your greatest weakness is your left side. Your right arm is overdeveloped. You need to stretch, to twist more, so your left side is better defended."

The general sitting next to Asheihi nodded. "He speaks the truth, old friend."

Asheihi shook his head, but didn't say anything. Norihiko moved onto General Kenika. "You have a formidable form," he told the smaller man. "Your swordplay is poetry to watch. But you don't move your feet enough. You're like a tree, powerful and massive, but vulnerable to great winds. You'll be blown over, sooner or later."

"Didn't I just tell you the same thing last week?" one of the other generals said, ribbing Kenika.

Norihiko felt the change in the room. The generals wouldn't follow him. Not yet. He still had to prove himself. He turned and walked over to a third general. "And you—"

A servant burst into the room. "Excuse me. I'm so sorry. Please, forgive me," the man said, over and over.

General Asheihi looked as though he could barely contain his outburst, but he managed to keep a civil tongue. "Before we behead you, you might as well tell us your message."

The servant gulped and paled further. "Lady Kayoku—she's dying." He turned to face Norihiko. "You must attend her. Now."

Without waiting to hear anything else the generals might say, Norihiko rushed from the room.

He would fight Masato with or without them. But he needed the heart of the mountain to keep fighting, too.

Kayoku had to get well.

The stench of Kayoku's wound made Norihiko wrinkle his nose, as if he could block the smell. She had gotten much worse, over the course of hours, not days. Priestess Ayumi had placed many sachets of sweetened *jinko* wood, and burned sweet candles as well, but they couldn't overcome the smell.

The room itself was dark. No windows faced the outside. Norihiko suddenly wished he could gather Kayoku up and take her out into the woods, to lay on a bed of fresh pine needles. He shook his head, confused. Had he done that with another lady in the past? The feeling of holding her in his arms made his entire soul ache.

"You came," Kayoku said. She wheezed, sounding much older than she was.

"Of course I did," Norihiko said softly. He automatically reached for the cloth covering Kayoku's forehead, dipping it in the bowl of cool water on the floor beside her, then gently returning it to her head.

"You must get better," Norihiko told Kayoku.

"I'm trying," Kayoku said. She coughed again.

Norihiko didn't like how it sounded. It wasn't a death rattle, not yet, but it had echoes of it.

"They said you were dying," Norihiko said, scolding Kayoku. "You shouldn't scare us all that way."

"But I am dying," Kayoku said weakly.

"You are not," Norihiko said fiercely. "You must get better. He…he would have insisted on it."

"He?" Kayoku asked.

"Iwao," Norihiko told her. He gently encased one of her hands in his. It was like holding onto a hot bag of coals. "He loved you, you know."

Kayoku shook her head.

"He did," Norihiko told her. "He did everything for you, my lady. He didn't care about his inheritance, about defending the mountain, as much as making it safe for *you*."

Tears started rolling down Kayoku's cheeks. "Is it true?" she whispered, her voice cracking.

"He wrote poems for you. Whispered them to me at night," Norihiko confessed. "Thought of you even when he needed to be working with me. I wasn't jealous of you. I pledged to defend you as well." He wiped away the tears from her cheeks. "So you must get better."

"I have been fighting it," Kayoku promised. "It's just that I'm so tired."

"Fight a little longer," Norihiko said. "I will find you a cure."

He left Kayoku sleeping peacefully. He knew he didn't have much time.

Without heed, Norihiko marched directly to Hikaru's rooms. She *had* to do something. Had to have some sort of magic that would at least halt the progress of Kayoku's demise.

No servants waited outside Hikaru's room. The *shoji* stood open. Nothing remained of Hikaru in the room either, not a poem or a single ribbon. Even her scent had been swept away.

She had said she'd leave. Figure out how to purify her magic. Then come back.

Norihiko felt a flush of shame, how he'd hounded her already.

Then his back grew more straight. She didn't know how serious the matter was. He was going to have to go after her. Make her understand that she was needed more than ever.

Not that he needed her. But that she had to use her magic to help them. Or else.

Three

Summer Rains Give Way

Hikaru

*Summer rains give way
To cold winds, fading hope
Drowns even mountains*

I didn't think I had any more tears left after mourning for my love. For what had become of Norihiko and me.

I was wrong.

There was nothing for me here in these cold, human rooms. I longed for the wild places that only the *kitsune* could find. I couldn't stay here. I'd made too many mistakes. Kayoku would die soon and it would be my fault. The mountain would be overrun by Masato and his Buddhists, striving to push out the *kami* and the *kitsune*.

I shuddered to think of him, his foul breath, how I'd let him touch me.

I needed to go somewhere else. Start anew.

I called for my sisters, but they hadn't returned.

Even they had abandoned me. Or maybe my powers were so corrupt they didn't recognize my call. Or perhaps this was what Estu had seen in her prophecy, the time when I'd no longer be able to travel with my sisters.

I had Yukiko pack my robes, my jewels, even my hair combs. Other servants stripped the room bare of the poems and pillows that had made the outer rooms tolerable. They packed everything in boxes and I sent them along, not caring if I would catch up or not.

I carried all the possessions that mattered to me: Seiji's empty scabbard, that had once held so much hope, my mother's amulet that had saved my life, that I still wore, and a tiny hand mirror that I'd found, that Norihiko had once given me.

The rest of my life was in tatters. I would rend my clothes to match.

I knew better than to think about walking in the eternal lands. Even if I'd had the energy to take my own life, I had no idea how my corrupted powers would act. Would they escape and haunt the place where I passed, causing all who entered there grief? Or would they suck at my soul and hold it so that I could never die, though never live, either?

I had to find a way to purify myself. Even the most extreme of the human rituals—fasting, bathing in vinegar, and bloodletting—merely punished the flesh. They didn't clean something as fundamental as the force that animated them.

Finally, we were ready to leave. Just Yukiko and I, traveling as we had after the death of Norihiko and our traveling party. It wasn't safe to travel this way. I didn't care.

Yukiko had done as I'd asked, though, and gotten us a plain farmer's cart and oxen. We would be slow. I would hide us with my magic, if I could.

The summer day was overcast, and I could feel the chill of autumn on the winds. Or maybe that was just me. Yukiko sat stubbornly beside me, her lips pressed tightly together.

The silence between us as grew too oppressive, even for me to ignore. "What is it?" I asked Yukiko. My voice was rough from all the tears I'd shed, still shed.

"You need to find your sisters," Yukiko told me firmly.

"I've called—"

"They won't recognize you," she said. "I barely recognize you."

I turned to look at her, astonished. Yukiko didn't have any magic. She was mostly human. She should have seen what everyone else saw. Then I reached up and touched my face. "Have I changed that much?"

"Not like that," Yukiko said, exacerbated. "Your spirit. The light that shines through your eyes. It's changed." She didn't look at me, but continued to face the road. "It's…unclean."

I shivered at that. Anger finally broke through my sorrow. How dare Masato do this to my powers? Though I knew it wasn't just him, but Junichi as well. It had to be the pair of them that had corrupted me.

How to clean the stench of death from what was once wildness and purity?

My mother would know, if I couldn't find my sisters along the way.

The road down the mountain wasn't wide, or even a proper road. It wasn't much more than ruts across the tall grass. It wound, turning back on itself often, as we descended.

Normally, we would have had to go along the side to get around the slower travelers, or wait on the side ourselves when larger, faster groups went by. But no one else traveled that morning.

I didn't know if that was because of the war—if there were fewer people on the mountain, or if everyone was just busy that morning.

We stopped to rest at an open meadow, with trees ringing the edges. Just beyond, the road dipped down again. The sun had dyed the grass blond. Butterflies danced across the bobbing leaves, birds sang in the trees just beyond, and yet, it all seemed barren and dead to me.

The sound of galloping hooves coming from behind us made my heart leap. Was it Norihiko? Had he finally remembered me? Was he coming to ask me to return?

I looked back, prepared to be disappointed.

It was Norihiko! He still sat so well on his horse as he came thundering up. I couldn't help but sigh.

However, I'd also grown wary of him. I wouldn't say wise. He didn't look happy to see me. He wasn't going to beg me to return.

He still didn't remember me, still couldn't look at me with love in his eyes.

I braced myself.

"You need to come back."

I could barely breathe when he said those words to me. Had I heard him correctly?

"You want me to return?" I asked. I cursed how breathless my voice sounded.

"You must come back. You must cure Kayoku," he instructed me.

I couldn't help myself. I laughed at him. Long and hard.

It was either that, or start crying again.

"I *cannot*," I told him. "You don't understand. If I tried to cure her, I'd *kill* her."

"Make me understand," Norihiko challenged.

"Fine," I said, getting down off the cart.

"Lady," Yukiko warned.

I waved her away. "Go. And keep going."

Yukiko stared at me for a long moment, her face as expressionless as granite. Finally, she nodded. "Don't burn down the mountain," she warned before she clicked her tongue and flicked the reins, starting the oxen moving again.

I looked around the field surrounding us. "Do you remember the first magic trick you were taught?"

Before Norihiko could answer, I replied for him. "Of course you don't! You're merely human, after all." I knew it was my fault that the spell hadn't worked as Etsu had crafted it, that it was my magic that had failed, but I was still angry about it.

"It was a protection spell. How to make a nest, someplace safe to hide," I told him. "It's the most fundamental spell for our people." Though Norihiko wasn't human, I still wanted him to feel some pride in the *kitsune*.

"Watch what happens when I try to make a nest," I told him. I pointed to a spot several feet away from me. "Stand there."

Norihiko stubbornly walked closer to me, to stand beside me while I tried to do the simplest of spells.

I shrugged. "It's your clothes," I told him.

I honestly didn't know what would happen. I suspected the worst, though. That instead of a warm soft spot in the center of the field, with the grass beaten down in a perfect oval, exactly the right size for a fox to curl up in, I would end up with a burned, scorched patch of earth.

I reached out my hand and waved my palm over the grass. I spoke the words of the *making*. It didn't take much, just an easy *push* of power.

The earth under my hand erupted, spewing dirt over both of us. We both fell back as bones asserted themselves, gathering above the earth where they'd been buried. Not just human bones, but rat bones, rabbit bones, cat and dog bones, bones of horses and mules and everything that had ever been buried around us probably for *li*.

I pushed Norihiko behind me, in case a chaotic skeleton of all the various bones came alive and attacked us.

But the bones settled onto the ground, lining the oval I'd created.

When they finished stirring, I had to give a bitter laugh. Instead of a nice, comfortable bed of grass, there was a perfectly formed bed of bones for me to lie in.

"Do you see now?" I asked Norihiko when I'd finished laughing. "Everything I touch turns to death. Even you."

"What do you mean?" Norihiko asked, taken aback.

"If you'd changed into a *kitsune* as you were supposed to," I explained, "you would have had an immortal's life. There's very little that can kill our— *my*—kind."

"You are more vulnerable than you think," Norihiko warned.

"The parts of me that are vulnerable are the parts you can no longer touch," I promised him. Though I would always love him, I was no longer willing to admit it. To allow any man to touch me.

"I could reach them," Norihiko boasted. He drew his sword.

I gasped. Maybe I had been living among the humans for too long, but his action seemed incredibly rude. A man did not just draw his sword in the presence of a lady. There were too many associations with that other part of a man's body that sometimes resembled a tiny sword.

"You still can't reach me," I told him.

Without warning, Norihiko attacked.

He was good. Better than any I'd ever seen, though I'd really only witnessed the one battle. Had it been only a week before?

But he was only human. His sword had no magic either. I danced away, moving quicker than a thought.

Norihiko pulled up, his face a curious mixture of astonishment and grudging admiration.

He'd honestly believed that I wouldn't be able to evade him.

Again, Norihiko leaped forward. Again, I avoided his blade.

At first, it was a close thing. But his patterns were easy to read. He no longer had the wildness of our kind. He was predictable, as only a human truly can be.

After a quarter of an hour, I tired of our dance and advanced on him without warning. I scratched his fine jacket, tearing at the threads, first across his bicep, then along his belly.

"You wouldn't last long if I used a real sword," I taunted Norihiko.

Instead of diving for me again, Norihiko pulled himself up straight. "I am one of the best swordsmen in Nifon," he said bluntly. "As Seiji, I learned everything there was about sword fighting."

I nodded, not surprised. What an advantage he'd have over anyone he fought!

Anyone who wasn't magical, that was.

"But I cannot fight you," he said softly.

My heart leaped in my chest. For the first time, Norihiko looked at me with something akin to kindness in his eyes.

"You're too wild," he said.

His disgust and hatred for me came flooding back.

"It isn't that I'm too wild," I told him. "It's that you're too straightforward. Being a sword changed you."

"Really?" Norihiko asked, his tone laced with amusement.

Pain stabbed my heart to hear that. If only he were *my* Norihiko! That teasing tone was far too familiar to me.

Maybe it was better that most of the time he talked with me, his voice was filled with disgust and rage.

"Sometimes guile, going around your target, not straight toward it, will win the day," I told him.

Norihiko snorted in disbelief.

I glided forward, dipping around him before appearing in front of him again, then lightly touched his chest.

Norihiko started and stepped back. "You are wrong," Norihiko said. "And if you were *human* you'd understand."

I stepped back, stung. "You assume I don't know what you're going through, or what you *are*." I nearly spat in disgust. "You know *nothing* about me. What I've gone through to get you back. The sacrifices I've made."

"You?" Norihiko asked, the derision in his voice clear.

"How do you think my powers got corrupted in the first place? I *gave them to Masato* so that I could take Seiji from him." I pressed forward. "I was human for a miserably long time. Then I let Masato touch me, *have* me, so that I could steal them back." I shook my head and pulled myself straight. "I've sacrificed everything for you. There is nothing more for me to give."

Norihiko nodded, thoughtful. "If what you say is true, then you have done many things to free me from the steel of my sword form. And I do thank you for that."

We both were quiet for a moment in the still of the afternoon, the sun beating down upon us.

If there was any justice in the world, at that moment, he would have remembered who I was. Would have taken me into his arms. I would have taken him as a human, accepted him, lived with him through his short human days.

Died a little with him each day as well.

But though he wasn't *my* Norihiko, he was still the stubborn Norihiko I'd always known. "I will still ask one more thing of you," he said quietly. "To purify your powers and come back to heal Kayoku. She doesn't have long."

Though I had bragged that he could no longer touch my heart, I had been lying to myself.

His request pierced me, through and through.

Iwao had loved Kayoku. It seemed that Norihiko did as well.

"I will try," I told him. "I owe Kayoku more than I can possibly say. But I can't guarantee that I'll return in time. My powers…"

"I know," Norihiko said. "Try."

He strode away, mounted his horse, then rode back to the estate.

If I could have, I would have created a nest, a safe place to stay, and curled up there to weep yet another river of tears.

But I couldn't. I would get my powers cleaned up. I would heal Kayoku if I could.

Then I would leave and never return.

The quiet clomping of hooves brought me out of myself. "Mistress?" Yukiko asked.

I shook my head at her. "Go to the inn. Spend the night there. I will come to you in the morning," I promised her.

Then I changed into fox form, something I hadn't done for what felt like years. It was an easy shape to fall into.

Too easy.

Yukiko gasped.

I wondered what my fox form now looked like. I still had merely four paws, a red coat, and a tail.

But claws stuck out of each foot. My fur was the color of newly born flame.

And when I licked my tongue over my teeth, I discovered fangs I'd never had before.

I wasn't merely a fox. No, I more closely resembled a true beast, something from nightmares.

It didn't matter, though. This was now my true form. And I had hunting to do.

Time to find my sisters.

Four

The Forest At Night

Masato

The forest at night was loud around Masato and Junichi, crouched behind a *sanzashi* thorn bush. Crickets called shrilly, frogs boasted in deep tones, and a constant wind clanked bamboo together in the grove to their right. A small clearing opened in front of them, covered in thick grass. Moonlight faltered, then failed, as clouds gathered across the sky. The rich smell of damp earth rose to greet them, full of promise.

Masato practiced his breathing, letting his senses expand to take in all of the night. He ignored how his knees cried out from being bent for so long, how his back hurt from sitting so still, how the echo of pain still laced his arms, despite how the skin had healed.

He would prove to Junichi that he was worthy. While at the same time, Junichi would prove his skill as a swordsmith.

The sword in Masato's hand—Fuko—hummed to itself, content. When Masato had bound himself to this length of steel, it had bound itself to him as well. No one else could wield the sword—it wouldn't allow it. It would work for one master alone.

Junichi had warned Masato that might be dangerous, that someone could take the sword away from him and use it against him.

Masato was willing to take the risk. The only one he knew with such power was Junichi himself. And while they might not always see eye-to-eye, Masato didn't think his old master would betray his former apprentice that way.

At least not yet.

Fuko vibrated in Masato's hand, the trembling moving up his arm.

His prey was near.

The creature that entered the clearing looked like a regular fox. The night darkened her coat, making it easier for her to slip in and out of shadows. She stepped cautiously, nosing in the dirt, looking for her own easy prey of field mice or rats. Her ears twitched and she stopped, looking up for a moment.

Masato held his breath, but the moment passed, and the *kitsune* continued her aimless search.

Stupid creature.

Soundlessly, Masato rose from where he'd been kneeling. Adrenaline coursed through his body, distancing all the minor aches that had been so distracting earlier.

Masato broke through the bush, charging into the clearing. The fox darted away but didn't leave the clearing, perhaps confused by the thorns that sprang up on the far side. It hissed like a goose at Masato, its hackles raised. It stayed low to the ground as it circled the clearing.

Fuko trembled in Masato's hand. Here was his prey. Masato matched the fox, circling the clearing, his sword raised high.

He'd asked Junichi for the ability to force a *kitsune* out of its fox form and into its human shape. However, Junichi had assured him he wouldn't need such an ability. The *kitsune* loved the sound of their own voices too much to stay in their animal form.

A young woman blossomed before Masato, tall and thin as spring bamboo. She wore a simple robe, off-white with no decoration. "What do you carry?" she asked warily as they kept circling.

She was beautiful, Masato decided, in that way that only her kind were.

A beauty that was a distraction. False. Keeping a man in the world, instead of reaching for the highest spiritual heights.

"Fuko," Masato said, introducing the blade. "He longs for the blood of your kind."

"It is evil," the woman insisted. She stopped. "You're evil."

The wave of magic that flowed across the clearing impressed Masato with its strength. The young woman was much older than she looked, and much stronger.

Fortunately, Fuko cut through her illusions. Masato felt them blow past him, like thick wads of cotton dissolving in a storm.

Masato laughed at her confusion, then neatly stepped in to attack. At first, the woman merely avoided his swings while scratching at him, throwing more ineffectual magic at him.

Of course, she didn't run. She had the arrogance of all her kind, thinking herself invincible.

And she did scratch Masato once, long claws down the length of his arm as she whirled away.

But he caught her soon after that, one hard stroke into her side, then a second, plunging the sword deep into her belly. The blood spurted like water from a fountain, merrily coating Masato's hands and face.

Smoke rose from Fuko as it burned the blood away, sucking the power into itself, then funneling that into Masato.

"Who are you?" the woman asked as she swayed, then fell onto her knees, her hands over her belly as if she could stop the flow of blood.

"The death of all your kind," Masato promised.

Masato rode into his camp the next morning, feeling victorious despite his exhaustion. He didn't remember the last time he'd slept through the night, his body still felt drained from the blood he'd "donated" to Junichi, and despite his best efforts, the stupid fox fairy from the night before had still managed to scratch him, giving him a nasty infected wound down his sword arm.

But he'd still beaten her, killed one of those who always boasted of being so hard to kill. Junichi had taken the bones to use for some spell that he'd tried explaining to Masato, but Masato had been too tired to listen to.

Fuko was his, and had worked wonderfully, both in the hunt as well as the kill. With this sword, Masato would surely win over the island of Nifon, and bring the Buddha here, get rid of the *kami* and *kitsune*. His vision of the Buddha stepping on this mountain was still clear.

The guards standing at the entrance to the camp barely glanced at Masato. He could have been anyone. And no one stopped him from riding his horse directly into the center of the group of tents.

Discipline had gotten far too lax. Did they think he'd never return? Or was it because his men had decided they'd won, and there was no reason to be on the lookout for spies?

What were they thinking?

The tents were in good repair, though. There wasn't a stench of sewage, at least not close by. But no one was drilling, sharpening their weapons, or repairing their armor. Instead, the faint smell of wine still lingered, and the camp had the air of being hung over.

Had he been gone that long? Of course, Masato hadn't announced that he was returning, so no one had prepared for his return, either.

A servant came scurrying up, ready to take his reins. Masato threw them at the boy, then slid from the horse with a sigh.

It seemed that no matter how much he paid his men, no matter what promises of reward or retribution, they required constant supervision.

Just beyond the ring of tents belonging to his generals stood Masato's own tent. It, at least, still had guards standing outside who looked sober and well rested. The tent itself—easily twice the size of any of the others—still appeared to be in good shape.

Then Masato's lead general stumbled out of Masato's tent, hastily tying his robes. From the disarray of his hair, Masato didn't have to come any closer to know the man reeked of alcohol and sex.

Masato shook his head as he walked forward. On the one hand, it was his fault. He'd been gone for far too long. His generals had forgotten everything. All that Masato was capable of.

On the other hand, really. The general should have known better.

If Junichi were there, he would be chortling, excited about the lives Masato was about take. Masato couldn't help but still feel tired. And curse the delay. It would be a few more days while he set order to his camp before he'd get back to Iwao's estate.

Masato rode angrily to the front of the line.

The scouts had been telling the truth. The long gate to the estate was closed to them. Trees had been cut down near the fence, making the estate more defendable. Well-armed guards stood in front of the iron and wood structure.

Iwao's generals had been busy.

A man Masato didn't know stood in front of the gate. He had an arrogant chin. His eyes bored into Masato. He stood without moving, as if he were a statue.

Fuko quivered once at Masato's side, then lay still.

This man wasn't a fox fairy. But his enemy was near.

The general who had already tried to remove the man from in front of the gate still lay to the side, bleeding. Along with the three other men. All of them would die soon, either from their wounds or Masato's hand.

He could, of course, just send archers to deal with the arrogant fool. But Masato had to show strength right now, show his men that he was still worthy.

"How dare you lock the gate to your rightful lord and master!" Masato thundered at the man.

"We do not recognize your claim," the man said, his voice echoing strangely, as if there were more than one of him speaking. "You are not the lord here. You have forfeited the estate through your inattention. It is mine, now."

Masato sat back on his horse, affronted. How dare this cur claim ownership of the estate?

"I am the rightful heir to Iwao," the man claimed. "You shall retreat."

How was that possible? Iwao didn't have an heir, had died childless.

Maybe he'd sired this cur in some dalliance. Masato sighed and shook his head, sliding down from his horse, taking Fuko out.

Again, the blade trembled in his hand. Where were the accursed fox fairies? It didn't matter. He'd come for them soon enough.

For the first time, the man smiled. "You, I won't kill. Not yet."

But the man didn't bother drawing his sword as Masato drew closer. "I won't make any such promises," Masato told him.

Only when Masato attacked did the man move. He drew his sword in one swift movement, so fast Masato couldn't tell he'd moved, just that one moment, Masato's blade was raised, and the next, it had been forced to the ground.

Fuko leaped up, drawing Masato forward, as if this man were a *kitsune*.

Masato held back, not giving the sword its head. He was the one in charge here.

The man didn't seem to notice as he pushed Masato back, step by step, away from the gate. Masato couldn't attack again. He was forced to defend himself.

"Is that the best you can do?" Masato taunted. He had to find some sort of advantage here. Perhaps he could make the man angry.

Instead, though, the man laughed. "You are no more important than a buzzing insect. And just as annoying." He pressed his advantage, making Masato back up another three steps.

Masato risked a glance behind him. In just a few more steps, he'd be backed up to the edge of the woods.

Fuko quivered again in his hands. Masato didn't want to give the sword its head, but he needed to do something.

He released his strict will and let the sword lead the dance.

For the first time, the man stepped back.

Now Masato laughed. He could see it. The man fought on straight lines, always directly forward.

Fuko was more wily. The sword needed to be, in order to defeat their common enemy.

Step by step, Masato forced the man back.

He was good. Probably the best swordsman Masato had ever seen.

But Fuko was better. The man certainly caught on, and was able to defend after a bit.

A lesser swordsman would have been killed. Masato certainly would have been killed if he'd wielded any other sword.

They finally reached the center of the opening, both panting from their exertion. Neither of them could gain headway. They could neither kill each other or walk away.

After a flurry of fast strikes that couldn't get through the man's defenses, Masato pulled back. He didn't want to declare it a draw. But he didn't see how to defeat the man.

"Will you yield to your rightful lord?" Masato demanded as he stepped back.

"Never," the man said. He kept his sword down at his side as he stepped forward. "I didn't allow you to wield me when I was a sword. Now, as a man, I won't serve you either."

Masato took a step back, blinking with surprise. "Seiji?" he asked, incredulous.

No wonder Fuko had twitched so hard in the man's presence! He'd once been a fox fairy, and the soul of the sword Seiji.

The man nodded. "I am Norihiko, the sword made flesh. Now go."

"I will not be commanded by one such as you," Masato sneered. "I go, but of my own will. Just know that we will return, with an army ten times any that you could muster."

Masato turned and walked to his horse, mounting in one swift motion, then racing away.

Damn him. Damn that stupid sword. Damn Junichi for using a fox fairy soul.

Masato was going to get back at all of them. And burn the estate to the ground. It would be an appropriate start for his temple, given the vision of the Buddha on fire.

Masato sat at his writing desk composing his formal declaration of war. He felt ridiculous. He'd already done this once, when he'd declared war against Iwao.

This time, though, Masato would leave nothing to chance. He spelled out the terms more completely, including demanding the lives of all the generals, the army, as well as the priests and priestesses of the Mori temple. Everyone.

He didn't care if he was going to leave the mountain without people. The mountain would survive. He'd bring in his own people, his own monks and farmers.

In his mind, he could already see the estate burning, the elegant wooden buildings collapsing with flames shooting out of the steep rooftops. The women there would be turned over to his generals, to use or discard as they pleased.

Then, once the estate was settled, Masato would go hunting. He'd find every single fox fairy in the entire land of Nifon and hand out the death such creatures so richly deserved.

Fuko shivered by his side. The sword slumbered after working so hard this morning, and dreamed of blood.

Masato then sent a second letter to Junichi. He kept the tone moderately firm, but accusatory, informing him of Seiji's transformation to a human, admitting how difficult it had been to kill him, and demanding his former master's assistance in creating a great army.

The men would complain about fighting beside the creatures that Junichi raised. They would fear, and rightly so, about becoming such creatures themselves if they fell in battle.

Masato planned on pointing out that that fear should just motivate them to do better.

After he sent off both letters, Masato rested. It had been trying, these last few days.

But he would do more training, later. He had to be prepared. He had to win.

The estate had to burn.

Five

How Strong

Hikaru

How strong I felt, moving through the woods! The night seemed to enfold me in her bosom, making it easy to slide between the shadows. Even the winds aided me, carrying interesting scents to entertain me on my quest: The cowering mice that curled together for comfort as I passed, the foolish rabbit who believed that standing so still would make me miss her, and the owls above that screeched their displeasure as I scattered their prey.

I wasn't certain how far away my sisters hid from me. Sometimes the trail seemed so close, as if I merely had to peer out into the darkness to see them. Other times, it felt like the trail was days old, and they had passed in a hurry.

It finally occurred to me that Etsu used her magic to hide their trail. Not from me, of course—they didn't realize that it was I who was trailing after them! But perhaps Junichi was on the hunt for another fox fairy soul to power his evil magic. Or maybe some other power had come into the woods seeking them.

No matter. Despite how corrupted my powers were—how much I feared, loathed, and relished using them—I still knew that I would have to use them in order to find my family.

I decided to do a proper calling of my kin. Like making a nest, it was one of the simplest, most basic spells I was taught as a child, so that family could always help in time of great need.

I didn't know how my powers would corrupt the spell, what else I would call. I had to risk it, though.

I needed my sisters.

I found a rocky outcropping far up the mountain. The trail to it was steep, narrow, and difficult. Few humans had ever been to this place. The moon smiled down on me from my high ledge. Just beyond the edge, trees tumbled down into a valley that was well tended, with fields and half a dozen huts gathered together.

I tried not to think as I raised my fox head to the moon and started singing. I knew the song was different—in addition to the yips were great howls, and growls erupted too.

However, the magic was strong, and I cast my net far and wide, seeking for my kin.

I don't know how long I sat and serenaded the clear sky and the valley. But the moon had long set by the time I heard something creeping through the bushes behind me.

I transformed back to my humanlike form immediately. I was ashamed of my new fox form, how monstrous I'd become.

A shadow slunk out of the trees. For a moment, I wondered what I'd called. Then it stepped further onto the rocks, and I saw a large fox before me.

"Etsu!" I cried, thankful that she'd finally come.

The fox looked at me with her head to one side, puzzled. Finally, she shook herself, and my sister stood before me. She looked tired, even in the sparse light. Her robe was plain, rust-colored, and her hair was tied with a simple string in the back.

But she didn't take me into her arms. Didn't immediately cry out my name. Instead, she asked, "Are you Hikaru?"

"I am," I told her. At her continued hesitance, I added, "Etsu. It's me."

Slowly, my sister nodded. She gave a single yip. A second figure came out from the woods, the fox form melting away as Cho took form.

Cho didn't hesitate. She came straight to me, holding me tightly. "You had us so scared," she whispered.

Scared? Was I that much of a monster?

I looked toward Etsu, who nodded. "You aren't yourself," she said flatly. "I barely recognized your call. Your scent is completely different. Only traces of the old you remain."

"I'm sorry," I said automatically. Then my anger flared up. Why should I be sorry for what had happened? I hadn't been the one who had corrupted my magic like this.

Except—I had let it happen.

Cho stepped away from me, backing up slowly while I struggled to contain myself. I was hurt, angry, confused.

And heartbroken.

"I need to purify myself," I told Etsu. "Purify my powers. Please, sister, can you help me?"

Etsu gave a great shudder and looked away. "I foresaw this day, you know," she said quietly. "Knew that it was coming. Please, do not ask me this of me."

"Why not?" I asked. Fright had now taken root, deep in my belly, and was sinking its spikes throughout my body. Pain laced through me, as if every word Etsu spoke was a magical arrow, scoring my flesh.

Finally, Etsu turned to face me. "From like, comes like."

When she didn't say anything more, I asked her, "What does that mean?"

"Your powers are corrupted by death," Etsu explained. "In order to be free of it, you must die a little. Give up that which is most important to you."

I blinked, surprised. "Norihiko?" I asked. Were all the sacrifices I'd made for nothing? Was I going to have to give him up as well?

Etsu shook her head. "I wish it were that simple. But he's not who you're closest to, not at this time."

'Then who?" I asked, already dreading her answer.

"Us. Your family. You have to give us up."

I shuddered, remembering Etsu's exact phrasing from what seemed like forever ago.

We'll stay with you as long as we can.

It seemed the sundering had finally come.

I railed at Etsu for the rest of the night as well as all the following day. Despite the beauty of our surroundings, the bright sunlight painting the valley in different colors and shades as it moved across the sky, the piercing blue sky above us, the wise pines and oaks surrounding us, all I saw was gray.

It wasn't fair. I'd already sacrificed so much. Lost my mate. Lost my innocence. Now I had to lose my family too?

"Even mother?" I complained. True, while she had constantly overreacted to everything, and not always been a part of my life, I couldn't lose her.

"All of us," Etsu said, her voice colder than storm wind. "You will believe yourself orphaned at a young age, raised in the wild."

"Mother certainly accused me of that often enough," I complained, bitterly. "But why?" At that point, I wished I could change everything. Norihiko had changed my life, cursed it from the moment I first saw him.

But I never would have known love, without him. As much as I wanted to deny it, I couldn't forgo him.

"You can get another love," Etsu said, her voice softening for the first time. "You can even build a new family, choose sisters of the heart. But your birth family is irreplaceable. And you must give them up, give up that essential, core part of you, to clean yourself."

"I don't want to lose you," I wailed. I didn't care if my voice echoed down the valley, making the farmers there look up and tug on their protection charms. "I need you. Is there no hope?"

Etsu hesitated.

I couldn't help but pounce. "There's hope? I could regain you?"

Etsu sighed. "I don't want to give you even this slim hope," she said slowly. "You'll never recognize us as family. Whenever you see us, we'll remain dumb animals, to you."

"But?" I asked after she fell silent. There was hope!

"There is a slight, slim future where we might be reintroduced," Etsu finally admitted.

Before I could start pestering her for more details, she added, "However. You will no longer be the person you are now. You may have lost more, much more, before you see us again. In this future, though you may finally recognize us, you may not want us to see you."

I shuddered at her dire words. There was more for me to lose? More pain to twist me, meld my shape, until I could no longer recognize the being in the mirror?

"Must it come to that?" I whispered, my soul shrinking at the thought of what might lie ahead.

Etsu shrugged. "It may not. You may die first. Or we will. Or the future will take another twist or turn, and our paths will never cross again."

I didn't want tomorrow to come, the future where I no longer knew my family, my sisters.

However, I also knew I couldn't remain as I was. My corruption was growing. Despite the beauty of the day, I found myself looking forward to the night.

Cho had spent part of the afternoon raising wildflowers from the dirt, making them spring up, following her hand as if it were the sun. I couldn't make a single thing grow. If I tried, I ended up killing it, driving a plane of ash across the beautiful clearing.

I knew I had no choice, and slim hope.

"Let us part, then, my dearest sisters," I told them sadly.

We cried together, then, with both of them folding me into their arms for the first time. I would have held onto them forever, if I could have. But the night was coming, and already I could feel my face turning toward it.

I turned away first, as I knew I would.

"I will always remember you," Cho declared. She took one of her beautiful, blue-and-green enameled hairpins and placed it in my hair.

"And I," Etsu said. She gave me a crooked smile. "As the most stubborn, obtuse, wild sister one could ever have."

"Thank you," I told them. It meant a lot to me, that though I was cutting them away from my life that they wouldn't cut me off from theirs.

"And we will continue to help, whenever we can," Etsu promised.

It was more than I could have asked for. I almost backed out, asked for them to stay with me, for one more day, to never let go of their hands.

But I had my own future to face. With or without them.

Etsu nodded when she saw the determination in my face. "Then let us begin."

Etsu made me sit close to the edge of the outcropping, so I could look down into the valley below. The last of the sun's rays still stirred the heavens, painted the clouds in orange and purple. It surprised me that there wasn't that much I was supposed to do for the spell. That at least half of it came from Etsu and Cho.

Maybe the sundering had always had to be both ways.

Cho and Etsu held hands and sang softly behind me. I could barely catch the words. But it seemed like some sort of lullaby. It made my head feel as though it was wrapped in cotton, and my body encased in warm blankets.

While they sang, I plaited together the long stems of the wildflowers Cho had grown. With each one, I attached a little thread of magic, unraveling it until I could find the corrupt core, then wrap that piece around the braided flowers.

Once I had finished tugging out a corrupted piece of magic, tying it up in a flower braid, I tossed it over the side of the cliff, letting it fall into the canyon below. Merely rocks grew directly below my seat, a wild place where not many animals and no man would go.

Etsu had assured me that the magic wouldn't stay, that as the flowers decomposed and went back into the earth, the magic would be released. It wouldn't corrupt this canyon, or the valley below.

I had to believe her, though I suspected she was probably lying, as well. The rocks here would always be haunted, if not with my corrupted magic, then with the tears we'd all shed as we grew apart.

The piles of flowers beside me diminished as I kept braiding away the darker parts of me. While I went along, I realized how I could unravel more than just the dark bits. I could weaken myself, give away my powers.

Never again, I vowed, being more careful then.

I had given up my powers for Norihiko. I would never weaken myself like that again, not consciously. No matter what the price.

I'd finally learned that I needed to stay whole in order to be me.

As the sun rose again, making the clouds pink, I cast the last of the braided flowers off the ledge and down onto the rocks below.

I took a deep breath, afraid to reach for my powers. Did it work? Had that old woman been right? Had I finally been able to cure myself?

Tentatively, I reached out, encouraging my blood to warm my hand, drive away the night chill.

It worked. Instead of a rush of heat, or worse, a deadly, nighttime chill overtaking me, my blood rose as it always had, fresh and heady, the day full of possibilities again.

The sun looked so bright above me. When I thought of the night, it was no longer with longing. I was finally a daylight creature again.

I sagged where I was sitting, sighing greatly. I was myself again.

I pushed myself up to standing, swaying a little. I was exhausted from staying up all night, from unraveling every bit of darkness from my soul, from all that I had been through. It had only been months, but it felt like years since Norihiko and I had left his home to start our journeys.

I paused, looking over the outcropping of rock. I could see a few braided stems scattered there. Most had fallen further away, striking the trees below or falling to the floor of the woods. I prayed that they would decompose quickly, that no one would be haunted or cursed with that darkness that I'd carried inside of me.

A noise behind me made me start. When I turned around, I saw two foxes sitting there.

Had they been drawn by my song? Curious about my magic?

They almost seemed familiar, though I'd never seen them before. The *kitsune* rarely mingled with mere beasts. Even though I'd been orphaned as a child and raised myself, I knew that.

Still, they seemed friendly enough. "And a good day to you," I told them, bowing low. Then I giggled. Why was I talking with them? It wasn't as if they could understand me.

The foxes didn't bow in return, but they did nod their heads, as if to say goodbye. Then they turned and left, disappearing into the woods as only those born to it can.

Despite my exhaustion, I knew I couldn't rest. I needed to return to the estate. Kayoku needed healing. I could do that now. I felt stronger than I'd been before, though I knew I had to be careful.

I'd released all the darkness that had tainted my magic. But if I pulled too hard, or pushed myself too much, I was afraid I'd bring some of it back in. I would need to be careful, at least for a while, until I learned the edges of all that I was again.

I slipped into fox form myself. It would be the easiest way to travel across fields and roads.

No matter how well I felt, I had no hope that after I cured Kayoku that Norihiko would ask for me to stay. He hated me, hated everything I'd done. It didn't matter that I'd done it all for him, for there to be an *us* again.

I flowed through the forest and down the mountain. After I did my duty, I would leave. Maybe go to a coast, find myself a hut on the beach, teach myself to fish and swim.

Never see another person again.

Because seeing people would remind me of the choices I had made. Choices to be human, then to be myself again. Choices about losing myself for someone else.

Choices that I wasn't sure I'd make again.

Six

With a Smile

Norihiko

With a smile and a nod, Norihiko bid the generals goodnight and walked away from the council room. They'd taken to meeting in the Ceremonial Hall, eventually taking it over so that the maps of the mountain and the lists of able-bodied men could stay pinned to the walls.

Guards stood vigilant at the door to the council room. Norihiko didn't have to worry about their honor, or if they were bribable. These were men who had originally served with Lord Taiga. They'd rather die than be accused of being disloyal.

Quickly, Norihiko made his way back to his rooms. The hallways were empty, and the household mostly asleep. The few guards that Norihiko passed didn't even look at his face, but looked away, as was custom, to give their superiors privacy.

Two servants waited in the outer room. They'd been Iwao's servants. The rooms had also been Iwao's. Priestess Ayumi had blessed them, insuring that it was safe for Norihiko to stay.

Norihiko still frequently checked under the *tatamis*, to make sure no weakening magic had crept in.

The servants helped Norihiko out of his robes (though it felt odd—he was perfectly capable of undressing himself.) His sword was already sitting on its stand in the corner. No decorations marred the walls. Norihiko preferred the walls bare, so there were no distractions for him here.

After dressing in the lounging robes the servants provided, Norihiko insisted that they leave, get some sleep. It would be another early day tomorrow.

Finally alone, Norihiko went directly to the windows and flung them open wide. He didn't understand his need for the outdoors. It wasn't something that his time as a sword had instilled in him. He just found that he always breathed better when there was fresh air.

Then Norihiko sat down beneath the widows, his legs crossed, his spine perfectly straight—Priestess Ayumi had told him it was the ideal meditation pose.

Norihiko didn't know how to meditate. Wasn't exactly sure what it was, or why people did it.

He did need to think.

He had been so close to beating Masato that morning. Driving the warlord to his knees. Forcing him to beg for mercy.

But then the warlord had fought back. There was something about his sword—Fuko. Something frighteningly familiar.

Fuko had been made by Junichi, the sorcerer who had reforged Norihiko into Seiji. Norihiko had recognized their kinship as soon as Masato had unsheathed Fuko, and the sword had whispered its name.

It didn't contain a soul, that much Norihiko was certain of. But it wasn't normal, either. Most swords were dumb, only as alive as their wielder. Fuko had some life of its own, powered by Masato.

Once Masato had let Fuko have its head, Norihiko had been in trouble. But why? It wasn't just because Fuko was a smart sword. Norihiko should still have been able to combat that.

He'd been a sword. No other sword should be able to beat him.

Yet, if he was honest, Fuko almost had once or twice. Luckily, they'd been able to fight to a draw.

Norihiko went back over the fight, examining every stroke, every block. But he still didn't see why Fuko, in the end, had held an advantage.

And Norihiko needed to know. Or else the next time they met, Masato would win.

The letter arrived later the next afternoon, bearing the second formal declaration of war by Masato. Norihiko took it to Kayoku first. She was still nominally in charge of the estate. The generals weren't reporting to Norihiko, but they were finally willing to take his lead.

All the lamps and candles were burning brightly in Kayoku's sickroom. What had happened? Normally, it was considered polite to hide the condition of the patient from their loved ones. No one wanted the truth of an illness spread so that everyone could see.

Priestess Ayumi replied to Norihiko's puzzled expression. "Kayoku has slipped into a deep place. Few waken from there. She needs to turn around and come back to the light. How will she find it if there are no lights for her to see?"

It made sense to Norihiko. However, the brightness in the room showed how far the black poison from Kayoku's wound had spread, how it pulsed with her breath where it had crawled up her throat. She lay pale as fresh snow against her sleeping mats. Her maids had taken the time to perfectly do up her hair, so she looked like a carved statue, beautiful and divine.

Norihiko knelt down beside Kayoku and tenderly took her hand. The fire inside her still burned, but with less heat. It would soon be out.

"You must come back to me," Norihiko told Kayoku. "There is so much you have to teach me." He felt lost without her. Priestess Ayumi helped guide him when she could, but she was otherworldly herself. Kayoku was much more grounded and of the earth.

Much more human.

After Norihiko finished his mourning, he pulled back and addressed Kayoku formally.

"Kayoku, the warlord Masato has issued a second and final declaration of war against the estate. This time, he means to destroy everything and everyone, burn the compound to the ground and kill everyone who survives." Norihiko took a deep breath. He would not tire her more by reading the hateful screed out loud.

"We will go to war again," Norihiko told her quietly. "The generals will follow my lead. And this time, we will win. I will defeat Masato." He had to. He still didn't know what it was that Masato and Fuko had, what knowledge they held that made him so vulnerable.

He was determined to find out, though. Or to defeat them regardless.

"I will lead the armies in your name," Norihiko told Kayoku. "Lead them to victory."

He left soon after that, leaving Kayoku to the constant murmurs of prayers from the priestesses, the overly sweet smell of the incense burning in the room, hoping she would find her way out of the darkness and back into the light before he left for war.

She didn't.

For the first battle, Norihiko and Masato chose the same field where the first battle had been fought, between Masato and Iwao. The generals and Norihiko set up their dusty, brown canvas tents a few *li* from the battlefield. Norihiko refused to stay in Iwao's larger tent, but instead, took a smaller one for himself. He wasn't planning on being in the cramped, musty space very often.

Again, Iwao's servants followed Norihiko, assigning themselves to him. He wasn't quite sure what to do with them, but he let them do the things they felt he required, like cleaning his armor and his robes, stabling his horse with the others and seeing that it was well tended, bringing him tea when he required it.

Though Norihiko learned their names—Taro, Yasuo, and Fujita—they worked at staying in the background, effortlessly providing what he needed. It gave him an even higher regard for Iwao. He wished again that he could have met him, man to man.

Masato had been true to his word. His camp spread like a dark cloud over the fields behind him. Norihiko didn't know which reports to believe, but some of the scouts had counted as many as ten men to every one that Norihiko and the generals had been able to raise.

Not all of Masato's men were human, either.

The tactic for how to fight the creatures powered by magic had been given to every man in Norihiko's army. It would give them an advantage, one they hadn't had the first time they'd fought.

Norihiko and the generals argued over how to fight Masato. Should the archers go first? Traditionally, that was how every battle started.

However, they'd be useless against the animated beings.

One of the generals proposed that they should reverse the order of the men, and send in the heavy lances and axes first. No one wanted such disorder to the battle plans, however.

As the night drew on, Norihiko found himself constantly clearing his throat. He realized that the despair in the room was so thick he could taste it. Finally, he excused himself from the generals, claiming that he needed to take a walk to clear his head.

Clouds covered the night sky. Foul smells were carried on the winds from Masato's camp. No one talked in loud voices—everything was muted, heavy with anticipation and dread.

Norihiko strode past the circle of the general's tents and down the hill. Two guards accompanied him, but at a distance. He'd already taken them to task for following too closely.

However, walking among the first line of tents didn't provide Norihiko with much relief. The men who were still awake prayed for good deaths. No one prayed for a win, not through superstition, but because no one believed they could.

Norihiko still didn't know how to fight Fuko, how they'd win against such overwhelming odds, if Kayoku would survive. He didn't know if Hikaru would return, if he'd see her again. She still confused him, but he wanted to see her again.

Finally, Norihiko walked beyond the tents and the camp lights and closer to the fields that circled his army. Guards patrolled the area, though was it to keep others out, or to prevent his own army from deserting?

The moon broke through the clouds for a moment, painting the field before Norihiko a pale silver. In the distance, a fox yipped, then another.

Norihiko grew very still. He'd been told that it was disturbing how motionless he got—that people always fidgeted or moved, even monks when they meditated, even if ever so slightly.

Norihiko didn't care. He needed to concentrate all of his senses on the creatures out there, hidden by the night.

The moon disappeared behind her shroud of clouds again, but not before Norihiko spied the foxes sitting a few yards away.

Glancing back, Norihiko saw the guards standing at attention. Did they see the creatures? He suspected they didn't. That somehow, they'd appeared just for him.

The two foxes began to sing, a soft, yipping song. It surprised Norihiko how rhythmically they sang, what a strong beat the music had, despite the lack of tune or words. He found himself nodding in time with it. It seemed familiar somehow. Where was it from?

One of the inner selves gifted Norihiko with a memory, like a small puff of snowflakes blown out of the palm of a hand. It showed Norihiko in formal red robes. He understood them to be his wedding clothes. The two foxes danced with him, a circling pattern, weaving in and around and back again, that seemed both familiar to Norihiko and utterly foreign at the same time.

Then the memory was gone, dissolved like a cloud by the hot summer sun.

What did it mean? Hikaru had told him he'd once been a fox fairy, had once been her mate. Why did her sisters show him these things?

He kept coming back to the dance. It seemed so familiar. It wasn't straightforward at all. Even the steps themselves curved.

Where had he learned it? Was that what they were trying to tell him?

But no, it wasn't that. With a swallowed gasp, Norihiko recognized the pattern of movements.

Fuko had used a similar weaving pattern when he'd attacked. Never straightforward. Always curving and coming in from the side.

The music the foxes sang changed abruptly, and Norihiko remembered that as well—how they'd easily merged from one form to the next, always shifting, always changing.

Fuko had done that as well.

The despair Norihiko had been infected with from the camp finally lifted. Following any sort of pattern, along any straight lines, was the quickest way to get them all killed.

They were going to have to plan a completely different attack.

Norihiko bowed low to the sisters, thanking them for helping him see.

Only as he was walking back did he realize that his memory didn't include Hikaru at all. He felt her there, though, a void to his left side.

Determined, Norihiko pushed the memory away. He knew what he needed to do.

He couldn't allow himself to get distracted, not by his former mate or anyone else.

"We must change the order of the men," Norihiko announced as he walked into the command tent.

General Asheihi looked up from where they had the maps spread out on the table. "Again?" he asked, scowling.

Only eight generals remained. Lamps had been allowed to burn down, letting shadows grow in the corners. The heavy canvas walls held in the sour scent of fear and tired men.

"The only way to defeat Masato is to surprise him," Norihiko stated as he took a candle and walked around the edges, lighting every lamp.

"Where have we heard that before?" General Kendo asked.

Norihiko knew that Iwao had led them down this path before.

And that he'd been successful as well.

"We must first move the archers to the rear," Norihiko stated. "They shoot after the first wave of attacks."

"Attacks?" General Asheihi asked.

"Eight squads," Norihiko said. "Attacking from all sides. Like the rivers flowing from the mountain."

The generals looked at each other. "Dividing the men that way will weaken them," General Kendo argued. "I can see maybe two or three squads. Eight will leave each group too vulnerable."

"We will lose some men," Norihiko acknowledged. "Some very good men. But the attack will be completely unexpected. There will be chaos."

"There's always chaos on the battlefield," General Asheihi said dismissively.

"Not like this," Norihiko insisted. "Each squad will be self-directed. They can attack in the way that best suits their situation, that will guarantee their success."

"That won't work," General Kendo insisted. "We must—"

"General Asheihi," Norihiko interrupted. "Would you attack an army on a hill the same way you'd attack one in a valley?"

"Of course not," General Asheihi replied.

"Part of our problem has always been the terrain," Norihiko pointed out. "We aren't just fighting in flat fields. We need to each attack our own section of land, our own enemy, in the way that will best match."

Some of the generals were nodding, but Norihiko knew he hadn't convinced them all. He wished he could show them the dance of the foxes, how they'd woven together, each separate, but working together.

Norihiko walked to the front flap of the tent and threw it back, letting in the fresh air of the night. Ghostly moans still echoed on the wind, but the air still smelled clean. "The old ways won't work," Norihiko insisted. "We will still coordinate from the top, here, when we can. Watch over all the separate squads. But we must try something new as well. Or we are dead."

General Asheihi looked at General Kendo, the pair of them communicating in a way that Norihiko could recognize, though he couldn't hear any of the words.

Finally, General Asheihi nodded slowly, as if his head had suddenly grown heavy. "We will do as you suggest," he said. "If we succeed, this battle will be spoken of for all the ages."

Norihiko understood that if they failed, the battle would also be remembered, and ridiculed.

"We will win," Norihiko told them sincerely. "The mountain demands it."

The generals worked out a few more details then went to their separate tents, to sleep, to pray, to plan more madness.

Norihiko went back to his own tent to sit motionless, listening to the wind, hearing the quiet yipping of foxes in the distance, ready to commit his soul to the mountain, though he hoped he would live.

He needed to see Hikaru again.

Seven

The Gates

Hikaru

The gates of the estate were firmly locked against me, and there were fewer guards than I'd ever seen before. What had happened? I didn't recognize any of the guards either, and they all seemed older as well. It was late afternoon, the sky turning crimson. I didn't hear much noise coming from the compound, not even the muted sounds of the cooks in their outdoor kitchen.

Instead of trying to go straight through, I went around the side of the wall, trying to find a place where the woods would hide my approach. However, the trees had all been cut back. The wall was much more defensible than ever before. Even the places where it had once sagged had been shored up.

I finally recognized some of the guards toward the back of the estate. They stood diligent, mindful, and armed.

Were they defending the estate against Masato?

Merely locked gates and guarded walls wouldn't stop me, however. I found a place that was marginally less defended and flowed up and over. It was more difficult to hide myself from humans who were consciously looking for anything and everything. I still managed to find a hole and wormed my way in.

Maybe I should have waited until it was fully dark before I tried getting into the compound. I didn't want to wait, though. Hopefully I wouldn't be too late for Kayoku.

I found her in her rooms, the stench of her wound choking me, despite how many candles and lamps were lit. Priestess Ayumi knelt beside her, praying earnestly. She looked old, much older than I'd realized.

I finally realized her true age. How had she kept it from me, from everyone? Why had she hidden it?

She didn't gasp when I appeared beside her, or cry out. Instead, she looked at me with hopeful eyes and asked, "Can you help her?"

I nodded, not trusting my voice. I threw back the fine sheet that covered Kayoku, then gently opened her robe.

Now Priestess Ayumi gasped. The poison from the wound had darkened Kayoku's entire middle, and tendrils of black grew everywhere, up her neck, across her shoulders, down her arms, all the way to her toes.

I hadn't thought before about how I would cure Kayoku. I didn't have a spell prepared. I still reached for her, holding my hands over her skin.

I shuddered when the poison reached for me, too, licking at my palms. I drew my hands back, hoping it would follow.

It didn't. It sank back into Kayoku's skin. She gave a small groan.

"Was there anything that worked against this?" I asked Priestess Ayumi. As always, I longed for someone truly magical who I could call on, a sister or a mother. That familiar gap ached deeper than before.

"Nothing, my lady," Priestess Ayumi replied. Then she paused and shook her head.

"What is it?" I pressed.

"It may not be anything," the priestess warned. "But even in this deep sleep, she seems comforted when her hair is being combed."

"Thank you," I told the priestess sincerely, the image and spell springing clearly to my mind. "Could you help me sit her up?"

The priestess nodded, puzzled, but she helped me move the unconscious woman so that she rested against me, her head lolled to one side.

"Could you please hand me her comb?" I asked.

Priestess Ayumi picked up the comb reverently. It was beautifully carved out of sandalwood, with a pattern of peonies along the edge. She passed her hand over it and said a brief prayer to the *kami*, asking that they aid this instrument in every deed. Then she formally handed the comb to me, with both hands, her head bent low.

I took the comb with as much solemnity as I could, then began to comb out Kayoku's fine black hair.

It wasn't as thick or soft as my own. It was thin, fine, with many hairs that would fly away, not fall back with the rest.

I scraped the teeth of the comb against Kayoku's scalp while my magic enfolded her body, gently squeezing, pushing the poison up, back out of her torso, up her spine, and out the crown of her head.

I had to stop every once in a while to shake the comb free of the blackness that gathered there. Then I went back to steadily combing and drawing up, ridding her body of the poison.

Priestess Ayumi gave a soft cry when she saw the magic working. She began to pray again, her soft words matching the rhythm of my rising and falling hand.

Kayoku started to breathe more deeply as the poison loosened its grip. The stench of it was overpowering, but I didn't stop. It tried climbing over the comb in a desperate attempt to poison me as well.

I laughed softly at its feeble attempts. I gave it no opportunity to slide into my skin, forcing it into the air where it had nothing to hold onto.

Finally, Kayoku's skin was clean. She moaned and shifted in her sleep, her breathing deep and regular.

"She'll awaken soon," I told Priestess Ayumi as she helped me lay the first wife back down on her sleeping mats.

"Thank you," the priestess said, catching at my hands as I started to get up.

"I caused her illness in the first place," I told her. I hadn't done it on purpose, but I still felt ashamed.

"You came back when you didn't have to," Priestess Ayumi said, letting go of my hand. "Where will you go now?"

"I…I don't know," I told her truthfully. I knew Norihiko would be happy I'd cured Kayoku, and happier still if I hadn't stuck around.

"You know they're in the field of battle again," Priestess Ayumi told me. "The final one. Masato declared war on us again. But the consequences were much more dire. He'll burn the estate to the ground and kill every man, woman and child if he wins."

"I'll help your people escape," I told her sincerely.

"Thank you," the priestess said. "But I don't know many who will go. The mountain is their home. If they leave, it will be the same as dying."

"Then Masato can't be allowed to win," I told her.

"I'm not sure you can stop him, child," the priestess told me.

"I can," I told her, though even I could hear the hollowness of my words.

"Only by becoming something you aren't," Priestess Ayumi warned. "Think long and hard before you decide to go down that road."

I paused, thinking. The words she said had a strange echo, as if I'd heard something similar just recently.

But I couldn't remember anyone else issuing such a warning. I hadn't seen or talked with anyone for ages. I'd been off by myself seeking a cure for my corrupted powers.

"I will," I promised the priestess.

I realized as I flowed away, over the wall and away from the estate, that this time, I meant it.

I might actually, finally, think before I acted.

If I had a mother, she would have been so proud.

I let the winds direct me to the battlefield. I couldn't follow Norihiko's scent—there were too many men, too many horses, too many conflicting scents for me to do that.

I could, however, follow the stench of Masato's camp. Junichi's magic hung heavily in the air. He was creating more beasts and creatures than Norihiko could ever fight. Their cries carried on the wind, no doubt to strike fear in the hearts of Norihiko's men.

The hill where the final battle would take place felt strangely open. It was close to where Iwao had staged his final fight, where he'd fallen, due to my interference.

This time, I wouldn't interfere. At least not with Norihiko. I couldn't approach Masato and distract him tonight.

But in the morning, ah, that would be another matter. I would do all that I could to stop him, to cause Junichi to fail.

I created a small nest for myself, a comfortable place to rest for the night, well protected by magic so no one would see it or stumble across me. I didn't know if I would sleep. Off in the distance, I heard the yipping of foxes. I took that as a good sign as I settled in, the warnings of Priestess Ayumi still troubling me.

I knew what she'd meant by her questions. Would I be able to remain myself? I would certainly try. But I wasn't certain I'd be successful.

I wasn't prepared to kill. Not yet.

But I had no idea what the morning would bring.

Eight

Sunlight Flickered

Kayoku

Sunlight flickered across Kayoku's face. A breeze caressed her skin. She felt as though she lay at the bottom of a flat bottomed boat, the waves rocking her gently. Or maybe she was in Iwao's arms again as he murmured words of love that he'd never speak at any other time. The smell of incense surrounded her, and off in the distance, faint prayers were being said, too quietly for her to hear.

For the first time in a very long time—possibly since her mother had died—Kayoku felt safe.

But that was foolish. She was at the estate. She'd been lying on her sleeping mats for far too long. There was work to be done.

It was time to get up.

Rising out of sleep felt like climbing out of a cave, or as if she'd been buried in the heart of the mountain. She fought, one layer at a time, to climb out of the darkness. The light on her face helped, as did the rhythmic stroking of someone combing her hair.

Kayoku would climb for a while, her legs never tiring, however, her will would grow weak. Then she'd stop, rest, regain her strength, and climb some more. She kept expecting her calves to ache from all the steps she took, but they never did.

Finally, Kayoku reached the very top. She hesitated for a moment. There was so much work to be done! And she would be so alone. Iwao was gone. So was her mother. She was so far away from her family.

She'd made a new family here, though. Chieko and Priestess Ayumi. They were counting on her. She was the most senior wife, still.

Kayoku opened her eyes.

The sunlight she'd been dreaming of didn't exist. However, brightly lit lamps and candles surrounded her, lined up against the walls as well as perched on stools all around her sleeping mat. The air smelled of incense and fresh flowers. The beams of her ceiling hadn't changed.

Then she focused her eyes. Cobwebs! She was going to have to take her servants to task. How could they allow cobwebs to grow in the corners of her room?

Or had she been so sick for so long that they hadn't had a chance to clean?

Kayoku shuddered. She had no idea what day it was. She turned her head slowly, her body telling her that she hadn't moved in quite some time.

Priestess Ayumi sat on the floor beside her mats, her legs crossed under her, her head drooping. Instead of greeting Kayoku, she gave a soft snore.

How much work had she done for Kayoku? Had she left her side in days?

Kayoku looked critically at the top of the priestess' head. She stifled a gasp. The priestess dyed her hair! There, along the part, were pure silver roots.

How old was Priestess Ayumi? Kayoku had always assumed that they were the same age.

When the priestess raised her head, she looked directly into Kayoku's eyes. "Welcome back, my lady," she said softly, her voice still sounding young.

Kayoku swallowed all her questions. Priestess Ayumi deserved her respect and her silence. "How long was I asleep?" she asked. She took a deep breath, then realized that the pain in her side was gone.

She hadn't just been sick. She'd been injured, and the wound had been poisonous. Carefully, Kayoku looked down.

Her skin was unblemished. She knew that when she undid her robes, not even a scar from the wound would remain.

"Hikaru?" Kayoku asked.

The priestess nodded. "She came yesterday. Full of magic and life. I've never seen someone so…so…"

"Beautiful?" Kayoku suggested, the word tasting bitter.

"Of course she's beautiful. But I was going to say so much in transition. She's like a child, still learning the world, and herself," Priestess Ayumi said. "She said she'll help people escape from the estate if they need to."

"Need to?" Kayoku asked.

"Ach, that's right! Please forgive me," the priestess said. "Masato issued another formal declaration of war. Norihiko came and read parts of it to you. He's leading the army today. If they lose—"

"Let me guess. Masato will destroy everything, right?" Kayoku asked grimly. That would be exactly the sort of thing he would do, like a petulant boy stomping on an ant hill.

But he might be surprised. There might be a scorpion or two located in that nest.

"Burn down the estate and kill all the people," Priestess Ayumi confirmed.

"We're not just about to roll over and let him walk all over us," Kayoku told her. She started pushing herself up to sitting, but faltered. She was so weak!

"My lady…" Priestess Ayumi sounded as if she was about to reprimand Kayoku, then she sighed and merely helped Kayoku to sit.

Kayoku felt better sitting. She was growing stronger. It would be a few days before she was back to normal.

If she had a few days.

"When is the battle taking place?" Kayoku asked as she breathed and rested.

"Today," the priestess admitted.

"Then there's no time to lose," Kayoku said.

She remembered, sometime before being sick, wanting to walk in the eternal lands.

No more.

It was time to fight, to live, even if it was for a very short time.

Time to make a difference.

Nine

From Atop A Hill

Masato

From atop a small hill, Masato surveyed the armies beneath him. His own men spread out like a great storm cloud, filling the valley and beyond. Norihiko's army looked puny in comparison, a few lines of men that would get wiped away before noon.

The air hung heavy over the field, rain promised for the afternoon. Storm clouds gathered on the horizon. Junichi still worked at Masato's camp, raising more spirits to join his already invincible men. The smell of decaying leaves and limestone graveyards swept over Masato, bringing the promise of victory.

Masato's generals had proposed a similar arrangement of squads and men as the last time they'd fought Iwao's generals. As it had worked the last time, Masato had agreed. Despite Norihiko's influence, he knew the old generals would fall into familiar patterns.

As people always did.

Masato was looking forward to this war finally being over. It would take some effort, but burning down the estate was going to be so satisfying.

And Junichi would be pleased, and handsomely rewarded, with all the lives Masato and his men would take.

It was going to be a great day.

The rallying cry from Norihiko's army startled Masato out of his thoughts. It wasn't time for the battle to begin yet, was it?

Just like the other young cur, Iwao, Norihiko was going to start early. Damn him! Masato had assured his generals that Norihiko wouldn't do such a thing, that he would obey the strictures of the war proclamation.

He'd been a sword, after all, and sworn to order.

Masato's men farther up the line scrambled to get ready. The ones at the front already were, Masato noted with pride. If any survived, he'd have to be sure to reward them. Or the generals in charge of that unit.

Then the sound of fighting rose up from behind Masato. What fresh hell was this?

Masato turned to see that a small division of Norihiko's men had already started their attack, from behind.

They were sure to get slaughtered. Masato didn't need to worry about them.

However, a second unit attacked from the side, riding in on horses. It didn't make any sense for that group to be attacking, until Masato realized that Norihiko was attacking his archers.

Another attack started, with a loud cry. Then another.

How many units had Norihiko divided his army into? Didn't he realize that without full support, each would be wiped out and all his men would die?

Masato whirled around as yet another group attacked. They were closer, now, than Masato was comfortable with.

One of Masato's newly promoted generals broke ranks, screaming as he charged.

An arrow knocked him off his horse. Masato recognized it as coming from his own archers.

All around Masato the battle raged. Men screamed and died. Norihiko's army was making headway up the hill. He watched a foot soldier bearing a long pike effectively gut one of Masato's own enhanced warriors, killing him with a single thrust into his center.

Junichi had crafted at least half of Masato's men into unstoppable killing machines. They could lose a limb and still fight on, until the loss of blood finally stopped them.

But Norihiko's men had found something to stop them. Masato's enhanced men were being killed before him.

This had to end. Or Masato would have no one left for his next battle.

Masato cried for his horse to be brought to him. It was time to end this farce. Time for Fuko to taste the blood of a former fox fairy and drain it all.

Time for Masato to challenge Norihiko directly.

As much as Masato wanted to charge directly into battle and find Norihiko, he'd learned some patience. He sent scouts ahead, racing through the battle lines, avoiding all those who would kill them, then coming back to him with reports.

It was sloppy. Not the best communication. Masato waited impatiently on the sidelines, listening to men and horses die, grinding his teeth. His generals seemed confused, uncertain what to do. Go after the advancing archers? However, that would leave them open to the horsemen. The lancers had at least pulled back, but wave upon wave of infantry had filled in. (And where had Norihiko gotten so many men?)

How Norihiko was attacking didn't make any sense. There was no pattern in it. It was almost as if he'd divided his army and set each unit to attack on its own. But that would have been suicide. Masato would never give his generals that much autonomy.

Finally, a scout returned, mud-covered and spattered in blood, but with a maniacal gleam in his eye. His commander brought him before Masato, obviously hoping to glean some of the credit himself.

"Sir, this man claims to have found Norihiko for you," the officer said.

Masato glanced at the officer, then dismissed him. The officer hadn't been out fighting, but had stayed behind, merely directing.

Masato would deal with him later.

"What did you find?" he asked, speaking directly to the scout.

"I found him. On the field," the scout claimed. He wiped the dirt and gore from his forehead with the back of his sleeve. "Up there, on that hilltop."

Masato nodded. Of course. That was close to where he'd killed Iwao. It would be the place where Norihiko would go.

So he, too, could be sacrificed.

"Thank you," Masato said. "Go. Clean up. Get ready to celebrate our victory."

The scout bowed deeply and raced off, obviously relieved that his duty was over. Masato nearly called him back in order to test the man, see how much will he had remaining.

But today wasn't that day, at least not for him.

It was time for Masato to put his own mettle to the test.

An elite squad of men fought in front of Masato, clearing a trail through the melee to the hill where Norihiko stood. It all felt very familiar, particularly the way the opposition melted away once they realized where he was going.

Was there some kind of magic at work? Clearing the way?

Maybe Junichi had been informed of Masato's task, and had decided to help. That must have been it.

Norihiko waited at the top of the hill. He wore very plain armor, Oyoroi style. Brown ribbons plaited the shoulder armor to his arms. Iron scales made up the front and side skirts, also laced together with brown ribbon. The leather piece that covered his chest was also brown, with the symbol of Mount Shirayama stenciled on it.

Masato slid easily off his horse, Fuko already in hand, eager to take the lead.

They were finally going to deal with this upstart and bring peace and order to the mountain. His first Buddhist temple might be built on this very spot.

"Come for another lesson, cur?" Masato taunted Norihiko.

The man still didn't move. Many yards behind him and down the hill a ways both their armies fought. Steel thumped soundly against armor, men screamed and cursed. The ghost winds from Junichi howled around them.

Yet, as Masato took another step toward Norihiko, it felt as though the swirling battle around them faded, the noise dying down.

Masato sent quick thanks to Junichi for providing him with some quiet, so he'd be able to concentrate more.

"You know what your problem is?" Norihiko said, turning his head to one side, no longer even watching Masato. "It isn't that you're lazy and undisciplined. It's that you know you're right, and refuse to change."

"I am right," Masato said, stung. "Buddhism will sweep over Nifon."

Norihiko nodded, finally turning to look at Masato. "True. It might. But not in the way you believe. There's always a merging. Both ying and yang. Push and pull. Straight and sideways."

Masato shook his head. "You're wrong. The pure Amida Buddha will save you all."

Norihiko pointed at Fuko with his chin. "Not all of us," he said softly.

Masato raised Fuko high. "Those who are deserving, will die." Once he finished this battle, it would be off to the greater war, destroying all the *kitsune*.

"And who decides who is worthy?" Norihiko challenged.

"We do," Masato replied. How dare this upstart question him? Without another word Masato rushed forward, attacking.

He *was* right. He would win.

Masato gave Fuko his head almost immediately. While he wanted to fight Norihiko, punish him, maybe force him to his knees to beg for mercy before Masato killed him, he also didn't want to take the time.

They needed to win this battle. Kill Norihiko, then start the slaughter of all his men, all those who called the mountain home. Purify the region. Bring in his own priests.

Plant the Buddha's feet firmly on the mountaintop. Let the burning begin.

Norihiko seemed more prepared this time for Fuko's wildness. He sidestepped Masato's wild swings, attacked using steps that defied patterns. Then he'd change, flow straight forward again, then change again.

Masato wanted to scream as his sword arm grew tired. Fuko was taking everything Masato could give, eager to win, to start the devastation against his sworn enemy.

But Norihiko refused to accept the demise Masato had promised him. Again and again he slipped out of Masato's grasp, answering with his own punishing blows.

Masato couldn't fight to a tie this time. It had to be to the death.

It wasn't until the very last moment that he realized it was to be his own.

The killing blow came from above, when Masato had been ready to block a lower thrust. Norihiko had reversed blow from low to high without warning, cutting deep into Masato's neck and shoulder.

Masato stumbled back, shocked. "This isn't how it's supposed to be!" he complained.

Norihiko showed no mercy. He stepped forward and thrust his sword directly into Masato's center, in a chink in his armor that he hadn't realized was there.

"I think the *kami* would disagree," Norihiko told Masato as he stepped back.

Junichi was going to have a field day between Masato's life force and all the soldiers dead on the battleground.

The arc of Norihiko's sword was perfect as it swung around. At least Masato had died at the hands of a worthy swordsman.

Then his head toppled from his body, and the world was no more.

Ten

Like Autumn Leaves

Hikaru

Like autumn leaves, the heads went tumbling.

Or at least that was what I tried to tell myself. The first time I'd been in a battle, just before Iwao died, I saw men getting killed. Heard the screams, smelled the blood, tasted their fear.

But it didn't really affect me. They were merely humans, after all. They were destined to die after a short while.

This time I felt their pain. The devastation as each man lost his life. How cruel it was for the potential in each individual to be cut short. How awful the waste.

Could I have stopped it all with just a wave of my hand? Ended the destruction? I was magical, full of my powers, stronger than ever before.

However, I knew I couldn't. My magic didn't work that way, not on a mass scale. I couldn't influence a large crowd, let alone entire armies. All I could do was help one man at a time, turn a sword stroke away, give him another chance.

Let him thank his luck.

From my nest, I watched many men die, the air heavy with fall rains and anticipation. Grass had sprung up since the last conflict, hiding the scars of the previous battle. Men trampled it again, then ground it into the mud. I moved around, staying hidden, watching and waiting.

It was midday before Masato finally realized he was losing. He had more men. He had more ghosts and wraiths who drove fear into the winds.

But he couldn't compete with Norihiko's brilliant wildness. My Norihiko, who had finally tapped into his true nature.

Watching him climb the small hill where I hid made me weep. He was already covered in mud and gore. Exhaustion lined his face. His eyes still shone as he surveyed the field. Scouts and messengers came running up to him with news or questions, and Norihiko directed them, made suggestions, and also waited.

Masato came riding up behind a unit of well-trained fighters. I made the way easier for them, clearing other men off the hill, distracting them, turning them away.

How I shuddered when Masato went striding up the hill! Not because of fear. My hands had formed into claws and I found my teeth bared. I hated him. I wanted to make him suffer. I'd let him touch me. He didn't make me unclean—I'd washed all of him from my skin, my soul, and my magic.

I just didn't want him to live, to breathe the same air.

The sword he carried was evil as well. I hissed at it, glad to be hidden from its evil gaze. It seemed to sense me anyway. I would have thrown it into the deepest sea to be rid of it.

The battle between Masato and Norihiko took longer than I would have expected. I don't believe Norihiko was playing with him. He was, however, showing Masato just how talented a swordsman he was, how outclassed Masato truly was.

In the end, when Masato's head also went rolling away, I thought that was it. I waited for the relief I should feel.

It never came.

Though the man no longer lived, I would always carry his actions with me. I was the one who had to let go, to not let them define who I was.

I stumbled down the hill, weeping with joy and sadness.

The estate was safe. Masato had been defeated.

I was who I was, alone again in the world. Norihiko had just been a dream, a brief time when I hadn't been on my own.

A dream that I also had to let go of.

The battle didn't cease immediately. It took time for the word to spread to Masato's generals.

In the meanwhile, I made my way to Masato's camp. I wasn't planning on any destruction there. Maybe a little mischief, though.

Few men remained in the collection of tents. The ones who were there weren't staying. They looted the flimsy, unguarded shelters, stealing blankets, clothes, tools, anything they could carry. Most of them were grimy from battle—many of them injured.

Why weren't they going to the priests' tent to get healing? I made my way to the tiny black canvas tent. No guards stood watch. The stench was worse than a graveyard, containing not just putrefying flesh but the smell of foul magic that clogged the back of my throat.

The door of the tent had been tied open. Inhuman groans and cries issued forth. I peeked inside. It was as bad as I feared.

Three animated creatures stood in the corner, moaning, bumping into each other. They'd been men, once, but were now mindless beasts. They knew nothing but destruction and chaos. There was no reasoning with them. All they would do would be go out and kill, until they'd been slaughtered.

Two priests wearing dirty brown robes worked on a third such creature lying on the table between them. The fat one carved esoteric runes into its belly, while the older one poured a magical mixture of tar, blood, and rotting herbs into the wounds. They both chanted a spell of power, a harsh song that promised pain and suffering to all those who came across the being they were animating.

Were they just planning on letting these creatures go, to terrorize the mountainside? There was no way to direct them. It wasn't as if they were creating guards who could defend them.

More mischief than I would tolerate.

I stayed hidden, but caused a great wind to gush into the tent, making the one priest curse as he lost his grip on the bowl with the nasty concoction, dribbled it down the side of the creature and splashed the robes of the other priest.

This disrupted the song they sang, as the priest with the knife cursed the other.

The wind also caused the creatures in the corner to stir, groaning loudly in complaint. They must hate all life. So I caused a second wind to blow, directing it at them. They turned as one, staring out the open door.

The two priests didn't notice. They had begun their chant again.

I crafted a spring wind, the kind that makes young lovers sigh, and directed to the three in the corner. They grew restless and agitated, crying out for their own lost lives and the destruction of all those around them.

I didn't know how to stop these three beings, except maybe to sing them to sleep.

First, though, they had a job to do.

I continued to blow winds at them, happy winds, winds that stirred the blood and carried promises of green growing things and hope. I also protected the priests, letting them focus and concentrate on their other creation.

Finally, the beasts had had enough. They erupted out of their corner, attacking the only other living things in the tent—the two priests.

The priests were caught off guard, as I'd hoped they would be. I made myself watch their deaths: I had caused them, after all.

I put a barrier up against the door so the mindless creatures couldn't escape and cause more harm. Once they were finished doing my will, I did sing them to sleep. They would expire before they awoke, the magic bled away.

I sent a quick prayer at them as well, for the poor men whose souls had once inhabited those hulks.

As I finished, someone behind me said, "Well done, lady."

I whirled around. There stood Junichi, a terrible, maniacal grin on his face. He held a box in his hands. I instantly recognized it. It wasn't the same one that had encased Norihiko's soul, but it was a sister to it, a box designed to hold the soul of a fox fairy.

Junichi looked fat, like a leech that had spent all night supping on blood. His off-white robes were streaked with tar, blood, and gore. He held a glittering knife in his hand—the light it gave off chilled my very soul. I could taste the magic even from a few feet away.

It, too, was meant to work against my kind.

"Thank you for taking care of those two idiots before I had to," Junichi said. "Now, are you going to come along nicely, or are we going to have to do this the hard way?"

"Do you truly believe I'm just going to lie down and die, so that you can take my soul?" I asked, incredulous. Really, the arrogance of the man!

Junichi just shrugged. "It doesn't matter one way or the other to me. I'll still have your soul in the end."

I shivered at his assurance. I didn't know how to fight him. I'd never really trained with a sword. The *kitsune* battled with words or misdirection. Not with action.

Still, I drew my shoulders back, ready to face him, determined to win.

Norihiko wasn't the only one who had learned. I would defeat this sorcerer. Finally get my revenge for him killing his love and my one chance for happiness.

I couldn't lose. No matter how alone I might be for the rest of my days, I wasn't about to die.

Even if it meant killing him.

Junichi attacked, swift and hard. I swirled away, dancing out of range.

It suddenly occurred to me that I didn't need to stay. That I could just flit away. I didn't actually have to fight him.

But this was the man responsible for Norihiko's death. For the creation of Fuko, the sword that lusted after all my kind.

If I didn't take care of him, he'd just continue to cause me and my people harm.

So I stayed. Engaged the madman. Watched carefully how he held his knife, how he fought. Stayed out of his way while I sent my winds at him, trying to confuse him, to distract him.

But how was I going to harm him? I didn't want to get close enough to use my hands. I had no weapon other than my wits and my magic.

So I used my words.

"She must have been beautiful, the one who rejected you," I taunted him. I allowed him to swing very close to me, but still miss. "But always out of reach."

"She was nothing," Junichi declared. "Just a blight. Like you. Like you all are. None of you deserve to live."

"Did she promise you immortality? The hope of never dying?" I asked as I brushed by him, coming close enough for him to smell my perfume. "Or did she promise you love?"

"She didn't promise me anything," Junichi said. "I was going to take it all from her."

"She defeated you, didn't she?" I asked. "And that bothers you most of all. Defeated. By not only a woman, but one of my kind."

"She should have just given me what I asked for," Junichi admitted. He drew himself up. "Like you will."

Did he really believe that I didn't know there were creatures behind me? Even enhanced, these former-men couldn't hide their stench.

I had to laugh at Junichi's surprised face when the man missed grabbing my arm by several feet.

Then I had to whirl faster to get out of the way of a second. These creatures were a threat. But I had watched Norihiko's men disable them.

With a quick burst of song, I directed strong winds to swirl around their centers, push into the flesh of their core, and disturb the characters carved there.

The creatures were far enough past life that they collapsed, falling hard, like old oaks whose roots had failed.

I knew it was just a matter of time before more came to join us. Perhaps Junichi was right, and I would lose.

But the animated beings gave me an idea.

Junichi's long life wasn't natural either. He used the lives of others to extend his own.

He probably didn't have characters painted on his skin. They were likely to be imbedded there, with ink and needles, like the warriors from the far off islands.

However, I would bet everything that he did have them. Covering his round belly. I just had to get at them.

The most direct way would be to stop the fighting and seduce him, get him to remove his clothes for me.

I shuddered at the thought as I slipped. Junichi's last pass with his knife came dangerously close.

I would never seduce another man like that again. No man would touch me unless I truly desired him. I would not hurt my soul like that again.

But then Junichi slipped on the same patch of blood-stained ground. I didn't know who had died there, but I guessed it was one of Masato's own men, killed by his own hand.

And that gave me an even better idea.

I slipped again and started panting, as if I was tiring from our little dance. Junichi immediately pressed his advantage, as I hoped he would.

With a cry of despair, I struggled back, out of the way.

Junichi paid no heed at all to where I was directing his feet.

It didn't take much. Just a quick wave of my hand behind me to slick up the grass.

Junichi slipped as I'd planned.

With only the slightest effort, I turned his hand at the same time, directing the blade straight at the core of him.

Junichi slipped again as the blade easily parted his robes, like a fish diving for water.

With a gasp, Junichi asked, "What have you done?"

His face contorted horribly, growing gaunt, like an apple shriveling. He dropped his accursed knife and put his hands over his belly. It reminded me of Ume, trying to stop the flow of blood back in the carriage so long ago.

But blood wasn't pouring out. Or rather, not just blood. Black filmy clouds also puffed out, smelling like a rotting monastery, with putrefying walls and souls just as corrupt.

"Please, please! Save me!" Junichi cried. He clawed at his armor, trying to get it open, maybe to heal himself. Then he reached for the box, that dreaded box that would hold souls, behind him.

"Keep me alive," he begged.

I didn't want anything to do with his black magic. Deep inside of me, however, whispered a dreaded truth: I could use his soul for magic. As he'd used Norihiko's.

Not for evil, not as he had. But for honest good.

I dragged myself past the wounded sorcerer, staying well out of his reach. Even though he was on his knees, he was still as dangerous as a snake.

The box felt cold in my hands, and heavy, as if it already carried something inside. It was beautifully carved out of mountain ash wood, with a lovely red polish rubbed into it, to make it shine. Bas-relief decorations surrounded the lid and sides, mainly of the *sanzashi* thorn bush, showing it blooming with its sickly-smelling flowers on one side, and with its great thorns on the other.

I carried the box back in front of Junichi. His breathing was labored, his once dark hair had gone gray, and spots lined his wrinkled hands.

"Open it," he said, his voice gravelly and rough.

I did as he said.

With a sigh, Junichi leaned forward. I could tell he was willing himself into the box, willing his soul to live on.

It wouldn't be enough. Too much was dribbling away.

I gave my own sigh and called up yet another wind, a gentle, cleansing wind, to carry the rest of Junichi's soul away and into the box. It flowed faster now, encouraged to slide into its new home.

It wasn't enough.

At the end, I had to start tugging gently, pulling on the soul to make it leave Junichi. Finally, like pulling a thorn from a wound, I jerked Junichi's soul free from his body and snapped the lid shut on the box as the sorcerer fell on his face.

I was surprised that the box didn't seem any heavier now. Was it just Junichi's soul had so little weight? Or were all souls as solid as sunlight and steam?

Regardless, I knew that Junichi's soul was a heavy responsibility, a burden for me to carry until I decided what to do with all that power.

I felt the familiar ache, that hollowness inside me, that longing to turn to a sister or a mother for advice. I had no one to ask, though, except the wind and the moon and the wilds.

As I turned away, it occurred to me that I had finally done it. I had killed a man. He wouldn't have died without my misdirection, or my pulling on his soul. It was my deeds that directly caused his death, not just indirectly. Just because it had been a gentle death didn't mean it wasn't a death.

And that, too, was a burden for me to carry to the end of my days.

Eleven

As Much As

Norihiko

As much as Norihiko wanted to celebrate Masato's death, he knew he had another responsibility first.

Fuko, the sword, lay quivering on the ground beside his wielder, malicious and angry.

Norihiko remembered being in that position, as Seiji, after Iwao had been killed. How he had raged against Masato and Hikaru. How he'd vowed vengeance.

The men closest to Norihiko gave a ragged cheer when they saw him standing alone, victorious. The sun stayed hidden behind gray clouds that bunched across the sky, but the air still felt lighter, suddenly. Messengers who had been waiting nearby sprang up, eagerly running to Norihiko for instructions to carry to his generals.

All the while, Fuko seethed.

A guard formed around Norihiko, to discourage any of Masato's men from deciding suddenly to be a hero and attack anyway. Only then did Norihiko approach Fuko.

Masato lay on his side, his head already gathered up to be shown to his generals. His body stank, already putrefying, probably due to some foul spell that Junichi had placed on him.

Norihiko ignored it, concentrating fully on Fuko. The sword had lost a lot of its strength and will with the death of its wielder. They were connected, forged together with blood.

It still had enough of its own mind to make itself heavy when Norihiko tried to lift it, to bind itself to the earth.

Norihiko would not insult Fuko by laughing, though its efforts were puny compared to his own. He did, however, prove to the sword that he knew more. He found the perfect balance point and lifted the sword from there, breaking its grip on the earth.

"What am I to do with you?" Norihiko asked both the sword and those others inside of him, the ones who remembered being Seiji the most.

The answer came quickly. There was no way to reforge the sword, or to free it. It was bound to, and powered by, its original wielder, not a separate soul. It had no purpose beyond the destruction of the *kitsune*, of Hikaru and her sisters. It would never accept a second wielder.

The most merciful thing Norihiko could do would be to kill the sword immediately.

Norihiko hesitated. Fuko was a thing of beauty. Junichi had learned crafting Seiji, learned more with Fuko. The blade was elegant and sleek, still clean despite having rested in the dirt. The edge was sharp enough to cut a silk sleeve while floating in the air. Golden snakeskin covered the haft. A diamond pattern of hair wrapped around it—Masato's hair.

It would be a shame to destroy such an incredible artifact. A few of the voices inside Norihiko wondered if they could work with Fuko, tame him, train him to work differently.

But Fuko had aligned itself with a single purpose: to kill all the *kitsune*. To get it to give up that cause would leave it brittle, likely to break with its first blow.

Norihiko took a risk and ran his fingers along the smooth side of the blade, tracing the channel in the back.

Fuko shivered and complained, trying to twitch hard enough to at least nick Norihiko.

Norihiko sighed. As shameful as it was to destroy such a beautiful sword, the real shame was in how it had been made, full of vengeance and hate.

With great care, Norihiko stroked the blade again, seeking its weak spots.

Fuko understood what Norihiko was doing, and tried to hide the places where the metal hadn't flowed together evenly when it had been doubled and doubled again.

There weren't any soft spots on the blade. Just a few places where it wasn't as strong. Norihiko chased those until he found the perfect spot to apply pressure.

With a great cry, Norihiko raised Fuko over his head, then brought it down on his knee, snapping the blade in two.

A loud cheer went up, startling Norihiko. Why would his men celebrate the destruction of such beauty? Then he realized it wasn't the death of Fuko that caused them to rejoice, but the final destruction of Masato, the last symbol of Masato's power.

Only Norihiko would mourn Fuko. No one would understand why he regretted having to do it. Possibly not even Hikaru.

Would he see the fox fairy again? He'd gone to battle to make the mountain safe for Kayoku, but he'd destroyed Fuko for Hikaru and her sisters.

Hopefully, his efforts weren't wasted.

Norihiko couldn't believe his eyes when he saw Kayoku standing just inside the gateway of the estate, smiling and healthy.

It was the day after the final battle, the sun finally clearing away all the clouds and promising a very warm afternoon. Clearing up the remains of Masato's army had taken longer than Norihiko would have liked, particularly after runners came to tell him that Kayoku had been cured.

Many of the animated creatures had dropped where they'd been standing, mysteriously dying in mid-fight. It wasn't until Norihiko got to Masato's camp and found the body of Junichi that he understood.

But who had killed Junichi? He held the knife that had punctured his middle. Had some other sorcerer caused him to fall on his own blade? But who?

It had been easy to divide Masato's generals into who would live and who would be invited to end their own lives—by their own magical abilities. The pure humans were allowed to live, if they would pledge their allegiance to Norihiko and defend the mountain.

The sorcerers, of which there were only two, passed on.

Norihiko slid from his horse and went over to greet Kayoku.

"Welcome home, my lord," Kayoku said with a graceful bow.

"Thank you," Norihiko replied, just as formally. "Tell me, what happened?"

"Hikaru returned," Kayoku told him. "She cured me. If the battle had gone differently, she'd also offered to help people escape the mountain, get away from Masato."

"Is she here now?" Norihiko asked eagerly. Though she confused him, he still wanted to see her.

"She isn't. She went to find the army," Kayoku said. "I'd thought she'd be with you."

"She isn't," Norihiko said, restraining his sadness. It was better that Hikaru rejoined her own people, left the humans to their own lives.

He stubbornly put aside the strange ache in his heart at the thought of never seeing her again. What did it matter? He wasn't her mate, now. And never would be again.

The celebrations went on for the next two days. Everyone at the estate joined in. The cooks in the kitchen outdid themselves preparing delicacies such as wild pheasant cooked with its own eggs, grilled octopus, and *kubotsuki*. Norihiko wasn't certain where all the pots of wine came from— he suspected some had been liberated from Masato's army—but he didn't begrudge anyone their reveling.

Only Priestess Ayumi noticed that Norihiko sometimes looked off, not seeing anything in front of him.

"She'll return," Priestess Ayumi assured Norihiko as he left the festivities early the second night, going back to his rooms.

"Why should she?" Norihiko asked bluntly. "There's nothing for her here." He didn't add *no one*, though he was certain the priestess heard his words anyway.

"That isn't the way of the heart," the priestess assured him.

"I don't want her to return," Norihiko said. Because while he did want to see her, she also still confused him so much.

Priestess Ayumi fixed him with a hard stare. "She's done more for you than she'll ever tell you about," she said. "You should at least give her a chance."

"I didn't ask her to," Norihiko replied. He knew he was sounding petulant, but he didn't know how to fully express what she did to him.

"Would you have wanted to stay a sword for the rest of your days? Drown in the sea?" the priestess asked in return.

Norihiko didn't have an answer.

He still didn't know what to say the next evening, when he heard the sound of soft yipping at his window, and he knew that Hikaru had returned.

Norihiko left the estate halls and went out back, to Lord Taiga's garden, certain that Hikaru would track him there. The night was cooler than he'd expected, the wind blowing cold fingers along the back of his neck, raising the chicken flesh there.

Or at least that was what he told himself.

Norihiko carried a lamp with him, easily following the trail through the tumbled rocks, finding a patch of solid ground to sit on. The smell of rich earth rose up, along with traces of sweet pine. An owl hooted in the distance, and a clump of gnats quietly buzzed together just to his left.

Hikaru appeared before him, as if she'd gathered her form out of the mist and darkness. She shone with her own light, her sweet perfume soothing him even as her smile caused his stomach to turn uneasily. She wore pale yellow robes that seemed as though they'd been spun out of sunlight. At her side hung a large, red canvas bag.

Norihiko bowed his head to Hikaru, hoping to hide his anxiety. "Good evening," he said formally.

At least Hikaru smiled at him and didn't laugh.

"Good evening, my lord," she said, her voice sounding like soft bells in the night. "Congratulations on your victory over Masato."

"Thank you," Norihiko said. They sat in the quiet of the night for a moment until Norihiko couldn't stand it any longer.

"Why did you come to see me?" he asked, cringing. She was going to tease him about being too straightforward again, wasn't she?

But again, Hikaru just smiled. "I bring you a choice. I do not expect your answer now. I wouldn't take it even if you gave it to me. You need to think and decide in the fullness of being."

Norihiko nodded gravely. He couldn't imagine what she was about to propose. "I will be patient," he promised, though he knew in his heart that he wouldn't be. He would decide immediately, as he always did.

Hikaru pulled a large wooden box out of the bag and placed it between them. Though it was made out of wood, Norihiko had the impression that if he placed his hand on the thorn bush carved on the top of it, it would feel cold.

"I fought the sorcerer Junichi on the morning of the great battle," Hikaru told Norihiko. "I caused him to slip, for his knife to injure him, then I helped his soul escape." She cleared her throat and looked beyond Norihiko, out into the night. "I killed him."

Norihiko nodded, finding that he was neither shocked or surprised.

"My kind don't kill," Hikaru finally added, looking back at Norihiko, her eyes seeming to plead with him to understand.

"Not ever?" Norihiko asked, puzzled.

Hikaru sighed. "Sometimes. At great extremity."

"Junichi wasn't a good man," Norihiko told Hikaru gently. "Killing him wasn't a bad thing."

"When we were first married, there was a fortune teller who warned me how our marriage would change things," Hikaru declared.

Norihiko didn't remember, of course, but he believed Hikaru. "More than a few things have changed," he said wryly.

Hikaru looked down at her hands, her shoulders shaking.

Was she crying? He hadn't meant to make her cry.

When Hikaru looked up, she did have tears in her eyes, bright dew points on her cheeks, but she was also laughing.

"You're right. A few things have changed." Then she grew sober again. "As I said, I have brought you a choice. This box contains Junichi's soul."

Norihiko couldn't help the hiss he gave or how he started back.

"It's safe," Hikaru assured him. "At least, for now." She took a deep breath. "His soul is very powerful. And it was freely given. Well, mostly freely. It can be used to power great magic."

"What magic would you use it for?" Norihiko asked, his heart leaping up. Was she about to propose becoming human for him? Could she be his mate again?

"I can use it to transform you back into a fox fairy," Hikaru said instead.

Norihiko almost told her that he would never do that, but then he remembered her request to think about it. "Why would I do that?" he asked. "I enjoy being human." He liked the duties of the estate, the way the generals, and now the farmers, would ask him for help. He was looking forward to spending the rest of his days here, on the mountain, learning her moods and needs.

"I was human for a while," Hikaru admitted.

"You were?" Norihiko asked. When had that happened? Was this what Priestess Ayumi had hinted about?

"While it has its charm, I won't ever give up my magic again," Hikaru said seriously. She looked hard at Norihiko. "Not for you. Not for anybody."

This gave Norihiko pause. Had she given up her magic for him? Someday, he'd like to hear the full story.

"I see," Norihiko said. "What will you do with it if I refuse?"

"Go talk with Priestess Ayumi. See if there's something she needs," Hikaru said.

That made sense. It might actually be wiser for Hikaru to just go and talk with the priestess now.

If he became a fox fairy, what would he do? Would he remember his former life? His friends and family? He was building a life here. Did he really want to start over again, from scratch?

"I will consider your proposal, as you asked," Norihiko said when Hikaru didn't add anything more. Though he already knew his reply.

Hikaru seemed to know it as well. Norihiko couldn't point to exactly what the change was in her, but her internal light seemed to dim. She put the box carefully back into the bag and rose. "You know, if you become a fox fairy again, you'll be practically immortal."

Norihiko nodded. He hadn't considered that, but knew that he should.

"You'd be much better able to take care of the mountain if you lived forever," Hikaru said before she bowed one last time and disappeared into the night.

Norihiko stayed where he was sitting, considering her words. More than one lifetime protecting the mountain. It was a dream he'd never even realized he had.

Suddenly, his answer was no longer clear.

He couldn't help but grin.

Hikaru continued to confuse him. And probably always would.

Norihiko didn't bother to go and consult with Priestess Ayumi. He knew what she would already say, that he should go and be with his former mate.

Instead, he went to see Kayoku. She looked well, still, as if she'd never been sick. She met with him in the formal greeting hall. All the old poems about the Kitayama family and the mountain had been returned. Sweet pine incense burned on the altar in the corner, dedicated to the *kami* of the Mori shrine.

Kayoku wore a pale pink robe, the color of cherry blossoms, with bright green bamboo leaves embroidered on it. She'd been wearing her hair down, ever since her illness. Norihiko thought it suited her.

After greeting him and serving him tea, Kayoku finally asked, "How may I be of assistance?"

"Hikaru…" Norihiko started, then paused.

"Hikaru?" Kayoku prompted. Though she only gave him a soft smile, her eyes laughed at him.

Was he destined to go through the rest of his life with women laughing at him? Was that a human thing? Or a man thing?

"Hikaru gave me a tough choice," Norihiko said. "She has offered to make me a fox fairy again." He didn't want to give the details of the magic—those felt too intimate. Particularly that it would involve using Junichi's soul.

"That's fantastic!" Kayoku exclaimed. Then she paused. "You don't want to take it?"

Norihiko sighed. "I've been human for such a short time," he admitted. "I'm just settling in. I don't know what it will be like to change forms again." To lose all the knowledge he'd gained about being human.

"Change is hard," Kayoku said. "But you know that whatever form you take, you'll be welcome here."

Norihiko felt tension he hadn't realized he was carrying release. "Thank you," he said. He had known that, but it was also good to have it spoken aloud.

"So what will you do?" Kayoku asked after the stillness had grown into a long silence.

"I don't know," Norihiko lied.

He knew. He just didn't know how to tell Kayoku and the others that he'd be leaving soon.

Hikaru had Norihiko lie down on a *tatami* mat in his front rooms. Priestess Ayumi had blessed the space earlier, weaving together incense and prayers, leaving sweet smelling sachets of herbs in the corners. Now, candles and lamps burned along every wall, making the room daylight bright.

Norihiko was determined not to shudder or shake as he lay, vulnerable, in nothing but lounging robes in the middle of the room. Hikaru wouldn't hurt him, not knowingly.

And while he enjoyed being human, if he was honest, there was something missing, and not just his sword form. An ache that only came up in the dark of the night, when the winds blew playfully, stirring the trees and his soul.

Kayoku had agreed to help with the spell, Hikaru assuring her again and again that there was no possible way harm would come to her this time. But she needed a second set of hands with the weaving—she couldn't do it alone.

Hikaru had gathered many, many bright strips of cloth, some cast off from old robes, others from uncut bolts of cloth. None was wider than a fist across, while some were just a finger's width. All were long, at least the height of a tall man.

Kayoku started placing them one by one across Norihiko's body, from right to left, then left to right, laying the warps of their weaving.

Then Hikaru came through, laying the weft, weaving her strips in between Kayoku's, softly humming and singing.

Norihiko started when he heard another voice join in. Then he realized it was just Priestess Ayumi, adding her blessings.

Norihiko wasn't certain how long the women wove a blanket to cover him. It might have been an hour, it might have been most of the night. He felt cocooned and warm.

Then a coolness spread over his entire body. He wasn't sure what it was. It felt like mist spreading out across wet grass, early in the morning, before the sun rose.

Then the mist dipped down, seeping into his skin, and he realized what he felt was Junichi's soul.

Most of the personality of his former Maker had been stripped away. A little of his greed and his blackest fear—of dying—remained.

The impression of Junichi remained for merely a moment, then vanished as the cold sank deep into Norihiko's bones. He shivered as his core absorbed the changes.

Then changed.

A furnace started up inside Norihiko's belly. It burned hot and fast. He couldn't see anything beyond its flames, feel anything except its heat.

He recognized it as a kin to Junichi's kiln, where he'd been forged into a sword.

Norihiko struggled to get away, but how could he? The furnace wasn't in front of him, but inside him, a gaping hole where his belly used to be.

He wept as he had wept before, his tears streaking off his body and forming sparks as a gray, ghostly form assembled in the flames. It wasn't that it hurt, not like the reforging.

However, the change was upon him, and he had to let go.

Without thinking about it, Norihiko reached out his own hand to grasp the gray figure, pull it out of the flames even though it was only half baked.

Pull it further into himself.

The blessed heat soothed him, chasing away the coolness that had remained of Junichi's soul. His blood sang with a wild abandon as it bubbled up. Magic cruised through his veins, carrying the knowledge of what he could do, what he had done.

Parts of Seiji, that endless chorus of selves inside of Norihiko, stilled and gelled, forming a more solid core. There were still a few individuals, but mostly they grew silent, pouring all of their tightly held knowledge together.

Norihiko suddenly remembered. Not everything about his former life. But some things were suddenly returned to him, like his own family and friends, the other mountain he loved, where he'd grown up, and a few shared memories of Hikaru, the way they'd passed poems to each other when he'd been courting her, as well as their wedding.

He remembered their love, but it wasn't him experiencing it. It seemed an outside, foreign thing to him.

He still held onto every memory tightly as it came flooding back in, determined to never forget again.

Twelve

How Brightly The Sun

Hikaru

How brightly the sun shone that morning! I sat quietly on the porch outside Norihiko's rooms, hidden from all prying eyes by magic. The humans would have been shocked at the state of undress I was currently in, though really it wasn't much—just my sleeves tied back above my elbows, and the sash on my robe loosened so much of my chest was exposed.

I didn't care. I needed the sun to kiss my skin, the winds to play with my hair.

I'd crafted the greatest magic of my life the night before, bringing Norihiko back to his true, fox fairy form.

I'd never doubted that I would be able to do it, though releasing Junichi's soul had been tricky, keeping it trapped in the weaving Kayoku and I had created, not letting it leak away to cause mischief.

Norihiko had shaken so after that, quaked with the magic racing through his body and reforming him. For a while I had worried that maybe he had changed his mind and was rejecting the spell.

But the night passed and he quieted, breathing easily as his new form grew strong.

I didn't wait for him in the room after the spell was finished. I waited outside, to give him time to come to himself. What would he be like now? I knew he wouldn't be the same.

Then again, neither was I.

Where would I go now? I had no real home to return to. Maybe I would go to the sea, leave the mountains behind. Learn to call the fish out of the water for my dinner, weave nets out of seaweed, sing to the waves.

Finally, I heard Norihiko stir. I closed my eyes and breathed in deeply, trying to capture his scent. It had changed, too. It was still sweet and masculine, but held deeper notes, now.

After a short while, Norihiko joined me out on the porch. "Thank you," he said, his voice hoarse, as if he'd been shouting all night.

"It was my pleasure," I told him honestly. He looked fit and hale. His shoulders had stayed broad and his chin well-defined. However, his lips now held a sensual smile and his eyes twinkled with laughter.

Norihiko sat down beside me. He had kept the stillness he'd acquired as a sword, a motionless quality that monks would envy.

I didn't bother him with questions or try to fill up the space with frivolous observations about the sun, the clouds, or even the estate.

It hadn't been that long ago when I would have.

"I remember more about you," Norihiko said softly after a timeless time.

My breath caught. I didn't dare to look at him. Had he come all the way back to me? Was everything I'd done, all I'd sacrificed, finally going to pay off?

"Not everything," he added after another long pause. "And not fully. It's more like I'm watching myself do those things. Marrying you. Not as though I'm the one who is doing them."

Of course. "You're not the same as you were."

Norihiko gave a soft laugh. "That's the truth."

I finally turned to look at him. He still knelt with his back as straight as an iron bar, his hands loosely resting on his knees. But he smiled and his face was relaxed. He looked more comfortable in his skin than he ever had.

"So what will you do now?" I asked, deliberately not asking about us, about what *we* would do.

He might remember our love, but he was obviously no longer in love. It was, as he said, someone else who had courted me night and day, who had shown me such tenderness.

Norihiko nodded, growing more serious. "I pledged to take care of the mountain," he said. "When I was Seiji. It was the only way to survive Junichi's reforging." He paused, then added, "So I will stay here. Make this my new home. Become another *kami* protecting this land."

I nodded. I had expected as such.

I didn't know how I would answer him when he asked me what I would do. I was so prepared for that question that I started when he eventually said, "You could stay here with me, you know. Guard the mountain with me."

I didn't know how to reply. That he might offer me a place here, to stay with him…it went beyond my reckoning.

"I know you'll want to go see your sisters first, but after—" he started.

"My sisters?" I asked, interrupting. "I have no sisters."

Norihiko blinked, startled. "Of course you have sisters. Two of them. They visited me before the battle. I danced with them at our wedding."

"I don't have sisters," I told him, horror building. "I've always been alone."

"You have sisters," Norihiko insisted. "Did you give them up? Because they would never have let you go."

I had sisters? Maybe a mother? There were no memories left, just the constant loneliness and wishing I did.

"I could call them. They would like to see you, I'm certain," Norihiko added.

"I'm not the same as I was," I told him. Also, I wasn't certain. I'd killed a man. The weight of it still dragged at my soul.

"None of us are," Norihiko pointed out.

I sat back and looked back out, over the wall of the estate, toward the trees. There were many wild places on the mountain, many places I could easily call home.

"Please," Norihiko said. "Stay with me. Help me protect the mountain."

I couldn't help but shake my head and laugh. Before, I'd never had to worry about another turning Norihiko's head. Though it wasn't in the nature of our kind to be monogamous, I knew he'd always return to me.

Now, I had a built-in rival.

"What is it?" Norihiko asked.

I had to share. "She's always going to be your mistress, isn't she?" I asked. I couldn't help but flirt with him. He looked so much like my love, smelled like him, felt like him. Would probably taste like him as well.

Norihiko laughed, then grew sober again. "I can't promise anything," he warned. "There are so many paths leading up and down the mountain. But I'd like to walk them with you."

"I would like that too," I told him.

It wasn't a declaration of love. He might not ever feel that way about me again.

But there was the possibility of love along those paths. Each day, a new sunrise. Each season, new colors for the mountain.

Finally, since that horrible day so many months before, I had hope.

About the Author

Leah Cutter currently lives in Seattle—the land of coffee and fog. However, she's also lived all over the world and held the requisite odd writer jobs, such as doing archeology work in England, teaching English in Taiwan, and bartending in Thailand.

She writes fantasy set in exotic times and locations such as Tang dynasty China, WWII Budapest, rural Louisiana, and the Oregon coast.

Her short fiction includes literary, fantasy, mystery, science fiction, and horror, and has been published in magazines as well as anthologies and on the web.

Read more stories by Leah Cutter at www.KnottedRoadPress.com.

Follow her blog at www.LeahCutter.com.

About Book View Café

Book View Café is a professional authors' cooperative offering DRM-free ebooks in multiple formats to readers around the world. With authors in a variety of genres including mystery, romance, fantasy, and science fiction, Book View Café has something for everyone.

Book View Café is good for readers because you can enjoy high-quality DRM-free ebooks from your favorite authors at a reasonable price.

Book View Café is good for writers because 95% of the profit goes directly to the book's author.

Book View Café authors include Nebula, Hugo, and Philip K. Dick Award winners, Nebula, Hugo, World Fantasy, and Rita Award nominees, and *New York Times* bestsellers and notable book authors.

www.bookviewcafe.com

Xiao Yen folds paper into the shape of an animal or object, then does
magic, so the paper becomes what she's folded.
Her problem?
She's lost her luck.
Set during Tang Dynasty China.
Available at your favorite retailers.

"Absolutely enchanting"—Booklist
"Cutter knows just what she's doing"—Locus
"An exceptional tale by an exceptional writer"—Dennis L. McKiernan